THE STEPSON

DIANE SAXON

B
Boldwood

First published in Great Britain in 2023 by Boldwood Books Ltd.

Copyright © Diane Saxon, 2023

Cover Design by Head Design

Cover Photography: Shutterstock

The moral right of Diane Saxon to be identified as the author of this work has been asserted in accordance with the Copyright, Designs and Patents Act 1988.

All rights reserved. No part of this book may be reproduced in any form or by any electronic or mechanical means, including information storage and retrieval systems, without written permission from the author, except for the use of brief quotations in a book review.

This book is a work of fiction and, except in the case of historical fact, any resemblance to actual persons, living or dead, is purely coincidental.

Every effort has been made to obtain the necessary permissions with reference to copyright material, both illustrative and quoted. We apologise for any omissions in this respect and will be pleased to make the appropriate acknowledgements in any future edition.

A CIP catalogue record for this book is available from the British Library.

Paperback ISBN 978-1-80426-489-8

Large Print ISBN 978-1-80426-488-1

Hardback ISBN 978-1-80426-490-4

Ebook ISBN 978-1-80426-486-7

Kindle ISBN 978-1-80426-487-4

Audio CD ISBN 978-1-80426-495-9

MP3 CD ISBN 978-1-80426-494-2

Digital audio download ISBN 978-1-80426-492-8

Boldwood Books Ltd
23 Bowerdean Street
London SW6 3TN
www.boldwoodbooks.com

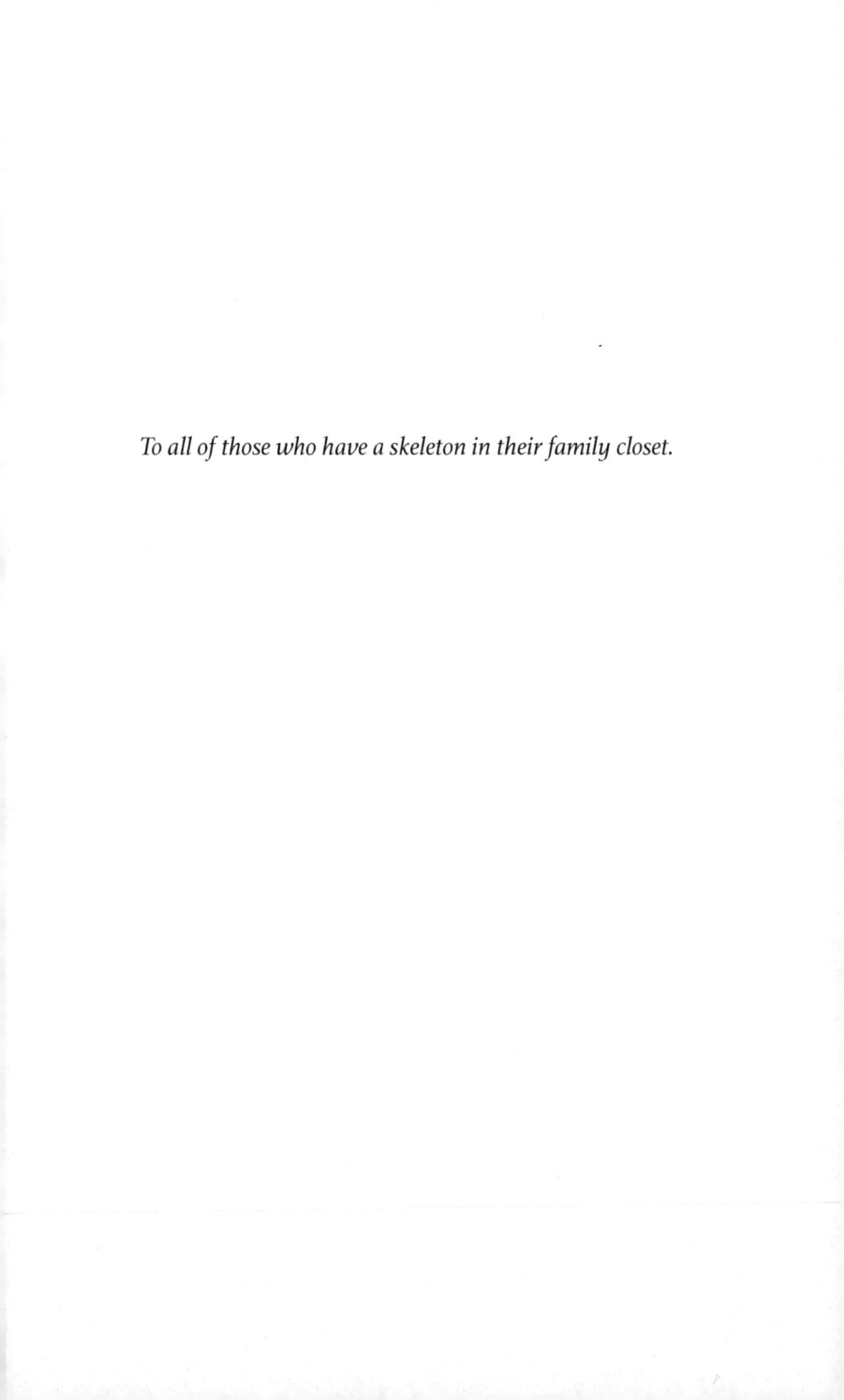

To all of those who have a skeleton in their family closet.

1

PRESENT DAY – TUESDAY, 6 JUNE, 3.23 A.M.

Sandra Leivesley twitched the curtains open a touch and peeped with one eye through the narrow gap she'd created. Her fingers gripped the material, ready to stitch the edges closed again with the speed of an electric sewing machine.

A car squatted on her drive. The orange glow from a distant streetlight highlighted a dull bloom on paintwork which had possibly been red at one time and gave a hint to how old it was. The engine rumbled for another moment, and then stuttered a gusty death rattle before quivering into silence.

Sandra let out a quiet breath, almost fearful she could be heard. Fairly certain she couldn't be seen, though, as she'd sneaked through on stealthy toes in the pitch black, certain of her way around the house she'd lived in for thirty years, even in the dark.

Motionless, she waited.

Nothing happened. No one moved. The car doors remained closed.

In the dim orange glow, she could almost believe it was empty.

Abandoned.

Sandra knew better. She narrowed her eyes to zero in on any

movement. Nothing. Except the vague definition of a pair of hands casually resting on the steering wheel. One finger moved. Tapped.

The soft cloud of her warm breath puffed over the chilled window to blur the image.

She jerked her face away from the narrow gap, fear gripping her.

Heart racing, she pressed the curtains closed and sank back on her haunches.

The soft mattress gave under her slight weight, and she pushed the palms of her hands down to steady herself.

The pattern of intertwining pink roses and olive-green leaves on the curtains wavered before her tear-filled eyes.

What was she to do?

What would Henry have done? Henry, her husband of thirty-two years, who'd always been there. Her rock. When she fell apart, he'd always stayed solid.

She listened for footfall up to her front door, the quiet crunch of leather on gravel and dried brown leaves that had whipped up in the autumn in piles along the edge of the drive and still resided there as winter gave way to spring, and then teetered on the edge of summer. Leaves Henry would normally have got the leaf blower on.

That had been his job. The garden, the drive, the cars. All abandoned recently.

She waited for the doorbell to ring. Prayed it wouldn't.

Sandra edged back off the bed and pushed to her feet. She glanced at the clock radio on her bedside table.

3.25 a.m.

The time she woke most nights since Henry had gone. Not so much hormones kicking in. They'd almost subsided except for the occasional rev as they tried to start up, sending sharp tingles and hot flushes.

These days it was more the scrape of guilt scratching the surface in dreams of dread and fear that disturbed her. Fear that surfaced at her weakest moments.

Tonight, it had been the dull throb of that engine on her driveway, sending a soft vibration through their 1960s house to disturb the light sleep she hovered on the edge of.

She checked the clock again.

3.26 a.m.

Too early to phone her daughter. She only lived a ten-minute drive away. One of the newbuilds near Trench Lock. It was so convenient for both of them. Usually.

Lorraine was going to think she'd gone mad. She'd seen the sideways glances her daughter cast when she thought Sandra wasn't watching. Concern dappled the love in her daughter's eyes. Ever since Henry had died. Lorraine's dad.

Sandra covered her mouth with both hands and squeezed her eyes closed to try to block out the memory, but it forced its way in.

His dad.

The creak of a car door swinging wide on rusted hinges halted her thoughts.

'Oh, no.'

Her breathing quickened.

'He's coming.'

Sandra reached for the phone in her dressing gown pocket. The one she'd slipped in when she'd gone to investigate.

She'd known this day would come.

Footsteps approached the front door with the quiet grind of pebbles beneath a heavy sole.

Terror gripped her as she hovered a shaking finger above her daughter's number.

The footsteps halted.

Sandra held her breath, not daring to take another peek.

Would he think twice? Would he go away?

It was him.

It had to be. Who else would turn up at this time of night, uninvited?

Her heart quickened with a sickening thought. One that slammed in to haunt her as she waited for the knock at the door. The bell to ring.

What if he didn't need to ring the doorbell? What if he had a key?

She let out a quiet whimper. 'Oh, God.'

She'd bet her life he had a key.

How stupid. She should have had the locks changed when Henry died. She'd never given it a thought, too absorbed in her own guilt and grief to care. To be aware.

Her tongue thickened in her throat so she could barely swallow as the phone dialled through. Two, three, four times.

'Hello?' A gravelly whisper. Her daughter wouldn't want to wake the children. Sandra didn't want to either, but who else did she have? No one.

'Lorraine.'

'Mum?' The soft shuffle of bedding as she imagined Lorraine bolting up in bed. 'What's wrong?' The edge of panic crept into her daughter's voice.

'He's here.'

'What? Mum, speak up. I can't hear you.' Irritation snapped through the panic.

'He's here.'

'Who?'

'Your brother.'

'My...? What did you say? Mum? Are you drunk?'

It wasn't an unreasonable question. She had been on occasion when the pain of loneliness since Henry died had crippled her.

She'd phoned Lorraine then, but it had always been at a reasonable hour. She'd cried down the phone, but she'd never been so inebriated that she'd not known when to stop. Known when to let her daughter get on with her own life.

A life that hadn't taken the easy road either.

It was hard.

She'd thought herself so independent. So strong.

Turned out she was wrong. All that independence and strength had seeped out of her when her husband died, to leave her an empty vessel, bobbing on a sea of loneliness.

When Henry had been alive, she'd thought it was her strength that had made them safe. Without him, she knew different.

Henry had kept her safe. Her and Lorraine and their first grandchild. Sweet five-year-old Sophia.

They'd grouped together, a tight-knit unit, when Lorraine's husband had left her ten weeks before she gave birth to their second child. It seemed he was more enthusiastic about the young childless woman he'd apparently fallen for at work. One who would probably want children of her own in a few years, so they'd thought, until they learned better. Turned out that she already did. A baby due just a few weeks after little Elijah.

Lorraine had seethed. Then she'd settled.

Until her dad had died.

Grief had smashed into Sandra and Lorraine. Shocking. Unreasonable.

Lorraine's ex hadn't bothered to come to Henry's funeral, nor visit his newborn son. Not then and never since.

The tragedies piled up. But the fatal car crash was something Sandra just could not come to terms with. The grief counsellor assured her that it was a natural process. The seven stages of grief. Time would help. But time wasn't flying on swift wings. It had stuttered to a halt for her somewhere around shock, denial and anger.

There would always be the guilt that riddled her entire being. Guilt would never go.

Not so for Lorraine. She'd moved on. With two children, she'd had to. She'd managed to override any sense of depression. Nothing like her mother.

Sandra had nothing but admiration for her daughter.

It didn't mean she could move on, though.

She wallowed. She had always wallowed.

The horror of a nagging thought scratching at the back of her mind.

A thought she was now convinced was correct.

She wasn't drunk. Not tonight. She wasn't paranoid. Paranoia held its basis on a rampant imagination. Her conviction wasn't imagination.

She was right.

Henry's car crash hadn't been an accident. Nor had it been a moment of distraction.

She knew that.

She'd believed otherwise at first. Full of horror at her own actions.

The rising panic dissolved into acceptance. There was nothing she could do for herself, but she could protect her daughter and grandchildren.

Her mind snapped into focus.

'Listen very carefully to what I have to tell you. I have little time, so just believe me when I say you and the children are in danger.'

'What? Mum... I don't understand.'

'Quiet. Listen. Your dad was first. Now it's me. I'm so scared, but mostly for you and the children. Because once I'm gone, you'll be next.'

2

FIFTEEN MINUTES SINCE PHONE CALL

The sense of unease about her mum exploded in a cloud of confusion and terror.

Was she drunk? She'd not sounded it. Her words hadn't been slurred like they'd been a couple of weeks ago when she'd called with a tearful outpouring of anger and denial. The natural responses to her dad's death, according to the counsellor. Eventually, she would move on, settle on acceptance. That's what the woman had told them. Sadly, her mum didn't appear to be able to move on. She was stuck on repeat, going round and round.

Numb by the time she hung up, Lorraine swung her legs out of bed. She sat for a long moment in the silence, listening to Elijah's soft breaths.

Lorraine stared at her mobile phone. Her mum had one. She'd used it tonight, but she normally insisted on using the landline, declaring it had much better reception. So, where had she been when she'd phoned? The landline was in her mum's bedroom and the living room. She'd normally reach for that.

She rubbed shaky fingers across her lips. Should she call the police? Her mum hadn't said she should. She'd just insisted Lorraine listen. Listen to something incredible. Unbelievable.

She might have listened, but it was garbled and confused, and Lorraine truly wondered if her mum hadn't ingested some hallucinogenic. Perhaps the doctor had prescribed something stronger for her mum's depression. Maybe mixed with a glass of wine, it hadn't suited her.

This hadn't seemed like depression, but a manic episode.

Could you call someone for that? The counsellor would know.

Lorraine glanced at the time. 3.40 a.m. Her chest ached with holding in the terror. She couldn't call at that time of the morning. It wasn't an emergency service. The counsellor probably only worked nine till five.

Was this an emergency, though? Enough to call 999?

What was her mum talking about? A brother? Lorraine didn't have any siblings. Nor did her mum, so why would she talk about a brother?

Nor one of her uncles on her dad's side. To her knowledge, he never kept in contact with them.

Should she call someone else, other than the emergency services? But who?

She came to her feet and padded silently across the room in a practised move so that she didn't wake her baby boy in his cot by the window.

Her lowered voice on the call hadn't woken him, nor the gentle buzz of the phone by her bedside that had her instantly awake, but the sharp creak of a floorboard would.

If it did, that would be it for the night. No more sleeping. He wasn't a bad sleeper, but once he'd had four hours, he was a supercharged dynamo, ready to play. If she left him undisturbed, he still woke supercharged, but more tolerant and happier.

Not that it mattered. She was never going back to sleep now.

Not with everything her mum had said churning around in her mind. Frankly, she was surprised she hadn't woken Elijah, her voice bordering on an hysterical hiss.

She glanced at the digital toothbrush timer above the sink as she sat on the toilet and emptied her bladder. Only 3.50 a.m.

What was she supposed to do?

Was her mum okay?

Elbows on knees, she buried her face in her hands, desperate worry snaking through her.

Without any back-up, she could hardly swing around to her mum's to check on her. She couldn't leave the children in the house alone, even if it was only for a short while. Her mum lived a ten-minute drive away, but that hardly mattered. She had no idea how long she'd be there once she arrived.

Nor could she wake them both and take them with her. It wasn't fair on either of them. Sophia was at the age where anything out of routine would make her anxious. That was the knock-on effect of her dad leaving without a word.

In any case, if she woke her now, Sophia was going to be exhausted and naggy by school time.

Lorraine stood once she'd finished on the loo, letting her nightshirt fall back down her thighs as she twisted around and almost flushed the toilet. At the last moment she hesitated, her hand hovering above the button on the top of the tank. The sound would wake Elijah. She hated not to flush the toilet, but occasionally, it wouldn't harm. She'd do it when they were all awake and squirt some bleach around the rim.

She tiptoed back into the bedroom and stared at the shadowed face of her son. His lips made a soft suckling noise as he slept on. Perhaps the smell of her subconsciously disturbed him, reminding him that his food source was close at hand.

What if she called Simon? Would he help?

Unlikely. He'd not even wanted to see his own son. He'd not bothered with Sophia either, leaving her little girl in a state of complete uncertainty. Lorraine had needed to take him to court to get any kind of child support for Sophia. She'd have to do it again for Elijah.

She might have been stupid not realising her husband was having an affair, but the other woman was stupider still for believing him when he said he wasn't sleeping with his wife. The one who was quite evidently pregnant when Lorraine went around to confront his new girlfriend. Who turned out not to be that new.

Funny how it was Lorraine who'd lost all her friends when they split up. Fear that she might lean on them, maybe. Foist her children on them with tears of self-pity.

There was no one she could call. No one who was close enough to drop everything at – she glanced at the clock again – 4 a.m. and dash around to help out. Her neighbours hadn't been the same since Simon had left. He'd always been the one to socialise with the three other couples they lived near. Two of them younger without children, and then there was Doreen and Keith Stroman. Both too frail and aged to ask. They were always lovely enough to take in the post, but that was probably as much as Lorraine could expect of them. Certainly, they wouldn't know how to handle the children. Their own children were grown men now whose visits were few and far between.

She'd barely spoken with the girls from work since she went on maternity. There was nothing much to say. She really didn't want all those coy looks and pity-filled speeches once they found out her husband had left. She hated the idea of being gossiped about. So, she'd told no one there that Simon had left. She'd kept to herself and put off any visits to her house.

Where had that got her, though? She had no back-up. No one.

The Stepson

She'd always relied on her mum and dad. Her dad was no longer there, and her mum, it appeared, had lost her mind.

Had she really? Was she sick?

Lorraine chewed on the side of her thumbnail. Was her mum sick in the head? Did she need help? Urgent help.

It was all a bit melodramatic to call an ambulance. Wasn't it?

What would she say? Hi, my mum's rambling like a mad person, words I really don't understand falling from her mouth. Yes, she's depressed. No, she's not suicidal. Is she?

As time ticked by, she stared at the phone in her hand. 4.22 a.m.

Her mum wasn't suicidal. Definitely. But there was something really wrong.

She hit her mum's number and let the phone ring out, turning the volume down and holding the phone close to her ear so Elijah didn't wake.

Her fingers trembled as it went to answerphone at her mum's end.

Lorraine paced back to the bathroom and lowered herself onto the toilet seat, the chill of it soaking through her thin nightshirt and sending her skin icy.

She shivered this time as she dialled her mum's landline. Not through the cold, but from fear as it gripped her.

Her dad's car accident had been just that. An accident.

Hadn't it?

That's not what her mum seemed to be saying.

Her mum wasn't it any danger. Was she?

And what about Lorraine? Was she in danger herself? And the kids?

It made absolutely no sense.

The landline went to answerphone too.

'Mum? Mum. Pick up, will you? You've got me desperately worried. Pick up.'

She waited as the static pricked at her nerves and then a long tone sounded.

Lorraine disconnected.

Helpless, she stood up and pulled her dressing gown off the hook on the back of the bathroom door.

There was no way she could go back to bed.

Worry curdled in her stomach.

Her mum was sick.

Lorraine needed to get an urgent meds review for her.

She tiptoed downstairs in the dark, then turned on the mood lighting in her little kitchenette, keeping it low. She filled the kettle and switched it on, her fingers tapping on the bench as she listened to the shushing noise getting louder as it came to the boil.

As she sat at the small table in her living room, her mug of tea cupped in her hands, her logical mind kicked in.

Her mum must have gone back to bed. She was asleep. She had to be. The tirade she'd had on the phone had worn her out. Otherwise, she would have answered when Lorraine called back.

Lorraine sipped at her tea, wide awake. Thoughts tumbled over in her mind, stumbling over each other, confusion overlaying all of them like a thick coat of dust.

If she got dressed now, organised things, fed Elijah and changed him, she could drop Sophia off at the 'before school club' when it opened at 7.30 a.m. and then go straight around to her mum's. She was supposed to pre-book the club, but they'd understand if she explained her mum was ill.

Perhaps they needed to make a doctor's appointment.

Find out what was going on in her mum's head.

Because whatever it was, it wasn't right.

She finished her drink and glanced at the time. Almost 5 a.m.

No matter how hard she'd tried to be rational, the notion that her mum was right still niggled. Her words sounding in Lorraine's ears.

'I'm so scared, but mostly for you and the children. Because once I'm gone, you'll be next.'

3

FOUR HOURS, FIFTEEN MINUTES SINCE PHONE CALL

Lorraine hitched Elijah higher up her hip as she juggled with the bunch of keys, grasping the one to her mum's front door and then jamming it into the lock. She pressed the doorbell at the same time, just to give her mum warning someone was there. She didn't need her dying of a heart attack because she wasn't expecting Lorraine at this time of the morning.

Only 7.45 a.m., Lorraine had managed to dump Sophia and run with the child barely even aware she was leaving as Sophia headed straight for the sandpit to bag the best sieve and shovel before the other children arrived. Karen, the team leader, had greeted them with a little confusion which soon turned to sympathy as Lorraine quickly explained that her mum was ill and she needed to get to her. It wasn't exactly a lie. But she didn't need to divulge the whole truth.

Lorraine swung the front door wide, removed the key and slipped the bunch of them into her cardigan pocket. She'd yanked her coat off and slung it on the front seat of her car after she'd dropped Sophia off. Mild compared to the weather lately, she'd overdressed.

'Mum?'

The unnatural stillness could just be her imagination, but the air pressed heavy with it.

Used to seeing her mum immediately, often with the front door wide once she heard Lorraine's car draw up, a vague suspicion that all wasn't well nagged. Even if she wasn't at the door, she'd be up, showered, dressed and making a cup of tea.

Lorraine glanced at the alarm box, knowing that it wasn't set. Her mum and dad had never used the alarm. They didn't like the thought of disturbing the neighbours if it went off accidentally. That was the kind of people they were. Private. Never wanted to draw attention to themselves. Naive, believing they'd never be broken into just because they never had been. Yet.

She'd inherited that trait from them, which was why she had no one to turn to now.

'Mum?'

She leaned her backside against the door and pushed it closed, the loud click of the deadlock filling the silence as she raised her head and stared up the flight of stairs, expecting to see her mum at the top of them. A look of confusion on her face and asking what Lorraine was doing there so early.

'Mum. Hiya. It's me. Are you up?'

Silence sent a flutter of anxiety through Lorraine's stomach. 'Oh, God.'

She gave Elijah a reassuring squeeze as though he was the one who needed comfort. There was nothing. Not just a lack of sound, but a decided emptiness. No radio, no washing machine, no movement.

Had she made a serious mistake not calling for help the night before?

Lorraine made her way from the short hallway to the door on

her left into her mum's living room. A living room not only empty, but cloaked in darkness.

One-handed, Lorraine tugged back heavy patterned curtains her mum would normally have opened by now.

The niggling anxiety turned into a kernel of fear as pale sunshine dappled through windows Lorraine had failed to notice her mum hadn't cleaned lately. A fastidious woman normally, Lorraine baulked at the fact she'd not noticed her mum slipping before she fell.

She circled around, her gaze touching on the furniture, the surfaces. Checking if there were more signs she'd missed.

A tall bookcase in stained oak served as a partial dividing wall between the sitting room with its brown leather settee and matching wingback chair her dad had always commandeered.

A chair that managed to make her heart squeeze at its barrenness.

Perhaps that was it. The absence of not only her mum, but her dad too. A room charged with emptiness.

Lorraine smoothed her hand over her little boy's bare arm. He'd felt warm too earlier, but his skin had cooled now.

She made her way through to the connecting dining room, with its impeccable neatness, as her mum barely ever used it. Only when Lorraine and the kids visited for midweek dinner and Sunday lunch did the room get used.

Last night's newspaper lay open, the crossword almost finished, three clues not yet completed.

An inch of blood-red wine, probably a Syrah, her mum's preference of late, sat heavy and dark in the bottom of the glass next to the open pages.

Had she had too much? Had it conflicted with her medication?

Lorraine pulled the highchair her mum had bought when Sophia was a baby away from the table and slipped Elijah into it.

The Stepson

She shrugged his changing bag from her shoulder and grabbed out a teething ring before the whinge rose in his throat. His arms and legs thrashed with excitement as she pulled his floppy white toy rabbit out and snuggled it against his chest while she blew soft raspberries at him. She slipped his arms through a cardigan, one at a time, so quick he barely noticed.

Contented gurgles accompanied drool as it slithered from around the teether he'd shoved into his mouth. A happy child, it didn't take much to appease him, as long as she kept him entertained.

She smoothed a hand over his dark hair. 'I won't be a minute, munchkin.'

She considered reaching for the remote control to turn on the TV in the sitting room but decided against it in case it masked any other sounds in the house. Sounds she was straining to catch.

With one last glance at her son, she left him in the living room and sprinted up the stairs, a pain that refused to go away tightening her chest.

'Mum?' She kept her voice light and airy, but concern fluttered, the panic of a moth's wing in her stomach.

Was her mum still asleep? Surely not. Never in her entire life had Lorraine known her mum to sleep in. She should be up. Dressed. Drinking tea.

All four doors from the landing stood wide, as her mum always liked them. To let the light through. Only the light wasn't spilling from the three bedrooms and single bathroom. The curtains and blinds were still closed to leave an eerie grey light shadowing through.

Lorraine peered into each room. Her mum would never go out without opening the curtains.

Lorraine glided them back and let the light flood in.

She stared at her mum's double bed with the duvet smoothed

flat as though her mum had just stepped out, leaving the bed perfect as she always did. Her slippers missing, though, from under the bedside table.

Lorraine placed her hand underneath the duvet, but the sheet was cold. Her mum hadn't just slid out. It looked like the place had been abandoned. Like she'd never been there.

There was no point calling her mum's name again. She wasn't going to answer.

Guilt knocked on the side of mounting terror.

She peered into the empty bathroom, fully expecting her mum to be passed out on the floor.

Regret and shame formed a hard knot.

Her mum had called in the middle of the night. For help.

Lorraine had done nothing about it.

What was she supposed to have done?

Called the police?

Paramedics?

All based on what assumption? One hysterical phone call. All too melodramatic then. Not so, now.

Lorraine slipped through to the front bedroom where Sophia slept when she stayed over with her grandma. The one she'd always considered hers, until her daughter came along and claimed it for herself. They didn't often all stay together at her mum's house. Her mum was supposed to come to her at Christmas this year. Their roles were changing, evolving. Since her dad had died, Lorraine felt a deeper sense of responsibility for the woman who had always been so strong, so independent, but whose health had deteriorated since her husband had gone. Her mental health more than the physical.

The imprint of what she assumed were her mum's knees dipped into the centre of the pretty pink unicorn duvet. The matching curtains still shut tight against the pale yellow sunshine.

Without leaning on the bed, Lorraine reached over and snapped the curtains open so she could peer out over the driveway where she'd parked her three-year-old two-tone Ford Puma with its smart black roof and special edition ruby-red body. Lucky she'd bought it when she did, because she couldn't afford a new car now. She'd paid the loan off when Simon had left, with a quiet personal loan from her dad. Interest free. Her mum had been horrified in case she racked up a load of debts once there was only one salary coming into the house.

She still owed the money, but her mum had told her not to worry until she started back to work. Which would be imminent because she couldn't afford to stay off any longer. In the meantime, this car would have to a last a number of years yet.

She frowned as she looked out at the ordinary day with people in the street going about their ordinary business. Children in uniform at the school bus stop. The same one she'd stood at when she was that age.

There was nothing wrong. And yet everything was.

'Where are you, Mum?'

Her heart thudded as she gazed out, looking for a familiar figure as people passed by. The vague sound of their voices floating up to her.

An explosion of glass shattering split the silence apart.

'Elijah!'

Lorraine screamed out her son's name as she whirled and ran for the stairs.

4

FIVE HOURS SINCE PHONE CALL

Elijah's screams rent the air in two as Lorraine charged into the living room and skidded to a halt.

Face puce with horror, scrunched up as he let out another howl.

'What happened, Elijah?'

She ran to the highchair, snatching him out to hug him close to the heart almost beating out of her chest. 'It's okay, it's okay. Mummy's here. I'm here, baby, I'm here.'

His legs thrashed against her belly as his spine stiffened. He wedged his arms between them and pushed back against her until her own arms burned with the effort of hanging onto her hysterical child.

'Elijah!'

Her gaze darted across the small sliding patio doors and then over to the dark wood Welsh dresser and the glitter of hundreds of shards of glass. Elijah's teething ring hovered on the ledge.

'Oh, no. Elijah.'

Her breath held in her chest as the immediate threat melted into the background. There was nothing to fear but her own mum's anger when she found her husband's delicate crystal whisky glass smashed to smithereens, the heavy base of it broken into unequal thirds. A victim of Elijah's strong left-handed lob. He may become a star cricketer in later life, but right now, he was nothing but trouble.

'We are in such a pickle.'

Lorraine rocked her howling little boy until his sobs petered out into snotty snuffles with the occasional hiccup.

'It's okay. Don't worry, Elijah.'

Lorraine grasped the back of the chair with one hand and pulled it away from the glass shard-littered table. None of it appeared to have sprayed over his highchair.

Exhausted, he barely objected as she slid him back into the seat. She dipped her hand into the open changing bag and then whipped it back out again. A pinprick of blood bloomed on her middle finger as she picked out a tiny splinter of glass. 'For goodness' sake.'

She drummed up a quick smile as Elijah's plump lips made a downturn. 'It's okay, darling.' In desperation, she grinned and wondered if that wouldn't upset him more. The image of his mother's face turning feral. 'Would you like one of Grandma's biscuits?'

'Mamma.'

'Grandma.' She felt the sob in the back of her throat. 'Oh, Grandma.'

Elijah reached out a hand and flexed his fingers in a 'give me' motion.

'Hold on, Elijah.'

She whipped through to the kitchen and swiped the biscuit barrel that her mum kept especially for the kids off the bench just as Elijah's whimpering started up.

'Mummy's coming. I have Grandma's biscuits.'

She wrenched the lid off and thrust the tin at Elijah, barely even blinking as he dipped one chubby hand and then the other inside to come out with three biscuits.

Normally, she would have handed him one. Just one.

With a fat tear still hovering on the ledge of his eye, ready to plop over, Lorraine couldn't take the risk. She pushed the lid back on the biscuit tin and forced another wide smile.

'You eat those, darling, while Mummy sweeps up this.'

The dustpan and brush under her mum's sink would have to do.

Each tinkling laugh of the glass hitting the dustpan made her think of her mum.

She didn't care if her mum was going to be angry with her for breaking the glass.

She just wanted her back.

Lorraine raised her head and stared at the patio doors and frowned.

All the curtains and blinds in the house had been closed. Except the vertical blinds across the patio doors. They were pulled open. Not all the way. Just the width of a person.

A person coming in?

Or one going out?

5

THIRTY-ONE YEARS EARLIER

Sandra forced eyelids, thick with lack of sleep, open and grunted as she attempted to roll onto her side, until the dull ache in her abdomen turned to a sharp stab as a quick reminder of the caesarean section she'd undergone ten days earlier.

She listened to her shallow breathing for a moment before reaching out to touch the cold side of the bed where her husband normally slept.

She'd been so exhausted from the night's long vigil with the baby crying, crying, crying, she'd not even heard Henry slide out of bed earlier to sneak off for his first day back at work.

She could have done with his help a little longer, but he was up to his eyes in it. With no thought of his wife having undergone a major operation, work demanded he return.

Even more so, she'd wanted to show her support by getting up with him, seeing him off with a wave to reassure him they'd be fine.

They would be fine.

But she'd not had the energy to move.

A long groan huffed from her lips as she edged her way to the side of the bed and then propped herself up on her elbow.

It was all very well Henry suggesting she ask friends to call in, but most of her friends were at work. Besides, all she wanted to do was sleep while the baby did. Not that she had much chance. Not while they had eleven-year-old Trevor living with them.

That was an unwelcome surprise, if ever there was one.

She didn't want to be a bitch, in fact she'd kept her feelings very much to herself. Just because she hid them didn't mean she didn't have them.

Twenty-six weeks into a pregnancy that had happened somewhat quicker than anticipated, in fact on their honeymoon, the last thing they'd bargained for was to be saddled with Henry's son from his first marriage. A marriage that had ended when Trevor was ten.

Uncomfortable with him, even when he only came to stay once a month for the weekend, Sandra barely knew the child. The boy came to see his father, not her. He made that very clear. He barely even acknowledged her existence, despite her best endeavours to engage him.

There was a possessiveness to Trevor, an insistence that he get between Sandra and her relatively new husband. The thin end of a wedge becoming insidiously wider.

Not that she could blame him. He'd just lost his mum in an accident. He was bound to cling.

Somehow, though, Sandra knew it was something far darker than that. It had existed from the moment Henry introduced her to his son.

Where she should feel sorry for him, a young boy who'd not long lost his mum, there was a coldness to him. Even when tears tracked down his sallow cheeks, there was something dead in his expression as it met hers over his dad's shoulder.

He's mine. I'm not going to share.

His arms would tighten tenaciously around Henry's neck, his thumb childishly poking between his lips.

He sent a chill through her when that cold stare turned to ice and he refused to look away.

And now she was stuck with him. A man in a child's body. Too cynical already. An underlying ripple of malevolence just hovering below the soft surface of innocence.

She knew she wasn't alone in her opinion of him. Even his maternal grandparents wouldn't have him during the final two weeks of her pregnancy to give Henry and her a break. Nor did they entertain having Trevor overnight after she'd had her caesarean.

Henry would have had to drive an hour each way to pick his son up from them. A factor they used to their own advantage when they said they were too old to travel that far to pick Trevor up from school for a few days. Only a few days. That's all Henry and she had needed while she was in hospital.

The child had tagged along with Henry, the simmer of annoyance shimmering in his dark expression as he glared at the little bundle his dad cradled in his arms. The baby who was getting everyone's attention when he needed it. He'd lost his mum, hadn't he?

He had that. It didn't make any difference, though. He'd always been an awkward child. Now he was awkward and sullen.

Sandra couldn't even attribute it to him being sad.

He was permanently angry.

She sighed as she swung her legs over the side of the bed. Despite the heating ticking over on low, she shivered as she padded into the bathroom to relieve herself.

The timing had been so wrong. If only she'd not had preeclampsia and needed a caesarean. If only the baby hadn't been four weeks early. If only Henry hadn't needed to go back to work at the beginning of half term so she was left with an eleven-year-old who she could do nothing with. Had nothing in common with.

She was too exhausted to entertain him. With a bright intelligence, he would soon be bored. Disruptive.

He was always disruptive. Demanding. Attention seeking.

It wasn't as though she could farm him out to someone with kids of his age. She didn't know anyone. He'd not long started at their local school, and she'd barely had time to get to know the parents of his classmates. He'd certainly shown no interest in any of the children in his class.

Not yet.

A little stab of guilt made her stop. Think again.

She needed to be patient. He needed time.

It wasn't easy.

She washed her hands, pausing with the towel wrapped around them as she cocked her head to one side, caution igniting a faint flicker of concern in her chest.

A sinister hush hung in a thick cloud. Claustrophobic and stifling so she could barely breathe.

Suspicion awakened in her.

Sandra dropped the towel into the sink, her breath catching in her throat.

Something was wrong.

The house was silent.

The baby was silent.

Trevor was silent.

6

SIX AND A HALF HOURS SINCE PHONE CALL

Lorraine gave the clerk on the front desk of the police station a strained smile.

'Will they be much longer?'

The middle-aged man stopped typing up the information she'd briefly given him and peered at her over half-moon glasses that perched halfway down a long, narrow nose.

A flicker of confusion passed through his eyes.

'They?' He stroked the hank of fine grey hair back from his wide forehead. 'They who?'

'The police officer? To look into my mum's disappearance.' She jiggled Elijah higher up her hip as the weight of him became a strain. 'Will the police officer be much longer?'

The man's brows twitched together. 'I think you may be getting ahead of yourself, madam.'

Elijah let out a squeal and shoved two dribble-slimed fingers into the corner of Lorraine's mouth, instantly stopping her from replying.

She took the child's hand in hers and placed a gentle kiss on his palm, before tucking it between them so she could talk uninterrupted. 'What do you mean?'

Aware of the stickiness around her mouth, Lorraine dipped her hand into her pocket to retrieve the ever-present tissue and wiped it over her lips and cheek, before doing the same to Elijah, ignoring his objections.

As she stuffed the tissue back into her pocket, she caught the quick flash of impatience on the man's face.

'I need a police officer. To investigate my mother's disappearance.'

He gave a slow shake of his head. 'That's not how it works, madam.'

She shifted Elijah again, a little peeved with his use of the word madam. It grated. 'I don't understand. I've just told you my mum is missing.'

'Yes.' He nodded. 'So, I'm going to take some details from you first, and then we'll see if you want to report this.'

'I do want to report it.' Panic rose in her chest. For God's sake, why wasn't he taking her seriously? Why else would she be there?

He pushed the glasses up his nose and returned his attention to the screen. The reflection of white light bounced from his lenses so she could no longer see his eyes, but she assumed they were intent on reading whatever it was he had tapped into the computer. She'd given her name and her mum's name so far. And date of birth. Just her mum's.

'Address?'

'Mine?'

He sighed. 'Yes. To start with.'

She reeled off her address and then waited in painful silence as he entered it onto the computer, taking so long, Lorraine had to shift the baby from one hip to the other, and regretted not carrying

Elijah in his car seat. She'd wanted the comfort, his small body pressed against hers.

A telephone rang at the back of the compact room. Sharp and persistent until it jangled on her nerves.

'And your mum's address?' His glasses flashed a reflection of light as he glanced up and then back down again.

Lorraine almost ground her teeth as the phone in the background continued to shrill. 'Pardon?'

'Address.' He raised his voice. 'Your mum's address.'

She raised a hand and brushed a lock of hair back from Elijah's forehead. 'Do you want to get that?' Her voice came out a waspish snap to match his and the clerk raised his head in jerky surprise. His glasses slipped down his nose again, so sharp blue eyes pinned her with disapproval.

'No. I can only deal with one task at a time. Lucky for you, yours is my priority. Someone else will get that one.' His lips pinched tight. 'Now, madam. Shall we continue?'

'Mrs Pengelly.'

'Sorry?'

'That's okay.' She forced a smile. 'But it's Mrs Pengelly, not madam.' Madam inferred that she'd not given him her name and she had as soon as she walked through the front door of the station. It may have been in a breathy gush, but she'd given it. He should at least have the courtesy to acknowledge who she was. 'And you are...?'

He gave a slow blink, evidently taken aback by her attitude. Perhaps he was used to outright aggression or sobbing victims. She was neither. She simply wanted someone to find her mum, but here she was talking to a clerk, not a police officer.

She gave Elijah a comforting pat on the back without taking her eyes off the man behind the security glass.

'Mark. Mark Hearn.' He pushed his glasses up with his middle finger. 'Shall we get on with this?'

A woman walked into the office behind him, and the phone stopped ringing with an abruptness that brought nothing but relief.

Lorraine nodded.

'Your mum's address, please, Mrs Pengelly.' He stressed the last two words.

'Thirty-four Westacre Drive, Ketley Bank.'

Her jaw tightened as he input the address with painful slowness, but she held her tongue.

He stopped typing and glanced up. 'What makes you think your mum is missing?'

'I told you.' Admittedly it had been a panicked garble as she walked through the automatic doors, fear in her heart. 'She telephoned me last night. She was panicky, like something bad was about to happen. Then I went around this morning, and she wasn't there. It was all very odd.'

Mark Hearn took his hands from the keyboard and gave her a direct stare. 'Could she have gone to the shops?'

Lorraine's face stiffened. He didn't believe her. 'There was something not right.' How could she explain? She knew in her heart that something had happened to her mum, but how did she portray that to this man? 'I went there this morning, and something wasn't right. The place seemed...'

The man's steely eyebrow raised. 'Empty?'

'Yes.' He'd nailed it. Even when her mum wasn't there, the house had never felt empty. But it had this morning.

'Is your mum registered as vulnerable?'

'No.' But she was vulnerable. She had been ever since Lorraine's dad had died.

'She's sad. A little depressed since my dad died.' She didn't want to make it sound as though her mum had something wrong with her, surely she only needed to tell him information that was relevant. 'Her GP prescribed antidepressants,' she blurted.

He gave a nod. 'And how long do you believe she's been missing?'

Lorraine frowned as she took Elijah's fingers from her mouth again. 'She phoned me early this morning in a state. Almost half three.'

Mark Hearn gave a slow nod. 'And you didn't go around at that point?' Everything about the man epitomised stiff disapproval as though he considered she should have rushed around at the time to check on her mum. The very moment she'd put the phone down on her. That it was her responsibility.

Guilt gnawed at her. It was. She wished she had. And now she had this man judging her. 'No. I couldn't leave my children.'

He slipped a glance over Elijah. 'Your partner at work?'

Heat slid over her cheeks as she held onto her son's hand. 'No. My *husband* left us. Last year. I couldn't leave my children.'

'And you didn't feel at that time it was urgent enough to call the police?'

She squeezed her eyes shut for a brief moment and then looked at him again. It was bad enough she was riddled with guilt without him making her feel like a foolish moron. 'Look. This is not normal for my mum. She's disappeared. I'm telling you. I don't know where she is.'

'But she called you last night in a state and you were unable to go around.' He held his hands, palms out to her. 'I'm just being devil's advocate here. When she called, had she been drinking?'

'No. Yes. I don't know.'

'So, your mum called you last night, she may have been drinking. She's on medication. You couldn't get there, so, she called someone else?' he suggested. 'She went to a friend's place? She woke up this morning and met someone for coffee and a chat? Maybe she feels foolish, selfish for waking you in the middle of the night and she's not yet ready to face you.'

Frustration rolled in her chest. He didn't understand. Her mum was panic-stricken when she phoned. Frightened. She didn't have friends. She spent most of her time with Lorraine and the children. Her circle of friends was not a circle. Lorraine could barely remember her mum ever mentioning anyone. She'd been a devoted wife, mother and grandmother. Most of her time had been with family.

'Look.' He leaned on the counter to bring himself closer to the partition between them, his face softening with understanding, or so he thought. 'Your mum is an adult. She has every right to have her own friends and do her own thing.'

'No, but...'

'Mrs Pengelly.' His tone stopped her dead. 'Your mum is probably perfectly safe. There will be a logical explanation. After her phone call last night, she probably realised that you have your hands full,' he stared pointedly at Elijah, '...and decided to find someone a little less... busy. Someone with time to listen.'

How could she explain that she and her mum had such a close relationship? They weren't just mum and daughter. They were best friends. Even closer since Lorraine's dad had died, and her husband had left her. They were inseparable.

It was hard to conceive her mum would have gone elsewhere. She didn't have that many friends.

'Look.' Sympathetic eyes stared at her from over his glasses. 'Here's my advice. Go home. Ring your mum. Don't run yourself ragged by spinning around in circles. Be logical.' Implying she hadn't been so far. 'Make a list of her friends and ring them. Check the places she would normally go. She may have just wanted to get away. Take a break from everything. Perhaps it's all got a bit much and she needs some thinking time. Think of where she might stay overnight. For comfort. Solace. Somewhere maybe your dad used to go with her. She may just want to be alone.'

How could she explain their relationship to a man who evidently didn't have a clue? 'I know my mum. She wouldn't.'

'Grief can make people act in strange ways. Change them.'

'That's what I'm concerned about. She said some really strange things. Something about a brother.'

'Your brother?'

She shook her head. 'I don't have a brother.'

'Your mum's brother?'

'No. She said she was in danger. He was coming to get her.'

'Who?'

'My brother.'

He lowered his chin. 'But you don't have one.'

'She sounded scared.' Crazy.

'And this was around about three thirty this morning, yes?'

'Yes.'

'You mentioned she's on medication. And she'd been drinking. I'll bet she feels dreadful, guilty that she woke you. It sounds like she mixed booze and drugs and had a bouncer of a nightmare.'

'No. Yes. Oh, I don't know, Mark. I just know she was frantic and I couldn't go around.'

He let out a sigh and gave her a pitying smile. 'And you feel guilty because you weren't available to dash to your mum's side.' He tapped at the keyboard again and lifted his fingers with a quick flourish as though he'd just typed 'the end'. 'I'm sure there'll be a perfectly logical explanation once your mum turns up. In my experience, there nearly always is.'

The doors behind her slid open to let a gaggle of loud teenagers and a sharp gust of wind in.

Frustrated with the barrier this man had raised between her

and a real police officer and the interruption, she clenched her jaw. 'So, you're not going to investigate?'

She could barely hear his reply as the kids' chatter rose to hysterical proportions. She heard the words 'shoplift' and 'nick' as she waited for the counter clerk to reply. All she wanted was to get out of there, get away from them all.

Didn't they realise she had a real problem? Possibly a crime.

Not that she had any evidence. She could see his point, but she was reluctant to acknowledge it.

'Look, I've put your mum on the system, just to save time. Give it a couple of days and I'm sure she'll turn up. Unless you consider she's at risk.' He paused, his grey eyebrows rose into a crinkled forehead. 'Is she at risk?'

Well, was she?

Filled with self-doubt and a foolish feeling that her mum was going to wonder what the hell she was doing, Lorraine gave a mute shake of her head. Her eyes stung with the hot tears she held back.

Mark Hearn's voice turned gentle.

'She'll be fine. Believe me, we have this kind of thing happen all the time.'

She clenched her teeth.

'And how many do you find a week later face down in a ditch?'

A wince passed over his face, but she was beyond caring.

Lorraine backed up, almost swallowed by the group of kids. She gave a nod and turned away, horrified at her own rudeness. She cuddled Elijah tight as the kids, oblivious to her, barely left a gap to let her squeeze through.

The cold hit her as she stepped through the door and drew in a breath of fresh air she'd not realised she was craving.

He was wrong. Her mum wasn't coming back.

Lorraine knew it. Felt it in the depths of her soul.

7

THIRTY-ONE YEARS EARLIER

Sandra pushed the door to the nursery open with one finger and let it swing wide.

Weak autumn sunshine fought to cast a pale finger of light through the narrow break in the curtain across the darkened room.

A room Henry had poured his heart and soul into decorating ready for the new arrival. As they'd not known the sex of the baby, he'd decorated it in a beautiful pastel wallpaper they'd chosen together. Sweet baby elephants blowing trumpets of rainbows across the wall.

She approached the cot, her gaze skimming over the white broderie anglaise sheet that had been thrown back across the baby-blue blanket with its satin edging to leave the cot empty.

Fear clutched at her throat as she held her breath. A breath she released in a rush as a soft sound behind her had her turning on her bare heel. Nothing more than a whispered gasp, barely audible in the cotton-wool silence.

A sob built, only to lodge in her throat.

In the shadowed area between the open door, corner of the

room and the wardrobe with his back to her, as though trying to hide, Trevor's shoulders hunched up to his ears.

'Trevor?'

She wondered if he'd even heard her, he held so still.

'Trevor.'

The boy turned. He cradled the baby to his narrow chest with such tenderness her heart skipped in relief.

'Thank God,' she whispered.

She took a step towards him, only to come to a sudden halt as he raised his face to her.

His eyes met hers over the top of the tiny bundle. 'I can't hear him breathing.'

Sandra stood rooted to the spot. Terrified at the look in Trevor's eyes, she stretched out her arms. 'Give him to me.'

He shook his head. The baby's legs dangled loose from Trevor's small hands, his head flopped over Trevor's arm. 'He's not breathing.'

Hysteria grabbed Sandra's throat until she almost choked. 'Give him to me, Trevor.' Her words through lips that barely moved hung leaden in the room between them.

She stepped forward and reached out cautious hands to take her baby's slack body from the boy.

Relieved of the weight of the baby, Trevor's arms flopped to his side.

She stared down into her precious baby's face, stepped over to the window for a clearer view.

Blue-tinged lips, chalky white skin.

Her legs gave way, and she sank onto the thick new baby-blue rug they'd recently laid in the bedroom. It gave no comfort.

Sandra touched the tips of her fingers to her son's icy cheek as a tear fell onto his skin.

She raised her head to stare at the boy hovering above her.

'He's dead, isn't he?' His voice, filled with flat conviction, held not one iota of despair while hers raged in her chest.

Tears streamed down her face as she met Trevor's eyes. 'What did you do to him?'

The only indication he'd heard her was a slow blink.

'I said...' She raised her voice. 'What did you do to my baby?'

He remained silent above her, freckles stark on pale skin with flags of red slashed across high cheekbones. Purple bruises smudged under the dead eyes of a monster.

'You've killed him.'

Unable to struggle to her feet, she glared up at him, her voice a piercing shriek of primal pain.

'You've murdered my baby.'

8

EIGHT HOURS SINCE PHONE CALL

Lorraine drew her car to a shuddering stop on the pebble-stoned drive of her mum's house. She glanced over her shoulder at her son, fast asleep in his car seat, and blew out a soft breath as she lowered both front windows an inch to let in some fresh air before switching off the engine.

With the radio still playing softly in the background, she combed shaking fingers through hair she'd not even brushed as she'd dashed out that morning.

What must Mark Hearn have thought when she pushed through the automatic doors of the police station all dishevelled and hysterical? No wonder the man hadn't wanted to take her report seriously. It wasn't him who'd made her feel like a fool. All he'd done was make her re-evaluate herself and the situation.

She leaned her head back against the headrest and closed her eyes, too exhausted emotionally and physically to even move. 'God.'

What an idiot.

Of course there was a rational explanation. She'd not even checked the garage to see if her mum's car was there or not. Her mum left it on the drive during the day on the infrequent occasions she used it, but every evening without fail, she put it away in the garage. In case there was a heavy frost. In case someone broke into it. In case it was stolen.

Lorraine hadn't made the assumption that because it was so early, the car was still away. No, she'd simply panicked and never gave it a thought.

Nor had she checked to see if her mum's phone was missing.

She gave Elijah a quick glance before she opened her door and slipped out, hoping the soothing sound of the radio would disguise the heavy clunk as the door closed and clicked as she pressed the lock. It would probably only play for five minutes before the battery saver powered it down, but that would be sufficient.

It wouldn't take her a moment to check on her mum again. To see if she was there.

Hope tremored in her throat.

She pushed the key into the lock of the front door and turned it.

Without entering, she already knew.

Oppressive silence pressed down the moment she closed the front door behind her.

'Mum!' she called out with a bravado she didn't feel.

There was no reason she should feel insecure in what used to be her own home. The place she'd known all her life, been brought up in. But her mum's phone call the night before had changed all that. Discomfort niggled at the back of her mind, setting her nerves on edge.

This time when she went through the house, quick and efficient, eyes scanning for clues, she found her mum's handbag with her purse inside tucked beside the armchair where her mum believed no burglar would look. It was probably the first place. But it was there.

If there'd been a burglar, they certainly hadn't looked there. Nor on the carved wooden owl keyholder Lorraine had bought her mum years before. From it dangled a bunch of keys. The front door key, the back door key, the shed key and the car key. A neat little bundle her mum never failed to pick up as she left the house.

Lorraine moved further into the small galley kitchen and pulled open the 'bits and pieces' drawer crammed full of rubbish. It grated along the metal drawer guides and stuck halfway. Her mum had never emptied it since her dad had died. She'd never got around to sorting anything out as she slid into a black hole of depression. A depression she'd tried to hide from Lorraine and the kids.

Lorraine knew what she was looking for, though, and dug her hand inside, pushing aside a couple of passports, to pull out the old rectangular tin that had once been crammed full of fudge when they'd bought it on a visit to Looe in Cornwall.

She prised the lid free and stared into the box where her mum kept all her spare keys. They were all there. As far as she could tell.

How could her mum have left the house without anything? Keys, handbag.

She took out the second, smaller tin. The one her mum kept her 'emergency' fund in. Notes she squirrelled away on the off-chance that something she wanted was so expensive she didn't want her husband to know. Not that Lorraine's dad had ever denied her mum anything. But just in case.

The notes unravelled in her hand, and she stared at them. How the hell would she know how much money her mum kept in her secret stash? The little tin her mum had taken out from time to time and slipped Lorraine a couple of notes. 'Get yourself a haircut, our Lorraine. Treat yourself, love.'

Lorraine's throat constricted.

'Buy our Sophia something nice, she's been an angel today.'

Lorraine folded the money back up and pushed it into the tin. She hadn't a clue. There looked to be quite a bit in there. Surely, if her mum was going to take off, she'd have taken it all with her.

She grated the drawer closed, turned on her heel and headed for the front hall.

Her mum's coat was there.

She raised her hand to her mouth and listened to the sound of her own breathing wisping through her fingers.

The doors had all been locked.

She could have walked out the front door. That was a Yale lock. It would have automatically closed behind her.

Lorraine opened the door and stepped outside to check on Elijah.

Her car was parked further back on the drive than normal.

She halted.

Right underneath the registration plate of her car was a large dark patch.

Lorraine crept forward and then hunkered down right in front of her car. She leaned in close for a better look.

She rolled onto her knees and did a half downward dog, her nose almost touching the drive as she squinted at the mark.

Had it been there earlier? She hadn't noticed. Then again, she'd not been looking and perhaps she'd pulled her car further forward when she'd visited earlier.

She stretched out and touched it with her fingertip. Brought it close to her nose to smell it.

Wet. New. Sticky.

Thick black oil.

She sniffed as she straightened, scanning the area as she dipped her hand in her pocket for a tissue to wipe her finger clean. She pulled out a small pack of wet wipes. Every mother's essential item.

As she contemplated, she scrubbed her fingers clean.

It was a relatively quiet neighbourhood. Most people would be out at work having taken their children to school.

Lorraine peeped in the rear side window of her car to check on Elijah. His face slack and peacefully asleep, she sighed with relief.

She stepped away from the car, strode down the driveway, and back up next door's drive which was separated by a knee-high sickly-looking hedgerow that had been staggering on, barely alive for the past six years as far as she could recall. The only time it ever looked good was at Christmas when her mum strung a set of bright white lights along it. With a good dousing of snow, it looked even better. Right now, it looked as though the long, frosty winter with temperatures dipping below freezing for long stretches had taken its toll and dried the evergreen leaves to a dull, brown crisp that would never recover.

Mrs Tindall, her mum's next-door neighbour, answered her door after a long, hanging silence as she made her way through the short hall, her large frame slow and lumbering. A shadow through her frosted front door panel.

Lorraine plastered on a smile. The woman's penchant for other people's business had kept her mum from associating with her on all but a very shallow level for years. At the age of eighty-seven, though, Mrs Tindall had become more needy recently, and Lorraine's mum felt obliged to help out in the absence of the woman's three sons coming to visit.

'They're such busy boys, you know,' the old woman frequently told Lorraine's mum, as if she had nothing better to do than look after her elderly neighbour so they could get on with their lives.

They rarely visited, but was that more of a case of you reap what you sow? How much had Mrs Tindall encouraged them to come? She wasn't the most sociable of people either. Pleasant enough, but she kept to herself. Until recently when she'd required a little more assistance from her neighbour.

None of her boys had arranged for Mrs Tindall to have carers call around to make sure she was coping. They seemed to leave her to it. Perhaps they believed she was managing.

As the door cracked open a fraction and the old lady poked her face through the gap, her eyes filled with fear, guilt scratched at Lorraine.

'Hello, Mrs Tindall. Are you okay?'

There was a moment of silence until comprehension flooded the old lady's face and she swung the door wide. 'Oh, it's you. Come in, come in.'

'I'm sorry.' Lorraine waved her hand in the direction of her parked car. 'I've got Elijah asleep in the car. I can't leave him.'

The old woman's face dropped, and the guilt stabbed again, deeper, so Lorraine stepped closer, her voice soft. 'I just wondered if you've seen my mum today.'

Mrs Tindall's papery skin crinkled in thick weathered lines across her forehead. 'No. I'm glad you've come, Lorraine, love, I thought she said she would do some shopping for me, but she never called this morning for a list. I haven't seen her. It's not like her, you know. She usually comes when she says she will.'

Her face turned morose. 'I don't see as much of the neighbours these days. I'm not as mobile, you know. It can get a little lonely.'

She stepped closer to the door to peer up and down the empty street. 'No one out doing their gardening. The kids are all in school and the weather's been so wet lately. So unusual. You'd think by June it would have stopped raining. I think we're going to be afloat soon. Where's Noah and his ark?' She chuckled at the weak joke. 'We should look on the bright side. It can't last forever.' She leaned against the doorframe and Lorraine feared she was about to settle in for a good gossip. 'And my boys are so busy. They have their own lives to live, you know.'

Torn between tearing around in her car trying to find her mum and comforting an old lady for just a few minutes longer, Lorraine forced a smile. 'I'm sorry she's not been around. Can I get you anything, Mrs Tindall?'

The woman's face brightened. 'Just a minute. I'll get you my list.'

She hobbled off down the short, dark hallway, her breath huffing with each step. She needed a hip replacement, should have had one years before, but she was probably considered too old now even if she'd agree to one.

As she returned, holding out a long, thin piece of paper, Lorraine stretched out to take it, her gaze skimming over the items, surprised at how long the list was.

Mrs Tindall offered her an apologetic smile. 'My youngest, Gareth, is coming later. I thought I'd better get some treats in. He's always hungry, that one.'

What the hell? Speechless, Lorraine almost handed the note back to her.

Perhaps precious Gareth should take his own mum shopping, or phone her first and ask if she wanted anything picking up, Lorraine thought with a stab of spite. She wondered if it showed on her face as Mrs Tindall took a step backwards, her hand on the door as if to close it.

'I really appreciate it, Lorraine. He's always so busy,' as if Lorraine wasn't, with a young child and a baby to look after. No wonder her mum got irritated with Mrs Tindall, always making excuses for her three lazy-ass sons.

'It'll be a flying visit.' A small smile showed thinning, yellowed teeth. 'I bet he turns up in one of those boy racer cars of his.'

The Stepson

Lorraine clenched her jaw shut on the rude rejoinder swirling in her head.

They weren't his, they belonged to the garage he worked for. He'd probably been asked to deliver it to a customer and was taking advantage by diverting to his mum.

Lorraine took another step back and motioned to her car, stuck now with a list she simply couldn't give back. 'I'd better get going before Elijah wakes. I won't be long.'

It would take her flaming ages. Maybe she'd see her mum wandering around the supermarket aisle, though.

She glanced at the list. Hardly the kind of staple food Lorraine and the kids ate. She'd be searching the shelves forever. Jaffa cakes and syrup of figs. She wasn't even sure she could get that in the supermarket. If she couldn't, then Mrs Tindall would just have to wait.

A vague glimmer of hope sparked at that thought.

She turned on her heel and set off along the short length of the garden path. 'I'll see you later, Mrs Tindall.'

'Oh, Lorraine, that reminds me.'

Lorraine ground to a halt, taking a deep breath before she turned. The old lady only wanted company, she was lonely, but Lorraine really needed to get on. Find her mum. She mustered up a smile. 'Yes?'

'Talking of cars, I did hear something in the night...'

Lorraine frowned as she stepped her way back up the path. 'You did?'

'Yes.' She rubbed gnarled fingers over her dry lips as she squinted, deep in thought. 'It's just coming back to me. I got up in the middle of the night for a glass of water. You know at my age my mouth gets so terribly dry at night...'

Lorraine just wanted her to get on with it. 'Yes.'

'Well, I remember I heard a car engine. Very loud, it was. Not one of these nice quiet purring ones my lads have these days. You can't even hear them when they arrive. Always take me by surprise. More like when Gareth was a youngster and used to fix old cars on the drive here. They'd grumble away and he'd work on them all hours until the neighbours complained.' She shot Lorraine a gimlet stare, challenging her to say anything.

Gareth was at least twenty years her senior; Lorraine had no memory of when he lived next door.

'That must have been a long time ago, Mrs Tindall. Cars are very different now.' Like her dad's MG BGT which both of them skirted mentioning, the pain of the memory too fresh.

'I know, dear, and they call it progress.' Mrs Tindall ran a cracked tongue around the inside of her bottom teeth, making Lorraine's stomach lurch. It was very possible it wasn't the woman's age, just rotten teeth that seemed to have scraped her tongue raw.

Mrs Tindall moved her weight from one foot to the other and a flash of pain darkened the woman's expression. 'I'd better go in, my legs are killing me.'

Lorraine threw the car a quick regretful glance and then stepped over the threshold into Mrs Tindall's house. There wasn't a sound from Elijah, she'd have to take a chance, just for a moment. She couldn't miss the opportunity to question the woman further. If she left it, Mrs Tindall's memory might not hold. She'd not have thought about it, if her son's enthusiasm for cars hadn't triggered something. Lorraine couldn't risk the wisp of memory slipping away.

'Come on, Mrs Tindall, I'll help you to your chair.'

'Close the door, mind. I don't want to let the cold air in.'

Lorraine pushed it to with a loud click as the Yale lock clunked into place. She hesitated. The same lock as her mum had. So, if she'd gone out the front door, she'd have locked herself out. Her first thought had been right.

Why would she have done that? Locked herself out.

Unless something had panicked her. Why hadn't she phoned Lorraine again? Had Lorraine been so off when her mum called that she'd been reluctant to phone back? Not answer the phone to her own daughter. Or had she fallen back asleep?

Regret tumbled from her as Lorraine turned and followed Mrs Tindall into her sitting room. The smell of stale cigarettes and urine hung in the air.

'Sit down, sit down.'

'I'm sorry, I can't stay,' Lorraine reminded her. 'I have Elijah in the car.'

'Oh, yes, off you go then.' Disappointment hung between them.

'I'm sorry, another time.' Lorraine raised the list. 'I'll go and get your shopping.'

'Shopping.' The woman's face brightened. 'Ah, yes, Gareth is coming.'

'I'll be back soon.' Lorraine took a step backwards and kept her voice casual. 'Did you say you heard a car next door last night?' She gave the woman a gentle reminder.

The slide of confusion drifted from the older woman's face as she heaved herself back in her chair and a mangy old cat leaped onto her lap before she'd even settled. Maybe the smell of urine wasn't from Mrs Tindall but from the four cats that loitered around the dingy lounge. A mirror image of her mum's house but cluttered to the point where Lorraine imagined the woman could barely move between the piles of boxes containing cat food and piles of magazines on healthy living. The irony of it struck her, but she didn't feel inclined to smile. The damp smell of cardboard came from boxes stacked three high lining one flock-wallpapered wall.

'A car. Yes, I did. It was a little after 3 a.m. Like I said before, I got up to get a drink. It must have been the sound of the engine that disturbed me. I'd been dreaming about Gareth tinkering out there and what the neighbours would say.'

Lorraine wished she'd get to the point instead of having another snide stab at neighbours who evidently had every right to complain about her precious son fixing cars on the drive. Her dad had never done that with his old classic. He'd taken it to his friend's workshop years ago and spent the weekends there tinkering with it. In more recent years, it had stayed in the garage most of the time with him buffing the paintwork to a high shine.

'Anyway.' Mrs Tindall's scratchy voice pulled her back to the present. 'When I turned the light on, I looked out the window and there was an old car in your mum's drive. I couldn't hear the engine no more, but it started up again and off it drove. It might have been the light from my window chased them away.'

'Them?' Lorraine jumped on the woman's words. 'You could see them?'

A twitch of frustration crossed Mrs Tindall's face at the interruption, and she circled her fingers in the air. 'No. No, I couldn't see anyone. I don't think.' She closed her eyes, shook her head as she opened them again. 'No.' Her voice was stronger, more definite. 'Just the reflection of the streetlights on the windscreen as the car reversed. It could have been one, or two.' She shook her head again and the folds of loose skin around her chin wobbled. 'I don't know for sure. Do you think your mum went somewhere?' Her lips pursed. 'Maybe she decided to go on holiday. She'd been talking about it. Taking a few days away on her own. Maybe it was spur of the moment.'

Lorraine blew out a breath. 'She's not gone abroad.' Her mum's passport had been in the stuffed drawer she'd just rifled through. Unless it was an old one Lorraine had seen. She wouldn't be surprised. Her mum and dad had kept all their old passports from year dot.

A deep throb pulled and the let-down of her milk had her raising both hands to her breasts. 'Oh, Mrs Tindall. I'm so sorry. I have to go. Elijah's awake.' Her body perfectly attuned to her son reminded her of his needs.

The woman's face creased. 'How do you know?' Her eyes dipped from Lorraine's face to her breasts and despite her age, the memory obviously still lingered of baby days. 'Ah, off you go now. He'll be needing his feed.'

Lorraine turned, mild panic speeding her through the hallway. 'I'll let myself out. I'll be back later with your shopping.' She slammed the door a little harder than she'd intended as she dashed out. A slide of dread in her stomach at the thought of going back into her mum's house to feed the baby.

She opened the rear door, unlatched a keen Elijah from his seat and moved instead to the driver's seat, shoving it back away from the steering wheel so she could feed her son there.

She stared at the blank windows of the deserted house.

'Where did you go, Mum?'

9

ELEVEN HOURS SINCE PHONE CALL

Gareth stepped from his car at the same time Lorraine drew hers back into the adjacent drive after her quick sojourn to the shops.

He gave her a dismissive glance, a slight raise of his eyebrows in recognition and then turned to make his way to his mum's front door.

Despite the exhaustion, she leaped from her car and called out to him. 'Gareth.'

Surprise registered on his face. She couldn't remember the last time she'd seen him, let alone spoken to him.

He'd aged well. Wide shoulders and a slender body spoke of a private gym membership, most likely. The thick mop of blond hair had thinned, receding slightly at the forehead and turning grey at the temples to give him more of a sophisticated look. No longer the thuggish young man she remembered, he had an elegant confidence that took her by surprise. The private registration spelling his name GA3 3TH made a mockery of Lorraine's assumption that he'd be driving past in a drop-off vehicle.

'Hi.' Her confidence dropped away in light of his self-assurance as he raised an eyebrow.

The Stepson

'Hi.' The air filled with an uncomfortable silence for a long second as he observed her, his eyes giving her a quick assessment.

Self-conscious, Lorraine thumbed over her shoulder to indicate the boot of her car. 'I have shopping for your mum.'

His face cleared. 'Oh, right. Thanks. Just bring it in.'

Her mouth dropped open. He didn't recognise her. Did he think she was a carer? A paid helper who was just about to cart in a boot full of shopping. Someone he considered beneath him and his help. Even so, surely he could show a little more compassion.

As he turned his back and made for his mum's front door, Lorraine called out again, sharper this time. 'Gareth.'

With a weariness displayed in the droop of his shoulders, he swivelled back around.

Lorraine almost bared her teeth as she forced herself to grin. 'I'm Lorraine. Sandra's daughter. I've just done your mum's shopping for *you*.' She hoped the neat little stab would hit its target. 'Would you like to give me a hand to bring it in?' For better effect, she continued, 'I've got my baby in the car and I'm in a bit of a rush. I have things *I* need to do.'

He dipped his hands into his perfect suit trousers, a sharp crease down the centre of each leg, and jiggled his keys before nodding.

'Sure.' He stepped effortlessly over the small hedge between the drives as Lorraine popped the boot open.

She indicated the pile of bags on the right side of the boot. 'They're your mum's.'

'Jesus.' He rubbed his perfectly smooth-shaven jaw. 'What the hell has she bought?'

'Cat food, mostly. Cat litter. Cat treats. And a few Marks and Spencer ready meals – for your mum, I assume. Not the cats.'

He breathed in a heavy sigh as he leaned into the boot and

started to collect up the bags. He grunted as he looped his fingers through the fifth bag.

'I'll bring the rest,' Lorraine volunteered.

'It's okay. I'll manage, then you can get off.'

'No problem.' It had cost her just over sixty-five quid, an amount she could hardly waive in her situation, she barely had enough to survive on day to day as it was. Her own mum had to help her out since Simon left. In the absence of his income coming into the house, it was even more thinly stretched now. According to him, he'd bung her a few quid here and there when he could. A few quid would hardly suffice, but she'd had to apply for child maintenance in the absence of Simon voluntarily paying anything and that all took time. Meanwhile she was having to survive on maternity pay, making plans to return to work early just to make ends meet.

Despite her mum's reluctance to look after baby Elijah, she was going to have to. She'd said it was too much asking her to look after a baby. Lorraine couldn't afford private nursery fees. She was currently up to her eyes in applying for help with childcare costs, universal credit, childcare vouchers, working tax credit. All of it so confusing.

Her mum hadn't looked after Sophia, reasoning that she didn't want the responsibility and that she wanted to spend more time with Lorraine's dad once he was retired. Now he was gone, perhaps her mum would be happy to help out.

If ever she could find her mum.

Lorraine scooped up the remaining two bags and followed Gareth by trotting down her mum's drive and up Mrs Tindall's. By the time she arrived at the front door, he'd already disappeared into his mum's house.

Huffing slightly, Lorraine carried the bags through the lounge into the kitchen. 'Hi, Mrs Tindall. I'm back.' She punched a level of cheer into her voice she was long past feeling. She'd check on her mum's house again, but she needed to pick Sophia up from school shortly. She'd barely had time to make a quick sandwich earlier after she'd fed Elijah. Guilt stole her appetite, but she knew she needed the strength while she was breastfeeding. More than anything, she could have done with a nap when Elijah had his, but so far that opportunity had eluded her.

She looked around for somewhere to put the bags. In the uncomfortable silence, her attention was drawn to Gareth.

White faced, he stared around as though he'd never been in the place before. 'Shit.'

'Is everything okay?'

His mouth dropped open as he focused on her. 'Okay? Okay?' His voice dropped to a vicious whisper. 'No, everything is not bloody well okay. I thought your mum was looking after her.'

'My mum?' She dumped the bags on the floor at her feet. 'No.' Lorraine shook her head. 'No. She does the occasional shopping for her, but she doesn't look after her. Your mum is not her responsibility.' She felt her hackles rise.

His spine went ramrod straight. 'Evidently.'

The sharp sting of fear hit her. She wasn't up to this. She had a new baby, a missing mum. Somewhere along the way, her backbone had wilted.

She held up a hand, palm outwards and took a step back. 'Look. This has nothing to do with my mum. She's not your mum's carer.'

'Well, if she's not, who the bloody hell have I been paying for the last six months?'

10

THIRTY-ONE YEARS EARLIER

Sandra pointed a shaky finger at her husband, so it almost stabbed at the end of his nose. 'I'll not have him here, do you understand? It's him or me, but I can't live in the same house as that... that demon.'

Henry reached out conciliatory hands, but she jerked back out of his reach.

'He's not a demon, love, it wasn't his fault.'

'Not his fault?' Her face went numb with disbelief. 'Henry, he killed our son, your son.'

He reached out again and this time she let him put his hands on her forearms in a gentle entreaty. A face wreathed with his own pain, he kept his voice gentle. 'Now, Sandra, you know that's not true. They said it was SIDS, love. Sudden infant death syndrome. They can't explain why an apparently healthy baby suddenly dies but they think it's more common to babies born underweight or premature. Alexander was both. Did you hear what they said about it occurring more often in boys than girls?'

She shook her head, adamant that the so-called 'professionals' were wrong. He'd only been a couple of weeks premature and slightly underweight. They'd released him from hospital, hadn't they? There was nothing wrong with her baby boy. He'd been healthy. Normal.

'You didn't see Trevor. His face when I walked in. Those eyes, Henry. He's evil. He killed our baby. I know he did.'

Henry flinched as spittle flew from her lips and splattered his face. 'I'm sorry, love, but you're wrong.'

Enraged, Sandra raised her hands, jerking his touch away from her. 'I'm not wrong! You're wrong. That crazy little bastard murdered our little boy, and all you can do is stand there and tell me *I'm* mad.' She threw her arms wide. 'That these things happen. Well, I am going out of my mind, but it's not with grief and hormones as they insist on telling you. It's fear. Absolute bloody terror.'

'There's nothing to fear from him, Sandra. He can't harm you. He wouldn't.'

'I'm telling you, I'm next and we certainly can't even consider having more children with him here.' She'd stopped making sense, even to herself, but how did she make him believe her?

Bordering on hysteria, tension tightened already thinned lips. 'You get rid of that child, right now, or I won't be responsible for the consequences, Henry.'

The slight weight of a hand on her shoulder had her spinning around.

Dr Williams took a hasty step back, the hand he'd touched her with flying to a strand of thinning hair to push it back from his face with shaking fingers. He was supposed to be there to help, to give her something to calm her down. He'd arrived at Henry's behest, not hers. Well, she didn't want to calm down. She needed to stay alert. Aware.

'Now, Sandra, this isn't doing anyone any good.'

'It's doing me no good having a murderer in my house.'

'Perhaps you should consider leaving the house for a few days, maybe if we admit you…'

His gaze trailed to Henry and back again.

She whipped her head around just in time to catch her own husband giving some kind of consent.

How dare he!

He was siding with that little shit. The cuckoo in the nest.

She narrowed her eyes and bared her teeth at him. 'Traitor.' She flung herself towards him, her fingernails reaching for his face.

Henry's eyes shot wide, filling her with a wild satisfaction that at last he was taking notice. He had to listen.

He took a step back and Sandra's body was slammed to the floor. A restraining hand pinned her head so she couldn't move, a weight lay across her legs, but she still felt the sharp nick of a needle as it pierced her skin.

Henry's voice came from a distance somewhere above her. 'I'm sorry, love, I'm sorry, Sandra.' He drew in a jerky breath, his voice fading. 'What have you given her?'

The doctor's voice was mild. 'Two milligrams of lorazepam. It's a sedative. Five milligrams of haloperidol, an antipsychotic drug.'

'She's psychotic?' The fear in her husband's voice tore through her.

'No.' The feral growl escaped her lips. She bucked but the restraint was secure.

'As we discussed, Henry, this can happen to some women after giving birth, especially in light of losing the baby, too. It's for her own protection. And that of your son.'

Her son was already dead.

They were talking about Henry's spawn. Not hers. Never hers.

Her baby was dead. Murdered.

Tears streaked down her face as she attempted to raise a head too heavy to hold up.

Her muscles melted as black waves washed over her. There was nothing she could do now, he was going to get away with murder. The strong hold on her slackened and she slipped into oblivion.

* * *

The atmosphere hung thick with concern as Trevor curled himself into a tight ball, his bony knees digging into his thin breastbone. He hugged a small brown paper bag stuffed with clothes to his empty stomach. He was so hungry and yet he couldn't eat. Nausea gripped at him.

Clothes he'd outgrown to a great extent since his mum died and no one had noticed, so preoccupied with the imminent arrival of his half-brother. A half-brother who was now dead. Just days after he'd been born.

Adult voices lowered so he barely heard them, just catching the occasional word. Enough to fill him with fear.

'Not for long, Henry…'

'Psychosis…'

'…a danger to herself.'

'He's been through enough.'

'Sandra is never going to accept him.'

'Temporary…'

'Just until things settle down.'

Trevor raised his head to try to catch his dad's gaze. He wouldn't look at him but scrubbed a hand over a face streaked with tears as he wiped a ruddy nose.

'I dunno. What's for the best?'

Trevor's bottom lip trembled. 'Dad.'

None of the adults looked at him, but one of them must have heard, surely?

'Dad?'

'Do you have parents who will have him?'

'No.' He shook his head. 'It's not practical. They still have my younger sister at home. There's nowhere for him that would be...' He recalled the words his father used. '...appropriate.'

The long silence hung as though the others held their collective breath waiting for more, but nothing came.

'What about his other grandparents? On his mum's side? Will they have him, just for a while?'

'I doubt it. They wouldn't even help out while Sandra was in labour. Maybe if they had, none of this would have happened.' He shook his head. 'They said he was too much of a handful for them.'

He lowered his voice, but it still carried to where Trevor hunched over. 'She changed as soon as he arrived. Thought he had it in for her.' Bitterness crept into his dad's voice. 'It was fine when he just came for short visits, but since his mum died...' He huffed out a breath. 'He's been very demanding, needing attention all the time. If he thinks I'm paying too much attention to Sandra, he... well, he acts up. He can be really... naughty.'

Trevor lowered his head back down to his knees. Not with fear and trepidation this time, but to disguise the boil of anger.

It was her fault. He'd known it was her, but he thought his dad loved him.

He'd never realised his dad didn't want him, either. He'd thought it had been that stupid, fat hysterical woman who kept giving him the stink eye. Every time she'd looked at him, there was something there. Fear. He'd coped with that. Found it a little funny at first. Until her looks became more guarded. Suspicious.

But he had his dad. Or so he thought. He'd been mistaken.

Neither of them wanted him.

Nor did his grandparents. None of them.

Nobody did.

The sharp sting of disillusionment branded him for life.

The Stepson

'Trevor?'

He jerked his head up and met soft eyes filled with concern as he held onto his terror before it consumed him. The woman in the grey suit, matching hair in a neat bun at the back of her head, leaned down.

What were they going to do with him? Would they send him to prison? How old did you have to be to go to prison?

He sucked in a deep breath, swallowing down tears that threatened to choke him.

'It may be good for you to come with me for a little while. Let things settle down with your stepmum. She's very poorly right now. All she needs is some peace and quiet.'

'Why can't she go away?'

A flicker of a smile curved her lips. 'Because the doctor has decided she'll heal better at home. In her own environment.'

He dipped his head to his knees to hide the cold satisfaction at the thought of his... of Sandra, because he couldn't think of her as any kind of mother to him... of her lying upstairs in bed. Drugged so hard, her head had lolled to one side so she looked like she had a broken neck. Now, he could have his dad to himself. If only they would let him. He raised his head and met her gaze.

'I don't want...'

The soft eyes of the social worker turned flinty.

Trevor's muscles stiffened as he withdrew and fell silent. Would she hit him for talking back, for expressing an opinion?

Like his mother used to.

The same look that hovered in Sandra's eyes when she glared at him over his dad's shoulder. Such anger. It lurked beneath the surface so no one else could see. But he knew. He saw.

Retribution had never come fast and direct but simmered like a well-seasoned wine. And then wham. His mum would get him.

The day she fell down the stairs, lying at the bottom in a tangle of limbs, her head crooked at an unnatural angle, was the day he thought to celebrate his freedom.

Until he realised Sandra was cut from the same cloth.

It was only a matter of time before she also showed her colours. Not to everyone.

Just him.

And she had started to. The day she brought his baby brother home, Sandra had changed from mild and slightly scared, to full-on raging protector of her newborn.

And now this woman, this official, who was determined to take him away from his dad. Another one.

He clamped his mouth shut, looking at hers for the tell-tale indication.

Lines feathered out from tightened lips.

That was it. The dead giveaway.

She'd not get him now, but later. When there were no witnesses. When his dad was no longer there to protect him.

And he wouldn't be. Couldn't be.

They wanted to take him away.

Away from the only protection he'd ever known.

Away from his dad.

This wasn't the way it was supposed to be.

11

FIFTEEN HOURS SINCE PHONE CALL

For the fourth time, Lorraine returned to her mum's house, in between all the other jaunts she'd done, including picking her daughter up from school. She was exhausted.

Still her mum wasn't there and it wasn't fair on the children. She needed to get them to bed.

Surprised to see Gareth's car still parked in Mrs Tindall's driveway, Lorraine hesitated. She needed to ask for her money but didn't see it would be forthcoming while Gareth was around. It wasn't fair. He'd not been paying her, but her mum. It's not like she'd made off with it.

Nor was it like her mum.

So out of character, she just didn't understand it.

How could she take money for a job she wasn't even doing? She thought of the roll of notes in her mum's drawer. Far more than Lorraine remembered seeing there previously.

Lorraine turned around in her seat so she could see her children.

'I won't be a minute, Sophia, just stay in the car with Elijah.'

'I want to see Grandma.'

'Grandma isn't here right now. I'll only be a minute. I just have to pick something up that I forgot.'

Sophia's bottom lip poked out.

'Grandma's gone away for a couple of days.' Lorraine rushed to stop that little drama before it developed.

'With Grandad?'

Lorraine paused, a catch in the back of her throat as the memory of her dad flashed up. How had things got this bad? It had all started with his death. 'Grandad?' She tried to keep the tears from welling in front of her daughter. 'Grandad's in heaven, Sophia. Grandma can't be with him.'

She hoped to hell she wasn't.

Sophia dipped her head and pinched her plump bottom lip between her thumb and forefinger. 'I think he's come back.'

Her voice was so low, Lorraine wasn't sure she'd heard right. 'Sorry?'

Sophia looked back up at her. 'I think Grandad has come back down from heaven to visit us.'

Lorraine clung onto her sanity by a thread. This was all getting a little too surreal. She had to keep calm otherwise Sophia would clam up.

'What makes you think Grandad has come to visit?'

'I saw him today.'

'Where?' This time she couldn't stop the question from punching out and Sophia's eyes went wide.

'He was outside the school at playtime.'

'Who was?'

'Grandad.'

Everything inside Lorraine stilled. Her entire body went numb as she stared at her daughter. She forced a swallow. She opened her mouth to speak and then closed it again. Sophia hadn't mentioned her grandad in ages. She sometimes said she missed him, but that was normally after she'd been with her grandma for a while and memories of him were dredged up. They didn't make it a point not to speak about him. He was part of their lives and Sophia had adored him. She'd also been devastated when he died. Old enough to understand that he'd gone, but quick to recover, as children do.

Lorraine had no reason to believe that her daughter was lying, but how could she have seen him? She didn't want Sophia to think she didn't believe her, even though it wasn't possible. She clung onto the calm that settled like a cloak on her.

'Where exactly did you see him?'

Sophia rolled her eyes as though she was deep in thought. 'I was looking through the fence.' She clawed her fingers to show how she'd linked them through the playground mesh fencing. 'He was under the big tree in the sports field.'

'The oak tree?'

'Yes.'

It was distinctive enough. There was only one oak tree with its enormous trunk and branches spreading wide to throw shade on an otherwise treeless field that was lined with hedgerows and wrought-iron fencing.

It was also far enough away from the playground that Sophia could easily have been mistaken. You'd have to have eyes like a shitehawk to see anything other than an indistinct figure from that distance. She glanced at Sophia. The child did have good eyesight.

Lorraine breathed out slowly. She wasn't about to make her daughter feel foolish for saying such a thing. It was a genuine mistake. The fields next to the school weren't council owned, but private land with a public right of way all the way across where locals walked their dogs. Her daughter could have seen anyone there. As long as they hadn't been hovering outside the school; from the sound of Sophia's explanation, it seemed like he'd just been leaning against the tree.

'Perhaps he just wanted to make sure you were all right. A quick visit from heaven.'

There was silence for a moment in the car, apart from the rattle of Elijah's teething ring as he bounced it up and down in rhythm with his legs happily kicking.

'Mummy, do you get younger when you die and go to heaven?'

'Ummm, what makes you ask that?'

'Grandad looked a lot younger. More like his photographs when he had more hair.'

Lorraine blew out a breath and cast a relieved smile at her daughter. The recent image of her grandad had obviously faded, but the photographs Grandma had framed and hung on her walls of him were of his younger days. It was false memories jogging Sophia's mind.

'Except he was bigger. Much bigger.'

Lorraine blinked. It was all too weird. Everything was weird.

'Do you think you grow when you go to heaven?'

Lorraine lowered her head and rubbed her hands over her face. 'Quite honestly, Sophia, I really don't know. But next time you see Grandad, you be sure to give him a wave from me.'

She pulled at the door handle and forced a smile as she turned to her children.

'Okay. I'll be just a minute. Just got to grab something from Grandma's and then we'll go home.'

She slipped from the car, locking the doors as she went, a sense of unease hovering at the edge of her mind. Uncomfortable at leaving her children alone in the car even for a moment while she slipped back inside the house to check if her mum had returned. It was never something that had bothered her before, but now the atmosphere of threat shadowed them.

In the silence, she circled around.

'Mum, where the hell are you?'

Her whispered entreaty went unanswered.

12

TWENTY-SEVEN YEARS EARLIER

Raucous, rattling snores filled the house, so the internal walls visibly shook.

Trevor inched open the door to the bedroom and stepped his bare feet gingerly past the creaky floorboard, so the sleeping man didn't waken.

The snores stopped abruptly, and Trevor's breath caught in his throat as he stared through the mirror on the opposite wall at the bear of a man in the bed. The duvet cover was flipped over with the man's sturdy leg thrown over it. His back to Trevor was covered in thick, wiry black hair. A bear. A beast.

Trevor swallowed, desperate to run in case the man stirred, but frozen to the spot with horrified fascination.

It wasn't a man. It couldn't be. Could any human really have that much hair? And on their back? Their arse?

His dad had barely any hair and where there was on his legs it was finer, lighter. Trevor couldn't ever remember being conscious of his dad having a hairy back. This man was more like a gorilla.

He acted like one too.

An animal.

The cruel twist of his lips exposed square teeth, large and gapped, when he stared at Trevor through narrowed eyes. Definitely a gorilla.

Trevor sidled back, as silent as he could, and then tiptoed through the small bungalow to the kitchen.

Garlic from the previous night's take-away meal hung with a sickly sweetness on the air.

He poked at the boxes lying strewn across the stained draining board. Congealed food stuck to the bottom of three of the metallic tubs. Food he could have had, if only the man would let him.

Trevor had been sent to bed as soon as the man arrived, with a stomach protesting its hunger and a groan of dismay stifled as Shell stared at him, fear dashing through her eyes as she watched the front door bounce open.

He hadn't seen her in the small double bed. Maybe she'd slipped out and gone to the shops while they both slept. Maybe she'd left.

Shell was his fifth foster carer in four years. They shuffled him along anytime something happened in the homes of the fosterer. Like he was the problem, not them.

The first one had been nice, but she fell unexpectedly pregnant and her interest in him suddenly waned. Children's Services couldn't get him out of there fast enough. With a new baby on the way, he assumed they took his past record into account. Their trust in him tarnished by Sandra's unfounded accusations.

The second fosterer succumbed to old age and a bad temper. She'd walloped him across the face just as the social worker was due a visit. The imprint of her palm on his cheek had been livid and undeniable.

He couldn't be blamed for that one. After all, there was no

excuse for swiping a twelve-year-old. No matter what her argument. Surely, he couldn't be blamed for the disappearance of her cat. A house cat that was never allowed out. Who'd ever heard of one of those?

It seemed like a cruelty to him, so he'd let it run wild and free. It wasn't his fault the mangy thing had no road sense. If she'd cared to look in her bin, under the bag of rubbish she'd told him to take out, the woman would have realised what had happened. Lazy, ignorant cow. It seemed to him she'd only asked to be a fosterer so someone could run around after her. Making her tea, feeding her precious cat. A cat that liked to claw at him whenever he tried to stroke it.

He could hardly be held accountable for a pure accident.

The third fosterer didn't like the way he stared at her all day. It unnerved her. Made her uncomfortable in her own home. It only took a week before they moved him on. He'd not so much as spoken a word to her during that week. It hadn't been hard to do, not once he noticed that flicker of unease when he pinned her with his gaze.

He'd quite liked Shannon and her partner Ricky. They'd been fun. For all of fourteen months, they'd had a wonderful time. Ricky took the lead, always playing games. Football all summer long, bowling. They went to the cinema. They'd had so much fun.

Until they went on a skiing holiday and Ricky broke his leg in three places. He could no longer continue his self-employed fitness business, the money had run out and Shannon had fallen to pieces with the stress of keeping them all afloat.

She'd blamed Ricky for not having insurance. Trevor hadn't understood until the day she walked out, and Children's Services arrived once more to rehome him. After all, he couldn't stay with a single male who needed personal and physical care.

His fifth placement had been good. For a while. Shell had been nice to him. A quiet woman, living on her own, she'd shared everything, despite it being meagre. She worked part time at the infant school as a dinner lady, so the hours worked well and they got along nicely. She was quiet spoken. Generous with her time. She coaxed out the best in him.

Everything had been fine until the man had come along.

Trevor had never had any issues with males before. In fact, he tended to get along better with that gender.

Not this one, though. This one wasn't human.

Trevor scraped the scraps from the tins into a small glass dish and then nuked them in the microwave until they sizzled and spit. It wasn't enough food for a growing teenager, but his stomach ached with hunger. Since the man had arrived, the food had been in much shorter supply. He'd virtually cleared the cupboards out and Shell barely had enough money to keep them both reasonably well fed.

He'd been happy, though. She'd have given him her last, often did. Until the man came.

If social services got a whiff of what was going on, they'd have something to say. They'd probably move him on again. He didn't want to be moved on. Shell and he were settled. He just needed for the man to go.

The microwave pinged and Trevor opened the door.

'What the fuck do you think you're doing?'

With guilt in his heart, Trevor spun around.

Mean, rheumy eyes glared at him from across the kitchen.

Trevor swallowed, his voice a harsh whisper as it came out. 'Just... just tidying up.'

The man cast his gaze around at a kitchen that had been neat as a pin until he arrived. Three weeks ago, he'd turned up, and since then, he'd returned every evening and stayed every night. Harsh, animalistic grunts coming from Shell's bedroom.

Her face, when Trevor looked at her, had become pinched and worn.

Trevor didn't even know his name. He didn't want to. The man was mean.

Even Shell had started to take on the weary, waxen look of the exhausted.

The man glanced at the bowl through the open microwave door. 'Give it here.'

Trevor hesitated, not wanting to pass the man who stood between him and the tea towel he needed on the other side of the counter. 'It's hot. Too hot to touch.'

'Give it here, or you'll be wearing it, you useless turd.'

Trevor reached his hand into the microwave and gulped. Heat pulsed from the dish.

This was going to hurt.

He took hold of the dish with hands that shook. He gritted his teeth and turned, the burn from the dish singeing his flesh, but it was only a short distance between himself and the only small square of kitchen bench visible. A whimper seeped from his lips and his eyes teared up as he met the man's hard gaze.

'Wimp!'

The man reached out and clamped his hands onto the back of Trevor's and pressed the boy's palms into the searing scald of the glass.

'Let go, and I'll beat the ever-loving shit out of you.' His narrowed eyes burned into Trevor's.

'Noooo.' The tears spilled over and ran down Trevor's cheeks. 'Let go. Please let go.'

'You fucking good-for-nothing scrounger. You're pathetic. You know that, don't you? Coming here and living off Shell. Eating her food, like it was your right. Little turd.'

'Let me go.' Trevor's knees started to buckle and all that held him up was the pressure from the man's hands, a vice around his.

Trevor sniffed up the snot that started to drizzle from his nose onto his top lip. 'Let me go. Pleeease.' The bitter taste of humiliation coated his tongue.

It was a power struggle. One boy could never win over man.

Disgust wreathed the man's face and with a hard shove, he pushed Trevor backwards as though the boy's weakness repulsed him.

Trevor stumbled, collapsing onto the floor, the back of his head smashed against the kitchen table leg with a sickening clunk and bright lights flashed behind his eyelids.

The glass dish flew from his tender hands to splinter into shards across the old red floor tiles.

'You stupid little shit.'

Trevor scrambled back. 'I didn't mean it.' He curled himself as tight as possible under the table where the man couldn't get him.

But he could.

He reached under with a fist the size of a spade.

Trevor grabbed the closet thing, his raw hand closed around a long, thin shard of glass. He palmed the thick square end and shot his fist out, ramming the spike deep into the man's hand until its bloodied point shot out the back between the bones, tearing through skin, tissue and veins as thick, viscous blood bubbled from the injury.

The man's scream tore through the house as his legs folded under him. Shock making his pale blue eyes bulge until they almost popped out of his head.

Trevor crawled tentatively out from under the table, his attention fully on the fallen man before him.

Crouched on the floor, gripping the wrist of his injured hand with the other, the man bobbed his head up and down as if in prayer, as he called out for his god. His saviour.

A sluice of ice ran through Trevor's veins as he stared down at the writhing form.

He came to his feet. Stood tall above him, not one iota of regret in his heart.

'Who's pathetic now?'

13

TWENTY-FOUR HOURS SINCE PHONE CALL

Lorraine turned onto her side and stared at the orange glow of streetlight that sneaked through the chink in the curtains to climb up the wall as a passing headlight swept by.

Her mind, in a turmoil, wouldn't allow her to sleep despite her exhaustion. Her mum's words circled around in her head, a whirling, continuous torment.

'Quiet. Listen. Your dad was first. Now it's me. I'm so scared, but mostly for you and the children. Because once I'm gone, you'll be next.'

She rolled over onto her other side and closed her eyes to block out the light, the thoughts, the anxiety. She shuddered as she tucked her knees up until she curled into a ball.

What more could she do? Nothing tonight. She needed sleep so she could start the search for her mum in the morning.

Lorraine forced her muscles to relax. Shut her mind down from thoughts of her mum.

The image of her dad appeared behind closed eyelids.

How strange that Sophia claimed to have seen him. A coincidence, surely. But why now? What made her child's mind think of her grandad now when Lorraine's mum had gone missing? It couldn't be connected. Lorraine hadn't even told Sophia about her missing grandma. Why would she? It would only stress the little girl out. She loved her grandma. They were so close.

Lorraine flipped over onto her back this time and watched the swathe of white light from the headlights of another passing car wash across the ceiling and down the wall before it plunged her back into darkness again.

She huffed out a breath.

When could she go to the police again? Why didn't they take her seriously?

It was all very well that man, Mark, who wasn't even a police officer telling her that so many people disappear.

It wasn't in character for her mum to go missing. Never in her life had she...

Lorraine shot up in bed, her hand flying to her mouth, her eyes straining to blink away the darkness as she pulled her knees up to her chest.

She glanced over at Elijah, asleep in his cot, and hoped her thrashing around hadn't woken him.

There had been a time. Her mum had disappeared once before. Lorraine racked her brain but for the life of her she couldn't dredge up the memory of where her mum had gone. Lorraine had been a child. Possibly ten or eleven. Her recollection was cloudy, but...

'No, Henry. I've told you. I will never, ever allow that boy into our house.'

'But...'

'Over my dead body.'

'But, Sandra, be reasonable. He only wants to come and meet us. It's been years.'

'I don't even want him to know where we live. We moved house so that he could never contact us again. Those awful, begging letters he sent. They were disgusting.'

'They were the outpourings of a child in pain.'

'Pain? What about my pain? What about my anguish?' She hugged her hands against her chest.

Lorraine pushed her face up against the spindles of the staircase until her cheeks squished. She could just about see her mum through the gap in the living room door, but her dad wasn't visible at all.

His quiet voice made her strain to hear. 'Sandra. Have some heart.'

'Heart? Heart? After what he did? And that was when he was a child. What do you think he's capable of now as an adult?'

'Shh, keep your voice down.'

'I will not! Don't you tell me what to do.'

'I didn't think you wanted Lorraine to know anything about him.'

'I don't!' The screech came from lips that had tightened into a thin line.

'Then be reasonable. If you shout, she'll be curious. She'll want to know all about him. What child wouldn't?'

'Not my child.' But her voice had lowered. 'Henry. If you allow that boy...'

'Man. He's almost twenty now. He's been gone a long time.'

Her dad stepped forward so Lorraine could see him through the gap, a sheaf of papers in his hand. 'He's been writing to us. Social services sent me his letters through Caroline.'

'I don't care. I don't want to know. I wish he'd stayed in the gutter where he's been hiding all these years.'

'Sandra. He's had the most horrific upbringing. All because we never gave him a chance...'

Lorraine's mum's head shot up. 'Because we never what? Gave him the chance to murder another...'

'Sandra! Shh. You'll wake Lorraine.'

Silence hung in a solid blanket. Lorraine edged back, her cheeks aching from where she'd had them pressed against the stair rails.

'Just give him a chance. Please, for my sake. He disappeared when he *was fourteen. Fell off the grid. They've not heard from him in years, and now he wants contact.'*

'No. I'm not having it.'

'Then I'll meet him. Away from here. Just me. I need to know where he's been. What happened to him after he disappeared that morning. I'll arrange to meet him at Caroline's house...'

'Caroline! That bloody sister of yours. Can't keep her nose out of our business.'

'It's not her fault, she just wants...'

'To interfere. To make decisions on events she has absolutely no knowledge of. She was a girl. A child. She knows nothing of what happened and quite honestly, Henry, you'd be better off cutting all ties with her too.'

The silence drew out until Lorraine could no longer hold her breath waiting for a reply. When it came, her dad's voice was low and level. *'I won't be doing that, Sandra. Not even for you. That's my baby sister we're talking about.'*

Lorraine didn't want that either. She loved her Aunt Caroline. She was always such fun. She wanted to say something. To protest, but she knew better than to get in between her parents in a row she had nothing to do with.

Lorraine skuttled back at the sound of movement from the sitting room. The rattle of keys.

'Right, then. If that's your last say on the matter, I suggest you have a hard think about what you're asking of me, Henry. When you're ready, let me know and I'll come back. You know where you can find me. Until then, don't bother speaking to me.'

Lorraine scurried further up the stairs into the shadows as her mum burst from the lounge and strode down the hall to the front door. She wrenched it open, shrugging into her heavy woollen coat as she stepped through and then slammed the door with enough force to rattle all the windows in the house.

Lorraine cupped her face in her hands. The memory of pressing her cheeks into those spindles almost physical.

What boy? What man?

The memory splintered into a million pieces that refused to fit together.

'He's here.'

'Who?'

'Your brother.'

'My...? What did you say? Mum? Are you drunk?'

It was hardly something she could take to the police. 'Oh, by the way, I just remembered something from when I was a girl.' They'd think she was making it up, just to get attention.

She sighed. Surely there was something there. She hadn't imagined it. It wasn't a false memory.

Her mum had been away for days, or so it felt like to her.

They'd barely coped, her and her dad, who was a useless cook. Mum had never left them before, to Lorraine's knowledge.

Her dad had remained tight-lipped, uncomfortable reassurances which sounded vague and not reassuring at all.

She'd squirmed with discomfort at his obvious embarrassment.

'When is Mum coming home?'

'She's gone to visit relatives.'

'Yes, but when will she be back?'

'I don't know. Eat your breakfast.'

Cereal was fine for breakfast. Only they'd run out. And then they ran out of bread. It was then that Lorraine realised that her dad had never once done the shopping. Or run a hoover over the carpet. Or changed a bed. He always washed the dishes after dinner, but he really didn't have a clue how to cook and once the meals Mum had frozen had gone, it was scrambled eggs and pasta with a tin of tuna dumped in. It was Lorraine who had to tell him to add sweetcorn and mayonnaise just to make it palatable.

Then, one day, Mum was back when Lorraine returned from school. A face wreathed with smiles and hugs hard enough to break bones. No explanation. Lorraine had struggled not to ask, but she didn't want to cause another argument. She just wanted peace between her parents. As though nothing had happened, life returned to normal. But the atmosphere had changed and there was a strangeness about her dad. Like he was treading on eggshells, worried in case her mum scarpered again.

She never did. Not as far as Lorraine knew.

But she had now.

The question was, who was the boy, the man, they'd spoken about? She knew for sure she never had a brother. She'd have remembered. So, who was he?

Was this the person her mum told her about the other night?

Had her mum gone of her own free will? Or had he taken her?

14

TWENTY-FIVE YEARS EARLIER

Dressed in shabby jeans slung low on narrow hips, not because fashion dictated, but because he hadn't had a decent meal in weeks, Trevor pulled the collar on his puffa jacket up against the persistent drizzle that found its sneaky way down his neck.

From the doorway of the charity shop he'd managed to snaffle his coat from a few days earlier, Trevor focused weary eyes on the street.

He'd thought it was bad living with foster carers, but this was worse. So much worse.

When he'd left Shell's house, it had been in a desperate rush, and he'd picked up nothing of his meagre goods. Until then, he'd never stolen in his life. Never needed to. They may not have been rich, but his mum had always provided. Put food in his stomach. He'd been warm and safe. Even when he'd lived with his dad and Sandra, he'd not realised how privileged he'd been. A roof over his head, food in his belly and a place to shower, if he'd felt the need.

He felt the need now. He could smell his own dried-on sweat. Sweat he'd worked up as he cowered in the corners of back streets and doorways, desperate not to be found. Technically, he was still underage. He'd been homeless now for almost two years, dodging and diving. Living on friends' sofas to start with, the few he had, until they'd become fed up with him. Some turning him away in case they got into trouble having a kid hide in their flat. What if social services came by? What if the police were looking for him?

Unable to get work apart from occasional dish washing at a local restaurant that paid cash and didn't ask questions, weight had dropped from him, until he was stringy.

Always aware he was on the run. In trouble. They'd send him to prison. He was old enough. It would have been youth custody if he'd given himself up back then. Two years previously. Now, he'd probably get a prison sentence if they caught him.

* * *

'Oh, my God, Trevor. They're going to put you away for this. This is not good. Hold on while I call an ambulance, then I'll have to speak with Children's Services and see what they're going to do with you.'

She'd crawled out from the bedroom where she'd been hiding so the man didn't hit her again. The skin around her left eye black and shiny. Purple fingerprints necklaced around her throat as she hitched her dressing gown high to cover them.

'Don't, Shell, don't tell them.'

'I have to, Trevor, they need to know. You can't stay here. Not after this. They won't allow it.'

With a slow, deliberate move, he turned his hands palm upwards for her to see what the man had done.

She clapped a hand over her mouth. 'Oh, Trevor. What did you do?'

'It wasn't me. He did it.' His voice cracked as he pointed to the prone man whose howls had petered out to quiet sobs. 'He held my hands against the bowl until they burned, Shell.'

Shell shook her head and then held up one hand. 'Ambulance, please.'

She stared at Trevor as she recited the information the emergency services requested and within minutes a siren echoed in the distance. How was it every adult in his life always chose to believe another adult instead of him? Adults lied too. This wasn't his fault. He was guilty of nothing but defending himself against an animal.

The man raised his head, a drizzle of snot smeared across the bushy moustache on his upper lip. Trevor stared at that, rather than the injury the man had sustained. The injury Trevor was responsible for.

'When I've had this seen to, kid, I'm coming back here and I'm going to kick the shit out of you.'

Trevor's gaze skittered to Shell's and caught the terror streaking across it as he did.

No, he wasn't going to hang around, he'd rather risk it out on the streets than be around a woman who had no control over a man who hated. Not just him, but everyone.

As the man's face turned cruel, Trevor slipped his shoes on and pushed past the paramedics as he opened the front door for them.

Shell barely noticed. She probably thought he'd be back.

But he wouldn't. His life with her was done. Over.

He closed the door with finality.

* * *

He regretted it now. He'd never realised how hard life could be on the streets. The things he'd witnessed. It wasn't just girls who weren't safe from sexual predators, the underworld was full of them. He'd managed to avoid them so far, but what he'd witnessed from behind a dumpster down a back alley filled him with fear.

Who knew there were such animals on the loose? Beasts who roamed under the cover of darkness.

He'd thought he was a badass, that he could look after himself. He'd defended himself, hadn't he? Stabbed the man with a shard of glass. That was thinking on his feet. Or so he'd believed. But it hadn't been. It had been pure defensive reaction.

This was a whole different world.

He had to be far sneakier now. More than just thinking on his feet.

If he didn't want to be the prey, he had to become the predator.

15

TWENTY-NINE AND A HALF HOURS SINCE PHONE CALL

The car engine ticked over while Lorraine stared through the rain-streaked windscreen at the primary school beyond. She'd street parked as she always did, battling with the other mad mothers for a space close enough to the school. She'd never been one to park across a private driveway, or access.

She watched now as one of the 'privileged' screeched at an elderly lady, arms gesticulating as though it was her right to block homeowners in with her luxury four-by-four. The desperate rush to her early morning Zumba class obviously a priority. Lorraine had seen the same woman do it on several occasions, oblivious to the fact that she had no right. Her precious little boy came first. A little boy who was swiftly becoming a thug even at his tender age. Not surprising in light of his own mother's entitlement. Her insistence that no one was as important.

Perhaps she should leave home a few minutes earlier.

Elijah rattled his teething ring and made happy noises in the rear of the car as Lorraine sat, giving herself a moment to let her racing heart calm down.

She was hardly in a place to criticise someone else for leaving it until the last moment to make the school run. This morning her mind had been so sluggish, she'd barely remembered to make up Sophia's packed lunch for the school trip.

She watched as a coach pulled up outside the school gates, barely able to squeeze in as the caretaker came to remove the 'no parking' bollards he'd used to reserve the space. The normal chaos of the day had turned frenetic as women desperate to get to work, or Zumba or swimming, found themselves unable to find a spot to pull in.

Tracey Fuller, one of the mums Lorraine had come to know and avoid, double parked, and her two independent kids leaped out, toast still grasped in their hands, jam smeared up their cheeks. A scary individual, she'd told Lorraine back in September, as she skimmed a critical eye over her, that the most important thing in the morning was to put her face on before she set off for the executive job she had in Birmingham. If the kids did without breakfast, it was just tough. Evidently, it was one of those mornings for her too.

If Lorraine had been feeling generous, she would have pulled away and left her parking space for some desperately late parent. She had no idea what compelled her to wait. Her mind sat in a state of limbo as though it was waiting for some kind of revelation to pounce. A lightning strike.

An only child, it wasn't as though she could go to anyone to tug on their memories. Her mum had also been an only child. Her dad had a big, extended family but once he'd moved from Liverpool, he'd left them behind.

They'd visited often enough when her grandparents were alive, but the contact had dwindled. She'd been in her early teens, and they'd died within a year of each other. Her grandmother first, followed by a frail old grandfather who no longer had the will to live without his beloved wife.

The eldest of five, her dad had already made his move away

from a family that had once been close. From memory, Lorraine thought he'd loved them and had been particularly close to his younger sister, who must have been barely a teenager when Lorraine's parents married.

Her aunt had attended her dad's funeral, but not stayed, not spoken to her mum. Her gaze had slid over Lorraine, and she'd given a slight incline of her head in acknowledgement, eyes brimming with tears, before she'd slipped away.

Lorraine squinted through the windscreen at nothing in particular as thoughts crammed her mind, stumbling over each other like enthusiastic children vying for her attention. There was something on the periphery. A memory that just didn't want to come forward in her sluggish brain.

Lorraine stared blankly, not taking notice of the parents who made their way back to their cars, pulling away from the kerb at various panicked speeds, some of them bordering on the illegal, to leave the street quiet once more.

As the privileged woman's car pulled away with a screech of tyres, Lorraine narrowed her eyes. Leaning forward, she peered through the windscreen at the elderly lady who reached into the post box suspended on her gate and retrieved a handful of letters.

She flapped them with annoyance at her neighbour while she appeared to relate her run-in with the entitled mum. In full rant, she seemed oblivious to the fact that the other woman looked as though all she wanted to do was get off to the shops with her wheelie trolley.

Lorraine narrowed her eyes. The flapping letters triggered that elusive echo which niggled at the back of her mind.

Letters.

She drew in a long, slow pull of breath.

Letters.

The night her mum and dad had rowed, and she'd left, it had been about some letters.

Lorraine closed her eyes and let another piece of the puzzle slide into place to give a bigger picture.

* * *

'She had no right. None at all passing these on to you. Disrupting our lives again. I can't believe she'd interfere.'

'She wasn't interfering, Sandra, she was just doing as he asked.'

'She could have kept them to herself. We didn't need to know.' Sandra's temper erupted. *'How dare she? I'll never speak to her again. What a cow.'*

'Sandra! That's my sister you're talking about.'

'Is your sister more important than me? These letters more important?'

She hurled them in his face. 'You need to reassess your priorities,' she hissed under her breath, so Lorraine barely heard. 'Me and Lorraine, or them.'

* * *

A dull drizzle started to fall as she stared through a windscreen streaked with rain. She wiped the back of her finger across eyes that had turned wet and realised the tears leaking blurred it even more.

A dark figure separated itself from where it had been leaning against a tree, unnoticed. She blinked away the tears and scrabbled to switch on the windscreen wipers as she leaned forward, peering through the rain-streaked windscreen at the familiar shape.

Her heart raced, clogging her throat until she could barely breathe.

Her fingers shook as she hit the start button on her car and the engine revved to life. The wipers gave one lazy swish, as though they had all the time in the world, and the screen cleared just as the figure stepped behind the coach and disappeared from view.

'Dammit.'

She gripped the steering wheel until her fingers ached as she stared, waiting for him to emerge again.

She snatched at the door handle and flung open the door. Out and running as the door slammed behind her, she hit the lock button on the key fob.

Lorraine dashed across the road and along the footpath that had been obscured from view by the coach from inside her car.

She followed the curve of the path and then skidded to a halt alongside the rear of the coach.

The path ahead of her was empty, except for a short, rotund man, hands cupped around his mouth as he lit a cigarette and leaned back against the front wing of the coach, blowing out a cloud of smoke that wafted off with a soft gust of wind.

The relief washing over his face was short lived as he raised his head.

'For fuck's sake.' He hauled in a quick last, desperate pull of the cigarette and then dropped it on the floor. He killed it with the heel of his boot, a waft of smoke clouding from his lips as the crocodile line of kids streamed through the school gates towards the coach, voices lifted in excitement.

Pulled to her senses, Lorraine slipped back behind the coach and dashed back across the road, hoping Sophia wouldn't catch sight of her.

She wrenched open the door and flopped into her seat, her hand covering her mouth.

She was going insane. She could have sworn the man was her dad. The breadth of his shoulders, the gait of his walk.

Her dad was dead. There was no doubt about that. He'd died. She went to his funeral. To his cremation. There was nothing left of him but dust which her mum kept in a container on the fireplace.

'Oh, Dad.'

A small sob escaped her. He was dead. She'd never seen him, except in her dreams since he'd died.

But Sophia had. Yesterday.

Was he one of the other children's dads? Someone who bore an uncanny resemblance to her own dad, who'd managed to conjure up images of him for both her and Sophia?

Perhaps he was nothing like her dad. It had only been a view from behind. She'd not got a good enough look at him. Just from the back in a coat familiar enough that the image had projected itself onto her memories.

Sophia had only seen him from a distance.

She closed her eyes and listened to Elijah's contented gurgles as though he had no idea how traumatised his mum was. Thank God. She could do without him getting upset.

Her heart fluttered like a wild bird as she slowed her breathing down.

It was all her imagination conjured up through panic because her mum was missing and maybe because of what Sophia had said the previous evening. It had left her mind open to suggestion.

It wasn't her dad. That was totally illogical.

Perhaps she was the one going mad.

She pushed the start button on the car and let out another heavy sigh. Where to now?

How much longer did she need to wait before she took it to the police again?

Did he say give it forty-eight, or seventy-two hours? She couldn't remember. All she knew was it had only been twenty-four hours since she first went in.

His words came back to her. *Unless you consider she's at risk. Is she at risk?*

She'd been too taken aback then. How could the police not believe her mum had gone missing? Why did they insist she would be perfectly fine? They didn't know her. Didn't know her habits. That she would never just take off and not say where she was going.

The memory slithered back to haunt her.

Only she had. Hadn't she?

In all honesty, could Lorraine be absolutely sure she should involve the police?

Her mum had taken off before. Disappeared.

Because of some mysterious letters.

So where were they now? What did they mean?

16

TWENTY-FIVE YEARS EARLIER

Trevor slithered down the slippery embankment to the river path. The thick, tacky mud sucked at his shoes and let out soft popping noises. Wet sneaked in through the thin, pock-marked soles to leave his toes icy.

The darkness closed in, a thick blanket as he stepped under the old railway bridge down by the Spital River to get out of the rain.

It hadn't been so bad living rough until the rain came down, plummeting temperatures with it.

He huddled at the entrance, the stench of urine filling his nostrils. Why were people so filthy? It was engrained in the red bricks, so instead of leaning against the wall, he hunkered down, sitting on his own heels.

'You're new.'

The rough gravel in the voice had terror shrieking through him as Trevor shot to his feet. 'Who the fuck are you?' On the balls of his feet, he curled his hands into fists ready to strike out at the darkness.

He'd survived the past few months by living off scraps from the bins and sleeping out under the stars, but he couldn't sustain that, not with autumn sliding into winter.

A dull click followed by a flood of bright light from a torch illuminated the area, bouncing off the low arched ceiling of the tunnel, and cast shadows of monsters to dance across oily water. Trevor took a step back, horror curdling in his stomach as he prepared to run.

Bodies littered the narrow pathway between the curve of the bridge wall and the fast-flowing River Spital that ran underneath. Horror filled him at the sight. A dirge of humanity huddled together for warmth under dusty, torn blankets and cardboard boxes. More people than he could ever have imagined. Homeless. Abandoned. In total around a dozen or more in that small space.

Most of them curled up away from the light, their faces hidden, disinterested in becoming involved in something that might escalate. Might attract attention.

There was a strange kind of regiment to them. Their makeshift beds lay in a ragged line along the wall away from the chill of the river, bags with discarded food and clothes spilling out were wedged between the bodies, presumably so they each could protect their own property. Rubbish had been abandoned to disgorge out each side of the tunnel and into the river where it bobbed with obscene threat.

Trevor's mouth dropped open.

'He's with me.'

A short, wiry boy stepped into the light, so his ginger hair glowed like a beacon and the freckles splurging across his face stood out in stark comparison to his white skin. Eyes glowed an unnatural amber.

'What's your name?' The towering presence of darkness above him made Trevor's muscles quiver. If he ran, they'd easily catch him. He might be swift on his feet, but not swift enough to outrun this guy. It looked as though most of them were disinterested, drugged, drunk or frightened to pitch in. The quiet shuffle of bodies moving away was testament to the fact that nobody would be willing to help him. Except this boy.

Trevor opened his mouth, but the dryness of his throat wouldn't allow any sound to come through.

'Your name, toerag!' The big guy leaned in close, his bald head glowing like a chestnut in the pale light.

'Rory.' The quiet confidence of the new voice thick with the distinct Wirral accent even in that one word had Trevor spinning around.

Diamond raindrops shimmered from the close-cut afro hairstyle as a tall, skinny guy dressed all in black stepped out from under the downpour. The light from his phone tossed a wide arc under the bridge combining with the torchlight, so the bodies scuttled further away, blinded by the light. 'Back off, Skin, he's one of mine. Just got the wrong end of the bridge, didn't you, kid?'

Trevor gave one sharp nod and the man's white teeth gleamed as he shot a wide grin. 'You too, Red, wharrah you doing here?'

The ginger-haired boy stepped forward, his shoulders hunching up to his ears as the sharp whip of rain hit him and he tucked his hands into the pockets of jeans that drooped low on his hips. 'Looking for Rory, Caid.'

Caid nodded, dark eyes glittering dangerously in the white light of his phone. 'We don't have a problem, do we, Skin?'

Skin stepped back, his hands spread wide as his light went out and he melted into the background.

Caid cast a look over the two boys. 'Follow me.' He turned on his heel, snapped the phone light off and plunged them all into darkness.

17

THIRTY-FOUR HOURS SINCE PHONE CALL

'Hello.' Lorraine stuttered to an awkward halt.

She hugged a cushion to her middle, her legs curled under her on the sofa.

There was silence on the other end of the line.

Lorraine had no idea what to do, no one she could turn to. Would the woman speak to her now?

Her own house had a hollow loneliness to it and Lorraine had no idea what to do with herself, other than pace back and forward. Sophia needed to be picked up from school shortly and Elijah was restless, not settling properly for his nap.

She'd brought him downstairs and popped him in his maxi seat. The gripe water Lorraine had given him didn't seem to have taken effect and flags of colour splashed one cheek. Teething, most likely.

She should have given him Calpol first before dialling her aunt. It would be rude to just hang up now, though. Now she'd made the call.

'Hello, is that Caroline?'

She'd taken her aunt's telephone number from her dad's phone when the police had returned his personal possessions, her mum too distressed to even look.

She didn't know this woman, her dad's youngest sister, very well. A vague recollection of her danced at the edge of her memory to tease her, but since her mum and dad had that argument all those years ago, they'd never seen her aunt again. Lorraine couldn't recall her name being mentioned in the house.

It hadn't occurred to her then to miss her aunt all that much. After all, Lorraine had friends of her own age, a life to live. Fun to be had. Their age difference had meant they had little in common.

Not until the funeral did she see her aunt again, which Lorraine had thought only right she should be invited to. Her brother had died.

It seemed her mum had no compassion or understanding of that.

'I've lost my husband,' she'd wailed.

'She's lost her brother.' Lorraine's tolerance snapped. 'It's not all about you, Mum, she can't get another brother, I can't get another dad.' The unspoken implication that her mum could always get another husband.

Her mum had gasped, hands flying to her cheeks as though Lorraine had slapped her. Guilt surged, but for once Lorraine refused to let it melt her.

Her aunt had come to the funeral. Lorraine had not made any attempt to greet the woman, too concerned about her mum's feelings. She'd slid a few sly glances her way and thought she'd go over once the service was finished, but before she could, her aunt had gone.

There was no doubting the eyes. The same shape and colour as her dad's. Except his had that slash of a different colour through them. The same as Elijah's.

Other than that, there was little resemblance between her dad and aunt.

Short blonde hair framed a pixie face, with a sharp chin and nose. Her skin was smooth, alabaster. Make-up applied with skill. There was a certain aloofness to her, a serene sorrow.

Neither of her dad's surviving brothers had attended.

He'd lost two. Both to cancer. Of the remaining two, one lived in Spain, the other in Doncaster. Their wreaths had been beautiful, yet soulless without their presence.

It was then Lorraine realised how far her extended family had drifted apart. But for what reason?

'Aunt Caroline?'

'Yes?'

Now there was a long silence on the other end of the phone as her aunt waited for Lorraine to speak. Lorraine, who had no idea what she was supposed to say. She'd stabbed at the number she'd entered into her own phone when she'd called about the funeral. The action impulsive, born of terror, she now had no idea what to say.

'Hello, Lorraine.' The Scouse rise and fall a reminder of her dad's accent. One that had had the sharp edges and angles smoothed out over years of living in the mid counties but came over stronger as soon as he was on the phone. One that sounded like her aunt's now.

She held her breath, a thick lump tightening her throat.

'Lorraine? Is there something you wanted?'

'Yes.' The word rushed out in gusty desperation. 'Yes,' she said, more controlled. 'Could I come and see you?'

Silence filled the air so she pressed the phone hard against her ear, barely even hearing the static. 'Hello?'

'When?' The voice was quiet. Controlled.

'Where do you live?'

'Birkenhead.'

There was another pause as Elijah started to whimper.

Lorraine unfurled herself and gave the maxi seat a gentle rock with her foot to soothe him.

'The Wirral,' her aunt added, as though Lorraine might not know. She knew. That's where her dad grew up. She had a vague recollection of long journeys when she was a little girl. It hadn't occurred to her until recently that they'd suddenly stopped going. Her dad's family had been vague figures in a child's otherwise busy schedule.

'Tomorrow.' She couldn't go today. It was a three-hour round trip. At least. That was assuming the traffic was free flowing, which it never was.

Panic grabbed at her throat to stop her brain working. She'd need to drop Sophia at school and make a quick dash up the motorway. She could think of no other way. It wasn't a conversation she was prepared to have on the phone. She barely knew where to start.

'Can you text me your address? I can be there for around half ten.'

That would give her a couple of hours if she needed it. She did need it, she needed information, more than just a scant, uncomfortable conversation on the phone. She must see her aunt's face to know that what she was telling her was the truth.

'Is there anything in particular you're coming for?' Her voice had taken on a wary note.

Lorraine drew in a long breath. 'I need to know why Dad stopped talking to you. I need to ask what you know about some letters?' It all came out in a mad rush, a question rather than a statement as she'd intended, while Elijah went from whimper to howl. She raised her voice to be heard above it as she unstrapped him, looping one arm around him to pick him out of the seat, hugging him to her.

'I'm not sure how much I can help you. But I do have some letters. Ones I never passed on to your dad. I'll find them for you.'

'I'm sorry, what?'

'I have some letters.'

'I don't...' The wail filled her head so she could no longer think. She'd wanted to mention him. The man her mum was afraid of.

'I'll see you tomorrow.' The high-pitched screech obviously had the same effect on her aunt as Elijah placed his forehead against Lorraine's and bawled down the phone.

'Tomorrow. Yes.'

The phone went silent, but her son didn't.

18

TWENTY-FIVE YEARS EARLIER

'Rory.'

Trevor gave a low groan. Every bone in his rapidly growing body objected to him moving.

'Rory.'

Trevor slit open thick eyelids and grunted again. He was Rory now. Red had named him, and he didn't dare object or he'd be out on his ear in the cold and the pouring rain with his belly growling with hunger.

They'd fed him the night before from a carrier bag full of sandwiches from Costa and Starbucks. Donated to one of the lads who stood outside all day, every day, offering *The Big Issue* to passers-by.

He'd sold twelve copies and acquired enough food to feed the small army of youngsters sharing the two-bedroom flat Trevor had been brought to the previous night. There was no mention of any cash he'd pocketed. Presumably that was for him to keep in recognition of his hard work. Because it was hard. Standing out in all weather, waiting for someone to look. Just to catch their eye and hope they didn't duck their head and run.

Mattresses lined the floor with a boot's width between each so they could be reached. Six in the large bedroom, four in the smaller. Trevor had been shuffled into the larger room after he'd eaten and showered.

A shower. He'd not had one for weeks and just the sheer joy of sluicing the rot from his skin had almost served to rejuvenate him. He'd been told to make it quick. Five minutes max, they weren't made of money. He'd taken a little longer, but no one came hammering on the door. One with a lock on the inside that gave him confidence to strip off. More than he'd had, not just in the last few weeks, but for years. Not trusting one of the foster carers to not come barging in.

He'd felt truly safe, though, for the first time since he'd done a runner. Snuggled down under a quilt, he'd slept for more than twelve hours.

His stomach was grumbling, a loud protest now it knew there was food available.

'Oy, Rory.' The boot to his backside lacked force. He'd had worse. This was purely a bump, a call for attention.

Trevor rolled over onto his back and stared up at Red. The boy's freckles stood out even starker against his pale skin and his curly ginger hair almost glowed. He'd obviously been treated to a recent shower too.

'What?' Trevor grunted, tempted to stay under the quilt.

'Food.' Red threw a small paper bag at him, and Trevor caught it one-handed against his chest.

He struggled to sit up, leaning his back against the wall.

'No eating in the bedroom, lads,' the deep voice called from the open doorway.

Caid, the guy from the night before, leaned against the doorframe. Trevor could barely remember the man, but he remembered him stuffing two tablets in his mouth for him to swallow along with cola from a can he opened in front of him. He'd barely had the energy to enquire what the hell the tablets were and only vaguely remembered Caid murmuring that they were paracetamol, and he needed a hot shower as he was in danger of hypothermia.

Truth be told, he probably already had hypothermia by the time he reached the railway bridge. His mind had turned to mush. It could have been the cold. It could have been lack of food. It could have been terror. Most probably it was a combination of all three.

When Caid had pulled the quilt over him, Trevor had curled into a tight ball around the hot water bottle that had already heated the sheets. If Caid made a move on him, Trevor wasn't sure he even had the energy to fight him off as his eyes closed tight against the thought.

Caid hadn't touched him. Nor had anyone else.

Trevor slipped from under the quilt, the well-worn but freshly laundered pyjamas he'd been given the night before hanging from his skinny frame as he dragged his naked feet across the threadbare carpet into the kitchen. He clutched the small brown bag and felt warmth seeping through it.

'Whaddya get?' Red nodded towards the bag.

'Hmm?' Trevor wasn't sure he'd regained the ability to speak.

'Breakfast. What's yours?'

Trevor slumped into a wooden dining room chair and peered into the bag. The savoury smell of something warm wafted out at him and had his taste buds popping. 'Sausage, I think.'

'Ah, God, I wanted the sausage.' Red leaned forward and inhaled the scent.

Trevor hugged the bag closer, and Red barked out a laugh. 'It's okay, you have it, I've eaten mine. It was fuckin' tuna.'

Caid leaned against the short length of kitchen counter in front of the window, so his face was in shadow as he breathed out a cloud of cigarette smoke that wreathed around him.

Trevor took a huge bite of sandwich which had already started to cool and spoke around it. 'Where are the others?' He looked around the kitchen, empty except for the three of them.

Red shrugged and sneaked a look from under his brows as he picked up a mug of something steaming. It could have been black coffee, but it smelled of something richer and savoury.

Caid pushed away from the counter and placed another mug in front of Trevor. 'They're all out at work.'

'Work?' Trevor couldn't conceal the surprise. Some of the kids he'd seen the night before had been far too young to work legally. Hadn't they?

'Yeah.' Caid slipped into the chair opposite and took another long drag of his cigarette. 'If you expect to stay here, you have to do your bit.'

A dull weight settled on Trevor. Shit. What had he got himself into? Some kind of gang? Drugs? He didn't do drugs, didn't want to do drugs.

His mind came back to life, the quick dart of it whizzed through his options. Run now, or wait until his chances were better?

There couldn't be a much better time than now, while there were only two of them and him.

His eyes shifted to the kitchen door. A short passageway led to the front door, if his blurred memory from the night before served him right. His attention slid back to Caid. Trevor didn't stand a chance against the guy. Big, square and sturdy, he held himself like an army veteran. Hard to pin an age on him. From the guy Trevor had stabbed, he could chance a guess of about the same. Maybe forty.

Older than he looked, Trevor hazarded a guess. Maybe older than Shell's boyfriend by a couple of years. Where Shell's boyfriend had a face like a bulldog, this guy had a square jaw, wide-set eyes and a nose that might have been broken at one time.

But there was an openness about it. A face most people would trust.

Trevor shook himself and stared back at Caid, who'd started to talk long before Trevor had started to listen.

'All the boys have a job to do.' Caid ran a gaze over Trevor, quick, astute, assessing.

Trevor squirmed under Caid's scrutiny. The mouthful of food turned to stodge and refused to budge from the back of his throat. He let out a spluttering cough. Red's hand came down between his shoulders and the wad of bread flew from Trevor's mouth, skidding across the table. It stopped just in front of Caid's folded hands.

Caid never moved. Never flinched. His gaze narrowed imperceptibly.

'Red is a runner. Takes messages to and from me and the boys. He's fast. Reliable. He has his own skillsets the other boys don't.' Caid flicked a look up at Red, who'd moved to hover at his right side. A flash of anxiety filled the boy's eyes for a brief second as he stared at the gob of food on the table.

Caid ignored it, leaned back in his chair, raised his hand to his face and gave the short, greying stubble a rub so it rasped in the silence between them.

Trevor raised his chin, defiance winning over fear. 'Why me? Why did you pick me up? What good am I to you?'

Caid's lips drew up at one edge. 'You're bright. Fast. We've been watching you.'

A trickle of fear ran down Trevor's spine. Watching him do what? Steal? Break into abandoned buildings?

'I'd say following you, but you're good. Sneaky. I like that. You've given us the slip a few times. Even managed to get into places most of my boys would struggle to. You have some raw talents I think we can finesse.'

Trevor wasn't sure he understood the word 'finesse', but he got the general gist.

He dropped his gaze to stare at his hands encircling the sausage sandwich on the table as Caid's eyes bored into him. He'd learned early on when to withdraw, decline a challenge. It wasn't cowardice. It was tactics.

Caid drew in a long breath through his nose, making his nostrils flare. 'I think, Rory, we need a little time, our kid. You to decide on whether you want to join our team, and me to consider what your strengths might bring to us if we decide to keep you. Because you do have some interesting strengths.'

The veiled threat hit its mark as Trevor held the sausage sandwich in his fist, fingertips digging into the thick white bread as tension tightened every muscle.

'Caid.' The one word filled with appeal came from Red.

Caid shrugged and came to his feet, a lopsided grin on his thin lips. 'I'll tell you what, our kid. I'll give you a week. You fill your boots with all you can eat and give some thought as to whether you want to join us or make your own way. I won't ask what you's doing on the streets.' His perceptive gaze flickered over Trevor. 'That's not my business, but Red here has been trailing you for the past few weeks. You might have some strengths, but you don't look like you're making a success of it on your own. We can help you with that. Everyone here makes their own living. We share. We look out for each other. Each of us has our own job, and nobody slacks. If they do, they're gone.'

His mouth still empty, Trevor swallowed, his appetite evaporating. He wasn't sure if Caid was waiting for a response, but he nodded in any case.

As though satisfied, Caid blew out another lungful of smoke and then stubbed out the end of his cigarette in an ashtray on the windowsill. 'A week. You make yourself strong again, kid, and we'll have a chat about your strengths and weaknesses, see if we can find you a nice little job on our team.'

'I don't do drugs.' He almost bit his tongue off as he blurted the words out, but the guy needed to know. He was no druggie, no drug pusher. Never wanted to be. There was no control in that. And he needed control.

Caid gave a slow nod as he squinted down at Trevor. 'Good to know. No one here does drugs. If they do, they're out on their ear. Understand? You may not do them now, but there's always a temptation. It's not worth flushing your money down the drain. Or more specifically, our money. We're a syndicate. We all fulfil different functions. No one gets any more than anyone else. Except me.' He stabbed his thumb into his chest. 'Because I'm the brains of the operation.'

The one-sided smile flicked up once more, but Caid's eyes remained flinty. 'Red here has spoken for you. It's up to you now.'

Caid glanced at his watch. 'Get yourself dressed.' He gave a sharp nod at the sandwich. 'Eat up. Get your energy back. One week. If you don't want to join us, you're free to leave, no obligation. No payback required. It's a one-time offer, so think hard.' He nodded at Red. 'Our kid here will tell you I'm not normally so generous. If you want to stay, think what it is you can contribute to our society. In the meantime, relax.'

Caid swung around and headed for the outer door, pulling it shut behind him with a distinct click.

'Christ!' Red gaped at him. 'I've never heard Caid make that kind of offer. He must like you.'

Trevor raised his sandwich to his mouth. Or the man had recognised something in him like himself. Hard. Ruthless.

19

FIFTY-SIX HOURS SINCE PHONE CALL

Lorraine sighed as she pulled the car up to the kerb outside her aunt's house, vague recognition tugging at her mind. A tall archway at the side of the house leading to the rear garden was covered with wild pink roses in their first frenzied blossoming of the year. The sight of it teased at the edge of her memory. Heavy and overgrown with an abundance of blooms, she held a picture in her mind of dancing through it, with... who?

Her aunt? Had she danced with her aunt when she was little?

Uneasy at the stirring memories, she glanced over her shoulder at the sleeping Elijah in his car seat. He'd not made a sound for the entire journey, quickly slipping into the land of nod as they left behind Sophia's school. It didn't bode well for the meeting she was about to have if he woke now. He'd most likely want to dash all over the place on all fours. Sophia had never been that fast. She'd been an easy child, a good sleeper.

Easy he was too, but Elijah was exhausting when he was awake, full of vim and vigour. Or maybe that was just Lorraine's state of mind with all the crap she was dealing with. A dead dad, an ex-husband and an absent mum.

She touched shaky fingers to her lips. Panic threatened to consume her. If she let herself dwell on it, she'd fall apart.

All she could do was take each step at a time. Running screaming through the streets wasn't an option, even though that was the strongest of all her feelings.

She gripped the steering wheel and held on until the adrenaline subsided.

Two out of those three issues were beyond her control. What she could do, though, was track down her mum and find out what the hell was going on.

That didn't involve dancing through the rose archway with Elijah and her aunt. She was fairly certain, from the clipped way her aunt had spoken the previous evening, she'd just want Lorraine to ask questions and go. The rift between her mum and her aunt felt like a giant chasm. One she'd never had to give thought to until her dad died.

As she stepped from the car, Lorraine glanced up and down at the street-parked cars. She thought twice about leaving Elijah in the back seat, still asleep. She didn't know the area, but suspected it was far more bustling than where she lived in Telford. A small, relatively new housing estate. Nothing expensive or extravagant, but it was clean and new. Her mum's house was much older, with its own drive, and Lorraine would leave Elijah in the car as they could keep an eye from the sitting room window. Not here, though.

The short drive leading to her aunt's house was empty. The gate shut.

Lorraine unbuckled Elijah's car seat and scooped it out of the car, so heavy now with the combined weight of child and seat, she needed both hands to carry it. She bumped the door closed with her hip and touched her finger to the fob to lock the car.

She didn't expect to be too long, but in truth she didn't really know. She had no idea what kind of reception this woman would give her. An aunt she barely remembered. One who'd had nothing to do with their family for years.

Lorraine cradled the car seat handle to take some of the weight on her hip.

Perhaps it wasn't going to be so bad after all. Maybe he would stay asleep for the whole of her meeting with her aunt so they could sort a few things out, track down her mum. If the woman was willing.

Opening the gate, Lorraine walked down the short pathway alongside the drive to the front door. The heady scent of early summer roses teased her senses to invoke memories of a past long faded.

She pressed the doorbell and stepped back, her body swaying to and fro in the age-old habit of mothers as she rocked the car seat, baby and all, and prayed Elijah would stay asleep.

With no response, she waited a moment longer and then used the side of her car fob to rap on the wooden frame of the door. Elijah stirred, but with a gentle swing of the car seat, he soon slipped back into sleep.

With nothing but silence from the house, Lorraine stepped back from the door.

Confused, she hesitated. Her aunt had definitely said she would be in. Lorraine's memory wasn't failing her. It was only the night before that they'd spoken. She might have baby fugue, but there was no doubt in her mind that she was supposed to see her aunt today. The address was correct. Her aunt had texted it to her straight after their conversation and Lorraine had tapped the postcode into her satnav.

If she'd not recognised the place, maybe there would have been some hesitation, some doubt, but she knew.

This was it. This was the right address..

She stared up at the windows in the hope that someone might look out. Perhaps the woman had gone to the bathroom.

Nothing stirred.

A thought occurred that her aunt might be in the back garden and hadn't heard the doorbell, or the knocking.

Lorraine didn't know the woman well enough. For all she knew, she could be hard of hearing.

Although there'd been no issue the night before on the phone, she had hesitated, and her answers had been short to Lorraine's questions. Didn't hard of hearing people have 'the loop' in their houses now? Lorraine had no idea how it worked or if many people used it. But what if she hadn't heard, for whatever reason?

Lorraine made her way around to the side of the house, under the archway of roses to the garden gate. The scent floated over her senses as she turned the old-fashioned latch and pushed the wooden gate wide.

Olfaction, she recalled, was the link between a heightened sense of smell and distinct childhood recollections. Recollections that flooded over her.

With a small gasp, she stepped inside an immaculate garden. Crazy paving wound through borders of roses in varying stages from tight buds to delicate blossoms, and encircled a small, perfectly round patch of lawn.

If she'd had any doubt before, it was swept away in a rush of memory so intense she sucked in her breath. She held still as she absorbed it all while her emotions took a savage battering.

She hitched the baby seat into the crook of her arm. Her free hand automatically went to her son's head, and she stroked his hair as she gazed at the garden so familiar in that one punch of memory.

She'd played with her aunt here on many occasions, it had been her grandparents' house.

The Stepson

They had lived here all those years ago.

She attempted to drag the memories from her mind of weekends she'd spent but they refused to form from a blurred image into a clear picture. She'd been so young when they'd stopped visiting and she had no recall of why.

The vague recollection of an upset with raised voices, her mum, her aunt who must only have been a young girl. Her long pale plaited hair swinging as she skipped along the pathways, her hand holding Lorraine's with cool, long fingers and fuchsia-painted nails. A teenager.

Lorraine skimmed a quick gaze over the garden, barely changed from when she was last there. The rose bushes had been well pruned over the years, keeping them low. Many of them possibly replaced once they'd outgrown their beauty. Some of them were just coming to life as spring hovered on the cusp of summer, others already budding enthusiastically.

How old had she been? Maybe five, or six. She couldn't remember, but the sudden realisation that her aunt wasn't that much older than her hit her.

The drawn face she'd seen at her dad's funeral had certainly been younger than expected, but Lorraine hadn't had time to dwell on her then. She'd had her mum to see to. A daughter to pick up from nursery at the time and a newborn baby demanding all her attention.

Holding the baby seat, she slowly circled around on the spot.

Why had they stopped coming? She had nothing she could pinpoint. Nothing particularly that came to mind, but the sight of the stunning rose garden brought a flood of emotions to her.

The arguments her mum and dad had were so vague. Why would they have triggered the tearing apart of a whole family? A family she felt weren't hers at all. But they had been at some point. A point so far back in her memory it no longer existed.

With a sense of disloyalty to her mum, Lorraine felt the urge to hurry away. She clutched the baby seat and swivelled on her heel, heading towards the gate, when a movement in the house caught her attention.

Had she seen someone?

A quick flit she'd caught from the corner of her eye.

Sun reflected a pool of bright light across the patio doors as Lorraine squinted, trying to catch another flicker of movement behind the doors.

Was it someone watching her from inside the house?

Who would do that? Her aunt? Why?

Why wouldn't she just answer the door?

Lorraine placed Elijah's seat on the ground next to her and leaned in closer to the glass to peer through into the darkened living room.

Maybe her aunt was in there after all. Perhaps she'd taken a fall.

Lorraine pressed her forehead against icy glass, her breath puffed out to form a small cloud of condensation that blurred her vision.

She narrowed her eyes as she caught a movement from a doorway into the darkened room.

'Bloody hell, there is someone there.'

She balled her hand into a fist, raised it and on the first bang of the glass, a sleek figure surged out of the shadows, teeth bared as it launched itself at her, its long nails scratching on the pane of glass, the only thing between her and the monster.

Lorraine fell back. She stumbled over the baby seat, twisted so she didn't land on Elijah and hit the ground, her hip taking the full weight of her fall.

She let out a grunt of pain. 'Shit.'

As the savage beast rammed the window hard enough to break

it, Elijah's body went stiff in his seat. That nanosecond of time between a child sensing fear and then screaming their lungs out.

Claws scratched at the pane and Lorraine scrambled to her feet, terror squeezing her heart as every instinct told her to grab Elijah and run. Run for their lives.

She scooped up the baby seat and whirled in the direction of the gate.

As a figure stepped into her path, Lorraine stumbled to a dead stop.

'Who the fuck are you?' he growled.

20

FIFTY-SIX AND A HALF HOURS SINCE PHONE CALL

Lorraine's eyes shot wide, instinct screaming almost as loud as her son for her to run. Panic grabbed her as her way was blocked by a long-limbed teenage boy, his otherwise handsome face ravaged by acne.

Elijah's ear-piercing screams almost burst her eardrums. He thrashed his legs against the baby seat as she tried to cling on while he bounced up and down, twisting almost onto his side to escape the restraints.

She ignored the young man, his face dark and set as he glared at her, all badass attitude that only teenagers could pull off to any effect.

She plopped the baby seat on the floor, quickly unclipping the restraints and hauled Elijah into her arms.

'Shh. Shh. Elijah, hush, darling, it's okay.'

The instinct to comfort her baby vied with the one to run screaming from the place. But the mere presence of the teenager had a more calming effect. There was someone there. She was safe from the beast.

The boy rolled his shoulders forward into a slump as he tucked long-fingered hands into his jeans' front pockets, unperturbed by all accounts by the screaming child in front of him. His eyes narrowed as he stepped in front of the patio doors.

The ferocious dog stopped throwing itself against the window, but the timbre of his growl vibrated through the glass and left Lorraine in no doubt that he would savage all three of them, given the chance.

The boy looked over his shoulder, his voice, deep and controlled resonated above that of her own son. 'Quiet, Ghost.'

Maybe it would only savage two out of the three.

Lorraine glanced at the German Shepherd dog while she jiggled Elijah, who'd also miraculously quietened at the sound of the boy's command. The racket fell instantly from powerful lung bursts to shocked, hiccupping snivels which erupted in short intervals, ready to rev up again given the opportunity.

True to its name, the dog almost disappeared into the background of the living room as it lay down on a patterned carpet with his tones of blue providing camouflage. No wonder she'd not spotted him in the first place. He'd remained silent and deadly, possibly coming from the front door through the living room while she'd approached. She'd certainly think twice about entering a stranger's garden again. Because although the woman was her aunt, she was a stranger. Presuming her aunt was married, Lorraine didn't even know her last name.

The boy in front of her, also a stranger, continued to stare, his eyes a strange mix of colours, so like her son's and dad's she couldn't help but stare straight back at him. Hypnotised by the familiarity.

Heterochromia iridum, she'd been told by the health visitor when Lorraine had queried it. Not necessarily hereditary, but genetic. In their family's case, it seemed a strong gene passed through the male line because this boy was undoubtedly related.

As Elijah's soft sobs diminished, Lorraine stroked his back. 'I'm Lorraine.'

At the boy's deadpan look, she tried again. 'My aunt lives here. I think, your mum, maybe?' She put a question in it as she could only assume, even though she was convinced in her own mind.

'What's her name?' There was a hint of belligerence in the tone as if he didn't believe her. Like he thought a small woman with a young baby would break into the rear of their house, guarded by an enormous German Shepherd.

'Caroline.' Aunt Caroline. That's all she'd ever known her as. 'I'm afraid I don't know her surname now, but it used to be Leivesley.'

'Hamps. Caroline Hamps.'

Elijah struggled around in her arms to snatch a look at the stranger. Their eyes locked and the older boy's went wide. 'Shit.'

Their eyes might not have the same pattern, but the colours were almost identical. There was no disputing a connection.

'I'm Oliver.' A frown creased his brow as he continued to stare at Elijah. 'Mum's out.'

Lorraine blinked in confusion. 'I phoned her last night. She said she would be in. I've actually driven quite a way to see her.' She tried to clamp down on the irritation. Her aunt obviously had no appreciation of what effort Lorraine had gone to to get there. She looked at her watch pointedly. 'It's taken me an hour and half to get here.' Not to mention the cost of bloody fuel. 'She said she'd be here.' In the absence of anyone else, she directed her annoyance at him.

Oliver's stringy body melted against the doorframe, all uncaring attitude and ignorance. 'She didn't mention you.' The sharp little insult stung, but Lorraine took note of the way his gaze strayed back to her son as his expression softened. He gave a casual jig of his shoulders. 'She had to pick Lola up.'

'Lola?'

He frowned. 'My sister.' He paused. 'If my mum's your aunt, which makes you my cousin, how come I've never heard of you, and you have no idea who me and my sister are?'

'Umm.' Pressured into speaking, Lorraine paused. She was the adult here, and she was being questioned by some teenage kid with too much attitude. She needed to pull herself together but she couldn't stop the shaking in every muscle in her body. The aftershock of her near miss with the blue-merle-coated dog.

Lorraine settled Elijah on her hip and raised her chin. 'That's precisely what I'm here to discuss with your mum.' *And only your mum*, she left unsaid, but from the narrowing of his eyes, she knew he'd caught the inference. 'She knows who I am. So, where is she?'

His jaw flexed and then he shrugged again. 'I told you. The school called her. Lola, my *sister*,' he stressed, 'broke her arm first period, playing bloody netball. I told Mum she'd have been better off playing rugby. She's a thug, my sister.'

The art of netball wasn't for the faint-hearted in Lorraine's opinion, anyway, but she stayed silent. Now he was communicating, she didn't want to stop him.

'How long will she be, do you think?'

'How long's a piece of string?'

A smile twitched the corners of her mouth. Such an old-fashioned expression, but one so familiar to her. She'd heard her dad say it countless times. Maybe she wasn't so very far removed from this branch of her family.

He pushed himself away from the frame, his body appearing to be in the permanent slouch of teenage boys. 'I've only come home to grab my homework and let Ghost out during recess. If I get caught, I'll be slaughtered, so I'd better hurry.' The curl of Scouse turned to a jab as he dug into his pocket and pulled out a key, reaching to push it into the lock of the patio doors.

Lorraine's arms automatically tightened around Elijah. 'Don't let the dog out. I...'

Too late, Ghost surged out as the door slid wide, his smoke-like body swift as he raced towards her.

'Ghost. Here, lad.' The boy barely murmured the dog's name and had its tail wagging enthusiastically. 'He won't touch you. He's too well trained.' True to Oliver's word, the dog gave her a dismissive sniff and trotted off into the garden to pee enthusiastically up the side of a birdbath. 'Mum said she'd not had chance to walk him, so he'd be bursting. Silly sod. He doesn't like to go in the garden, unless he's desperate.' Oliver's lips twitched. 'And that dog is desperate.'

She swore she could see a look of relief pass over the dog's face as his leg remained cocked for an amount of time she couldn't imagine a dog peeing for. Not that she knew dogs. She'd never had one in her life. Her mum had been too fastidious.

'He wouldn't do anything in the house, mind, but he doesn't need to be uncomfortable when I can just whip across the road and let him out for a quick...' He paused, his eyes twinkling. 'Whizz.'

Her lips twitched. There was something about this youngster she liked. 'Handy. How close is your school?'

'Yeah, it is handy.' He shoved his hands back into his pockets as he bobbed his head at her. 'Literally over the road.' He glanced towards the closed gate as though expecting a teacher to walk through. 'I'm not supposed to come out, but I can always plead with them as it's their fault my sister broke her arm. Health and safety. Gets them every time.'

He spoke as though he had first-hand experience. He was a charmer. A wheeler-dealer.

The cold, wet nose of the dog slipped up the back of her leg to mid-thigh, so she stiffened, automatically squeezing her son in close.

'Ghost. In.' The boy straightened. He reached for the door as the dog slipped by him, silent as the name he was given, and slid the patio doors closed behind him.

'I'd better get off before I get caught.'

'Do you know how long your mum will be?' She thought he might be a little more considerate in his answer this time.

He dipped his head and looked at her from beneath lowered brows. 'Have you been to A&E in this lifetime?'

Her heart squeezed. Yes. When her dad died. It was a complete blur. It wasn't her dad she'd gone for, but herself. There was nothing they could do for him, he was already dead when they found him. Her mum was in shock. That same shock had sent Lorraine into labour.

She said nothing for a moment and then realised he was waiting for her to leave. She sighed as she turned towards the gate. 'Would you let her know I was here?'

He shook his head. 'Not bleeding likely. Mum'll knock my head off if she knows I've bunked off.'

'I thought you said it was recess? That she knew.'

'I never said she knew, I said she'd mentioned she'd not had time to walk him. Different, see.'

Lorraine studied him for a long moment and then bent to scoop up the empty baby carrier. 'I see. So that's how it is.'

His face went deadpan as he closed the gate behind them. 'Go have a coffee, come back later.'

Lorraine thought about the time it would take to drive home. How long a broken arm would take to fix, to plaster. 'I haven't got enough time. I've got to get home for my daughter. I'll give her a call. I have her number.'

He shrugged and dug his hands back into his pockets. 'Up to you.'

Her arms ached from the weight of the baby in them, and she hitched Elijah up while she juggled with the baby seat.

The boy reached for it, relieving her of one weight at least.

Elijah gazed up at Oliver and the boy hesitated. He nodded at him. 'Is he Trevor's kid? He looks just like him. Spittin' image.' His gaze cruised over her. 'I'd say you were a bit young for him, though.'

Lorraine paused at the end of the pathway and turned, the sun catching her eyes to make her squint.

'Who's Trevor?'

21

TWELVE YEARS EARLIER

'Trevor?'

Trevor raised his head and peered at Red through the dim lighting of the hallway. 'What?'

'Are you going in?'

'Why the fuck else would I be here?'

'You just stopped. You've been standing like a bell-end for the last five minutes. Someone might come.'

Trevor let the silence settle as he stared at the other man. When Red started to fidget, he whispered, 'I was listening. That's what I do. This is my job. Now, do yours, pal.'

He pushed the door wide and stepped back to reveal the inside of the penthouse suite he'd been targeting for the past two weeks. He touched his fingers to the small electronic device in his hand and smiled at the soft beep of confirmation that he'd deactivated the alarm.

That was his speciality, too. He'd honed his skill through years of being on Caid's team.

Now Caid was gone, succumbed to lung cancer, his body shrivelled within weeks of diagnosis.

Trevor hadn't seen him in the final few weeks of his life, he didn't want to witness the melting away of muscle tone Caid had been known for. But he still posted Caid's family a little money every now and then. A family only he and Red knew about. And only near the end.

The man had been good to him. Good to all the boys he'd nurtured into the trade. Never any girls. Caid had always contended that when you mix sexes, you'll have problems. He stuck to his philosophy. There were still problems. Not many, because Caid knew how to deal with lads.

Now Trevor was the team leader of a gang that no longer had any of the original members. Just him and Red. They still had their instructions from the top guy. Whoever he was.

Trevor didn't give a shit, as long as he did his own thing, earned his own money. He was a master at this. Never been caught, not even been under suspicion for anything.

He made it his business to never get cocky, never put himself under the microscope. Anyone's microscope, because there were far worse things that could happen in their world than being arrested. There were worse monsters in the shadows.

So, he remained alert. Cautious. Never overreached his abilities.

This job was a big one, though. Bigger than usual.

Still, he could take his time, get it right. He couldn't resist.

He watched, patiently tracking the resident's habits. When they came and went to work. The evenings they went out with friends.

A single male in his forties. Trevor didn't need to know his personal habits, but he liked to. He didn't like to be taken by surprise. He'd learned a lot in the past few years. He was the observer. The breaker. He found the places, watched them, broke in.

He left the rest to the team. Two of them, Red 'the real thing' McCoy, another Scouser who knew his business. Who had an eye for good stuff, valuables, jewellery, paintings. His best mate. The boy who'd rescued him, who was now the mate who worked only with him, side by side as equals.

Red's mate, Leon. Thin and wiry, with a vicious streak. He was the lookout, the carrier. Less predictable than Red, the drugs he'd taken to lately had made him twitchy, unreliable, impatient.

Trevor knew Leon's days with the team were numbered. The moment the big boss got wind of his habit, he'd be gone, like fumes, as though he'd never existed.

If Caid had still been there, the kid would already have gone.

Trevor had never been tempted. Never felt the need to sniff cocaine and as for injecting, his terror of needles kept that one at bay.

He liked his cigarettes, but the smell of weed made his stomach turn. The thought of dying of lung cancer, like Caid, had even curbed that habit. Not entirely killed it. But drugs had never been his thing. He'd stuck to his word from the beginning.

Apart from anything, he needed his wits about him. Wanted to be sharp, cunning, fast. That's how he'd worked his way up to second in command, now commander under the big boss. He'd preferred second in command, but he'd been Caid's natural replacement.

When he spoke with the boss about Leon, there would be no going back. Leon would disappear. Trevor didn't give a shit where to. He'd had his chance. If he'd wanted to be a member of the team, he needed to be there for them, not off his head on smack or whatever else he could get his thieving hands on. This would be his last job with them. Trevor regretted allowing him this time.

'Trev.'

At Red's hurried whisper, Trevor slipped inside the bedroom, his eyes going wide at the sight of a walk-in wardrobe of such epic proportions, his whole flat could fit inside it. The flat he'd moved into for peace and quiet from all the newbies settling into the team. He no longer needed to live there. He'd earned his right to a place of his own, with privacy. He liked the quiet. The big boss appreciated that. Trevor had earned it. Had earned his share of the profits. Enough to house, feed and clothe him. He'd bought his own furniture, TV, a mobile phone, just a cheap one he could dispose of at the drop of a hat.

And it didn't matter how much he trusted the boss, life had a habit of biting him in the arse. He'd never be homeless again, never be out on the streets, a frightened kid. He'd outgrown that. Made it his business to look after himself. With a bank account even the boss didn't know about. Especially the boss didn't know about. Every spare bit of cash went into it. So that one day he could go back, find his dad and show him just exactly what he'd made of his life. Just as importantly, he had cash stashed away. Just in case.

'What do you think?'

Trevor stepped inside, swept his gloved hand over the neatly hanging shirts, sorted in colour order from black through to grey and then stark white. Not a coloured one in sight. Silk ties in jewel colours dangled artistically down a centre console and on the other side hung suits. Jackets on the top hangers, trousers neatly draped over hangers on the bottom section. Navy, varying shades of grey from light through to dark. And then black.

'Fuck,' Red whispered in his ear. 'Who needs this many suits?'

A curl of uncertainty bloomed in Trevor's stomach, and he wiped the back of his wrist over a mouth that had gone dry. He'd made a mistake. He'd picked someone too rich, too powerful. Way above their game plan. The past years living on his instincts should have taught him better than this.

He had a bad feeling. His gut screamed at him. The guy he'd been watching had been discreet, executive. Not flash. This wasn't flash. This was big, big money. Bigger than Trevor cared to mess with. And he'd missed it.

Stupid.

He skimmed his gaze around the room.

He'd been too cocky. Too sure of himself. Without Caid to rein him in, he'd powered ahead, believing he knew everything there was to know. He was just starting to realise he didn't.

Red pushed back a curtain of what appeared to be kimonos and Trevor's heart notched up another beat.

A small safe embedded in the wall winked at him. Almost had him running from the room as he ran his tongue over his dry teeth. 'Shit. We need to go.'

'You're fucking kidding me, right?' Red squatted in front of the safe. 'This guy's got to have a fortune inside of here.'

'I doubt it.' Trevor knew in his gut that this man wouldn't keep his fortune here. 'There'll be jack shit inside of there.'

A hard hand fell on his shoulder, making Trevor's nerves dance. 'Don't tell me the infamous Trev's found a safe he can't crack.'

Trevor shrugged Leon's hand away. 'Fuck off, Lee...'

'Leon.'

'Trevor.'

He waited to see if the penny dropped but he suspected it had bypassed the less than intelligent Leon.

In the silence, he hunkered down next to Red. 'I can open it, pal, but I think we should back out of here without taking anything.'

Red stared at him, eyes filled with horror. 'The boss'll fucking kill us.'

Trevor gave a slow shake of his head. 'Not when I explain.'

'He won't give you time to explain. He'll have your fucking guts.'

'No. He won't.' Trevor pushed up from his crouched position. Certain now. 'But the guy who owns this will.'

He swivelled on his heel, his chest pounding with the age-old flight instinct. 'Leon, why aren't you on the lookout?'

Leon glanced around, his eyes glassy. He scrubbed at his nose with his forefinger. 'Fuck, that stings.'

Trevor's heart bumped back down. 'Shit! What did you just take?'

Leon swayed in the doorway. 'Cocaine. I think it was cocaine. Maaaan.' He flicked to indicate behind him. 'That shit's strong.'

Trevor darted a look at where Leon indicated. The place was immaculate. Nothing lying around. Nothing. Except that tiny see-through packet neatly left right in the middle of a small table of impeccable taste. Fine grains of white powder streaked across it, where before it had been clean.

Who would do that? Leave cocaine in full view. Not someone who lived in a place like this. Not unless it was deliberate. A set-up.

'You were supposed to be the lookout.'

Leon's eyelids slipped down over those glassy eyes that rolled back in his head.

'Shit,' Red murmured from behind him. 'He's fucking OD'd.'

Trevor grabbed Leon's arm as he slouched against the open doorway. 'Let's get him out of here. I don't like this. Not one fucking bit.'

Red slipped his arm around Leon, and they staggered their way towards the outer door. Leon was a lightweight, skinny addict. Red could almost carry him on his own, but the dead weight of his body made it difficult as they both hauled him through the penthouse, his toes dragging through the thick shagpile rug on the floor.

As they reached the door, it swung open.

The elegant businessman Trevor had been stalking filled the doorway, two huge men towered over his shoulders.

Narrowed eyes pierced straight into Trevor's. 'Good evening, boys. I've been expecting you.'

22

Trevor gingerly ran a dry tongue over teeth that felt loose in his gums. Stale blood coated them in a thick paste filling his mouth with a metallic taste.

Eyelids so swollen he could barely squint out of them pulsed in rhythm with the rest of his face, his mouth, his cheekbones.

As he inhaled, his breath caught in agony. He wasn't sure how many broken ribs he had. He'd passed out somewhere between the two giants' meaty fists hammering at his face, and their feet booting him across the multi-storey car park they'd chosen as their preferred place to beat the shit out of him, Red and Leon. Well, they wouldn't have wanted blood on the thick rug in the penthouse, would they?

'Red...' His voice broke from a throat thick and swollen. 'Red.'

A hoarse grunt came from close by.

In the shadowy car park, Trevor unfurled his tightly coiled body so he could peer at the guy lying a few feet away. 'You okay, mate?'

A low groan sounded.

'Red?'

'Yeah. I'm here.' The other man coughed out a breathless reply. 'Fuck. I hurt.'

Trevor rolled onto his knees, his forehead almost touching the ground, and held still as pain lanced through his lungs to paralyse him. 'Oh, God. For the love of all that is holy.'

The soft shuffle of Red moving was accompanied by guttural grunts. 'I never knew you were religious.'

Trevor let out a breathy chuckle. 'Not until now. I think I saw the light. Several times.' He placed his hands on the tarmac surface and on all fours, he raised his head so he could take in their surroundings. 'I thought they were going to kill us.' He could barely see through the fuzziness of tears and swollen eyelids. He was in too much pain to care about the tears tracking down his cheeks. Red wouldn't care. Wouldn't tell.

In the absence of a reply from Red, Trevor pulled himself up off his hands and settled back on his haunches. He wrapped his arms around his ribcage to stop it from creaking. 'Red.' He swivelled around to see the shadowy countenance of his mate. 'Can you move?'

'Yeah.' Red turned his head, his eyes dark pits in a chalky white face as he struggled to his own knees. 'But Leon can't. He's dead.'

This time, there wasn't even an attempt to disguise the tears as they welled up in a pained sob from the depth of him. 'Christ. Are you sure?'

'Yeah. No pulse, no breathing. Lips are blue and there's white foam coming from them. It was the fucking drugs. He overdosed.'

Trevor closed his eyes to let them rest for a moment while he waited for the fog to clear from his mind.

'Those drugs were meant for all of us. They thought we'd all take them. Probably surprised them when we were still standing.' He felt himself burbling on but couldn't stop. It had to be. They'd taken so little care when they'd bundled them out of the penthouse and down in the lift at gunpoint. If they'd believed they'd taken the drugs, perhaps they hadn't wanted to shoot them. Gun crime was so much harder to cover up than a simple overdose. Small-time gang beating up on each other was much easier to brush away. Less likely to attract attention. It definitely wouldn't bring the police down on the head of the big man. Whoever he was. All Trevor knew was he didn't want to come across him again.

He stared around at the scene, his squinting eyes stinging.

'We've gotta get out of here, mate. Before someone comes.'

Trevor leaned a hand against the white BMW he'd virtually rolled under to get away from his assailants as the distant sound of sirens grew closer. 'What's the betting that's not an ambulance?'

Red snorted. 'Unlikely anyone has called one. I'm not sure our mates want us to live.'

'But if we did, they might want us arrested for Leon's fuckin' overdose.'

'Shit. Or his murder, because his face looks like fucking chopped liver. I kid you not.'

Red pushed up from the ground and staggered over, his left arm dangling uselessly by his side. 'Fuck, come on, pal. Come on.'

He tugged at Trevor's arm with his good hand to encourage him up off his knees and they stumbled towards the exit, supporting each other.

The only evidence they'd been there was a single bloody, livid print of Trevor's hand on the wing of the white BMW.

23

FIFTY-NINE HOURS SINCE PHONE CALL

Exhaustion washed over her in waves as Lorraine pulled her car up in front of her mum's house again. She'd never gone back and forth so much in her life.

It didn't matter how many times she called her mum's phones, the landline just rang out and the mobile instantly went to answerphone, indicating that it was switched off. Or out of battery.

Her fuel tank had virtually been on empty, running purely on fumes by the time she'd filled it on her way back. Then she'd stopped at a Costa coffee shop further down the road to feed Elijah and herself, oblivious to the fact that she'd almost run out of money.

She was eating crap, she knew she was, but it couldn't be helped. She could have chosen from some of the salads they had on display, or even a soup. Instead, she'd opted for a high-calorie toasted baguette. She needed the energy. Usually, the treat would have filled her with joy, but it tasted like ash in her mouth as she fed Elijah, her mind racing.

Oliver had been in such a dash to get back to school before his mum discovered his deception that he'd literally called over his shoulder that Trevor was his cousin.

Just as she was his cousin.

It was feasible. After all, the gap between the various branches of the family tree had widened. She had no idea who any of her cousins were. She'd never heard of Oliver before today.

Lorraine pushed open the car door and climbed out, taking in a deep breath as she did. All she'd done lately was sit in her car, chasing around after people who weren't where they were supposed to be.

She was run ragged. Her chest ached with holding her breath all the time.

She never doubted that her mum hadn't returned. But she felt the need to go in again.

Once she checked, she was going back to the police station to make them listen. This wasn't normal. It wasn't in character for her mum to just disappear.

Lorraine's mind was in turmoil.

Only the niggling doubt that it might just be in character kept Lorraine from dashing straight back to the police and making a complaint.

The guy on the desk had asked if her mum was vulnerable. Well, dammit, yes, she was. She was at risk. Wasn't she?

She reached in for the smiling Elijah and thanked small mercies that the child was so affable. As long as he got his food and plenty of sleep, the boy was a charm. He also needed to stretch his limbs, he'd happily sat in the car for hours, barely making any objection, but he needed to move around now.

As she backed out of the rear door and turned, Mrs Tindall beckoned to her from her front doorstep.

Lorraine closed her eyes for a brief moment. She really didn't want to get into this.

'Lorraine, I've been looking out for you. Can you spare a minute?' Her voice warbled with a frailness Lorraine hadn't noticed earlier.

Was she upset? Was she going to have a go too, like her son?

Lorraine paused. She really didn't want to get involved all over again with the issues between her mum and neighbour. It was nothing to do with her. Lorraine knew nothing about it. Nor did she want to right now.

She couldn't give a damn. It meant nothing to her.

All she wanted was to find her mum.

She'd not even allowed her mind to go down the route that her mum could possibly be a thief. If that's what taking money on false pretences was classed as.

And there was another good reason not to chase down the police again. What if the police accused her mum of something so ridiculous?

What if her mum had done something wrong? Perhaps she couldn't face the consequences and had taken herself off somewhere. To hide.

Lorraine couldn't even imagine it. Not her mum.

There was no way her mum was a thief.

No. No. No.

If she'd gone of her own free will, then there was more to it than that.

She cast a quick glance around to check for Gareth's car. She didn't need to be cornered by him. He'd not exactly been aggressive, more abrasive. But she wasn't sure she could deal with his kind of abrasive at the moment as she hovered on the verge of tears.

There were far more important things, but each issue built until she thought the foundations of her sanity were cracking apart.

'Of course.' She ducked her head into Elijah's neck as she made her way to Mrs Tindall's front door.

'Come on in, dear. You look done in.'

'I am.'

'I've kept an eye out, but I've not seen or heard anything from your mum.' She unfolded her arms from where she'd wrapped them around herself and opened them wide in an invitation for Lorraine to walk into them.

Taken aback, Lorraine nevertheless accepted the offer and let the woman enfold both herself and Elijah in her welcoming arms.

It had been so long since she'd had a hug from the woman next door. Years. Probably the last time had been at Lorraine's wedding. Prior to that, Mrs Tindall had often given her a cuddle as she was growing up. Funny how she'd forgotten. The mists of time had swallowed those memories, until now.

She'd known the woman all her life. They'd never been overly close. She was just her mum's neighbour. Older than her mum, and with very little in common. But they'd never had any disagreements. They'd lived comfortably alongside each other. Apart from, evidently, complaints about Gareth's home-run garage.

The tears that had threatened earlier welled up for a whole different reason as the woman's gentle arms embraced her, offering her all the comfort she needed.

A poor substitute for her mum, but a substitute nonetheless. Lorraine leaned down to tuck her face into the woman's shoulder. The smell of old-fashioned soap and freshly scrubbed hair a comfort.

After a long moment, they pulled back from each other.

'Come on in,' Mrs Tindall repeated. 'You can put the lad down and save your arms.'

Lorraine considered how best to politely decline her invitation, but Mrs Tindall swiped up a throw and flicked it out, so it landed on the large, empty space in the middle of the lounge floor.

A plaintive meow came from one of the cats as the waft of air displaced it from the side of the fireplace. It bounded onto the windowsill and gazed at them through yellow eyes, wide enough to be disconcertingly intent.

With a twinkle in her eye, Mrs Tindall smiled at Lorraine. 'It's clean.'

Lorraine had no doubt. The fresh scent of washing powder clung to the air as she bent to place Elijah on the tartan throw.

'After Gareth threw his teddy out the pram yesterday, he sent for a gang of cleaners he employs. They descended like a colony of ants, marching through, scrubbing everything down.' She flicked her hand in the air with a dismissive wave. 'He owns cleaning companies that clean all the big offices he owns. Reckons it was cheaper to own the cleaning company than to employ one externally.' She tapped her temple with two gnarled fingers. 'He's not stupid, my boy. Not by any account.'

Lorraine said nothing. Evidently the man had more nous than his own mum had given him credit for.

'Would you like a cuppa?' The old woman looked hopeful, but Lorraine shook her head.

'No, thank you.'

As Mrs Tindall's face fell, Lorraine felt obliged to qualify what she'd said.

'I've just had a coffee at Costa.' She nodded to Elijah, who'd rolled onto his front and was now on all fours, making quiet huffy sounds to himself. 'I had to feed him, so I stopped for us both. Just for a while.' She didn't divulge why, or where she'd been. She didn't want Mrs Tindall gossiping about her affairs.

She straightened and watched her little boy. She had to make sure he didn't move off the rug if he broke into a kamikaze crawl.

Gareth might have had the place cleaned, but there was still the underlying smell of cat urine coming from somewhere.

She leaned down, plopped him onto his backside and just as his bottom lip poked out, she delved into the changing bag and plucked out an activity toy. As she placed it in his hands, he grinned. A drizzle of saliva hovered on his bottom lip before it tracked down his chin. 'He's teething,' she said in explanation to her mum's neighbour.

'He's a good boy.'

'He is.'

'He has the look of your dad.' Mrs Tindall's mouth tilted up in a sad smile. 'Especially those eyes. Spittin' image of him.'

Lorraine felt the catch in her throat and could only nod.

She sighed as she sank down to perch on the very edge of a wide brown fabric armchair with what may once have been gold thread woven through. Now a dingy beige.

Mrs Tindall lowered herself onto her own chair, pain etched across her features as she shuffled back. 'Gareth said he's getting me one of those special rise-and-recline motorised chair thingmabobs.'

'Nice.'

'A new sofa for when the family come to visit.' She waved a flippant hand in the air. 'He says he's having all the carpets ripped out and replaced because of my cats p...' A small smile of annoyance tightened her lips. 'Peeing. It's not their fault, they don't know any better.'

'Hmm.' Lorraine had no idea how to respond to that. Maybe Mrs Tindall should let the cats out to roam, instead of keeping them inside all the time. And so many of them. She'd counted four last time, but she was quite convinced the one on the windowsill hadn't been one of them.

Lorraine gave a surreptitious look around the room and caught sight of at least three more. All of them fast asleep. As a soft bump came from up above, she thought, four in the living room, but how many more throughout the house?

She gave a small shudder. She had no objection to cats. They were quite lovely, although the one staring her down was a little unnerving. She swore it hadn't so much as blinked yet. To have so many, though. Surely that couldn't be good.

Just as the cat did, Mrs Tindall made a slow study of her, until Lorraine almost squirmed with discomfort. Could she read her thoughts?

'I'm sorry about yesterday. He didn't mean to be so rude, you know. Gareth. I told him off. It wasn't your fault and you'd been helping me out doing that bit of shopping.'

Railroaded into it, more like.

Mrs Tindall nodded at a small white envelope on the mantelpiece. 'Your money is in there. I prefer dealing with cash. Which is why Gareth paid into your mum's bank. Save me keeping too much in the house. For my security. He's a good boy that way. Quite happy to pay someone to do his jobs for him.'

Lorraine wondered if the old lady knew what she'd said. From the lift of her straggly grey eyebrow, she guessed she absolutely did. Sometimes the elderly got labelled as stupid when they slowed down. This woman wasn't stupid. On the contrary, she was as sharp as a pin. It was the first time she'd let it slip, though, that she did consider her son less than perfect.

'I'm so sorry about Mum doing that to you, too. She should never have taken that money without looking after you. Not if you had an agreement.'

Mrs Tindall's thin nostrils flared while she hitched herself further back in her seat as though giving herself time to contemplate her next words. She made a soft humming noise in the back of her throat that had Elijah looking up at her. The noise stopped as she smiled at him. He dipped his head and continued trying to get the blue triangle shape into the green rectangle hole, becoming more savage as he whacked one against the other, the clacking noise making Lorraine's nerves jump and twitch.

'Your mum didn't want to take any money, but Gareth insisted. She was good enough to see me to bed on my off days, and make meals for me. Said it was no trouble at all seeing as she was making a meal for herself. The only reason the place is such a tip is because your mum brought all those small boxes down from the attic. My old man was a bloody hoarder. Everything he could get his hands on, he would save. Boxes and boxes up in the attic.' Regret shimmered in her eyes as they met Lorraine's. 'Your mum was trying to help me clear them all out. Some of the things we came across...' She stumbled to a halt as though it was too painful to discuss.

Lorraine really needed to get off. She had things to do. Just over an hour before she needed to pick Sophia up from school. That allowed for the ten-minute drive to get there.

She slipped onto the rug next to Elijah, picked up the green rectangle and offered it to him, swiftly wiping the drool from his chin with a tissue from her pocket.

'You need a spare pair of hands when you have a baby. Mine may be all grown up, but I still remember. Boys are a handful. Never still. Always on the go.'

Lorraine didn't reply. Personally, she felt Elijah was a gentle, happy soul. He had bursts of energy, but didn't every child? Time would tell.

Mrs Tindall grunted as she leaned forward and clapped her hands to attract Elijah again. He turned to look at her and she sat back, her lips compressed in a downward smile, her chin dimpling.

'Is something wrong, Mrs Tindall?'

Mrs Tindall shook her head and rubbed gnarled fingers over

her chin as though trying to smooth out the deep wrinkles. Her mouth made little puffing noises of indecision.

'I don't think it's my place to say.'

'To say what?' Her irritation rising, Lorraine was aware her voice carried a waspish sting. 'Look. I'm going out of my mind here. I have no idea where Mum is. You obviously know something I don't. What's been going on?'

The old lady raised both hands to her cheeks and shook her head. 'It's none of my business really, but you're right. With your mum missing, I think I should tell you.' She dropped her hands back onto her lap as she made up her mind.

'It hardly matters what she thinks, Mrs Tindall. I've been to the police, and they think she might have gone off on a jolly somewhere for a couple of days, or she's licking her wounds. While I was in Costa, I looked up statistics. Seventy-five per cent of adults turn up within twenty-four hours of disappearing. Eighty-five per cent within two days. Most of those just come back home. No wonder the police weren't overly concerned. They asked if she had any mental health issues. I think I should have said yes.'

'But she doesn't. She's sad about your dad. That doesn't make her mentally ill.'

'Doesn't it? She's on antidepressants, you know.'

Sadness rippled over the other woman's face. 'I come from a generation that never acknowledged depression.' Her wan smile never reached her eyes. 'No such thing.' She hunched her shoulders in a painful-looking shrug. 'But... she won't like it, and she'll probably never talk to me again.'

Without taking her gaze off Mrs Tindall, Lorraine automatically turned the toy around, so Elijah continued to play happily. There was no need to say anything. The dice was already rolling.

'I've known your mum and dad a long time.'

Lorraine nodded.

Mrs Tindall linked her fingers together. 'Ever since they first moved in next door.'

'Yes.' She really wanted to say move along, but she let the woman take her time.

'Your mum was pregnant with you when they arrived. I wanted to be friends, but she was... is... a very private person. But we got along. We're a whole different generation. My boys were already slipping into their teens.'

Her eyes turned mellow at the distant memories. 'Your dad spoke, and when my George passed, they were kind to me. Your mum and I became closer. Your dad always put my bins out. Never made a fuss, just did it without ever being asked. I thought he might stop after a while, but he continued. All the way up until he... died. He was a lovely man. So thoughtful and gentle, but...'

She clasped her hands until her knuckles turned white. 'I feel very disloyal even talking about this, but this is your family. You have a right to know, under the circumstances.'

Lorraine's face felt stiff as she clenched her jaw until it almost cracked. There was no rushing this woman, so she stifled the desire to give her a push.

'It turned out that your dad wasn't quite as thoughtful as we believed, and he didn't have life assurance.' Mrs Tindall unlinked her hands and spread them, giving an apologetic shrug as though it was her fault. 'Your mum was left to pay the remaining mortgage.'

Lorraine's locked jaw slackened as her mouth fell open. 'What? What?' Elijah's head went back at her sharp tone, so she lowered her voice again. 'I never knew. Mum didn't say a thing.'

'I know.'

'Why not?'

'She didn't want to worry you.'

'Worry me? I'm a sight more worried now.'

'You'd just given birth when she found out, and she would

never have blamed your father. It was an oversight, she said. They never gave it a thought. He always dealt with the money side of things, she told me.' She paused.

'But why keep it from me?' And tell her next-door neighbour, for God's sake!

Mrs Tindall spread her hands. 'She knew you'd be upset. That you'd try to help her out, when you weren't in the best place yourself.'

Not in the best place was an understatement.

Lorraine scrubbed stiff fingers through her hair, realising as she did how tangled it felt. 'I thought their mortgage was all paid up in any case. They've lived there forever.' She gave it some thought. 'No. I remember when we all had a little celebratory drink a few years ago because they got their deeds to the house. That's not true. They didn't have a mortgage. So, why would he need life assurance?'

Mrs Tindall leaned forward, her nose wrinkling with regret. 'They took out one of those... you know, when you take the money from the profit in the house.'

Lorraine leaned back. 'Equity release?'

'That's the one.'

'What for?'

'To buy his car. They needed one just as you got married. Remember the engine blew on his old one?'

Her dad had bought a brand-new MG. Nothing like his classic, he'd said, but he was delighted with it. The MG her mum found a little clunky for her, but she managed. She'd have been happier with a little Smartcar.

Not once had her parents mentioned they didn't have the money to give her. She'd never asked for money, they'd given it without a qualm.

Lorraine covered her mouth with her hand and squeezed her

eyes closed. He'd given her five grand towards the deposit on her house the year before she'd met Simon. Which was how she'd managed to keep the house when her husband left. The declaration of trust had been her dad's idea. One she'd not been keen on at the time, but truly grateful of once she'd discovered what a snake Simon was.

Her parents had lavished her with money they didn't have and kept it secret from her.

Guilt snuck in under the worry. Had she put her parents in debt? They'd helped to pay for the wedding, but she thought that came from savings.

She'd been so wrapped up in her own despair when her dad died, although she and her mum had clung together, Lorraine couldn't remember speaking about the practicalities. Why would she? Her parents were old-fashioned in that respect. She might tell *them* how little she earned, how much her mortgage cost, the price of living increase, but they never spoke about their own money in that manner.

Mrs Tindall gave a small head tilt. 'You were in no position for her to lean on. You're still not. Not since Simon the skunk left.'

'Simon the...?'

'Skunk.' Mrs Tindall's lips twitched in what could have been a smile. 'It's what your mum and I called him.'

'After he left me?'

'No. We've always called him Simon the skunk.'

Lorraine raised a hand to her forehead. 'Always? I thought Mum used to like him. Before he left me, that is.'

'She never liked him. Never trusted him. Thought he was a... well, a skunk.'

Lorraine blew out a breath. 'Well, she never indicated that she didn't like him. Ever.'

'Why would she?' Mrs Tindall's voice was calm. 'It wasn't her choice to make. He was yours, and she'd never dream of upsetting you by telling you that you'd made the wrong choice.'

'But she knew I had?'

Mrs Tindall inclined her head. 'Of course. But you needed to discover that for yourself. She did regret not speaking out sooner, though, especially when the skunk left you in the way he did.'

'Did she know about the other woman?' She couldn't help the shock in her voice.

'No. She said not.' Mrs Tindall pursed her lips. 'But she recognised the signs.'

'Signs, what signs?'

'He lost weight, started working out again, like he did when he first met you. He bought new clothes. Trendier. He shaved more often, changed his aftershave.'

Lorraine's mouth dropped open. 'How do you know all this?' She thought her mum barely spoke to her neighbour.

'Because we've always chatted.'

That was news in itself to Lorraine.

Mrs Tindall smiled as she evidently caught the sour look on Lorraine's face. 'Oh, we weren't bosom buddies, certainly not in those early days. We never lived in each other's pockets or even did afternoon tea. But we passed the time of day.'

Sadness rippled over her papery cheeks. 'Because when your dad died, your mum realised just what it was like to be lonely, and you were in a situation where she didn't want you to take on any more because you were struggling too.'

'But surely she had some kind of pay-out from his accident?' For all the recriminations about Mrs Tindall's sons not doing their bit, Lorraine realised just what a terrible daughter she'd been.

Mrs Tindall leaned forward with a delicate grunt for Elijah to place the red shape in her hand. She turned it over, possibly with the same thought as Lorraine had turning over in her mind.

'Your dad only had the old car insured under third party and thingy.'

'Third party, fire and theft.'

'That's it.'

'You're kidding.'

Mrs Tindall shook her head, handed Elijah the shape back and let out another longer groan this time as she sat back. 'Apparently, he didn't see any reason for anything more for that car when the other was fully covered. He barely ever drove it except on sunny days. Even then, not as much as he used to.'

'Jesus.' The word slipped from Lorraine's lips. 'I can't believe she'd hide this from me. I thought I knew everything, and then this happens. Now I feel like I know nothing at all.'

Shrewdness flashed through the other woman's eyes just before she dropped her gaze to study Elijah. But Lorraine had caught it. 'Before she disappeared, she phoned me. She said some strange things. What else hasn't she told me, Mrs Tindall?'

Mrs Tindall hunched her shoulders. 'Oh, I'm sure there's more. Parents don't always tell their children everything, you know. After all, most things are history. My boys wouldn't want to know the things I got up to in my past.'

'Did my mum get up to something in her past?'

'Not your mum so much as your dad.'

'My dad?' Now she was confused. She glanced at her watch. She'd need to go shortly. Another twenty minutes. That's all she had, and time had wings, it appeared, as she tried to hustle Mrs Tindall on.

'What did Dad do?'

24

FOUR YEARS EARLIER

Trevor stared up at the ceiling from the top bunk, boredom gnawing at him as his cellmate threw a small white table-tennis ball at the wall, where it bounced off, hit the floor and rebounded back into his hand.

Trevor had given up counting after the first fifty throws. It was driving him insane. Completely insane. Worse than Chinese water torture. The incessant tink, as it ricocheted off the wall, crack as it hit the floor, puh as it landed in Chris's hand.

Tink, crack, puh.
Tink, crack, puh.
Tink, crack, puh.
'Give it a rest, will you, mate?'
Tink, crack, puh.
Tink, crack, puh.
Tink, crack, puh.
'Chris, would you cut it out?'
Tink, crack, puh.
Tink, crack, puh.
Tink...

Trevor leaped from his bunk.

Crack!

He backhanded Chris across the cheek.

'Puh.' His fist ploughed into the other man's soft, pillowy stomach and he watched with dispassion as the other man crumpled to the floor.

Trevor crushed the small white table-tennis ball in his hand and then dropped it to the floor by Chris's body before he was tempted to ram it down his throat.

'I asked you to give it a rest, pal.'

Trevor climbed back onto the top bunk, raised his arms, folded them behind his head and lay back.

In the silence, he allowed his mind to roll over things he needed to sort out.

He'd sworn never to write to his dad again. Not since he'd been ignored. Ignored every single time he'd written. He'd excused the first few letters going astray once he heard from his aunt that his dad and that witch of a wife had moved house.

In his youth and ignorance, he'd believed the letters had been lost in the postal system. He knew better now.

No one was willing to pass the new address onto Trevor. A clean break, the social workers had told him. He hadn't wanted a clean break. At the age of eleven, he'd wanted his dad. Needed his dad. He wanted a stable life with a family who loved him. Like his mum had. In her way. Until she died.

His dad had adored him. They were good together. They would have done well. If it hadn't been for Sandra.

He'd written each time he'd arrived at a new foster carer's house. He couldn't say if they'd ever been forwarded. But he had written. There must have been dozens of letters somewhere.

Anger hovered just below the surface. Anger he'd been told was only natural when he'd been deprived of someone close. Someone precious.

He wasn't inclined to agree that it was natural for it to have continued for this long. He was old enough and wise enough now, though, not to discuss it with those in authority. He could keep it to himself. Anything to help get him out earlier than scheduled.

He'd be on his best behaviour.

He glanced down at the crumpled figure on the floor. Most of the time. When there were no eyes, no ears.

Chris wouldn't say a word. It was a quick spat. No one need know.

Besides, it had been Chris's fault with his Chinese water torture. It had driven Trevor to the edge of insanity. He doubted pleading insanity would get him off the hook, though, if the screws found out.

Chris would keep his silence. He had done before. He would this time.

All Trevor had wanted was a quiet afternoon contemplating his next move.

The last time he'd written to his dad had been the day before he'd been convicted of murder.

He had no idea how to contact him, except through his aunt. Not much older than Trevor, she still lived in the same house she'd been brought up in. She'd offered to forward his letters. She swore to him she had.

Still nothing.

Years it had been since he'd even tried.

The silence from his dad had been endless.

How could anyone ignore their own flesh and blood that way?

Tension stiffened his muscles and his jaw cracked as anger settled in.

With a restless shuffle, he rolled from his bunk, his trainers slapping onto the floor. He barely acknowledged Chris, who scrabbled onto his lower bunk and curled into a tight ball.

The lad was safe. Trevor was done with him.

He wasn't given to smashing the other inmates to pieces. In general, he kept to himself. Didn't bother with the others, provided they left him alone.

He raised his hand and touched square fingertips to the scar dissecting his top lip.

He knew what it was like to take a good thrashing. There was nothing *good* about it.

Trevor rolled his shoulders, the crack and pop of his muscles another reminder that despite his age, that kicking he'd taken had damaged his neck.

It had damaged Red even more.

* * *

'Red, you all right, mate?'

The guttural groans his friend let out had weakened over the past hour and Red's eyes were closed, his skin a sickly white. His eyelids had deepened to purple and those freckles that peppered his skin had turned a dull olive green.

'Shit. What am I supposed to do?'

In the absence of an answer, Trevor leaned over Red who'd flopped onto the sofa three hours earlier after they'd made their way home. The climb up the eight flights of stairs had nearly killed them both, but as the lift had been broken again by the little shites that ran the tenement hallways, they'd had no choice in the matter.

Red had not moved since. Barely grunted.

'Mate. Red.' Trevor touched the other man, his hand grazing across a stomach that was normally flat on the slim, wiry man.

A curling dread clenched at his chest as he parted Red's jacket and then pushed his hoodie up to reveal a belly distended and purple. He placed his hand on it. Heat pulsed through it like a heartbeat.

He snatched his hand back, nausea clawing at his throat.

'Fuck.'

He staggered to his feet and paced to the window of his flat to stare out across the darkened skyline with his arms wrapped around his middle to stop his ribs from cracking any more.

Lights gleamed from below, stars glittered from above. Blue lights flashed in the distance, and he knew in an instant what he had to do.

It was no longer about him. But about survival. Of his friend. He needed to do the right thing.

He dug the phone from deep in his jeans pocket and dialled.

'Ambulance, pal, and make it quick.'

* * *

Trevor pulled out the white plastic chair and sat at the narrow bench that served as a desk. He slid the small pad of lined paper towards him and picked up a biro. His handwriting had never been the best at school and hadn't improved since. He knew how to write, but it was a large, childlike scrawl. After all, when had he had the chance to practise? What need had he ever had?

He looked towards the cell door, closed now for the night. Perhaps he should join the educational programme. They could help him write a proper letter to his dad, instead of the crap he produced himself. There was an English language course one of the other lads had been on. Said it was cool. Said it had helped him to write letters to his family.

He cringed at the thought of the last one he'd written. Desperate, pathetic. Pleading.

It had been such a long, painful time ago. A lengthy missive inside a birthday card for his dad.

He wouldn't plead again. Never.

He shoved the paper away and pushed to his feet to pace the cell.

'Chris, mate. Can you write?'

'Course I can fucking write.' Chris barely moved from his huddle, his voice a low petulance. 'What do you think I am, a fucking neanderthal?'

Trevor had no idea what one was. He could take a guess.

'Not a stupid question, mate.' He hunkered down next to Chris's bunk, gave his back a prod with his forefinger. 'Most of the inmates here can't write properly. The authorities say that's half the problem. The uneducated.'

'I'm not uneducated.' Chris reluctantly unfurled his body and turned to face Trevor, sulky eyes not quite meeting his. 'I went to university.'

'No shit. To study what?' Trevor leaned back onto his heels and squinted at the other man.

'Law.'

Trevor snorted. 'How did that work out for you?'

Chris cautiously swung his legs over the side of the bed as if he was waiting for another smack on the head. It wasn't coming. Trevor had made his point.

'I dropped out at the beginning of year three.'

'What the hell for? You were nearly there, weren't you?'

'Yeah. But funding stopped for law graduates, and I didn't have the connections most the other students had at the time. Some of these guys have their whole family line practising law. Mine just go against it. I never stood a chance. So, in my youthful wisdom, I couldn't see the point.'

Trevor straightened and leaned both hands against the upper bunk. 'So, you're a rebel within your own family.'

'Yeah. Thieving gits, all of them.'

'But you're the one in prison.'

'Because they let me take the fall for their bungled burglary.'

'Oh, yeah?'

'Armed robbery, really. My prints on the gun.'

'How come?'

'Because the gits handed it to me, asked me to keep it safe. I refused and handed it back. The prints were already on it. Mum gave me hell, said I'd gone the way of the others and she'd never forgive me.'

'Didn't she believe you?'

'Course not. If a word comes out of one of my family's lips, it's gonna be a fucking lie.'

'You can't be in for long, for what? Possession. Going armed?'

'Murder.'

'No way!'

'Yep. They cocked up. Fired the gun. Killed a security guard. Framed me. Little bastards. I probably will do murder when I get out and track them down.'

'Your mum won't like that.'

'Nope. But then, she shouldn't have cased the joint and given them the job in the first place.'

'You're shitting me.'

Chris grinned. 'No, mate. Mums... ay.'

Trevor sniffed. 'I wouldn't know. I haven't got one.'

25

FIFTY-NINE AND A HALF HOURS SINCE PHONE CALL

Her face was frozen. Completely numb. She might have had a stroke. She felt like her soul had stepped out of her body and was hovering somewhere above her. A cool, distant spectre that had no emotional connection with the woman who sat on the settee, clutching at a limp piece of lined paper.

'Lorraine, love, are you okay?'

She couldn't raise her head, couldn't take her gaze from the letter.

Her body was disconnected from her mind.

Only her survival instinct kicked in and she sucked in a deep life-affirming breath, making juddering sounds in her throat as she did. Not so much sobbing as grabbing onto life.

The disconnect was gone and every colour in the dingy room flashed to bright whites and glaring reflections off glass cabinets, mirrors and windowpanes.

Elijah's drool glimmered as he smiled up at her.

'Lorraine?'

She turned her head. 'So, it's true. I do have a brother.'

'Half-brother.'

She was frowning so hard, her head ached. 'Why didn't they tell me?'

Mrs Tindall gave a shrug, her mouth compressing. 'Maybe they didn't think it should involve you.'

Aghast, Lorraine couldn't speak for a long moment.

Elijah flipped over onto his hands and knees and started to crawl, but much to Lorraine's relief, he grabbed an orange piece of the puzzle and plopped himself back onto his nappy-clad bottom. He rammed the orange plastic into his mouth and chomped down on it.

Aware it wasn't Mrs Tindall's fault, or even her business, despite the fact that she knew more than Lorraine, she tried to tether the hysteria threatening to run free.

She flapped the paper with spider-like scrawl running between the lines. 'Surely it was and is my business. I have a half-brother. One I had no idea about until...' Until the phone call the other night. Why hadn't she grabbed the kids out of bed and whizzed around to her mum's house?

Because like the police, she'd initially believed her mum had been drinking. Hadn't really listened to the garbled hysteria, because she was soaked in enough grief of her own.

Mrs Tindall rubbed her hands together. 'It was their decision not to tell you. Not mine, Lorraine. I had nothing to do with it.'

Lorraine blew out a breath. 'Nor did I. In fact, I had less to do with it than you. Why would they tell you, just a neighbour, when they couldn't even get up the courage to talk to me about it? I'm their *daughter*.'

The tone of her voice escalated, and her final word came out almost as a shout. Aware of the flicker of insult in the other woman's eyes, she couldn't stop herself.

She came to her feet and paced over to the front window.

She looked out through yellowing net curtains. She couldn't see her parents' house, the house she'd known all her life, from where she stood, but she could picture it in her mind's eye. Set back just slightly behind Mrs Tindall's house.

Lorraine turned and studied the old woman. 'When did you find out?'

Mrs Tindall shook her head, time-slackened jowls wobbling as she turned pleading eyes on Lorraine.

'It was when you were a little girl.' She unfolded her hands, wringing them together. 'Oh, it was horrible. Your mum and dad, they had such a fight. Our walls are fairly thick, we don't hear much, but oh my goodness, that day, they managed to rattle the windows in their frames.'

She stared at Elijah while she took a moment to draw breath. 'It wasn't really your dad. He was a quiet soul most of the time.' She looked up from under thinning, pale eyebrows. 'I've always thought he was a little downtrodden by your mum. Not that I'm criticising her, but he always did as she wanted. Kowtowed to her, if you get my drift. He was a peacekeeper, your dad. A nice man.'

Lorraine wondered if the woman was implying that her dad was lily-livered. A coward.

She turned it over in her mind. He'd been gentle. Quiet. Had he been abused by her mum? No, she thought not. She felt he'd always had his say, she rarely remembered them having words apart from that one incident. The one Mrs Tindall evidently also remembered, but he'd never been browbeaten. Had he?

She blew out a breath as she leaned over and handed Elijah another piece of the puzzle which he took with dwindling enthusiasm.

Sensing his loss of concentration, she rooted in the baby bag and slipped out a small box with an airtight lid. She peeled back the lid and set the box down in front of Elijah, allowing him to help himself to the sticks of cheese. A second small box contained

The Stepson 153

fingers of carrots, apple and cucumber. The apple had browned a little, but he was quite happy to ram it into his mouth and squish it through his fingers with the rest of the food. She often wondered how much he actually consumed and how much ended up on the carpet. Or in this case, Mrs Tindall's rug.

The old lady gave a small smile of approval and a nod as she resumed what she was saying.

'That day, I think your dad decided to have his two-penn'orth. They went at it hammer and tongs. My old man, George, actually went round and said he would call the police. At which point your mum stormed out.'

Lorraine frowned. Rubbing her brow, she found she simply couldn't pick at that memory. She didn't remember Mr Tindall coming around to their house while her mum and dad were arguing. Could it possibly be a different incident? One, like so much that was coming to light, she didn't have any knowledge of?

Mrs Tindall rubbed a chin speckled with short, wiry hairs. 'George felt awful. But your dad came around later and explained.'

'What did he explain?'

Mrs Tindall reached to the pile of paperwork stacked up on one side of her chair.

Her fingers clawed for a moment at a bundle, then she managed to get purchase on them.

'Here. I think this may be why your mum disappeared.'

26

EIGHTEEN YEARS EARLIER

Henry clutched the envelope in both hands and stared at the black scrawl on the front.

There was no address. It had been posted through his sister's front door. Or so she had said.

But Henry had a sneaking suspicion Caroline had been in contact with his son for longer than she'd admit. If only he'd had more time with her, he could have gleaned that information from her. The moment he'd stopped at the motorway service station on his way home and stepped out of the car to meet up with his little sister, Sandra had called.

As the phone burst into the theme of 'SOS' by Rihanna, his sister's eyebrows raised.

He tugged the phone from his pocket, his shoulders giving a defeated slouch.

'I've got to get it, it's Sandra. Maybe something's happened.'

'Something always happens when you arrange to see me.'

He gave an awkward shrug.

'Oh, for God's sake, Henry,' Caroline snapped as he weighed the phone in his hand, undecided whether to leave it to go to answerphone. 'You need to grow a pair and tell that wife of yours that you're allowed to see your sister.'

It was an on-going tug of war.

He cringed at the waspish tone, laden with Scouse, but it wasn't as harsh as Sandra's when his wife put her foot down and demanded he never speak with his own family again. For her sake. For the sake of their newly born daughter, originally. She wasn't newly born now, and he'd thought for a long time she should be told. But Sandra got her way. She always got her way. Well, mostly.

He'd complied at first, of course. Then he'd cajoled her into including his family into their lives again. That was until she found out that Trevor was in contact through them.

Ever since, he'd been barred from seeing his own flesh and blood.

It hurt too much and eventually he'd actually defied her for the first time in their married lives. Not so much openly defied as gone behind her back.

He hated dishonesty but found himself wallowing in it.

If Sandra knew, she'd hit the roof and disappear off again. Days she would be gone without him knowing where the hell she was. Worried to death that she'd deserted not only him but their daughter too. A child who needed her mum. Especially at this age. Lorraine's hormones had been raging for several months now. He'd like to think of Lorraine as still a child but there were signs that she was becoming a woman far earlier than he'd hoped. He couldn't hold back time on that front.

He smoothed the wrinkled envelope, thinking of the briefest of meetings he'd had with his sister.

In a hurried whisper, she'd said she'd had the letter for a few weeks. Didn't dare post it in case Sandra got hold of it. So, she'd waited until they could meet up.

'Has that woman got a bleedin' tracker on you?' She reached for the phone just as it started to chime again. He pulled it out of her reach.

It hadn't occurred to him that Sandra would do such a thing. Track him? Know his movements. Why? She wasn't paranoid. Was she?

His stomach clenched as the ulcer he'd had diagnosed gave a sharp twinge to remind him not to get stressed.

In defiance of his younger sister, he stabbed his finger on the answer button.

'Sandra. Hello, love.' He kept his tone calm, but sensed some of the weariness made its way through.

'Henry. I need you back home. Quick as you can, love. I've cut my finger.'

The ulcer flared again, maybe as a warning of the drama to come. He leaned forward and took a blister pack of Rennie from the centre console and with one hand flipped one into his mouth, followed by a second.

'Sliced it wide open, I have. Blood everywhere. I think I need stitches. I can't drive myself to the hospital.' Her voice faded so he pressed his ear close to the phone. 'I feel a little faint.'

'I'll be there shortly.' He looked at his watch, sheared off a little time for how long he would take to get there. Didn't quite tell her the truth so she couldn't calculate where he was. He could always say he'd been caught in traffic if she queried it once he arrived home. She'd probably be more concerned about getting to A&E rather than having a go at him for running late. 'Forty minutes, love.'

'Oh, God. That long?' Her voice hit a wailing note and he shot his sister a horrified look. 'I might have bled to death by then.'

He caught the look in his sister's eyes at his wife's histrionics and turned away. It didn't matter, she could still hear.

'I'm in the MG, love. You know it's going to take me a little while.' He turned as his sister tapped him on the shoulder and then frantically gesticulated beside him. He almost laughed as she mimed to tell Sandra to wrap her finger in a tea towel and hold it above her head and lie down.

After he relayed that, he touched the off button and sighed.

With a lethargy he often felt after dealing with Sandra, he spared his sister a quick hug, a kiss on the cheek and took the envelope before he dashed off home.

The injury had barely broken through the skin. Little more than a long, thin scratch.

All it had required was a good, thick plaster. But Sandra had taken herself off to bed for the rest of the evening with two paracetamol and a good measure of port, for shock, in the absence of any brandy in the house.

A sneaking suspicion edged in that his sister was right. She'd achieved her goal. He'd gone running.

Henry shrugged off the disloyal thought. Guilt and exhaustion hit him, so he sneaked past his daughter's bedroom door, slipped out of his clothes in the dark and crawled into bed without even cleaning his teeth.

It wasn't until the following morning he remembered the envelope which he pulled out of his abandoned trousers on the floor and tucked into his jacket pocket.

To Dad.

The writing didn't look any different from how it had when Trevor had been eleven. When he'd been taken away.

Another hot flame licked at his stomach, reminding him of the ulcer. One caused by stress. Because more accurately it hadn't been when they'd taken Trevor away, but when Henry had begged for his boy to be taken from him. That's what had started it.

Aware of Sandra's movement upstairs, he slipped the small penknife from his pocket. Slitting the envelope open, he let out a sigh at the thick wedge of pages he pulled out. He cast his eyes upward again. She was too busy getting Lorraine ready for school, she wasn't likely to come down and catch him.

Like a criminal, he furtively opened the folded pages and stared at the childish writing. His heart pounded in his ears to fill his head with a primal beat so he could barely hear the sounds upstairs.

'Oh, my God.'

He pressed his hand to his mouth and squeezed his eyes closed, holding back stinging tears.

Tears of guilt. Tears of regret.

If Sandra found out what he had in his hand, she'd hit the bleedin' roof. He wouldn't get a chance to read what his son had written, and she'd slide into that deep, dark place she had after...

He breathed out, leaping to his feet as the pounding of footsteps along the landing cut through his reverie.

'Come on, Lorraine, come on! You're going to be late.'

He looked out of the window to where the curve in the road disappeared up the hill and from where the school bus would sweep down at any minute.

His throat tightened. The letter would have to wait, but it was hardly inconspicuous.

As his daughter clattered down the stairs, Henry squashed the letter into his shirt pocket and smoothed his cardigan over the top.

Perhaps he'd go and sit with the old boy next door, and they could pretend to be gardening. It was the only time Sandra left him in peace. She thought he was playing his charitable part. The truth was, he enjoyed the other man's quiet, unjudgemental demeanour.

Henry stepped to the open sitting room door so he could give Lorraine a tight hug as she passed through the hallway before she went to school.

He loved his only daughter. But she wasn't his only child.

27

SIXTY-FIVE HOURS SINCE PHONE CALL

Lorraine unfolded the thick wad of yellowing paper and placed it on the small occasional table while she wandered through to the kitchen. Her heart pounded until it felt like it was about to jump out of her throat. Her temples beat the same rhythm.

After Mrs Tindall had given her the letters – dozens of them, it appeared – Lorraine had left. Numb to the very core, she'd been on automatic pilot ever since. She could barely remember saying goodbye after Mrs Tindall told her.

'They're from your brother to your dad.'

The shock hit her. A sucker punch straight to the solar plexus.

'A brother. So, I do have a brother.'

Who the hell was he?

Why had her parents kept this massive secret?

Blood drained from her brain to leave her light-headed. She'd taken a staggering few steps to the chair she'd vacated.

Mrs Tindall had wrung her hands together. 'Oh, I don't know if I've done the right thing.'

Nor did Lorraine.

She didn't want to know.

It was none of her business. There was no place in her life for a brother she had no knowledge of, no history with.

Her chest had squeezed tight from the very moment she'd been handed the letters.

She didn't often drink, being solely responsible for two little ones, but she'd called in at the local Co-op on her way home from picking up Sophia and used some of the cash Mrs Tindall had given her to buy a bottle of wine and a Margherita pizza. Neither of which could be deemed cheap.

Still, she'd considered it an emergency.

It seemed Mrs Tindall had put a little more cash in the small white envelope than her shopping had cost the previous day.

Lorraine would have to speak with her about that. Was it a mistake? Had she put extra in to cover mileage? If so, ten pounds was more than a little extra. Or had it been guilt money for the way Gareth had spoken to her? Whatever the case, she'd check with her, but right now the money came in handy.

It probably hadn't been a wise decision. Pizzas cost so much now, but she hadn't the brain power to think of anything else. Besides, she was on a junk food crash. She'd bring it back under control shortly, but right now, she needed all the carbohydrates she could get.

Once both the children were fed, bathed and in bed, there was no more procrastination. Nowhere left to hide.

She poured a small glass of red wine and took a sip. The warming liquid slipped down easily as she curled her legs under her and listened for a moment for movement from upstairs. Any restlessness.

Nothing.

Silence.

She gazed at the letters in her hand.

Faded black spidery writing sprawled over the lined pages. She would have guessed the age of the child to have been early teens from the style of it, but as she read, she realised that this was a man in his mid-twenties at the time the letters had been written. So, how old would that make him now?

An outpouring from a heart wrenched apart.

The letter had come from prison.

With each word she read, little shock waves had her fidgeting in her chair until she took a sip of wine, placed it on the side table and jumped out of her chair, letter in hand, to pace the room.

Dear Dad,

This is the fourth time I've written to you since I've been inside, and I have no idea whether or not you're even getting these letters. But I'll keep writing in the hope that one day you'll reply.

I decided to take up a couple of courses to occupy my time and expand my brain cells. I'm studying Science, which is really interesting and English Language, so hopefully you'll see an improvement in my style and grammar. I hope this makes you proud of me.

There's not much to say. Life inside seems to float along. I keep myself out of trouble in the hope that I'll be let out after my parole hearing, but...

Lorraine riffled through the pages, letting them flutter to the floor one by one as she tried to find the earlier ones. They were in no kind of order, as though they'd been hurriedly thrown together.

Hi Dad,

The Stepson

This one was written on smaller sheets, the writing blue and faded so Lorraine found herself turning towards the small table lamp to illuminate it better. She reached out a hand, took hold of her wine again, took another mouthful and placed the glass back down with a clatter.

She held her breath and waited a while, listening for movement from the children.

She turned back to the scruffy sheets of paper.

When can I come home?

I don't know what I did wrong, but I'm so sorry.

I just want to come home.

I don't like it here.

They don't eat the right food and the school is horrible. The big boys are always picking on me.

Can I come home if I tell Sandra I'm sorry? Even though I did nothing wrong, if I say I'm sorry will she let me come home to live with you? I promise to be a good boy.

How old could this child, who was now a man, be? Her older brother, by all accounts. How much older?

Lorraine clutched the letter in one hand and covered her mouth with the other, tears spilling over as she stemmed the sobs that threatened.

Oh, this poor little boy.

What had he done?

Why had he been sent away?

What crime could a child commit that was so bad, so awful, that his own dad had abandoned him?

To whom?

Where was Trevor's mum?

Lorraine dropped to her knees and scrabbled through the paperwork, reading an odd sentence here, a paragraph there.

Until she came across a white, unlined sheet.

Dad, can I come home? I really miss Mum since she died. I miss you. Can I come home? Please, please let me come home.

Lorraine's heart splintered. The crackle of broken pieces filled her ears until she could hear nothing.

She gathered all the pages, none of them making sense, into her hands and sat back on the edge of her chair, the glass of wine forgotten.

This was ridiculous.

How could something like this have happened and she remain completely oblivious to a life her parents had lived before her?

She needed answers, right now, and the only person she knew who held them was her mum.

She slumped back in her chair. Tremors rippling through her like aftershocks.

Where the hell was her mum? Was she safe?

Did this man, her brother Trevor, have anything to do with her mum's disappearance?

Evidently, he was her dad's son. Not her mum's. His mum had died.

That would make him her half-brother.

Her hands went slack around the letters, and they fluttered over her knees as she melted back into the chair. She closed her eyes, the last thing her mum had said to her clamouring to be heard.

'Now it's me. I'm so scared, but mostly for you and the children. Because once I'm gone, you'll be next.'

Lorraine's eyes popped wide, and she shot out of her chair, allowing the paperwork to flutter to the floor.

She snatched up her phone, dashed to the patio doors and checked the lock was secure. She checked the front door and slipped on the security chain.

With shaking fingers, she punched in the code for the alarm then sprinted upstairs as it beeped its five-second warning to set the alarms for downstairs.

A quick check reassured her that Sophia was fast asleep, but she left her door wide so she could hear any noise as she made her way to her own room at the front of the house.

She peeped in the cot at her son and then, leaving her clothes on, Lorraine slipped under the bed covers, pulling them high. Despite the mild night, she couldn't stop the judders consuming her, turning her blood to ice.

Her gaze slid to the blind that covered a window she would normally leave ajar for fresh air. It could stay shut tight tonight. She leaned over and switched off the nightlight with its soft warm white glow she left on for Elijah and then shuffled onto her knees.

As stealthily as possible, Lorraine put one eye to the side of the window blind and edged it up so she could peep out at the street without being seen.

Not fully dark, with streetlights glaring down every fifty metres or so, it was easy to take a good, long look at movement down there.

Several cars came and went. Loud music played and laughter came from the family four doors up with three teenagers. The middle-aged woman across the street dragged her red-top bin out for bin men who wouldn't be there until Monday, which meant she was going away for the weekend. Always a risky thing to do, in Lorraine's opinion. A good signal that the house was empty. Better to ask the neighbour. Then again, not all of them were neighbourly.

Faint shouts from the house on the end drifted. Another

domestic from them. If it went on long enough, someone would call the police.

If they did, Lorraine would be out there.

She could call them herself, but what could she say?

Her teeth chattered as she sank down under her covers, eyes wide.

If her mum was right, he might be out there now.

28

NINE MONTHS EARLIER

'Henry Leivesley, if you leave this house now, don't you expect me to be here when you return.'

'Sandra, for God's sake, I'm only going to take Betty for a run, I'm going nowhere.' Betty was his beloved classic 1971 MG BGT in Damask Red. The one he'd inherited from his dad and cherished like it was his second wife. Possibly his first wife...

He glanced at Sandra as he slipped into the driver's seat of a car he possibly wouldn't be able to get in and out of for much longer. The low-slung chassis almost had his backside on the floor. The endeavour of prising himself out of it had become an effort as his knees creaked and groaned. No longer able to keep up with his thirty-year-old brain, his sixty-eight-year-old limbs had succumbed to his real age.

But the pleasure of driving his beautiful Betty that his dad had bought brand new and handed down to him was next to none. Every Sunday afternoon, come rain or shine, he polished the immaculate paintwork whether it already gleamed or not.

These days, he only took Betty out on rare occasions. Her engine was immaculate, her mileage low for a gal her age. But he didn't like to risk her, only taking her out in dry, sunny conditions these days. A rarity at any time of the year other than summer.

Betty's thin tyres were a hazard on a wet road, especially with her incredible power. Her steering wasn't as accurate as a modern car, but he loved her all the same.

'Look.' He lifted a placating hand.

'Don't you "look" me.'

She stormed around the rear of the car and leaned over the passenger side, pointing her finger wildly at him. 'If you think for one moment I don't know what you're up to, you're sadly mistaken.'

'Sandra...' He tried pacifying, but to his surprise, she opened the passenger door, slipped inside the car and settled herself in the passenger seat with a startled grunt as her backside hit the low-slung seat, similar to the ones he gave when he got in too quick. She wriggled around to persuade the seatbelt from its retractor.

She yanked at it hard enough to make him cringe, her stiff, arthritic shoulders apparently forgotten.

'If you believe you're going on your own, you've a surprise coming, my man. I'll tell you what. I'll come with you and when we get to your sister's, I'll tell her exactly what I think of her poking her nose into our business. Again.'

'She's not...'

Sandra butted in once more, not giving him a chance to reply. 'She has no right, Henry. None at all. She was a girl, a child herself when this all happened. What does she know about it?'

'A lot more than you think,' he mumbled.

Defeated, he edged the car out of the drive, the long, low bonnet making him cautious. The visibility wasn't as clear as their modern-day MG ZS compact SUV. But that couldn't hold a candle to this beauty.

He glanced sideways at his wife, her cheeks flushed a mottled red.

If she was calling his bluff, then he was up for it. Although he checked his watch briefly as he turned onto the estate road to follow the long curves down to the main road.

With every hundred yards, he expected her to tell him to pull the car up and she'd get out, slamming the door behind her, and storm away back to the house.

She'd brought nothing with her. Not her bag, or her phone.

He glanced down. She still had her slippers on, but he noticed the house key gripped in her hand, her finger looped through the keyring. She'd not chanced going back to change into her shoes in case he'd driven off without her, but she'd made sure she could get back into their house independently.

'Sandra, this is nonsense. I'll take you back.'

'No. You won't.' She crossed her arms over her chest and settled back. 'Wherever you're going, I'm coming with you.'

This was not what he needed. He couldn't have Sandra with him. It was bad enough she thought he was meeting up with his little sister, but this was worse. Far worse. If she had any inkling of what he was up to, she'd flay the bleedin' skin off him.

Instead of heading down the motorway, he steered the car down a small country lane which would have been barely wide enough to fit his modern car, but the little MG sailed through.

If he could only throw her off the scent, he could loop around and take her back home. He just needed to calm her down.

'I'm not going to my sister's. I swear I'm not.' He wasn't a good liar, but this wasn't a lie.

Normally he managed to get past on avoidance rather than lying. The truth of the matter was he mainly hid behind his work and his daughter. She took most of the pressure away from him. If Lorraine was there, Sandra was happy, especially since little Sophia had come into their lives. And with another one on the way. Another few weeks only.

He wasn't given to violence, but he knew inside if he met Simon the skunk, as Sandra nicknamed the man who'd married their daughter, he'd like to bop him on the end of that smug, tipped up little nose he had. Not that Henry would.

Simon had never been a man Henry had taken to from the moment his daughter brought him through the front door into their living room. His wife called him 'the skunk' because she claimed she could smell something wasn't right about him.

A smug little prick.

Lorraine was a hard worker. She'd got a promotion at work, earned a good salary and even managed to buy herself a little two-bedroom starter home. All on her own. Except for the little bit of help they gave towards the deposit. She'd been a devoted daughter, giving much of her time to entertaining her mum.

Once Simon came along, the dynamics had changed. With Lorraine no longer there to keep Sandra company, his wife had started to rely on Henry. Question his movements. She'd wanted more of him. A situation he'd found stifling.

He'd had mixed feelings when the skunk had left his daughter just a few months from her due date for their second baby.

She'd been heartbroken, of course, and there was nothing Henry wanted more than to go around and kick that man's arse from one end of town to the next. Especially once he discovered the woman he'd left Lorraine for was also pregnant.

Literally, Simon the skunk had been between a rock and a hard place.

Two pregnant women. Who to choose?

Henry knew for a certainty he'd never had that dilemma. His previous wife had left him for a brief fling with her then boss. A fling that was never going to last. She'd lost both her job and the boss. A spiteful woman, she'd held onto Trevor just to keep the balance of power when she realised she'd lost her husband to no avail.

Henry had made a promise to himself that he'd kept for the entire duration of his second marriage. That he would never be unfaithful.

'Henry!'

He jerked back to the present time. It had been easier when Lorraine hadn't been so exhausted, and she'd come around in the afternoon. But now all she wanted to do was collect Sophia from nursery and go home so they could both have an afternoon nap.

Things would change again once she had the baby. Perhaps Sandra would be needed more to help out with the baby once Lorraine returned to work. That would occupy her time more.

He'd kept silent when Sandra had declined to look after Sophia when she was a baby, despite his daughter's indignation. He understood she didn't want the responsibility of a newborn. Especially after what had happened. How was Lorraine to understand, though, if they didn't tell her? Would never tell her because Sandra wouldn't allow her pain to surface again.

Not until Sophia was confidently running about the place did Sandra agree to have her, and only when Henry was available too. She'd claimed it was too much for her to be fully responsible.

'Henry.'

'Yes.' He couldn't help the snap in his voice as she shocked him out of his thoughts. A rare moment for him.

'Are you going back home?'

'Yes.'

'I thought we were going for a ride.'

'No. I was.'

'You're meeting someone! I knew it. You've got another woman, haven't you?' She gave his shoulder a hard shove, taking him by surprise as the little car jolted towards the hedgerow verge.

Without the same dexterity of steering as the modern MG, he found himself hauling on the steering wheel to guide it away from the ditch. It skimmed the edge and then bounced over the uneven ground.

The narrow wheels took traction once he had it back on the rutted lane but he regretted his decision to take that route after all. He should have stayed on the main road and chanced Sandra realising the direction he was taking.

'Sandra! Get yourself under control, woman,' he barked. She knew how to get under his skin. Deliver an insult he couldn't bear, because his morals would never allow him to look at another woman. She knew it, she simply wanted to wind him up.

Surprise made her voice squeaky. 'I am under control.'

'No. You're not.'

'More so than you. You've lost the plot. I should have you committed.'

He gave her a sideways look, astounded by her words. 'What are you talking about?'

'We agreed. You and I said we would never allow that boy, that *murderer* into our house ever again.'

Genuine shock rippled through him. 'I have no idea what you mean.'

'You know! I saw that letter. I was testing you. I'd rather you'd admitted to seeing another woman. That, I could have dealt with. I wondered if you'd say you were, because we both know this is far worse. This is a complete and absolute betrayal, and you've been had.' Her lips curled into a sneer. '*Dad, oh, Dad. Rescue me.*'

The blood drained from him. She knew. How the hell had she seen Trevor's letter? His heart gave a painful squeeze, and he raised his hand to his chest.

With a tone far calmer than he felt, he spoke to her. 'How did you find it?' She'd said 'that letter' which presumably meant she'd only seen one. Which meant it hadn't come from next door. That was a relief. The others were safely tucked away, although for how long, he wasn't sure. If anything happened to old Mrs Tindall, there was quite a bit that could come to light. Unless her sons simply 'tipped' the lot as they were likely to do.

George had been gone two years now, but no one had found the 'stash' of papers that belonged to Henry. He wasn't sure exactly where the old boy had hidden them, but George had been quite amenable when Henry had suggested it. He'd persuaded him with a bottle of port, a cigar and his company every Sunday afternoon.

It hadn't been premeditated. The pair of them had developed a comfortable routine from their unlikely friendship.

His foot pressed a little harder on the accelerator and they dashed around the next bend, skimming over the low grass verge and back onto the road.

Sandra scraped her hair back and held it with one hand, she raised her voice against the roar of the engine and the whip of the wind. 'You dropped it on the bathroom floor, you careless fool. I assumed it had been in your dressing gown pocket. So, I read it, then put it back.'

He remembered the hot slice of panic when he couldn't find it in his trouser pocket, and then the relief on checking his dressing gown. He'd been confused for a moment but could only assume a momentary distraction. Seemed he was wrong. He had dropped it from his trouser pocket. Sandra was the one who had slipped it into his dressing gown pocket without his knowledge.

'Why didn't you say anything at the time?' He cut her a quick glance.

'I wanted you to come clean. I gave you every chance to admit your disloyalty. Your treachery.' Tears welled in her eyes, big fat ones that threatened to roll out. He couldn't let her distress affect him. Not this time. He hardened his heart to her tears.

He swallowed hard and stared at the road, his speed slipping up another notch. 'You wouldn't have allowed me to see him. You would have given me your histrionics again.' He couldn't help the bitterness creeping out.

'And deservedly so. He murdered our son, Henry.'

'He says not. The experts said not. It was SIDS, for God's sake. When will you ever see that? When will you stop blaming Trevor? He's had an atrocious life, all because of y...'

Her expression could not have been more stunned if he'd slapped her face.

Her lips barely moved, and the wind whipped the words away as the hedgerows opened up for a moment and rolling hills became visible. Such beautiful countryside and yet they were mere minutes away from town.

'What?' He raised his voice to project above the sound of the wind thrashing through the knitted beanie he wore over his thinning hair.

'I said, you bastard.' Her pale face turned florid. Wild eyes glared at him with tears spilling over to roll down her cheeks and be snatched away by the wind. 'How can you put that evil monster before me? Before your *daughter*. And *granddaughter*.' Her voice lifted to a terrifying scream, broken only by the rough edges of tears catching in her throat. 'Our new baby on the way. If you let him into our lives, he'll do to them what he did to my baby. Our baby. Don't you understand? How can you be so bloody blind?'

'Stop! Just stop your stupidity. I've tolerated it for thirty years, woman. He's not going to harm anyone.'

'He is! You stupid, stupid man. He's been writing to you from prison. Prison. He murdered someone. Someone else! And now he's out.'

'It was manslaughter.'

'Manslaughter. Murder. Same thing in my eyes. He's going to kill us all!'

Her hands curled into claws and just as he hit the bend in the road too fast, Sandra turned in her seat to give her more leverage. She lunged at him.

'No! Sandra, no!' The scream tore from his throat as he jerked his elbow up to protect his face.

The car slewed across the dry, arid surface of the lane, smacked into a loose rock and careered up the slight embankment.

With a yowl of horror, Henry slapped both hands back on the wheel and wrestled to keep it on track, his arms straining to contain it.

Crack!

Something went loose and the steering wheel turned slack in his hands.

Sandra shrieked, her body flopped like a rag doll as she flung her arm across her face to protect it.

The car slewed sideways and mounted the grass verge, heading straight for the ditch.

The world tipped on its axis as his precious MG BGT flipped over onto the driver's side.

Henry never saw the branch which smashed through his window.

It lanced through his skull, splitting his head in two.

29

SEVENTY-EIGHT AND A HALF HOURS SINCE PHONE CALL

Lorraine paused outside the police station and ground her teeth. This time there was no way she would leave until she had the front counter staff's attention.

The dark-haired woman, Lorraine hazarded a guess in her late forties, stared at her with liquid brown eyes filled with sympathy. A whole different approach from Lorraine's previous encounter.

'My mum's missing,' she repeated, in case the clerk hadn't taken it in, as Lorraine placed a sleeping Elijah at her feet in the car seat she'd decided to bring this time instead of taking his ever-increasing weight for an interminable time.

The woman nodded.

'I came in the other day, but the...' She hesitated, not wishing to make an issue of it. She never was a troublemaker. She preferred to keep her head down, but this was a serious matter. 'The man here told me to go away and that she'd probably come back home.'

'Okay.' The woman nodded again. 'Ninety-nine per cent of the time people do turn up, come home. Provided they're not at risk. They normally come home.'

'She hasn't.' Lorraine's chest expanded and she clawed back at tears that threatened to spill. 'She's not back and now I've found out all these things.' She thrust the bundle of papers at the other woman and watched as they scattered through the hole in the Perspex window and across the front desk, one or two fluttering to the floor on the other side. 'I think she's in trouble. I think something bad has happened.'

The woman fumbled to grab hold of the letters, confusion passing over perfect tawny skin. She gave a hasty glance behind her while she gathered up the papers. As she turned back to Lorraine, she cast her a sympathetic smile. 'Give me a minute, would you, Lorraine? You did say Lorraine, didn't you?'

'Yes. Lorraine Pengelly.' The tears broke free and trickled down her cheeks as she nodded. She wiped her nose on the back of her hand and then sniffed as the woman turned her back and spoke to a uniformed officer behind her.

Astute eyes studied her for a moment as the clerk placed the letters in the officer's hand. A quick glance and the officer made her way to a side door leading to where Lorraine waited.

'Morning. Lorraine Pengelly, is it?'

'Yes.' She nodded as a small sob burst out.

'Okay, now, love, don't worry.' The officer bent and scooped up Elijah in his car seat as though she was an old hand at it. 'Let's go through here and we can have some privacy.' She bumped open a door with a well-rounded backside and edged her way in, gently placing the car seat on a small table. She leaned over the baby, a soft smile creasing her cheeks. 'Well, isn't he a darling. All quiet for Mummy.' She glanced up. 'And you look like you could do with it.'

Lorraine's pounding heart settled as she slid into the seat the woman indicated with a wave of her hand.

'I'm Sergeant Lisa Willingham. Looks like you arrived at the right time. I'm a trained Family Liaison Officer. I was just picking up some messages when you came in.' She hefted herself and her bulky uniform onto the chair opposite and kept her voice low in deference to the sleeping baby.

Lorraine felt the woman's quiet appraisal. Not judgement, merely a consideration, a weighing up of what she had on her hands.

A light knock at the door had Lorraine jumping for no other reason than her nerves were in tatters.

The clerk stepped inside, silently placed a small white plastic cup of water down in front of each of them and then sidled out, leaving nothing but a waft of perfume-infused air in her wake.

'Would you like to start at the beginning?' The police officer pushed a small box of tissues across the desk and Lorraine picked one out. She wiped her eyes and then snivelled in a shaky breath.

'My mum's missing.'

The concern in the sergeant's eyes almost had Lorraine in tears again as the officer leaned forward and placed her hand in reassurance on top of Lorraine's.

'What makes you think she's missing?'

Lorraine blew out the breath that had backed up in her lungs. 'She phoned me a couple of nights ago. She sounded all flustered. I thought she'd been drinking.'

There was a beat of silence. 'Had she?'

Lorraine's hackles went up in defence of her mum, but then she slumped back in the small chair. 'Yes. Possibly.' She met the other woman's eyes. 'It's complicated.' She covered her face with her hands. 'Oh, God. It's so complicated.' She spread her fingers to peep at the other woman, and then dropped her hands to her lap. 'My husband left me a few months before Elijah was born.' She rested her hand on the car seat. 'Then my dad died.' She paused. Swallowed. 'He was in a car accident. He'd taken his classic MG BGT out and ditched it. Unfortunately for him, there was a branch sticking out of the ditch.' She put her fingers to her head and quickly withdrew them, the graphic too much for her to endure.

She caught the quick flicker in the officer's eyes. 'Did you...?'

Sergeant Willingham gave a controlled nod, never taking her gaze from Lorraine. 'I attended. I'm very sorry for your loss, Lorraine. And obviously for your mum's loss too.' Her lips turned down at the corners, sympathy in every muscle twitch. 'Has she been acting strangely since?'

Lorraine raised shaky fingers to her lips. 'Yes.' She nodded, so reluctant to admit it to a stranger, but then again, who else did she have to speak with? 'I think she's suffering from depression. Everything has gone wrong. Ever since Simon left.'

'Simon? Your husband.'

'The skunk.'

The sergeant's lips quirked into a reluctant smile which quickly dropped away. 'Did your mum get along with your husband?'

'Ex.'

'Ex.'

'Technically, the divorce isn't finalised, but he's definitely my ex. To answer your question, no, not really. They didn't particularly have a relationship. Mum never criticised him, not in front of me at least. I always thought they got along. And then her neighbour told me yesterday Mum had never liked him.' She took a sip of water. 'It was a bit of a shock, really. That's when I found out they called him Simon the skunk. You know, they thought he gave off a bad smell, figuratively speaking. Apparently, Mum didn't trust him. Thought he'd do the dirty on me.' She raised her eyebrows. 'Looks like she was right.'

She took in a long, slow breath. 'If the truth be told, although I was knocked sideways when he left, I haven't really missed him. It might sound strange, but I think we'd already sort of separated by the time I realised I was pregnant. Mentally. Emotionally. He just hadn't made the move away yet. I have two beautiful children who he refuses to have anything to do with, which kind of knocks him off my Christmas card list.'

With a wry smile, she rubbed her nose again with the tissue as the truth of what she vocalised struck home for the first time. 'I believe his new partner...' just saying those words felt peculiar, 'his partner had a little boy by him a few months after I gave birth. So,' she indicated her son with a flick of her hand, 'my kids also have a half-brother.'

She caught the flash of surprise in the other woman's eyes. Shrugged away the pain that edged into her. 'He has his family. I have mine.' She spread her hands wide. 'He doesn't even contribute. Only sporadically. Seems to think that only planting a seed isn't enough to take financial responsibility.' Aware that she was rambling on as nerves made words spill from her lips, she straightened up in her chair.

Sergeant Willingham took a notebook from her pocket. 'It's a civil matter, but I might be able to have a word.' She scribbled a few words. 'What's his date of birth?' Lorraine told her. 'I don't suppose you know where he lives?'

Lorraine nodded, reluctant to admit that at first, she'd stalked him when he'd left, convinced he'd soon be back. That was until she saw the pretty woman a few years her junior with the obviously rounded belly of a heavily pregnant woman.

'So, your mum isn't likely to have gone to him for help?'

Lorraine snorted. 'No. Definitely not. He's the last person she'd ask for help. She'd rather...' She stopped just short of saying her mum would have been more likely to go around and belt him one. Maybe that wasn't the sort of thing you admitted to a police officer.

Sergeant Willingham put her pen down and leaned back, her uniform creaking as she crossed her arms over her chest. 'It sounds like both of you have been through an awful lot, lately. Was your mum being treated for depression?'

'Yes. She was on some kind of antidepressant.' She raised her hand to her forehead, guilt squeezing so hard. She thought they were looking after each other, her mum and her, when in reality, Lorraine realised, it had been all about her. Her mum had been left floundering, unable to tell Lorraine things that should never have been kept secret.

'Have you?'

Shocked at a tough question laced with empathy, she couldn't answer, Lorraine let out a small grunt in response.

Sergeant Willingham's furrowed brow cleared. 'Oh, Lorraine. I think you need help.'

Lorraine nodded, tears springing back into her eyes. 'I do. I want my mum. I'm lost without her. I want my mum... I can't find her, and I have nowhere I can think that she's gone. She wouldn't leave me. I'm sure she wouldn't.'

She hiccupped in between the words, barely able to get them out.

'Now then...' The officer handed her the box of tissues again and this time Lorraine plucked out several of the thin paper hankies and gave her nose a hard blow.

'Calm down, love. Don't upset yourself. It's not good for you...' she gave the baby seat a gentle rock as Elijah whimpered in his sleep, '...or the baby.'

Elijah settled with a soft snuffle and Sergeant Willingham smiled.

She picked up the white plastic cup and encouraged Lorraine to wrap her fingers around it. 'Let's see what we can do to find your mum. The probability is that she's fine but with the information you've brought us, we'll look into everything for you.' She shuffled some of the papers together, tidying them into a neat pile and putting them to one side as though they bore no significance while Lorraine wiped her eyes, blew her nose and gained some element of composure.

'Right. Let's recap so I get all the facts.'

Lorraine sighed and then took a sip of water. It all seemed to take so long. So much wasted time.

'Your mum has been missing for...?'

Lorraine glanced at the time on her phone.

'Seventy-eight and a half hours.'

'That's pretty precise.'

'I've counted every hour since she phoned me around 3.30 Tuesday morning.'

Sergeant Willingham smiled as she jotted down a note.

'Have you been around to her house?'

'Yes, lots.'

'Phoned her?'

'So many times, her mobile now goes straight to answerphone.'

'Which could mean it's switched off.'

'Precisely. She never allows that to happen. Never allows it to run out of battery. She's very... meticulous that way.'

The officer took in a breath.

'I'm assuming she has her phone with her. She's not left it at the house?'

'No. I had a look. I searched the house to see if there was anything unusual.'

'And was there?'

'Yes. Definitely. She'd left her cash, her handbag, her coat.'

'But not her phone. Which would give her access to her bank account.' She poked out her bottom lip and stared at Lorraine. 'Why do *you* think your mum disappeared?'

Lorraine's mind went blank as she stared into the officer's pale grey eyes. 'What do you mean?'

'I mean, what do you think the reason is that your mum has gone? Do you truly believe she's in trouble? Has she ever done this before?'

Lorraine gave a jerky nod and watched the police officer's eyebrows slowly rise.

'Okay.'

She took a breath in. 'I didn't want to say when I first arrived in case the man on the front desk thought she does this kind of thing regularly and didn't take me seriously.' She paused. 'He didn't anyway.'

Sergeant Willingham blew out a breath. 'He will have done, but unless your mum was believed to be a vulnerable individual, we wouldn't take action immediately. There are normally so many reasons why a person...'

'...disappears?'

'No.' Sergeant Willingham shook her head. 'Just take themselves off for a few days.'

'She did it once,' Lorraine blurted out. 'Once that I can remember.' She wrung her hands together. 'My aunt may know more.'

'Your aunt? You never mentioned an aunt. Could she have gone to stay with her?'

'Oh, God, no. Apparently, they didn't like each other. They've never spoken since I was a child.' She paused. 'I was going to visit her.' She looked at her watch as discomfort slid through her. 'I need to get going if I'm to be back on time.'

'On time?'

'To pick my daughter up from school.'

The sergeant sat up a little straighter. 'Ah, yes. You mentioned two children.'

'Yes. Sophia. She's five.' Lorraine gave a weak smile. 'She's not been at school long. Just September.'

'Okay.'

The sergeant jotted down another note.

'Just circling back. Why are you going to your aunt's?'

'Just...' Lorraine flopped back in her chair. 'Just to see if she remembers anything.' She flicked slender fingers at the pile of letters. 'In case she knew about what happened before.'

'Can I have your aunt's details?'

Lorraine nodded and reeled them off as she read the details from her phone.

'I'd rather you left it to us to see your aunt.'

'She's my aunt. You can't stop me seeing her.' She crashed headlong into the middle of the sergeant's suggestion.

The woman raised her eyebrows. 'No, but I wouldn't advise...'

'She's not done anything to her.'

'I didn't imply she had. For all we know, she may have some information she doesn't even know is relevant.' Sergeant Willingham gave her an understanding smile. 'We're good at this. It's our job.'

Lorraine fell silent. That was exactly the reason she was going, though. Aunt Caroline could have information that would lead Lorraine to her mum and no one was going to stop her. She nodded as though she agreed with the officer and tried desperately not to let it show.

'Do you know of anyone who might want to harm her?'

Lorraine raised her head. 'Not before I discovered she had a stepson no one told me about. And then Mrs Tindall told me she'd heard a car in the middle of the night.'

'Mrs Tindall?'

'Mum's neighbour.'

Sergeant Willingham was making frenzied notes. She looked up from under a heavy fringe. 'You do know you should have come straight back to the station as soon as you learned this.'

'But... the man...'

'You didn't give him this information at the time. We would have taken this so much more seriously if we'd been given these circumstances. It changes everything.'

Lorraine's eyes burned as they filled with tears. She dabbed at them. 'I'm really scared for her. I thought she was just rambling on, and I never took her seriously to start with. But now this.' She stabbed at the letters. 'I ignored her, and she was frightened. For her life.'

The words swirled around in her head. 'She said... "Now it's me. I'm so scared, but mostly for you and the children. Because once I'm gone, you'll be next."'

The sergeant leaned back in her chair, her lower lip held between her teeth as she made a mhmm noise. 'Let's go and have a look through your mum's house, shall we?' She shot Lorraine a tight smile as she pushed back from the desk and came to her feet.

'What, now?' Lorraine's eyes popped wide.

Sergeant Willingham tucked her pen into the utility belt and made for the door. 'No time like the present.'

30

NINE MONTHS EARLIER

Tremors radiated from her core until Sandra thought she might rattle apart.

Shock had frozen every emotion as she stripped, leaving her clothes where they dropped next to the almost threadbare slippers. The soles split and holey after the trek across the fields, over the main road and along the footpath to her front door. Not far on a good day, with good shoes. Barely a mile, she'd estimate. As the crow flies.

Devoid of feeling, Sandra had let herself in the front door and made her way up the stairs.

She stared at herself in her full-length bedroom mirror.

She'd just lost her mind. She'd killed her husband and here she was, numb, examining a naked body with barely a mark on it.

Apart from the red stripe across her shoulder slashing diagonally through her torso. Excruciating pain both there and horizontally across her belly where her caesarean scar was barely visible indicated she'd have severe bruising from the seat belt that had saved her life.

Some would call it a miracle.

She looked at it as punishment. Retribution for the evil she'd committed. Killing her own husband. To be left alive, with barely a mark on her.

She didn't even feel the desire to cry. To sob.

Her soul was empty. Numb.

Sandra stepped under the shower and let water thrash down on her head.

Trying to rid herself of the image of Henry, she blinked.

As Sandra had clambered out of the car and stumbled away along the lane, she'd glanced back. Even the car had been barely damaged. Or so it seemed from her viewpoint. On its side in the ditch, its wheels still spinning. Grass and dirt had been churned, leaving evidence of the skid in its wake. Rubber, bumpers, glass and chrome littered the verge and the shallow ditch.

If the branch hadn't been there, Henry would have walked away too.

She stepped from the shower, the heat of it failing to defrost the ice in her veins. She wrapped a large towel around herself and a small one turban-style around her head.

In a trance, she applied moisturiser and foundation. A touch of mascara to her eyelashes and a quick brush with blusher across her cheeks. Her stomach clenched.

She'd go to the police. Turn herself in.

She'd killed her husband.

Would they call her a murderer? Send her to prison?

She unwound the towels and dropped them into the linen basket ready to take downstairs and wash.

As she slipped on clean clothes, she looked at the pile on the floor. They wouldn't go in the wash. She'd never wear them again. They'd go in the bin.

The socks she slipped on over bruised feet failed to warm them and with no slippers, she couldn't imagine them ever feeling better.

Sandra picked up her hairbrush and stroked it through drying hair, then followed that by running her fingers through to give it a more natural look, instead of plastered to her head.

She bundled her clothing and slippers into one of the waste bags she kept in the bathroom cabinet for the bin and secured the top. She plopped the bag on top of the damp towels and made her way downstairs.

As she pushed the towels into the washing machine, dumped in a washing tablet and set the machine going, a curdling nausea burned at her stomach as the shock wore off.

She slipped on a pair of gardening shoes, picked up the bag with the clothes in and stepped outside the front door, making for the red lid bin Henry had taken up the drive earlier for collection the following day. Mrs Tindall's was level with theirs.

Sandra reached over and opened the lid to Mrs Tindall's bin and dumped her possessions in without thinking. The old lady always had less rubbish than them and they often used hers when theirs was full.

As Sandra reached the front door, a car pulled onto the drive behind her. She turned. A police officer stepped from the vehicle while her heart thundered.

Sandra's brow creased with confusion. She took a step towards the officer.

'Hello.' The officer's face was wreathed with sympathy.

Sandra hiccupped in a sob. 'What's wrong? What's happened?' Without a thought, the idea of confessing her sins slipped into oblivion as the police officer stepped closer and touched her arm.

'Mrs Leivesley? I'm Sergeant Lisa Willingham. Can we go inside?'

Sandra scanned the area to see if any of her neighbours were looking out of their windows at the police car.

One in her drive could only mean bad news.

Swallowing back tears as she led the way, Sandra closed the door both emotionally, and physically, with determined finality.

31

THREE YEARS EARLIER

Dear Dad

It's been some time since I've wrote you, but I've been busy trying to catch up on the education I missed out on when I was taken away from you.

I've had time to think.

I know Sandra won't let me anywhere near your house when I get out, which hopefully will be soon, but I wondered if you'd come and visit me in prison?

I never did anything wrong. I was imprisoned falsely for manslaughter because a friend of mine died while I was with him after he'd been beaten up. My only crime was not calling the ambulance soon enough. The police thought I'd been involved in the fight with a known drug dealer, but it had nothing to do with me. I hope you understand.

I really would like to feel that after all these years we can meet up and perhaps get to know each other.

If you're happy to do so, just let me know through Aunt Caroline, or direct and they'll make the relevant arrangements here.

I hope you can make it.

~~Best wishes~~
Love
Your son, Trevor x

Trevor placed his pen down and stared at the short note.

He normally scripted pages and pages before scrapping half of them.

This one would do. He'd learned a lot in his English lessons. Brevity was better.

He folded and enveloped it before he sat back in the flimsy chair. His chest squeezed. It was more than he could ever hope for that his dad would come and visit.

If Sandra got wind of it, she'd make sure he never saw his dad again. Heartless bitch.

He took the lined paper from the envelope and opened it up, flattening the crease with the side of his fist.

Forget brevity.

What was it you were supposed to put on the end of a letter once you'd already signed off?

He tapped the end of the pen on slightly crooked front teeth.

That was it.

PS

32

Henry sat opposite his sister in the small, steamy café and scrubbed his hands over his face. 'He wants me to go and visit him.'

Caroline said nothing as she cradled the white coffee mug between her hands, her eyes narrowed as she waited for him to continue.

'He says he wants to tell me what really happened that day.'

Her eyes bored into his until he looked away through windows dripping with condensation. 'She'd kill me if she found out.'

'What's new? She'd kill you if she found out you were meeting up with me.'

'No.' He shook his head and looked back at his sister. 'She'd be upset, but she'd get over it.' It was his way of justifying his actions. He could live with that. He hated to upset his wife.

She was his world. Always had been since the first day he met her. She'd placed his coffee on the meeting table in front of him and stared into eyes he knew attracted women. Each one a different colour. His left one with a stripe through it.

Lips the colour of raspberries slipped open and she'd seduced him with the slowest of smiles as her summer sky eyes melted his heart. He'd loved that colour lipstick on her. Still did when she deigned to wear it these days.

She'd been the partner's secretary at the solicitors he'd engaged for his divorce.

Three dates later, he'd known Sandra was the woman for him.

They'd had their issues. More than most. But he loved her as much now as he had then and there was nothing he would do to intentionally hurt her. Including making contact with a son he no longer knew.

Even now, sitting in this little café meeting up with his sister. If Sandra found out, it would rip his heart out that he'd hurt her.

Deliberately, he folded the letter and slipped it back inside the envelope.

He pushed it across the Formica table to his sister.

'I can't visit him in prison. It's not right.'

'It's not right that he's in prison.'

'We don't know that.'

'I believe him.'

'You don't know him.'

'No, you don't. You don't know your own son. You've had nothing to do with him since he was eleven. For God's sake, Henry, how could you have been so callous?'

Only a sister could say that and get away with it, he thought. No one else in his life had ever challenged him the way his sister did. Other than his wife.

She'd put her foot down on so few occasions, which meant when she did, he took notice.

Trevor was one of those occasions.

Henry had genuinely believed that once the baby blues, as they called it back then, lifted, Sandra would come round. They'd have Trevor back. The situation was only temporary.

Trevor had never killed their baby.

Alexander had died of SIDS. That's what the experts had told them.

Only Sandra had never believed it. She swore blind it was his son. Trevor.

The health visitor, that's what they'd called them back then, had reassured him.

'Henry,' she'd said, her cool fingers resting on his forearm. 'Sandra is suffering from what we call postnatal depression. She needs special care, a close eye. Probably antidepressants.' Her face crinkled with empathy. 'Especially under these circumstances. Losing a baby like this can be horrific for a new mother.'

'And for a new father. I feel the loss of our baby too.' He felt the breath catch in his throat.

She hesitated, afforded him a condescending smile and a pat of those cool fingers again on his arm. 'It's different for women. Your wife had hormones to deal with too.'

Did hormones make you grieve more?

He had no idea back then. What he did know was the devastation of his baby son's death had destroyed not only Sandra, but him. And, in consequence, his older son.

Trevor, who should have lived with them after his own mum had died. Trevor, who had his own emotional issues to deal with, had proved too much for them.

Guilt racked Henry.

Through his own grief, desperation and self-preservation he'd allowed his son, his firstborn, to take the brunt of all their heartbreak.

Look what that had brought him.

Trevor. His only son, in prison for a crime he never committed.

The letter explained it all. If you believed it.

'He says he's innocent,' Caroline said.

'All murderers claim they're innocent.'

Frustration ran across her features. 'Give him a chance, Henry. Do you think any of this would ever have happened to him if you and Sandra had kept him, instead of kicking him out to fend for himself? Do you?'

His hackles rising in defence, Henry glared back at his sister. 'We didn't kick him out. Everything we did was for the best.' He scrubbed a hand over his head.

'Best for whom?'

'Everyone,' he snapped back before she'd barely finished her sentence. 'Best for Sandra, me, Trevor and, most of all, our baby.'

'She's not a baby any more. You have no excuse.'

'She was still a baby when he absconded from the system. We would have had him back. Eventually.'

'Really? Are you trying to convince me, or yourself?'

The truth of her words sent a spiteful dig of guilt into his heart. Because she was right. He'd been so consumed with his wife and little girl, he'd barely given Trevor a thought. Each move he'd had in the foster care system, Henry had tried to raise the idea of him coming back home to Sandra. She'd not been ready for it. Not then. Not when he'd gone missing. When Henry had waited by the side of the phone for word from the police that his son, aged fifteen, was missing, Sandra had kept a steely silence.

Henry drained his mug and came to his feet. 'I've got to get going.'

'Of course.' Disappointment tightened Caroline's features.

'Maybe when he comes out...'

'Henry, Trevor's in for another two years. That's a long time.'

Henry shrugged into his thick jacket and glanced out of the window at the thrashing rain. 'Not so long really. It'll soon be gone.'

'Then you'll see him. When he comes out?'

He turned to face her and gave a grim nod. 'I'll see him. When he comes out. But not a word to Sandra. Not yet.'

33

SEVENTY-NINE AND A HALF HOURS SINCE PHONE CALL

Lorraine stepped inside her mum's house ahead of the police officer and made her way through to the living room.

She dragged out Elijah's highchair and plopped him in it, handing him a rattle he could bang against the sides. If he stayed in that carrier much longer, he'd be bored sick.

She circled around to meet Sergeant Willingham's gaze, her eyes wide at the sight of the other woman snapping on a pair of nitrile gloves. 'Oh, are they needed?'

'Just in case I need to touch something.'

'Do I need some?'

Sergeant Willingham shook her head. 'No. We can safely assume your prints are going to be all over this house. If we need to, we'll take yours for elimination purposes, but we're getting ahead of ourselves. Right now, we're looking for any evidence that might point to where she's gone. If it was of her own volition, or if we suspect foul play.' She gave a small smile. 'Now, should we start in here?'

The officer worked her way quickly and efficiently, through a living room that had little out of place.

She checked inside Sandra's handbag, the purse with credit cards in, before she replaced them. The TV drawer unit, the small occasional table with a thin drawer only good enough to keep the four remote controls her dad had bought for the one TV.

As Sergeant Willingham passed by Elijah, she gave him a smile which dropped from her face as she stopped. She crouched down, her uniform creaking as she almost touched her forehead to the carpet. She plucked something from the long fibres and stood upright. She held it up for Lorraine to see.

Heat flooded Lorraine's face as she stared at the long shard of crystal she'd evidently missed on her clean-up. She clapped her hands to her face. 'Oh, no. That was me. Well, no, Elijah. I was looking for Mum and he hit Dad's whisky glass with one of his toys and it went all over the table. Oh, my God. I was so concerned about Mum, I got the dustpan and brush and brushed all the splinters up and put them in the bin. I never even thought to get the vacuum out. I'll get it right now. Right now.'

Aware she was rambling, Lorraine moved past the policewoman, embarrassment at her thoughtlessness consuming her.

'Hold on.' Sergeant Willingham touched her arm. 'Don't bother vacuuming just yet.' Her eyes met Lorraine's. 'Just in case we need to do another sweep.' She let the silence hang while the meaning of what she was saying dropped.

With a long, drawn-in breath, Lorraine nodded.

Sergeant Willingham turned her back and made her way to the sliding patio doors. She gave them a tug. The doors never moved. 'Keys?'

'Yes.' Lorraine nodded. 'Where they should be.'

'Spares?'

'I have one. One in the kitchen drawer. Dad had one.'

'Where is your dad's?'

Lorraine frowned, her mind twisting through the possibilities of where her dad's keys could be. 'He would have had them on him when he crashed.'

Sergeant Willingham inclined her head. 'They would have been returned. To his next of kin. To your mum, in this case.'

Lorraine chewed her bottom lip. She shook her head. 'I can't recall seeing them anywhere.' Her mind racing. Who could have stolen her dad's keys? Had they used them to enter her mum's house?

'So, is it a possibility that your mum started to use your dad's keys? Maybe for sentimental reasons.'

Lorraine's runaway train screeched to a halt and a flush of embarrassment warmed her neck. She'd make a useless police officer. Her imagination would have her running down every dark alley instead of the calm, logical approach this woman was taking. She was right. It was her job. Lorraine needed to acknowledge that, stop fantasising, and keep her wits about her.

'That could be plausible.' She paused. 'She's started to wear one of his cardies. His favourite one. She says it brings her comfort.'

Sergeant Willingham gave a nod of understanding. 'It's another avenue to explore.' She touched the sliding door handle again. 'And was this locked when you came around?'

'Yes. Definitely.'

'Okay.'

Lorraine followed the woman through to the kitchen and watched her rummage through the cupboards and drawers, cringing as she started in on the first of the bits 'n' bobs drawers.

Sergeant Willingham cast her a sideways glance. 'We all have them. I've got three teenage daughters, you should see their dressing table drawers. Pure crap.'

She pulled out a small tin and prised the off the lid. Lorraine gave a gasp as money unfolded and almost popped out of the tin into the officer's hand. There was an awful lot there to have left behind. Why wouldn't she have taken it? If nothing else. Cash. Untraceable.

'You're right. Wherever she went, she didn't take her cash.' Sergeant Willingham raised her eyebrows. 'Nor any of her credit or debit cards from the look of her purse, unless she has one of those you don't know about.'

Lorraine shook her head, unable to take her eyes from the money. 'Not to my knowledge.'

'But then, you didn't know about this.'

Lorraine clamped her lips closed on the denial. She did. She'd had money from that tin in the past. Money her mum had slipped to her. She'd never gone in it herself, though. That would have been an intrusion. Had her mum always kept that much in there?

'It's been years since I lived here. It's still my home, but I can't remember the last time I looked in these drawers. Except the other day. There's never been a need. It would feel a bit like snooping.' She thought of Mrs Tindall next door. Of the money Gareth had been paying her mum. Didn't they tell her it went straight into her bank account?

Lorraine remembered the small white envelope. She wasn't about to tell the policewoman that insignificant detail. It wouldn't help if she mentioned about Mrs Tindall next door. Her mum was doing the old lady's shopping for her, paying for it on her card and taking the cash. Because Mrs Tindall didn't like to use her account, she'd told Lorraine that earlier. That was why Gareth paid her mum. Or did *he* pay her mum so she couldn't get into trouble for not being a registered carer?

As Sergeant Willingham delved further into the drawer, Lorraine kept quiet about the money. She didn't want to get her mum into trouble. 'I did have a brief look yesterday. Just for the keys and stuff, but everything looked the same as usual.'

'Apart from the money.'

'Well. She's always kept the tin in there. It was always, like... her pocket money. It was hers. She had a joint account with Dad, so it was for stuff she could just treat herself to once in a while.' She nodded at the wad of money. 'Not normally that much.'

The hot prick of tears stung her eyes unexpectedly, not sure if it was her dishonesty or just the memory. 'I wouldn't dream of going in that tin, but she has recently.' She sniffed and wiped her eyes with her fingertips. 'She's been helping me out since the skunk left. She pushes a couple of tenners in my hand every so often. But I know she can't really afford it, not since Dad died. She didn't work, you see, never has since she married my dad. Apparently, it didn't go down very well when they found out she was dating a client at the solicitors she worked for. My parents got married and she never went back to work. She enjoyed being just a housewife.'

The officer slanted her a look. 'Nothing wrong with that. Hardest job in the world.' She pushed her tongue into her cheek. 'I'd far rather face a criminal than an ironing board.'

Lorraine gave a faint smile and stopped herself from saying more. It was evident her mum could afford it if she had this much in her 'pocket money' tin. But how?

She gave a dismissive shrug as though it was of no importance.

But it was. She needed to give it some thought.

Sergeant Willingham folded the notes back down, clipped the lid on the tin and placed it on the kitchen counter as she continued to look through the drawer.

Her fingers slipped under a brochure in the bottom of the drawer, and she eased it out. 'Family holiday?'

Lorraine frowned. Mist descended on the vague memory, but she couldn't pull it to the fore. 'It must have been.' She touched the brochure. 'I can't remember going there.' But there was something about a narrowboat, she recalled.

'*Old Codgers.*' Sergeant Willingham tapped her finger on the name plate of the narrowboat. 'Lovely name. Does your mum like the canals?'

'Not to my knowledge. I don't think...' She paused. 'I can't actually remember.' She put her hand to her head. 'I'm sorry, it means nothing.'

'Okay, don't worry. It seems very old. Perhaps just a memento of a holiday your mum and dad took at some point.'

'That would be another thing they never told me about.' The bitterness slipped through her tone like a sharp knife.

The officer slipped the brochure back inside the drawer and replaced all the items. It may not have been tidy before, but she was pretty sure her mum wouldn't like to know a stranger had just rummaged through her personal possessions and then dumped them back in no kind of order.

Not that her mum was there to put it right.

Her eyes teared up.

She resisted the temptation to adjust the position of the money tin back to where it belonged at the back of the drawer.

Oblivious, Sergeant Willingham swept from the kitchen and made her way upstairs.

With a brief glance at her son, Lorraine sprinted up after her.

A quick scan of the bathroom revealed nothing special and then they moved into her mum's bedroom.

Sergeant Willingham paused at the door. 'Was this the way you found it?'

Lorraine frowned as she sidled up beside her. 'Yes.'

'It's impeccable. Like it's never been slept in.'

Lorraine shrugged. 'I don't know what you mean. This is the way Mum always left it.'

Sergeant Willingham sighed.

Lorraine hoped she never came to her house. Clean washing

still piled up on the dressing table waiting to be ironed, folded and put away. Dirty washing exploding from the linen basket.

She'd put a load in when she got home. Get things done while she waited for news from the police. Now they were taking it seriously.

She linked her fingers and squeezed them together. The internal shakes hadn't stopped from the moment she realised her mum was gone. She functioned out of necessity when instinct screamed at her to run. Run, search, find.

Sergeant Willingham stepped closer to the bed and then dropped to her knees. She ducked her head sideways, resting it on the carpet as she raised the pretty lavender valance sheet so she could peer under the bed.

With a grunt, she scooted closer to the bedside table on her knees and reached for something.

Lorraine held her breath as Sergeant Willingham came upright, resting her backside on her heels.

'Is this your mum's?'

Lorraine clapped a hand over her mouth to stop the pitiful wail from escaping her.

Sergeant Willingham held aloft between thumb and forefinger a phone. Lorraine instantly recognised the pink hydrangea on a rose-gold background cover and reached for it.

'It's Mum's.'

The police officer moved it out of her reach. 'Don't touch this.'

'But why? You said you could eliminate my prints.'

'We can. But we don't want you smudging any evidence, should there be any. When was the last time you handled your mum's phone?'

Lorraine squinted, her brow furrowing. 'I don't...' She shook her head as the other woman took a bag out of the thick belt around her waist. She rested it on the bed, put the phone on it, and with her gloved fingertip flipped open the cover.

The screen was black.

'Out of charge,' the sergeant murmured. 'We'll get it charged up at the station, get our experts on it and check if there's anything of relevance.'

Lorraine nodded. 'The screen's broken.'

Sergeant Willingham cautiously closed the phone and, holding the edge with her fingertips, pushed it inside the evidence bag. 'Was it before?'

'No.' Lorraine shook her head. 'I can't recall seeing it, but Mum would have mentioned. She would have mentioned it to me. I'm positive. Mum and I are really close.'

Pushing to her feet, Sergeant Willingham eyed Lorraine for a moment. 'So close,' she said. 'Close enough that you believe your mum would let you know if she was going away.'

With a vehement nod of her head this time, Lorraine indicated the phone. 'I believe she would have told me her phone screen was cracked.'

'Okay.' The sergeant sighed. 'Let's keep looking.'

Ten minutes later, they'd found nothing further out of place, nothing suspicious.

As they made their way down the stairs, the officer's boots giving a hard clump all the way down, Lorraine looked over her shoulder at the other woman. 'What happens now?'

'Now, I go back to the station and register your mum as missing and we start putting all the appropriate procedures into place. Do you have a photograph of your mum? One that is recognisable and recent?'

Lorraine turned as she reached the bottom of the stairs. 'I do. There are some on my phone.'

Elijah let out a small sob and she recognised instantly that tone.

'I need to feed Elijah.' That mother's instinct kicked in to speed up her heart rate and pull at her breast.

Sergeant Willingham nodded and reached for the door, pulling it wide, understanding in her intense eyes. 'Go and feed the lad, and when you're done, have a scan through photographs of your mum and forward one to me.' She dipped her fingers into her jacket pocket and drew out a business card just as Elijah let out a more demanding wail.

She smiled. 'I'm sure you'll keep yourself occupied, but I'll update you as soon as I can. Let me know if you hear anything from your mum, or anything you believe might be of interest to us.'

An almost ear-piercing shout came from the living room and Sergeant Willingham nodded, pulling the door behind her with a distinct click.

Released from her task, Lorraine dashed into the living room, a forced smile creasing her face.

Elijah didn't care. His milk train was here. The cries instantly dried up and he smacked his lips, holding his arms out for her. It wouldn't be long before he no longer wanted a feed from her. It tended only to be night-time and once during the day, if he was ready for a sleep.

Tiredness swept over her as Lorraine settled herself in her dad's armchair, a cushion under her arm and Elijah suckling voraciously. As his panic subsided, all tension flowed from her body, and she tipped her head back. Her eyes closed and she slipped into a soft, dreamy sleep.

'Mum, Mum. Can we visit Granny and Grandad?'

'No, love. They're not up to having you. They're not feeling well.'

'But I want to see their boat. The one in the picture.'

'Not now, Lorraine. Don't pester, love. When they're better, I'll take you. It's a long way just for a visit and we can't stay over, the boat's too small.'

'But Muuum...'

'Lorraine.' Her dad folded the newspaper he'd been reading and placed it on the floor by his soft leather wingback chair. 'Go and put your shoes on and I'll take you for a spin in old Betty.'

Thrilled at the thought of the wind blowing through her hair as her dad whizzed the beautiful car down country lanes, Lorraine dashed to the door. She turned and opened her mouth, but her dad had his back to her, staring down at his chair.

Lorraine blinked open her eyes, the image of her dad's face still filling her vision. 'Oh, Dad.'

She shuffled forward, the sleeping weight of Elijah heavy against her shoulder. She cradled him to her and pushed to her feet, repressing the groan, so it came out as a quiet puff of air over the top of his head.

She hitched him up and balanced him on one shoulder, reached for her baby bag and put it over the other.

Letting herself out of her mum's house, Lorraine opened the car and strapped Elijah into his seat.

As she straightened, she stared at the front door of her mum and dad's house. The same colour as his precious Betty. The same colour as that narrowboat.

She drew in her breath and made her way back inside, opened the drawer and withdrew the brochure.

34

NINE MONTHS EARLIER

'Mum?'

'Lorraine,' Sandra's voice choked out.

'Lorraine?'

Eyes wide with concern, Lorraine nodded as the police officer took her by the elbow and gently led her through to the living room in deference to her almost full-term pregnancy. Only another few weeks and the baby would be with them.

'Take a seat.'

Lorraine's beautiful face turned pale, her expression full of questions, but all Sandra could do was wilt into the chair and let the young officer deal with it. Sergeant Willingham had handed over so she could get back to the station... for something... or home. It may have been. She had no idea. It had all been a confused blur, Sandra had nothing in her head. Her mind had closed down. Like it had almost thirty years ago when her baby had died. Been murdered.

She'd remembered Lorraine would be calling around. She often did before she picked Sophia up from nursery. She wouldn't let Sergeant Willingham call her. Not in her condition. Not when she had to drive. Let her come, she'd be there soon enough in any case.

'What's happened?' Terror snaked through her daughter's eyes like a premonition had hit her.

'I'm PC Derry. I'm very sorry to tell you...' The young woman guided Lorraine to sit on the sofa next to her. 'But I'm afraid I have very bad news. Your...'

'Your dad's dead.' The wail burst from Sandra's lips. 'I killed him!'

Dual shock registered on both Lorraine's and the policewoman's faces as Sandra's words splurged out.

'I killed him. I killed your dad. I couldn't help it. He was going...'

'Mrs Leivesley.' PC Derry jumped up and knelt on the floor next to Sandra. 'No, Mrs Leivesley, it's not your fault.' She turned to look at Lorraine. 'It's not your mum's fault. I'm very sorry to say your dad has been in a terrible car accident. He was killed instantly.'

Lorraine's hand gripped at her throat as she looked from one to the other of them, horror flickering through her intense gaze.

'You're not listening.' Sandra placed her hand on PC Derry's shoulder and gave her a small shake. 'It's my fault. I killed him. We got into an argument, and I shouted.'

Tears tracked down her cheeks as she sobbed, determined that they would listen to her confession. It was her fault. She'd hit him and he'd driven into the ditch. She wrapped her arms around her aching ribs, finding it difficult to pull in a decent breath.

'Mrs Leivesley, Sandra. It wasn't your fault. There's absolutely nothing you did that caused this accident. It appears the steering column broke, the officers could see underneath from the angle it was at, we'll have more details at a later date, but it caused your husband to lose control of the car.'

'Which car?' Lorraine's voice grated as it came out.

PC Derry's mouth opened, but Sandra butted in. 'His MG, of course.'

Lorraine's face looked pinched as she winced, her hand going to her rounded belly.

Sandra flicked a quick glance over her, still consumed with the need to confess. 'But it wasn't that. It was my fault. I should never have...'

'Oh, Sandra.' PC Derry gave her arm a comforting touch. 'Please don't do this to yourself. It's not your fault. Something went wrong with the car.'

'He treated that car like a bloody goddess, there's no way there was anything wrong with it.'

Lorraine's lips compressed and she squeezed her eyes closed, a whimper slipping from her lips as she shot to her feet. 'Oh, Mum, my waters have broken.'

Sandra leaped up as the PC struggled off her knees, surprise grabbing them both. 'We'd better get you to the hospital, pretty sharpish. Looks like baby is on the way.'

Lorraine squeezed out a feral sound between her teeth and then panted. 'Oh, God. The baby's coming. He's coming.'

PC Derry shuffled her towards the front door. 'Hospital. Now. I'll drive. What about your husband?'

'No.' A guttural grunt came from Lorraine. 'He has a new partner.'

The woman's eyebrows raised but she never made a sound of judgement.

'Mum. Mum.' Pain flashed over Lorraine's face.

Sandra rushed to Lorraine's side. 'Yes, love.'

'I need you to pick up Sophia from nursery. She finishes any time now.'

'I can't...' Normally Henry would be with her. Fear gripped

Sandra. She didn't want a child. She didn't want the responsibility. She couldn't look after Sophia and keep her safe.

'Mum! You have no choice. This baby is on the way. Go and get Sophia. Mum, I need you.'

Sandra snatched in a breath, her whole body aching. They'd not listened to what she had to say.

Nobody seemed to care that she'd killed Henry. Murdered her husband.

It no longer mattered.

Her daughter needed her.

35

EIGHTY-ONE AND A HALF HOURS SINCE PHONE CALL

Lorraine pulled her car up outside Aunt Caroline's house.

She'd barely given the woman an opportunity to answer as she told her she was on her way, she'd be just over an hour. If she put her foot down. Lorraine hadn't wanted to give the woman a chance to say no. Time was of the essence. She had no more of it to waste.

The woman might be an aunt, but she felt like a stranger.

'Here we go again. Déjà vu.'

She slipped from the car and glanced at her son in the back seat. 'Just for a minute, Elijah.'

She closed the door with a soft 'clunk' and peered through to check he was still sleeping before she locked the car and walked up the short pathway to her aunt's front door.

Exhaustion dragged at her legs, but she had no choice. She had to come back. She had to see this woman. Look her in the eye and know the truth when she saw it. No matter what that police officer had said. There was no way she could leave it to them.

Only this time she wasn't about to risk the route through the garden with the terrifying Ghost an immediate threat. If her cousin hadn't been there... her cousin. A boy. Half her age.

She paused, her hand raised to knock on the door as she realised she'd not even processed that thought. She had a cousin. More than one. Family she never even knew about, just a vague mention in the distant past. So absorbed in her own life, she'd never given her extended family a single thought. Never even been curious.

The woman who opened the door this time gave her a long, considering look.

'Aunt Caroline?'

'Apparently so.' The smile was warm with all the familiar hallmarks of her dad's. 'I am so sorry about yesterday, Lorraine. You had a wasted journey, but it couldn't be helped. I had an emergency to deal with and I couldn't get hold of you in time. I did leave a message.'

Lorraine shook her head. 'I've not had anything, but then again if I was in a blackspot, I normally get messages three days later.'

Aunt Caroline tutted. 'That's the way of things, I'm afraid. I am sorry, though. Come in, come, don't stand on the doorstep.'

Lorraine's chest tightened. 'Elijah is asleep in the car.'

Aunt Caroline peered over her head at the car. 'Bring him in.'

'The dog...' Lorraine flicked a hand to indicate the dog that had just sidled up to her aunt's knee.

'Who, Ghost? He wouldn't harm a soul. Gentlest animal I've ever known.'

Doubt must have flickered across her face as her aunt chinned towards the car once more. 'Go and get the baby. Ghost won't touch him. I promise you that.'

As Lorraine returned with a bright-eyed Elijah who'd woken the moment she opened the back door of the car, Caroline held out her arms. 'Give him here, he'll be fine.'

Evidently, Lorraine's trepidation about the dog had communicated itself to Caroline and the other woman took immediate, confident control.

Without hesitation, Lorraine handed her little boy over, something in the woman's mannerism so calm and familiar that it put her at ease.

Until the huge wolf loped over, head lowered and piercing eyes connecting with hers.

'Ghost, in your bed.'

The animal turned, his body giving a leisurely swagger as he wandered over to a crate in the corner of the living room and settled himself with a disgruntled moan.

Lorraine squinted at him and then looked towards the wide patio doors at the other end of the room. That's where he'd come from, where he'd concealed himself the previous day, until he could stalk her.

Lorraine turned her head to look at her aunt, not about to confess that she'd already met the infamous Ghost.

A smile spread over Caroline's face as she sank into the sofa, Elijah held between both hands so he faced her. The moment his feet connected with Caroline's thighs, he started to bounce up and down.

'Wow, you're a strong lad. Bet you'll soon be tearing around.'

The wattage of the smile dimmed a little as she turned to Lorraine, who still hovered in the doorway. A shimmer of tears filled her eyes.

'I'm sorry about your dad. You must be lost without him. I know how much he adored you.'

Lorraine sucked in a breath and moved to the other end of the charcoal-grey corner sofa unit, wondering how the woman managed to keep it so clean looking. Then she remembered, her aunt's children were virtually adults. The dog was so impeccable, he probably didn't dare to shed.

Quick to cover up her thoughts, Lorraine swept in with a question. 'How is your daughter?'

Confusion flickered over Caroline's face and Lorraine remembered her aunt hadn't mentioned what the emergency had been.

Lorraine saw no reason for loyalty to her cousin. 'Your son was here when I arrived yesterday. He told me.'

'Oliver?' Caroline frowned. 'What was he doing here? He should have been in school.'

'He popped back to check on Ghost.'

'Hmm.'

'He didn't tell you he'd seen me?'

'He did not, which means he probably knew he'd be in trouble if I found out he was skiving.'

'Oh, he wasn't...'

'Believe me,' her aunt cut in, 'that child of mine was skiving. He knew I was stuck at the hospital seeing to his little sister, so he thought he'd slip off home. Only you were here, so the game was up. Believe me,' she repeated. 'I know that boy of mine.'

She leaned back and blew a raspberry into Elijah's hand as he tried to ram his fingers into her mouth. 'Anyway, she's fine. It's a greenstick fracture so she's back at school today.' Her mouth gave a sardonic twist. 'Now I know why her big brother offered to carry her bag for us. He knows he's in the mire when I find out.'

'Oh, please don't...'

'No worries, I won't say it was you. I'll tell him the door cam caught him and I was looking back to check when you arrived. Cheeky little bugger.' Caroline bounced Elijah up and down and softened her voice as though she was addressing him as he gurgled into her face.

She straightened, her gaze catching Lorraine's. 'But you haven't come to talk about my domestic situation. It's yours we need to be concerned about.'

Lorraine's throat tightened as Caroline squeezed her little boy to her chest and came to her feet in one fluid move. For a woman of her age, she was in remarkably good form. But then, Lorraine's dad had always been slender, athletic.

Caroline cupped the back of Elijah's head as she gave a soft sway, standing with the light from the front window behind her so they were silhouetted. 'So, Lorraine, would you like to tell me what the hell is going on?'

Lorraine squinted up at her. 'My mum phoned me the other night. She was terrified. I mean literally panic-stricken.' She blew out a soft breath and came to her own feet so she could touch Elijah, make contact with him to reassure herself. 'I couldn't go around.' She stroked soft fingers across his downy head. 'I have the kids. No one to look after them, certainly no one to help out in the middle of the night.' Did she need to explain about Simon? She didn't think she had the time or the inclination.

'There's absolutely no evidence of her in the house. As though she simply disappeared without trace. Nothing gone. Her toothbrush is still there, passport, car and house keys. Her phone.' Something made her stop short of saying the screen was broken. 'Nothing out of place, as though she's just down the bottom of the garden. When she called, she said some very strange things.' She didn't want to direct her Aunt Caroline's thoughts one way or another, she wanted her to voluntarily divulge information. After all, she didn't know the woman, she didn't know if she would become defensive. There was obviously history here between her mum and her aunt.

Lorraine circled around her aunt so she was obliged to face the light and give Lorraine a chance to study her expression. A frown furrowed her brow, but there was something there.

'What do you know?'

'About...?'

About everything, anything. But they needed to start somewhere.

'About my mum. She's done this before. When I was a child. Disappeared off. To somewhere.' Lorraine raised her hand to her own forehead and kneaded it. 'I have a vague recollection.'

Caroline placed Elijah on the floor and Lorraine's heart flipped as Ghost floated from his crate and lay down in front of her son. He stretched his neck forward and she stiffened. His shiny black nose twitched, and he sighed out a gentle whimper before he shuffled closer.

Elijah grabbed Ghost's ear with a shriek of excitement and just as Lorraine almost pounced on her son to rip him away from the dog, Ghost rolled onto his back, pulling the child with him. A gurgle of sheer delight erupted from her son. Terror shattered her heart.

A smile split Caroline's face as she went down on her haunches to join the two already on the floor. She reached out to scrub at the dog's pale, furry underbelly. 'Ghost loves children. He's a real sweetheart.'

Lorraine squatted next to them, still wary of the huge teeth the dog now exposed in something that could be a grin.

'I've never had dogs.'

'Your mum didn't like them.'

'How do you know?'

'I knew your mum.' Caroline bumped down onto her backside and hauled Elijah onto her knee as Ghost rolled back to the lying position and placed his huge head on the boy's knees so he could ruffle his fur.

'Henry... your dad loved animals. We always had them.' She nodded her head to include the house. 'Mum loved her English

Setters. I think they're the breed we always had. I've had Ghost since he was nine weeks old. He's now four.' She sent Lorraine an understanding smile. 'Despite his appearance, he's very gentle.'

Lorraine kept her opinion to herself of how gentle he'd appeared the day before, baring his fangs at the patio doors.

Caroline rested her back against the sofa, her body relaxing as Elijah continued to grasp Ghost's fur in his chubby fists.

'I loved your mum.'

Lorraine stared at her aunt in surprise. 'Then why…?'

'It's a long story. I was only a teenager when your mum met and married Henry. My brother was devastated when his previous marriage failed. I wasn't surprised. She wasn't a particularly nice creature.'

Lorraine pressed her lips together. 'I never knew he'd been married before. Not until…' she shrugged, 'now, really.' She raised her hands to her face, pressing her fingers together as though she was about pray. Instead, she touched them to her lips as she shook her head.

'It's such a shock. Everything. I don't actually know what the hell I'm doing. My head is spinning with everything that's happened over the past couple of days. After a frantic call from my mum, she's disappeared. She said such odd things. I then find out I have a half-brother and that my dad was married before. Before what?' She bumped down onto her backside and crossed her legs, dropping her hands down into her lap. 'I have an aunt I had forgotten.' She stared into Caroline's eyes and saw the hurt flash through them. 'I don't know how all this happened.'

'I can try and tell you what I know.'

'What do you know?'

'More than you. Less than your mum and dad. And Trevor.'

'Trevor.'

'Your half-brother.' Caroline picked up her mobile phone from the small side table next to her and glanced at it. 'It's a long story and I don't have much time, but I'll fill you in with as much as I know.'

Lorraine nodded. Her time was limited too. She needed to get back for Sophia. She probably shouldn't have come today, but she'd needed answers.

'Henry married Camille when they were both very young. Nineteen.'

Lorraine clenched her jaw to stop from asking questions she knew would only slow down where she wanted to get to, but her curiosity ground at her.

'I don't know much about it myself. I was only a little girl. Four... five. Your dad is... was a lot older than me.'

Lorraine inclined her head. It was quite evident.

'Anyway,' Caroline continued, 'it wasn't the happiest of marriages by all accounts. Camille became pregnant immediately.' She lowered her head, a faint smile quirked her lips. 'Rumour was Trevor was premature, a seven-month term. Well, that's how long they'd been married in any case, when he was born. Bit of a rush job, I understand. If you get my drift. Henry and Camille split up when Trevor was still young. Apparently, Camille met another man. And then another.' She scrunched her face. 'I'm only telling our family's side of the story, but according to my mum, Camille liked men. More than average, and she wasn't willing to let a child and a husband hold her back.'

Caroline allowed Elijah to wriggle off her lap onto the floor, his happy grunts bringing a smile to both their faces as he stretched out full length along Ghost's long back and scrunched his fingers into the dog's fur.

'So, your dad left her and while he was getting his divorce, along came your mum. She was the secretary at the solicitors' practice. He fell in love with her so hard.'

Lorraine couldn't help the smile. All her childhood memories were of her parents in love. All, except maybe...

'Your dad used to have Trevor then every couple of weekends. When it suited Camille and she needed a babysitter so she could go out partying. Otherwise, she was a manipulative woman, according to Mum.' Caroline stretched her legs out in front of her. 'Not just according to Mum. I remember. By this time, I was older and I do remember. He used to come here on those weekends.'

'Trevor?'

'Yes. He was great. There's only four, nearly five years between us. We used to tear around the place. With me being the youngest, it was like having a little brother. But without the angst. He'd come and play, and then off he'd go.'

'Like I did?'

Caroline took a long, drawn-in breath through delicate nostrils. 'It broke my heart when you were no longer allowed to come.' Her voice thickened. 'You were such a beautiful child. They used to let me babysit you. Of course, I was a bit young then, and I think Mum was probably about, but you were so special. I loved you.'

Lorraine felt her own throat tighten. Her memories were vague, and guilt touched her that she didn't feel the same emotion as Caroline evidently did. She didn't feel the loss. Could barely remember the girl who was now the woman in front of her.

Caroline steepled her fingers together. 'Of course, Trevor was long gone by then.'

'Why?' Lorraine made herself more comfortable as she reached down to stroke Elijah's head, and then cruised her hand over Ghost's soft pelt. The fear of this immense bear dissipated, but never disappeared. The slight tremble in her fingers was testament to that.

Or was it overload?

Could her mind take any more shocks and secrets?

She met her aunt's eyes. 'Why?' she repeated.

'Because your mum claimed Trevor murdered your older brother.'

36

ONE YEAR EARLIER

Dave and Specs sat on the fat, bulging sofa across the room from Trevor. He'd bagged the faux-leather armchair in the corner of the room, facing the window.

Roomie number four had never materialised. He'd obviously been there ahead of Trevor, as his belongings were spread around the largest bedroom in the house. Claiming it for his own.

A week later, when the guy never turned up, Trevor moved out of the box room where his feet touched the wall at one end and his head crammed up against the headboard of the bed at the other. He scooped up the guy's belongings, shut them in the box room and moved into the bigger room.

Dave and Specs, his remaining two housemates, never mentioned it.

He didn't give a shit as long as he had the room he wanted with a clear view along the main road.

Just as his seat in the living room did.

Trevor positioned himself so he could watch out of the window. See the comings and goings.

His housemates never queried that either. They had a reluctant respect for him. Kept a healthy distance and appreciated his silence.

He leaned back in the chair and squinted at the TV, trying to ignore the irritating 'click, click, click'.

Dave, left sock off, picked at his big toe using a thin wooden toothpick to clean the dirt out from under the nail.

Trevor considered taking it off him and stabbing him with the sharp little weapon. In the eye.

He ground his teeth. His hands gripped the arms of the chair and he pushed himself out, freezing mid-rise, his attention fully on the front window.

The small black car that glided up to the kerb outside their house wasn't from the surrounding area. Trevor knew that much. It was his job to. Always had been. The observer. The stalker. Old habits didn't just die. Nor was he even particularly rusty.

He sucked in a breath as recognition hit him.

'Probation officer!'

He didn't so much yell as project his deep voice, so Dave and Specs leaped to their feet, panic streaking through their eyes.

'Shit!' Specs raced away, clattering up the stairs as he yelled over his shoulder, 'Stall him while I stash my weed.'

Trevor's blood ran cold as he moved to the open hall doorway and glanced up the stairs.

Little bastard.

After three months in his first accommodation, manned twenty-four hours a day by probation officers, this was Trevor's first real taste of freedom. One he wasn't about to sacrifice for the sake of someone he barely knew.

If Specs had weed on the premises, they could all be in the mire. He wasn't prepared to go straight back to prison. He'd only been in the halfway house for the past couple of weeks. Kept his nose clean, made sure he turned up every time, on time, three times a week for his meetings with Ken, his probation officer. Nice enough guy. Another Scouser. Mild and easy-going on the outside. Heart of steel on the inside.

Trevor recognised that. Respected it. He could get along with Ken.

Trevor was never going back inside. He'd served his time. Had an education now he'd been deprived of before. He'd managed to make parole first time around. He had been good, kept his nose clean. And when he hadn't, he'd made damned sure the screws didn't know about it.

This little scrote wasn't going to mess it up for him. Not now, not ever.

His entire life had been ruined by other people. His mum, Sandra, not to mention grandparents who could have given his life a different path if only they'd helped out. And his dad. The jury was still out on his dad.

Right now, his priority was staying out of the slammer.

'How much, mate?' Trevor called up after the other man.

Specs leaned over the stair banister. 'Just picked the fuckin' stuff up this morning. More'n just personal. And some other stuff too.'

Trevor moved back to the sitting room, held his hand up in a halt motion as Dave went to race past him, one sock on, one sock off.

A stocky, grey-haired man stepped out the car and locked it, all the time looking up and down the street as though he expected to be pounced on by one of the ex-cons he'd come to inspect. There was no fear in his demeanour, just awareness.

Trevor lowered his voice as he gave Dave a hard stare. 'You got any?'

Dave's spine snapped ramrod straight. 'Holy shit, no.'

'Anything stronger? Something you shouldn't have?' He kept his voice low, deadly.

'No! No! Clean as a whistle, mate. I don't want to breach my licence. I don't want to go back inside. Not for nobody. I don't do drugs.'

'Nor me.'

As the grey-haired man approached through the broken-off gate and up the short drive towards the front door, Trevor placed his hand on Dave's shoulder. 'Then sit your arse back down and carry on picking your fuckin' toenails. I'll get the door.'

The solid double knock vibrated through the premises and Specs's feeble wail sounded from upstairs.

Trevor opened the front door and faced the probation officer. 'Hello, Ken, mate.'

He stuck out his hand and gave Ken's hand a firm shake. 'Good to see you. Come on in.' He opened his arms wide to indicate his openness to the visit. One they should all have expected now they'd settled in. They'd been forewarned that probation officers would make unannounced visits from time to time. Make sure they were coping. Keeping their noses clean.

'Hello, Trevor. I'm not here to see you. It's Spencer McAllister I've come to see.'

Trevor raised his eyebrows. Who the hell was that?

'Specs, he means,' Dave called from the living room where he picked madly at his big toe. Click, click, click.

Trevor closed the door behind his probation officer, his face deadpan, and held out a hand to indicate the stairs.

'I think you'll find him upstairs, in that case, Ken. Not seen him all day.'

37

EIGHTY-TWO HOURS SINCE PHONE CALL

'Brother? I never had an older brother. I'm an only child.' Heat almost choked her and all she wanted to do was leap up from her place on the floor and dash out into the cool air. Breathe it in.

She dropped her head down and contemplated her son, now fast asleep with his head pressed into the dog's thick fur as though he cuddled a soft toy.

Lorraine scrubbed a hand over her damp forehead and rolled softly to her feet. 'Oh, God.' How could a simple life suddenly change until it felt like she dangled over the pits of hell with only her less than perfect fingernails gripping on to a reality that was also slipping away? There was no longer any control. She'd lost it all.

She paced over to the back windows which overlooked the perfect garden she'd walked through the previous day.

She turned her back on it, her gaze meeting that of Ghost, who gave a lazy lift of his head to check on her without disturbing her son.

Every one of her nerve endings twitched, frayed.

Within less than a year, her husband had left her, her dad had died, she'd given birth, her mum had gone missing and now this.

Her parents had lied to her, her entire life.

She had a half-brother she'd never known about and now this was also sprung on her. An older brother. One who died?

Her chest burned.

How was she supposed to cope?

'Are you okay?' Caroline edged herself away from the dog and child and came to her own feet. 'I haven't even offered you a drink.'

'I don't need one.'

'I'd say you do. But right now, a stiff whisky would be the wrong thing as you're in charge of a baby and a car.' She moved towards a door Lorraine assumed led to the kitchen. 'You sit down, and I'll make you a cuppa. Tea or coffee?'

'Tea, please. Only a little milk, no sugar.' The response came automatically as it required no thought.

'Okay. Anything else?' She glanced at a wall clock as she said it. 'Tuna sandwich?'

Lorraine was about to decline when her stomach let out a low growl. 'Yes, please.' Otherwise, she'd be stopping on the motorway services or grabbing a quick drive-through Costa.

For one thing, she couldn't afford it. Neither the money nor the time.

For another, it was unhealthy. Well, the choices she made when she was confronted with all their tempting food was. She knew she'd forgo a salad for something high calorie.

She watched as Caroline disappeared from sight and let out a tortured whimper.

All her senses crackled and buzzed and with a weary sigh she sat back down on the sofa and stared at her own son. Like a strand of overcooked spaghetti, she had nothing left. No muscle tone, no energy.

What had happened? All those years ago, before she was born. What had happened to tear the family apart before she came along?

'Tea.'

Lorraine looked up, surprised that time had flashed past so quickly while she'd done nothing but stare numbly at her precious little boy.

'Bull's blood.'

'Excuse me?'

'Bull's blood – the tea. Means it's strong and dark, almost red.'

'Oh.' She took the mug from her aunt and placed it on a mat on the small table next to her in time to take a plate with a sandwich and a packet of crisps. 'Thanks.'

'Are you still feeding him yourself?' Her aunt nodded at Elijah.

Was that judgement she detected in her expression?

'Umm, yes. I am. Sporadically these days. Mainly at night and during the day if he wants.' She stuttered through, making excuses when there was no need. She took as much comfort from breastfeeding as Elijah did in being fed. Each child was different.

The fact she could barely remember the last time she'd fed him was irrelevant. He'd let her know when he needed more. In no uncertain terms. Right now, he was asleep, and she could eat.

'Mum said I should switch to bottle feeding, but truth be told, why would I? He gets all the nutrition he needs from me, and I'm not stuck sterilising bottles and warming them up in the middle of the night.' She knew she sounded defensive but that's how she felt. It was her decision, no one else's. It's not like she had a husband around to take turns.

'Well, you'll need all the energy you can get, love. Enjoy a moment of peace while you can.'

Lorraine looked at the sandwich with plastic white bread and could barely summon up the energy to lift it from the plate.

'Thank you.' Maybe Costa would have been just as healthy a choice.

It wasn't her son draining her of all energy right now. It was everything else.

Her aunt returned with her own mug of tea and plate and settled on the sofa.

'I don't understand why no one ever told you. But they didn't and that was their decision. When you were little, I could see why they wouldn't, but as you grew older, I have no idea why they never mentioned him.'

'It seems there was a lot they never told me.'

'Apparently. Which was also one of the reasons your mum and I stopped… talking.'

'Why?'

'Because I was young and headstrong and had teenage opinions which I believed everyone else should listen to.'

Lorraine smiled at the women's self-deprecation, although she couldn't remember days like those in her household. She'd not been given to teenage tantrums and rebelliousness. She and her parents had all got along very well. It had been peaceful in their house. Hadn't it?

'Anyhow. Little Alexander was born shortly after Trevor's mum died.'

'How old was Trevor?'

Lorraine could almost see the mental calculation going on in her aunt's head. 'Eleven.' She nodded. 'Yeah, he must have been around eleven. Henry, your dad, and Camille must have split up when he was nine, maybe. Then when Camille died, I think your mum was almost seven months pregnant. I know from what Mum and Dad said that she found it a struggle having an eleven-year-old around all the time, instead of just the odd weekend, but no more so than when Alexander came early.'

'I had a brother called Alexander.' Lorraine couldn't take it in.

'Yes.' Her aunt's voice was soft. 'He was born prematurely. Your mum had a caesarean.'

Lorraine gaped at her aunt. How in hell's name did she not know that?

In a breathless rush, she said, 'I wanted to name Elijah Alexander to start with.' She felt the blood drain from her face as her gaze flickered from her son to her aunt, unable to shake the numb disbelief.

'How sad. Your mum missed the ideal opportunity to have confided in you.'

Lorraine shook her head. 'It was all such a mess. Dad died and the shock sent me into labour with Elijah.' She nodded at her son, a faint smile on her face. 'I can't describe how it felt. The death and birth of two of the people I love most in the world on the same day.'

'And your mum said nothing.'

Lorraine shook her head. 'No, she didn't. She couldn't.' Lorraine's eyes filled with the memory, and she pressed her fingertips to trembling lips. 'She was beside herself. It was awful. The doctor had to give her a sedative to calm her down.'

Lorraine met her aunt's gaze. 'She blamed herself for the accident. Said she'd had a row with my dad.' She scrunched her eyes closed. 'Ah, now I know why. Why they argued that day.'

Aunt Caroline leaned forward in her seat.

'Why?'

'It was because of this. This whole mess.' She took a sip of tea too hot to drink and took comfort instead from holding it. She needed to re-wind. To know it all.

38

EIGHTY-TWO AND A HALF HOURS SINCE PHONE CALL

'Tell me what happened. What happened to my older brother?' There was a terrible disconnect in her mind, she could barely hold her thoughts together.

Her aunt wriggled to make herself comfortable, cradling her mug between her hands. 'He died not long after he was born.'

Lorraine gave a shiver as she took a bite of her sandwich, the heat from her mug doing nothing to warm her up. Despite the milder weather, chills still prickled her skin.

'They ruled it as SIDS. Your mum disagreed.' She took a sip of her tea as though her memories were too painful, and she just needed to get them into some kind of order. 'Everything was very vague and maybe because of my age, they didn't tell me all the details. I learned more as I got older. Apparently, your mum, Sandra, came into the nursery to find Trevor holding Alexander. The baby was dead in his arms.'

Lorraine's hand flew to her throat. 'Oh, God.' She moved her attention to her own son. 'How old was he?' She recalled her aunt had said he'd died just days after he was born, but exactly how many?

'Only a few days old. I wasn't allowed to visit him in hospital when he was born. Kids weren't allowed back then. Too full of germs. Little good it did him keeping him all swaddled away. I was due to go around the following day. I can only remember being devastated. I never even got to meet my nephew.'

The tuna stuck in her throat and Lorraine took a huge gulp of hot tea, almost spluttering it out as heat seared the back of her throat. Her eyes filled with tears she suspected her aunt believed were for her baby brother.

Sadness, she certainly felt that. But hardly devastation at an event before her time. Heartache for her parents and an aunt she barely knew was the dominant emotion.

Tears reflected in her aunt's eyes and Lorraine looked away, unable to take the woman's distress onboard when she already had enough to deal with herself.

'Your mum turned on Trevor. She blamed him entirely. Said he'd murdered Alexander in cold blood.' Aunt Caroline scowled. 'I was fifteen. I couldn't believe Trevor would do such a thing. He'd been traumatised by his own mum's death. He was eleven and devastated. He went silent. Catatonic, they called it. He came to stay with us on and off to get him out from under your parents' feet for a while, but he was a troubled child. Clingy with your dad. Didn't want to be with us. Couldn't sit still. Wouldn't sleep. We'd find him wandering around the house at night. Mum found him so hard to deal with.'

Caroline tilted her head. 'I don't know if you remember, but Mum was disabled. She had a problem when she gave birth to me and the base of her spine sort of crumbled. Your dad and my other brothers brought me up. I only ever remember her in a wheelchair.'

Lorraine nodded. Sadly, so did she. As a child, it had meant nothing to her apart from a free ride on what she'd thought of as a scooter. They'd maybe even told her that's what it was. Her memory of those times was vague, though.

Caroline shifted, crossing one leg over the other as she continued. 'She wasn't young when she had me, and Trevor was just too much at her age.' She let out a low murmur. 'Sixty-one she must have been. Dad was a bit older, and Trevor required lots of attention. He was very demanding. I did what I could to keep him entertained, when I wasn't at school. He was too difficult, though, and they couldn't get him to settle in school. They tried to help, but he kept doing a runner. He'd turn up here or at your mum and dad's house just any time of the day or night. He'd slip out the bedroom window and be gone.' She put her hand to her chest. 'You had to be there to really understand how shredded he was.'

Surprised she'd manage to nibble her way through the sandwich and crisps while her aunt talked, Lorraine placed her empty plate on the table and picked up her mug again, casting a quick glance at the perfectly content pair on the floor.

Perhaps she should get a dog. She'd always wanted one herself, growing up, but her mum would never allow them. She always had a reason, an excuse. The fur, the dust, the allergies. Perhaps losing a baby so young had made her entirely paranoid about everything.

A paranoia she'd known nothing of.

Except, Lorraine recalled her mum's overprotectiveness. Not to such an extent that Lorraine would have considered herself smothered by her mum's behaviour. Quite the contrary, her mum had been laid-back compared to some of the other parents. Or was that because Lorraine had never been an awkward child?

She moved her attention back as her aunt continued.

'Mum and Dad had their hands full with their own family without having a child with emotional issues to deal with. Both of them had medical issues too. Then Sandra became pregnant with you so quickly afterward. It surprised everyone. Everyone thought it would help.' She shrugged her shoulders. 'Make things easier.'

'But it didn't?' She sipped at her tea, allowing her muscles to relax as she sank back, aware she was doing all she could to find her mum, and thankful for a moment that didn't feel frenzied and exhausting.

The police were on it.

She was on it. Investigating, at least. Even if she wasn't racing around for one short hour, trying to find her mum physically, when all this information might just give her a lead, an idea, a nugget of inspiration.

'No. If anything, things became worse. Oh, God, I was a teenager, barely able to control my own hormones and completely oblivious to anyone else's. But Henry was my big brother and I loved your mum too. It was awful. Like a car crash.' She shuddered to a stop and put her hand on a flushed cheek. 'Oh, I'm so sorry, I didn't mean...'

Lorraine suspected Caroline was more upset by her own words than she was herself.

Caroline shook her head. 'I'm sorry. I only meant that nobody seemed to know what to do with each other. All hysteria and shouting. It was a battle. Henry, your mum. Trevor said nothing. I remember him sitting there with this warzone going on around him and he seemed to sink into himself. My heart shattered for him. He was like a broken toy, abandoned for a bright, shiny new one, when all he needed was to be fixed.' She closed her eyes as though preparing herself to be careful the way she phrased her next words, but they came out raw in any case. 'Eventually your mum won.'

Caroline took a drink of her tea and let the silence hang for a few minutes. 'Trevor was only supposed to go into a temporary foster home, just to help out. Give everyone space to think, to sort things out.' The strain showed on her face. 'But your mum wouldn't have him back. She didn't want him near you. She stuck to the belief that he'd murdered Alexander.'

Her eyes turned steely. 'There was nothing anyone could do to persuade her otherwise.'

39

ONE YEAR EARLIER

Nerves got the better of Trevor and he rose from his seat in the small café for the third time in forty-five minutes to go to the toilet.

The chair scraped against old red tiles that were chipped and cracked with age. The grating sound set his teeth on edge, as his muscles gave a quick spasm, encouraging him to run. Run now.

It wasn't that his dad was late. Yet. But it was getting close.

Trevor had arrived early. He'd nursed his second coffee while he waited, his gaze centred on the invitingly open doorway of the café.

Perhaps it was the zing of strong caffeine he was unused to. Prison coffee wasn't the same. In fact, he wasn't sure it could legally be classified as coffee at all. More like weak piss. He'd given up on it years before, preferring to stick to fizzy drinks. That way he knew for sure there wouldn't be any piss in it. No one could tamper with a can.

He glanced at the clock behind the counter as he passed by.

Another three minutes and it would be the designated meeting time.

He took a minute to look around the bustling little café. Just to be sure.

The man still hadn't arrived.

How was he supposed to recognise him? He'd not seen him for years. Not since he was eleven. He'd never seen photographs of him either.

The only communication with his dad had been via the social workers in the beginning and then Aunt Caroline, who'd said it wouldn't be right to let him have photos unless his dad specifically said she could. They never moved from that point. Trevor assumed his dad never gave permission.

So how the hell was he supposed to recognise him?

Would his memory serve him right?

Would he know his own dad when he saw him?

Trevor thought his dad might have been early too. Which was why he'd arrived extra early.

He paced over to the toilets and went inside. When he finished, he washed his hands and instead of waiting for the blower to dry them, he gave them a shake and then rubbed them on the thighs of his jeans.

As he made his way over to his table, a pair of keen-eyed teenagers loped over and pulled out the two chairs, making the same ear-splitting grating noise with the chair legs as he had, only doubled.

Trevor stepped up close. 'Mine,' he murmured in the ear of the closest boy.

Anger flickered over the boy's features until his eyes met Trevor's. The flame of annoyance died, as he recognised the expression of someone to be feared and he stepped away.

Trevor had had a world of practice dealing with kids like that. Kids far worse.

With no other tables free, the boys edged their way out of the door and faded into insignificance.

Trevor took his seat, his gaze still on the doorway.

He was a fool. How had he ever believed his dad would meet up with him after all these years? Who was he kidding? Only himself.

His dad had never so much as replied to one of Trevor's dozens of letters. Not in the beginning, although when he'd been in foster care he'd had a birthday card, a five-pound note and a Christmas card with the same. During the time Trevor stopped writing, his dad had never even tried to locate him, to his knowledge. Never shown interest. Not even enquired if he was alive. What kind of parent would do that?

If that was the man his dad was, why would he come now?

Except Aunt Caroline had said he would. Trevor trusted Aunt Caroline. As much as he trusted any human. She'd always believed him. If she'd been older when everything happened, she would have had him. Looked after him. They would have managed. But she'd only been fifteen herself and a bit of a rebel with her thick black eyeliner and short tartan skirts.

He stared at the clock behind the counter again just as a tall, slender man turned, coffee in one hand, slice of cake on a plate in the other.

Trevor must have walked straight past him when he had his eye on the two teenagers trying to hijack his table.

He didn't know how he'd missed him, though.

There was no mistaking him.

Trevor surged to his feet.

This time, the chair didn't so much scrape hideously as tip over backwards with a loud clatter. As it crashed to the floor, every customer in the place turned their attention to him.

He didn't care.

His eyes were only for the man cautiously coming towards him with a coffee cup brimming over so the contents sloshed into the saucer.

Placing it carefully on the table together with the plate, his dad straightened and looked him over. A slow, assessing look. Man to man.

Trevor recognised that, too.

Grateful for the fresh haircut and new clothes Aunt Caroline had provided him with, Trevor resisted the temptation to tug his jacket into place and smooth the curls he knew were creeping around his ears. No matter how short his hair, the curls would find a way. More like his mum's hair than his dad's, straight as a die and now peppered with grey and thinning on top. Unfamiliar wings of almost pure white streaked above his dad's ears. The face of a younger man he remembered was now lined with age, white creases scored through the lines around his dad's eyes and deep brackets curved either side of his mouth.

As though his dad had come to a decision, he stuck out his right hand for Trevor to shake.

As Trevor leaned in, his dad yanked him into his chest for a firm, manly embrace together with a hard slap on the back.

Emotion crinkled his dad's face as they both leaned back out of the hug, embarrassment tussling with overwhelming delight.

'Trevor.' His dad still gripped his hand as though he didn't want to let go. 'It's good to see you, son.'

Tears were not something Trevor dealt with. Not ever. Not since those first few years without his family. When they'd dried up, he'd sworn never to cry again.

He choked them back now, his voice coming out a raspy whisper. 'Dad.'

A smile he recognised as so familiar passed over his dad's face. 'It's been a long time. You might feel more comfortable calling me Henry.'

Trevor's heart went cold, and he slipped his fingers out from Henry's. His dad's. A dad who it appeared still did not want to acknowledge him as his son, despite using the word a moment before. It had been an acknowledgement. Not a recognition of his actual, real son.

The eyes, so similar to his own, met his and crinkled at the edges as though oblivious to Trevor's pain. 'Or Dad, whichever you feel happier with.'

'I've only ever known you as Dad.'

There was a beat of silence as though the man in front of him might say more in favour of his argument, but Trevor held.

'Dad it is, then.'

Henry pulled out one of the chairs, lifting it so it didn't scrape as though he was familiar with the place. He sat and stared at the spilt coffee swamping his saucer.

'I'll get you a tissue,' Trevor offered.

'No, it's okay.'

'I've got it.' Panic grabbed him by the throat. 'I need another drink anyhow...' He staggered backwards and then whipped around to make for the counter.

He needed to breathe. He needed just a moment to grasp his equilibrium. It was his dad. Really his dad. Here in the same room as him after all these years. Too many years.

A child again, he'd fumbled, stumbled, almost fallen.

By the time he reached the small serving counter, his fingers shook. He contemplated how close the door was, but decided it was cowardly to make a run for it.

After all, it had been him who had pursued Henry... his dad... Henry.

His mind staggered in drunken contemplation. He didn't want to call the man Henry. Like a stranger.

'Are you okay?'

'What?' His response was automatic.

'Would you like something else?' The small, bespectacled lady on the other side of the counter blinked up at him like an owl in shock. Faded green eyes focused on him.

'Yeah. Ta. I'll have a piece of cake, some of those tissues there...'

'Napkins,' she interrupted him, a benign smile on her lips. 'Anything else, duck?'

'Yeah. Umm.' He squinted at the drinks board. It wasn't easy to get used to a life outside of prison that had raced on ahead of him, while he stood still. All the time, with the education he'd received and training he'd taken inside, he'd believed he'd be ahead of the game, not a steam train on a slow track trying to keep up with the Eurostar on the high-speed rail.

He blew out a breath and raised both hands in defeat. 'Something without caffeine. I think I've had too much, my head is spinning.' He'd not talked so much in ten years.

'How about decaffeinated coffee?'

He'd not had it in prison. Just as he'd barely drunk coffee.

Trevor gave one sharp nod and dug into his pocket for the money his aunt had slipped into his hand as he left her place. He knew she wasn't well off, but she had enough to give him a little. Just until he got his feet under him. It wasn't easy walking straight out of prison into a well-paid job. Any money she gave him helped. And he was grateful for it.

It wasn't much. It wouldn't last long at this rate. Who knew the cost of a cup of coffee could be so much? He could have bought a two-course meal at the local Wetherspoons for that price. It would have been better for him, too.

He scooped up the tissues... napkins... and shoved them into his fake leather jacket pocket, picked up the decaffeinated coffee and his cake. Just like his dad's.

He placed them on the small round table, dug the napkins from his pocket and handed them to his dad, who had either drunk the coffee from his saucer, or poured it back into his cup. He took the napkins nevertheless and mopped up the remainder.

'I think I'd prefer to call you Dad.'

He didn't think he imagined the small light of pleasure on the other man's face before he picked up his cup with both hands and took a gulp.

When he'd swallowed, he looked Trevor in the eye. 'I didn't want to push it, son. You've had a long time away, one way or another, and I thought it might be awkward. If you're happy, I am.'

'Yeah. Well.'

He was older than his dad had been when he'd given him up.

They were strangers.

His dad pulled the cake plate close and picked up the fork. Not something Trevor would have automatically done himself. He was about to pick the whole slice up in his hand.

Instead, he followed suit and used the side of his fork to cut off bite-size pieces.

'What are you doing with yourself?'

He looked at his dad. Would he acknowledge Trevor had been inside for the past ten years? Was it something they would discuss, or would it be side-lined forever more as though it was a cloud of dust to be swept under the carpet?

Trevor only realised he'd not spoken when his dad continued. 'I would have met up as soon as you got out of prison, but it's not been easy lately.' A wash of pink coloured the older man's cheeks. 'My daughter's husband left her last week. Just as you were coming out.' He gave a furtive glance around at the closest tables as though he didn't want anyone hearing.

Was that about Trevor's term in prison, or his dad's husbandless daughter?

'I have a sister.'

'Half-sister.'

The little insult trembled between them, but it was never going to be easy. Leaving things left unsaid or tackling them head long. Which would be the best?

Candour was Trevor's way. Always had been. Get it out there. Let it be said. He'd changed since they'd last met. Learned to express himself. After all, the only thing he'd got by remaining silent was homeless. He wasn't going down that route again. He had plans.

He pushed the plate away from him, half the sickly-sweet cake still on it. The sharp clatter of his fork attracted attention. He kept his voice low, though. Out of respect for his dad.

'I know nothing about any sister.'

'Your stepmum...'

'She's not my stepmum. She chose that.' Technically his dad had chosen not to be his dad either, but you couldn't argue with bloodlines.

'Sandra. She was pregnant with Lorraine when...'

'When she decided she didn't want me.'

The awkward silence hovered between them.

'It was a difficult choice. We'd lost Alexander and there was just you for that short time. When she announced she was pregnant, there wasn't much of a choice. We needed to make decisions. She didn't trust you. She was hormonal.' He rubbed a hand over his face as though he hated to be disloyal. To her. His wife. But what about the loyalty he'd owed his son?

'I thought it was going to be a temporary fix. I never dreamed I'd never see you again.' His dad waved a hand at him. 'Not until now.' His dad pushed his own empty plate away and picked up his coffee. 'I'm sorry, son. No one could have predicted what was to happen. I know it was never anything to do with you, Trevor, but she was hysterical every time you came near. Alexander's death did something.' He tapped two fingers to his temple. 'It sent her off her rocker for a while. The psychiatrist said it was temporary. It was hormones. It was grief.' His voice faded on the last word. He placed his cup down on the saucer and it gave a harsh rattle. 'I had no idea she would never come round to trusting you. She associated you with Alexander dying. We never could understand.'

'There was no need.'

'I believe you.'

'Good. I would never have harmed Alexander. He was my little brother.'

His dad opened his mouth and Trevor wondered if he was about to correct him, that it was his half-brother. Instead, he closed it again and gave a sad shake of his head.

'I know that.' His dad's voice thickened as he leaned over to grasp Trevor's hand in his. 'I trusted you, son. I knew you never had anything to do with Alexander's death.'

Trevor returned the pressure and looked his dad straight in eyes strikingly similar to his own.

'No. I didn't.'

He took a breath, licked his lips. 'But Sandra did.'

40

EIGHTY-THREE HOURS SINCE PHONE CALL

'And did he? Kill him, in your opinion?' She felt strange talking about a baby, barely a few days old, who was actually her older brother. A baby who had been dead for the past thirty-one years.

Her aunt shook her head. 'No. Not in my opinion. I wasn't there, though. No one was except Trevor and Sandra, your mum. It was her word against his.'

'But...'

'The diagnosis had come back that he'd died of SIDs, but there was no persuading your mum. She was absolutely adamant that because Trevor was holding Alexander at the time she discovered her baby was dead, she couldn't unlink the two in her mind. No one else believed Trevor had anything to do with it, but there was no reasoning with her. Not then, and I suspect not now.'

Caroline leaned forward in her chair and clasped her hands together between her knees. 'Obviously, I was way too young to have an opinion then.' She met Lorraine's gaze, her brow creasing. 'Later, I formed one. Based on the truth.'

Lorraine leaned forward. 'Why?'

'Because Trevor wanted to confide in someone, and I was the only one who would listen.'

'But you were very young.'

'I was then. I'm not now.'

'No.' Lorraine sighed and leaned back, her full stomach sending a sleepy vibe through her body.

'I've still not changed my opinion, to this day. I believe your mum had a psychotic episode. I looked into it. It's called postnatal psychosis.'

Lorraine rubbed her eyes. 'Surely that's schizophrenia, isn't it. Psychosis?' She felt compelled to defend her mum, who had no way of defending herself. She was a good mum, a loyal mum. One who'd never displayed signs of schizophrenia. Not while Lorraine had been alive.

'My mum doesn't have schizophrenia.'

'No. I agree. Although I've not seen her for years. Since she discovered I started passing on letters to your dad from Trevor. Everything kicked off then too. But postnatal psychosis is different. It's a severe form of postnatal depression. It's more chemical than mental. She truly believed what she saw. In her mind, Trevor murdered your older brother and there is nothing that will convince her otherwise, even if she no longer has that psychosis.'

Lorraine's eyelids turned heavy.

She really wanted her aunt to carry on speaking, but she was struggling to keep track. The woman's soft lilting Liverpool accent seemed to soothe her.

'I hope to God I don't get postnatal psychosis. I haven't got time to deal with that shit as well.' The words slipped from her mouth without her meaning them to. It had just been a thought forming, then it was out there.

Aunt Caroline gave a soft snort. 'No, but if you don't have a sleep, you're going to struggle to look after two young children. You must be exhausted.'

She was desperate for sleep. She wiped the heel of her hand over her eyes. She'd normally swipe a lick of mascara over her eyelashes, and slick a bit of lippy on, but since she'd given birth to Elijah, she couldn't be bothered. Which was just as well under the circumstances. She'd have made a terrible mess.

Her eyes drifted closed. Her head lolled to one side and she felt the soft, downy weight of a throw being tucked around her.

41

ONE YEAR EARLIER

His dad hadn't believed him. Why would he?

He didn't know him.

Trevor had grown up alone. Not always on his own, but always lonely.

Curled up on the dingy brown sofa in the peaceful house now there was only him and Dave, he smiled to himself.

It didn't matter.

The dad he barely knew was back in contact.

Excitement tightened his gut, and he drew his knees up to his chest.

He got his new housemates today. Two of them.

They'd not turned up yet. Not while he'd been there.

His stomach rumbled. One slice of cake wasn't enough to sustain him, but the money he'd spent on three coffees was more than his daily budget.

He needed food, but as he hadn't met the new scrotes who were sharing the place yet, how did he know he could trust them if he bought a load of stuff? The cupboards were virtually empty. One of Specs's mates had turned up and cleared out the lot while Dave sat, no doubt picking his toenails. They'd come around to collect their share of Specs's weed, but they'd been too late for that, so they'd gathered what they could. Stripped the place clean. They'd probably have taken the sofa if Dave hadn't been sitting on it. Dozy sod just sat there and let them take it all. In fairness to Dave, there'd been three of them and they were hard little gits who were likely to have given him a thrashing if he'd opened his mouth.

Trevor regretted no longer having a team. A gang. Nothing could touch him then. Well, almost nothing.

Ken soon had the locks changed once Trevor put a phone call in to him.

A good guy, Ken did a lot for Trevor. They got along just fine. As long as Trevor turned up every week on time for his appointment. He could talk about anything with Ken. How he was going to go straight. His next job, as the one he'd tried out for hadn't worked out. The boss hadn't liked the way he'd looked at her.

It wasn't his fault, Ken had told him. He had strange eyes.

Eyes like his dad.

He'd not spoken about his dad, though. That was his little secret.

He wandered through the downstairs rooms and looked around. The fridge had been emptied too. He slammed the door on it and circled around.

It was a shitty little place, especially with four of them sharing, but he wasn't going to be there forever. He needed to find somewhere better. Somewhere of his own. He didn't need to be ensconced with a pack of ex-cons all vying for top-dog position. He'd been there, done that. Got the T-shirt and all that shit and now they expected him to put his trust in a load of guys straight out of nick.

Trevor stared out the front window and along the street.

He didn't.

He'd never trusted anyone. Not since the age of eleven.

That wasn't entirely true. There'd been Caid and Red. But they were long gone.

There wasn't a single person he could rely on for anything. Except maybe Aunt Caroline. She'd been good to him. Diligently wrote to him in prison every couple of months to keep him up on her family life. Even if she never mentioned his dad.

She said that was for her brother to tell. Not her.

Only his dad hadn't spoken with him. Not until today.

He said he would meet him again next week. Only Trevor didn't trust him.

It was obvious the man still loved his wife. That dozy bitch who'd turned him out of his dad's house. She still wouldn't have him back.

Begging was in his past.

A past which had been shaped by that woman.

He was an adult now.

No longer a frightened little boy who could be manipulated by a scheming woman. Perhaps all he needed to do was meet her.

If his dad would let him. Unlikely, as he'd not believed Trevor when he'd told him that Sandra had been the one who'd killed Alexander. Accidentally, of course. He'd not wanted to hear about Trevor finding the baby in bed with Sandra, already dead. At the age of eleven, he'd not been mature enough to realise that what he'd done by removing Alexander from her arms had been wrong. That there was no way he could have brought his baby brother back to life.

Doubt had flickered through his dad's eyes. A reluctance to believe such a thing could happen.

His dad wasn't about to let him meet up with Sandra.

Even if he didn't, there was always a way.

42

EIGHTY-FOUR HOURS SINCE PHONE CALL

The quiet murmur of her aunt's voice dragged Lorraine back to the surface. She blinked her son into focus and smiled as he rammed a finger of bread into a boiled egg, dunking it like he was a pro. Bright yellow glooped over and slid down the brown eggshell and over the back of his clenched fist.

He made content cooing noises as her aunt adjusted the lap tray over his knees and held onto it with one hand while she helped him with the other.

Ghost, the German Shepherd, sat quietly on Elijah's other side, possibly waiting to clean up after him. Possibly bonded for life.

Elijah had never eaten soft-boiled eggs and soldiers. Good grief, was he old enough?

Lorraine straightened. She was pretty sure there was some kind of rule that you should cook eggs until they were solid until a certain age, but she couldn't remember what that was. It was a bit of a blur. She'd been so pedantic with Sophia, every milestone measured, every trial tested. She'd forgotten it all where Elijah was concerned. She'd gone on instinct and memory of her firstborn, not rules and regulations. Second children were so different.

Still, he looked supremely pleased with himself. It wouldn't do him any harm, one undercooked egg.

Aunt Caroline smiled over at her. 'Hello, sleepy head.'

Lorraine rubbed both hands over her face. 'Oh, how embarrassing. I'm so sorry. I never even realised I'd slipped off.'

'I thought I'd leave you for a while. You obviously need the rest. All the strain and worry must be taking its toll.'

Lorraine coughed, and then dropped her hands down to her lap. 'I went out like a light. I can't even remember what we were talking about.'

'You did. I hope you don't mind, but I thought little Elijah was hungry and I didn't want to disturb you.'

'No. It's fine. In fact, thank you so much. I feel like a bad mum hauling him all over the place, and evidently,' she smiled at her son, reluctant to disturb him, 'he's ravenous.' She paused. 'He's not had eggs cooked like that before.' She hoped there was no rebuke in her tone.

'He's fine. Strong young chap like this. They're fresh eggs, I only bought them yesterday from the local farm shop.' She smiled down at him, stroked his cheek with the back of her fingers and came away with yolk on them. 'Oh, my goodness, I've not seen a child eat like this for a long time. He is enjoying himself. He's eaten the lot.'

Lorraine pushed herself forward in the chair, the first real smile she'd managed for days sliding over her face. 'He does like his food, unlike his big sister, Sophia, who's so finnicky about things...'

She gasped. Her hand flew to her mouth and she launched herself out of the chair. 'Oh, my God. What's the time?' She grabbed at the changing bag on the floor and fumbled for the phone inside it. 'Oh. God! It's almost two o'clock. I have to pick Sophia up from school at quarter past three.'

Panic raced through her veins as she whipped the bag off the floor and scrambled through it. 'I'll never make it in time, I'm going to be late. I'm going to be late.' She wasn't quite sure what she was looking for.

Aunt Caroline swiped a wet cloth over Elijah's face, cleaning off the residue of yolk, without protest from a child who would normally cry the place down the moment a wet cloth swiped over his face.

She gave him a smile, and then looked up at Lorraine with calm, placid eyes. 'Phone the school. Let them know you're running late. They're not going to put a child out on the pavement. Don't worry about it. You won't be that late.'

She came to her feet in a lithe move, pushing the lap tray to one side and picking up Elijah. 'Honestly, Lorraine, calm down before you upset yourself and Elijah. He's been awake now for quite a while. I changed his nappy and he's fed. You're fed. You just need to stay calm, stay safe. Don't get in a car all panic-stricken.'

Lorraine choked back the sob. 'Okay.' She wished she felt as calm as her aunt was.

'How late will you be?'

Lorraine checked her phone. 'Fifteen, twenty minutes.'

'It's nothing, love. They'll understand. Give them a quick call now. Then you can settle down. You have a long enough drive ahead of you without making it a panicked one. Better late than never, as the saying goes.' She gave Elijah an affectionate jiggle.

Lorraine nodded as she pressed the quick dial to the school.

Once she'd spoken to the school secretary, she blew out a relieved sigh. 'Oh, my God. I can't believe it. I'm such a bad mum.'

'No.' Her aunt gave her arm a brisk rub. 'You're a good mum. You're just running late and there's a lot going on in your life.'

Ghost slipped to Lorraine's side and touched a cold, sympathetic nose into the palm of her hand. She wanted to sink to her knees and bury her face in his beautiful, lush fur, taking all the comfort she could.

She swallowed down tears that threatened and straightened her spine.

'Can I use your loo before I go?'

'Of course.'

Aunt Caroline indicated through the door to the left with her free hand and smiled at the happy Elijah. 'You know, if you ever need a babysitter... What a star he is.'

'I wish I lived closer. I'd definitely take you up on that. He's truly bonded.' She smiled. 'With you and Ghost.'

She nipped through the hallway into the toilet, her mind racing.

Once she'd finished and washed her hands, she opened the door to find her aunt waiting with Elijah on her hip and the changing bag on her shoulder.

'I've put you a bottle of water in, in case you're thirsty. It's a long drive and you've only had a cup of tea and that was before you fell asleep.'

Lorraine smiled at the woman's thoughtfulness and gave her a swift hug while she took Elijah from her arms. 'You know, I really do wish I lived closer.'

'Your mum and dad used to.' Caroline's mouth turned down with regret. 'Sad, really, that they moved so far away.'

'They didn't have a choice. It was for Dad's work.'

Aunt Caroline's brow wrinkled as she sent Lorraine a curious look. 'No, it wasn't. Your dad *had* to find a new job. Your mum made him.' She gave her head a slight shake. 'Something else they evidently never told you, why would they, when they'd kept everything else secret?' She stepped out of the door, and they walked together down the short path to Lorraine's car.

Lorraine strapped Elijah into his car seat and clunked the door shut. Her mind spun with information overload. She needed to phone Sergeant Willingham, she could do that on the way to pick Sophia up, provided the signal was good enough.

She thought of her mum's phone call a couple of nights before and hesitated before telling the other woman the details of it.

'So, where is Trevor now?'

Caroline pressed her lips together before replying. 'He lives not so far from here. Has done since he came out of prison.'

'Prison? What prison?' What little blood she had in her brain drained out to leave her light-headed.

Her aunt frowned as though she only just realised that if Lorraine didn't know of his existence, then she knew nothing of his history. 'Trevor was convicted of two counts of manslaughter almost twelve years ago.'

Aghast, Lorraine swallowed the horror as the impact of her aunt's words hit her.

'You never said he was a criminal.' Because her aunt had said he'd been accused of the murder of her brother, but that he was innocent. At the age of eleven. Cleared by all but her mum. 'Who did he murder?'

Her aunt hunched her shoulders as though she regretted bringing up the subject. 'Not murder. Manslaughter. A couple of gang members.'

'Gang members? He was a member of a gang?' There was so much more she needed to know, but she also had to go. She pulled the driver's door open, her chest squeezing so tight she wondered if it was possible for a person to actually shake themselves apart. Implode.

'He had an atrocious upbringing, your brother.' Aunt Caroline stepped close to the car as Lorraine slipped into the driver's seat.

Lorraine wanted to shout out that he wasn't her brother. Just because he had some of the same blood running through his veins didn't immediately make him family. Not her family. Never. She was this many years old when she discovered he existed. Thirty-one years without him and she wished to God she'd never heard of him now.

'Lots of people have poor childhoods, it doesn't make them criminals.'

'It wasn't his fault.' Her aunt was insistent. Defensive.

She'd heard her say that before. She'd repeated it. Was she trying to convince herself or had she really been duped by this man? This relation? Did her own guilt at not being able to save him taint every scenario? Make him an innocent in her eyes?

Was he?

Lorraine punched the start button and gripped the wheel, refusing to look at her aunt, her jaw so tight she thought it might break. 'How long has he been out?'

She waited for an answer, but when it didn't come, she risked a look at the other woman.

'Almost a year.'

Aunt Caroline crossed her arms over her chest.

Lorraine put the car in drive, her foot still on the brake. 'Did my dad meet with him?'

Aunt Caroline nodded. 'Yes.'

'How many times?'

'Twice. I think. Then...'

'Then my dad's car crashed and killed him. And you still believe this boy. This man that you can't even begin to know, you believe he's innocent?'

'I do. Circumstances haven't been kind to him, but none of it is his fault. If your mum hadn't...'

She stared at her aunt. 'What? Got him out of our house, our lives? Why do you think she might do that?'

Aunt Caroline's eyes narrowed as they contemplated Lorraine, for the first time a flicker of doubt entered her expression. 'To get away from your brother. Your mum believed she needed to protect you against him.'

Lorraine revved the engine and reached for the door. 'Too damned true. Looks like she may have been right.'

She slammed the door and took off down the drive, turning the car without looking. The blare of a horn behind her did nothing but spur her on, homeward.

There was a man out there who might well be looking for her.

She recalled Sophia mentioning a man by the tree near school. Grandad, she'd thought.

The quick flash of a figure who reminded her of her dad.

Her mum was right. He was after her.

And her daughter.

She punched the quick dial for the number she'd input for Sergeant Willingham.

43

NINE MONTHS EARLIER

Anger burned so hot in the pit of his stomach that flames licked into his veins to make his blood boil.

He'd never felt this much fury since the day his mum had banned him from going to see his own dad.

'Trevor. Every time you come back from your dad's, you have "attitude". He allows you to get away with murder.'

'But Muuum.'

'Don't but Mum me,' she mocked. 'He has no control of you. No discipline. He simply doesn't understand you the way I do. That you need a strong hand.'

She raged on, gesticulating wildly as he watched, tears brimming in his eyes until the sobs he'd held inside all the while she was yelling erupted.

She bent and picked up the laundry basket, letting out a grunt at the unexpected weight of the wet towels he'd slung in there when he'd let the bath overflow the night before.

She was angry about that. Fuming. But that wasn't the basis of her anger. No. Her anger was rooted elsewhere. On his dad. That he'd found a happy life, despite it being her who was the one who'd left. He'd never *been so happy.*

He followed her out of the bathroom and along the short landing to the top of the stairs. 'You're jealous.'

'Jealous?' She whirled on him, hitching the basket onto her hip, her eyes narrowing with reluctant comprehension. 'What have I got to be jealous of, exactly?' Her lips thinned and her voice dipped into a low, threatening whisper. One he would normally back away from instantly.

Today, however, she'd caught him just wrong. He was going to his dad's whether she liked it or not. His dad would make sure of that.

As if he wasn't important enough to wait for, she turned her back on him and made her way towards the top of the stairs.

He didn't care. She wasn't going to stop him this time.

Dad was already on his way, wasn't he? She was just going to let poor Dad draw up outside the door, sit there for ten minutes and when Trevor didn't come out, he'd get out, a weary droop to his shoulders, and walk through the front yard to the door.

Trevor had seen him do it before when Mum had locked him in his bedroom. Tears of frustration had soaked his cheeks then. But he didn't dare cry out.

Not today, though. These tears were absolute fury. He was going to be with his dad. He jutted his chin out.

'You're jealous because Sandra's pregnant. She and Dad are going to have a new baby. And he won't let you push him around any more.' He'd overheard Sandra telling his dad that. He'd overheard more than that.

'She's having the baby you always wanted.' She'd wanted a second one after him, from what Trevor had overheard.

Chalk-white, his mum turned to glare at him, her dark eyes piercing through his soul before that low voice turned to a threatening growl.

'Go to your room right now, you little shitbag.' His eyes widened. His mum never swore at him. Oh, he knew she swore, but not normally if she thought he was within earshot.

She straightened, her fists white around the laundry basket.

'I'll let your dad know when he arrives you won't be going around in future. Ever. I'll tell him you don't want to. That it was your decision.' Her voice turned sly. 'That you don't feel comfortable there now there's a baby on its way.' She tilted her head to one side. 'I'll think of an appropriate punishment for your behaviour later, but right now, you go to your room.'

She turned and placed her slippered foot on the first step down.

'I won't go to my room, you horrible bitch.' He'd heard Sandra use the word before.

His mum turned furious eyes on him and drew in a long breath.

Before she could issue more vitriol in his direction, he stepped forward and with both hands pushed with all his eleven-year-old might.

The washing basket with the weight of dirty, wet towels upended and tumbled down the stairs, white plastic splitting as it smashed against the wall before it continued on its way.

For a second, Trevor thought she might snatch at the banister and hold on, but her foot slipped out of the back of one of her mules and her arms pinwheeled, holding her suspended. He almost laughed. She looked like one of those cartoon characters, running on the spot in mid-air. But not for long.

Head over heels backwards she went, a wild scream tearing from her, echoing all the way down until she lay broken and silent at the bottom of the stairs.

He waited, thinking how loud that scream had been. Would anyone come running?

If he stayed where he was, just for a minute... Just to make sure.

Their connecting neighbours wouldn't have heard. They'd gone away on holiday to Greece. The ones on the other side were rarely there. They worked long shifts, his mum had said when she wanted to shush him at any given time.

'Don't disturb the neighbours, Trevor. They eat, sleep, work.'

He held on a while longer, then Trevor picked his way down each *step, placing his feet carefully between the bundled-up washing, his hand clinging to the banister in case he met the same fate.*

He studied the strange form sprawled over the bottom two stairs. His mum. But not his mum. Her body posed like a manikin, fractured and inhuman. Arms twisted at peculiar angles.

His attachment to her frayed, snapped.

Brown eyes stared sightless at the ceiling, no longer narrowed and following his every move. But frozen. Her feet twitched in erratic spasms before they came to rest, each of them pointing at a different angle.

Her newly streaked blonde hair spread in wild disarray across the bottom step, her head at a strange angle as though she was making one of her super sarcastic enquiries. Her lips, with perfectly applied lipstick, gently parted as though she was about to smile.

Trevor stepped over her, scooped up the backpack in the hallway and looked at her again for a long moment, his mind empty except for one thing.

'Mum, can I go and see Dad now?'

With no objection from her, he slipped through the front door, closing it with a distinct click behind him and made his way to the side of the road just as his dad's car pulled up, ready to take him away for the weekend.

He dashed tears he never realised were falling with the back of his sleeve and slipped into the car. 'Hi, Dad.'

'Trevor. Everything okay, son?'

'Yeah. Fine.'

His dad waited patiently for him to buckle up before he pulled away from the kerb. 'How's your mum?'

'Oh, same as usual.'

His dad snuffled a breath out of his nose. 'Stiff. Unyielding?'

Trevor leaned back in the seat, his backpack between his feet. 'Yeah, you could say that.'

She had not been discovered until Trevor and his dad returned on the

Sunday evening. With no lights on at home, his dad had used Trevor's front door key to let them in.

The shock of seeing her after a whole weekend of lying dead in her own urine at the bottom of the stairs, exactly where he'd left her, had sent Trevor into a catatonic state.

After all, it's not every day you find your mother dead.

Authorities put it down to shock at being witness to finding her body. The time of death showed it must have been shortly after he left the house.

They never questioned the silence that shrouded him for weeks.

That same silence blanketed him now. It wasn't distress.

It was pure fury.

44

EIGHTY-SIX HOURS SINCE PHONE CALL

Every single traffic light hit red as she approached.

Despite the school's reassurances, the tremor of anxiety still ran through her as Lorraine pulled the car up against a now empty kerbside and leaped out.

The other parents having already collected their children and the majority of the street residents possibly still at work left the place deserted and eerily quiet.

In a way, she could only be grateful there weren't any mums there to witness her shame. Her failure.

With not even any stragglers outside the school, the proof of her lateness screamed at her.

It couldn't be helped.

Traffic had backed up behind an accident on the motorway and by the time Lorraine negotiated her way through the chicane the police had set up, another twenty minutes had passed. There was nothing she could do but tap on the steering wheel, sip water from her bottle and listen to Elijah's happy gurgles from the back seat. At least she could thank her lucky stars he was such an easy child. Perhaps all second children were easier than the first due to necessity. They couldn't be wrapped in cottonwool. They had to be dragged all over the place to accommodate the first child.

Lorraine leaned in the back of the car to pluck Elijah out of his maxi seat, and grinned at her little boy, who'd remained awake, chirruping in the back of the car, the entire way back. He'd talked to his teddy, rattled the bunch of plastic keys and cooed at the tactile book. All of which she'd managed to lodge around his legs so once he dispatched one to the back seat or floor, he had another to pick up.

'You've been a champion, my darling.' She placed a soft kiss on his forehead and let out a relieved laugh.

With a quick scan around to make sure no strange man lurked in the shadows, she dashed through the still open school gates, clutching Elijah to her chest. She was even later than she'd estimated.

She buzzed the front door of the junior school to be let in by some mysterious person still in one of the offices.

Her heart still pounding, she made her way through the hallway once she'd announced herself. Her hands trembled as she transferred Elijah's weight from one side to the other.

'Hello?' She poked her head around the door, expecting a tear-drenched child to fling herself into Lorraine's arms.

Instead, she was greeted by vague disinterest from a child whose attention was firmly on the sandpit and water she was playing with.

The wave of relief hit Lorraine with such force, she almost sank to her knees with gratitude.

The teacher looked up from her kneeling position on the floor next to Sophia. 'Mrs Pengelly, how lovely to see you. Sophia and I have been having such fun.'

Lorraine drew in a breath to fill her lungs until they burned. The same burn that threatened behind her eyes. She sent the teacher, Miss Fennell, a wobbly smile as the other woman bounced to her feet.

'Sophia, wash and dry your hands and then collect your book bag and coat. It's time to go home now.'

Without protest, the child also leaped up, a wide grin on her face as she raced across the classroom to do the teacher's bidding, barely batting an eye at her own mum. Relief touched Lorraine's heart that her daughter was so confident and secure. Under the circumstances, she could be a gibbering wreck, if Lorraine hadn't kept all the drama from her. There was no need. Sophia was too young to take on life's cruelties yet. The time would come. She'd already had Daddy leave and Grandad die. She didn't need any other responsibilities yet. The secure school life was so good for her.

Miss Fennell stepped closer and lowered her voice as she touched gentle fingers to Lorraine's arm. Her smooth brow furrowed. 'Is everything okay?'

Lorraine nodded, barely able to speak. 'My mum's missing.'

She wanted to snatch the words back, but they were already out of her mouth.

The teacher's eyes widened. They slid sideways at Sophia as she approached with her coat over her arm and lunchbox in hand, and then back again. 'Sophia.' She raised her voice and shot the child a wide smile. 'Why don't you help yourself to an extra book?'

As Sophia turned to the bookcase to make another choice, Miss Fennell took a step closer to Lorraine, her voice a soft hush. 'I'm so sorry. Sophia's grandma is such a lovely lady. Is there anything the school can do to help?'

Lorraine shook her head as tears thickened her throat. 'No. The police are involved. Now.' She'd had to leave a message on the number she'd been given and hope it got through. Otherwise, she'd ring again in the morning. 'But it's taken a couple of days for them to take it seriously. They thought she might just be out shopping or something.' Lorraine stared at her daughter and then shook her head. 'I'm so sorry if it upsets you too, but I wanted you to understand why I was so late. I'm not a bad parent.'

'You certainly are not. I can tell. Sophia is a very bright, well-adjusted child considering everything you as a family have gone through this last year or so.'

Lorraine nodded.

'Do you think she's okay, your mum? Has she ever done anything like this before?'

Lorraine hesitated. The temptation to pour her heart out to this woman she barely knew almost overwhelmed her. She reined in the compulsion and gave a sad smile. 'No. Not that I know of. She's had a lot to cope with lately with Dad dying. It's only been nine months. It's been hard on her.' She sent Sophia another quick glance. 'I'd better get out of your way, I'm sure you're desperate to go home.'

Miss Fennell placed her hand on Lorraine's and gave it a light squeeze, her warm fingers defrosting Lorraine's. 'Don't worry. I was going to be here anyway. I have more lesson plans to create than you could shake a stick at since they decided to change the curriculum at the beginning of term.' She smiled. 'Still, that's nothing in comparison to what you have to deal with. Just let the office know if Sophia needs to stay late any day, I'm normally the last one here apart from the janitor and I'd never leave before you got back.'

'No. Thank you. It shouldn't be an issue. Only today, I had to travel to see family and check with them.'

'Wouldn't the police do that?'

Lorraine huffed out. 'Yeah, they will. But I needed to do it myself. Just to be sure.'

She turned her hand over in the other woman's and squeezed back. 'Thank you,' she repeated.

Over Miss Fennell's shoulder, she called out to Sophia. 'Let's go home now, sweetheart.'

Sophia turned, her arms full of books. 'I can't decide which one.'

Lorraine shot the teacher an apologetic glance. 'I'm sorry, she loves books. She seems to lose herself in them. You should see how many we get from the library every week. She doesn't just look at the pictures. She reads them. Again, and again.'

Miss Fennell gave a gentle smile as she reached out for the pile of books, taking them from Sophia. 'There's no need to apologise. I wish every child loved to read as much as Sophia.' She placed the books on the table and spread them so all their covers could be clearly seen. 'Choose four, Sophia, and the others will be ready waiting for you when you finish and return them.'

Sophia grinned. 'Thank you, Miss Fennell.' She took her time, pointing with care at each one of the four books she was about to take home.

'And so, how many books do you have altogether?'

Sophia counted, stabbing each one with her index finger. 'One, two, three, four.'

'Plus, how many already in your book bag?' The woman had such a way of making it interesting, her tone full of excitement.

The child's eyes lit up and she rolled them towards the ceiling as though she was envisaging the books in her bag. 'Five, six, seven, eight.'

'Well, you're going to be hard pushed to read eight books over the weekend, aren't you?'

Lorraine wasn't so sure. Her daughter steamed through them. She read way beyond her age.

The teacher was obviously aware of that too.

'Sophia, slip your coat on, it's quite chilly out there.' Lorraine watched as Sophia picked her coat up from where she'd left it on the desk nearest the bookcase. She slipped her arms through the armholes which made one less item for Lorraine to carry out to the car while she juggled the increasingly heavy Elijah in her arms. Maybe she should have kept him in the carrier, but truth be told that was getting heavy to carry one-handed, it was easier sometimes just to hold him. Apart from anything, he didn't always want to be in his carrier these days.

Miss Fennell must have been of the same mind about Sophia as she picked up the book bag and pushed two of the books inside. 'They won't all fit, Sophia. Do you think you can manage to carry them while Mummy carries your little brother?'

Sophia nodded with enthusiasm, desperate to please her teacher as she tucked two books under her arm, slipped her fingers through the handle of her book bag and then swiped up her presumably empty unicorn lunchbox, giving it a jaunty swing.

'Good girl, Sophia. I bet your mum is so proud of you being such a helpful girl.'

Lorraine's throat tightened again, and she had to swallow hard.

God, she was a mess. She wanted to burst into tears at the slightest kindness.

She adjusted Elijah and straightened her shoulders, sending Miss Fennell a wobbly smile. 'Thank you so much. I appreciate everything you've done. Have a lovely weekend.'

'Thank you, I will.'

Miss Fennell touched her arm as they made their way to the classroom door, she opened it wide, her hand on Sophia's shoulder, and took Lorraine by surprise as she walked down the long corridor to the front door with them. She gave Lorraine a pointed stare. 'I hope everything works out for you. If you need us, please ask.'

Lorraine bobbed her head at the woman as she closed the school doors and walked through the playground to the huge black metal gates that stood wide.

Movement by the car caught her attention and she snapped her head up, gaze fixed on the tall, slender man who leaned against her car, back to them. The familiar-looking black donkey jacket snug across wide shoulders she'd recognise anywhere.

Her footsteps faltered as Sophia skipped on ahead.

'Sophia, wait.'

The thick pump of blood as it drained from her head turned everything into slow motion. Elijah's body became a lead weight in her arms as her face turned numb.

As though he sensed her presence, or maybe he'd heard her voice, the man pushed away from her car and started to turn.

She knew it wasn't possible, but...

'Dad?'

45

ONE YEAR EARLIER

After his mum was buried, he thought his dad and Sandra would take him into their fold. That they would nurture him, smother him in sympathy and give him some kind of special treatment. After all, his mum had gone. The accident had been a tragedy. He was a child who needed attention, understanding and love.

But that bitch of a woman had driven a wedge between Trevor and his dad long before his mum was dead. Still, she continued to do so. She'd kept them apart for years and just when he believed he might re-establish his relationship with his dad, Sandra wedged herself between them.

Only this time Trevor wasn't a child. He was an adult with skills he'd learned on the street, expertise he'd honed in prison.

The time had come to put one of those skills to use because he knew what to do with a car. Not these new-fangled electric hybrids that hadn't even existed when he went in. He'd dabbled in mechanics and knew how to fix old cars. Real damned cars. Cars that were interesting, fixable. Like his dad's precious MG B fucking GT that he'd had for years.

It wasn't difficult to gain entry into the garage of his dad's house. He'd watched and waited until his dad went out with Sandra.

Trevor bided his time to make absolutely sure they weren't going to return immediately and when that time was right, he slipped in over the fence, along the length of the garden, taking care that the nosy neighbour next door didn't see him because after all, he might be a little rusty, but it was his trade to break and enter.

The lads back in the day had all said he had eyes in the back of his head. Lads he'd not seen for years. Lads who had disappeared like rats up a drainpipe once he'd been sent to prison. No matter. It meant nothing to him. He needed none of them now. He was utterly independent and could start all over.

He'd never been caught for breaking and entering. That had never been an issue. It was his skill. His livelihood.

He'd fouled up elsewhere. Been committed for manslaughter. Not picking locks.

He'd never have been caught if it wasn't for the arse that had found him in his apartment. That was one guy he never wanted to come into contact with again. Never wanted to see. Hoped the guy never knew he was out of prison. Because if he did, he might just come after him again.

Only when he was inside did he realise the extent of his cock-up. The man he'd targeted was the head honcho of a diamond-smuggling operation. Not someone their measly little team would ever have come across, never mind targeted. If Caid had been alive at the time, he would have steered them well clear of him.

Naivety had made him arrogant. He'd never make that error again. He was lucky to have got away with his life. The prison sentence was his punishment for his conceit. He'd considered himself lucky the head honcho hadn't sent anyone after him while he was inside. He'd kept his head down, his mouth shut and realised he was never important enough for the guy to send anyone after him. That was another lesson in humility. He was worth nothing.

He slipped inside the garage in no time at all, not even having to pick the lock to the door that backed onto their garden.

People believed that because they lived in an enclosed area, no one would scale the fences and let themselves in. A nice neighbourhood wasn't a safe neighbourhood.

It hadn't taken him long to tamper with the steering rack on the old MG BGT. A few bolts to loosen. It wasn't that complex.

Perhaps his dad would have been wise not to have shown it off, bringing his pride and joy to flaunt in Trevor's face the last time they'd met. Something Trevor had been less than impressed with. An inanimate object that his dad appeared to have more affection for than he did his own son.

'Trevor, remember this?'

Trevor had a vague recollection.

His dad smoothed a gentle hand over the wing of the shiny red car, inviting Trevor to do the same.

Look what I've got, his attitude and body language screamed. The pride his dad displayed was more than he'd ever shown Trevor.

All these years, Trevor had never thought for one moment that his dad didn't love him. He'd been convinced that the dad he worshipped had been kept away from him first by his mum, and then his stepmum. By Sandra.

He'd wasted an entire lifetime waiting for approval, for love, when he could have done so much more.

He could have been so much more if he hadn't been concentrating on the love he'd poured into the one person who didn't deserve it.

The deep burn of fury gathered in Trevor. Not the wild flames his childhood self had experienced before he pushed his mum down the stairs, but a slow, smouldering heat that wasn't about to dissipate.

The one person he'd thought, when all obstacles were out of the way, would love him unquestionably was his dad. That man had made it clear he never wanted to see him again. His own child, his breath, his blood.

His dad's heartless cutting of all connections was the epitome of evil.

After their second meeting, Trevor had sensed a withdrawal. His dad had wanted to know about his past. Until he didn't. Perhaps as the colour had drained from his dad's face, Trevor should have taken the hint. That had only been the beginning of his tales. Stabbing the beast through the fingers. Perhaps he should have stopped there, but he made that error of judgement again. Underestimated how much his dad actually wanted to know. Trevor had made his life a boast, so it sounded more exciting than it was. Put in too much detail. Instead of being a dirge, he'd made himself out to be a hero.

Not long after, that pathetic letter arrived through Aunt Caroline, because his dad still hadn't given him his address.

Not that he needed to. Trevor had that after the first time they met. It wasn't hard to follow someone home. Especially a someone who would have no idea. An innocent.

An innocent who had sent him a blow in the form of a letter.

Trevor had read it so many times, he could almost recite it.

Dear Trevor,

It's been really great to meet with you these few times and I'm so pleased to know that you're getting your life together and have plans for the future. Sadly, and I am sure you will be disappointed to read this, but I feel it probably isn't the wisest thing for us to continue to develop a relationship. One that I feel obliged not to tell Sandra about. I know if she discovered my disloyalty to her, she would be devastated. I can't risk that. We've been married now for over thirty years and we're partners in everything. I cannot find it in my heart to deceive her.

I wish I'd been able to do more for you when you were a lad, but that time is past and there is no going back. You're now a man, full grown, and I am sure you will find your own way, but I need to do the same with my family.

I hope that you can find it in your heart to forgive me and move on.

Perhaps we can meet one last time to say goodbye and to give you some mementos of happier times when you lived with your mum.

Same time, same place, next Thursday?

Yours,

Henry – your dad

46

ONE YEAR EARLIER

Henry! His fucking dad!

Hate elbowed its way through, shoving aside all the childish promises he'd made himself and the hope he'd held onto all these years. To meet up again. To be reunited. For that dad to show remorse for his past and pride in his future.

What a waste of time.

Trevor slipped through the interconnecting door from garage to house it appeared they never locked and took the opportunity to scope out the rest of the place. He moved wraithlike through the small house, his gloved fingers touching the framed photograph of their precious fucking daughter, hand holding that of a little girl whose big brown eyes stared directly into the lens of the camera. His half-sister's belly was swollen with a baby inside. A baby he could only imagine would take all their love and devotion. They would spoil a child, undeserving of the love he'd been deprived of.

He riffled confident fingers through stuffed drawers in the kitchen for something, anything of use. Something of interest. Maybe spare change. After all, his dad owed him big time. More than he could ever get from a few loose coins at the bottom of the kitchen drawer.

Mementos of his time with his mum he could do without. He wouldn't thank his dad for them. It was money he needed until he was able to retrieve his own.

Trevor had spent all his available money getting to meeting places, waiting for his dad. Ordering unnecessarily expensive coffee. His dad hadn't even offered to pay. Hadn't thought that times might be tough for someone straight out of clink with no job set up yet.

He started work next week. Pot washer in one of the local hotels. Keeping behind the scenes and out of trouble. Away from humans. Mostly. He'd done the job before, but not since he was a kid on the streets. They paid cash back then, and less if they thought you didn't have a parent at home to come in and complain at the pitiful wage.

Still, it wouldn't kill him to do it again.

He'd never been one to shirk hard work.

He narrowed his eyes and took his time making sure not to displace things in the small drawer. He edged it closed and opened the one next to it. Another junk drawer. Everyone had them. This family seemed to have more than most. The kitchen was only small.

He reached inside.

He knew this job inside out. This was his job of old before he'd been inside. He knew exactly how to fly under the radar, cover his tracks. Never leave any prints. He'd had that one hammered home when he'd left one fat, bloodstained handprint on a white car. That's how they'd caught him.

Gently, he removed the keys, one bundle at a time from the drawer. How long had they lived here? They had so many abandoned keys. Surely they weren't all for this house. He placed them back inside, exactly where he'd found them. Raised his head to listen for any kind of sound.

Nothing.

He closed the drawer and opened another. More crap. Vestiges of living a pathetic life.

As his fingers touched on a small tin, he hesitated, then slipped it from the drawer, knowing what he would find, what he always found in little tins kept in kitchen drawers.

It was more than he'd expected.

The thick wad of ten-pound notes unfurled in his hand, the Queen's head uppermost. Every single one of them. He imagined they'd been counted and turned the right way like a bank teller had counted them. He did the same now, quick and efficient. Two hundred and twenty quid.

He huffed out a breath. He couldn't take it all. If he took it all they would know someone had been there. But if he just creamed off enough so that if it was counted anytime soon, they would doubt their own sanity, think maybe the other one had taken some and not said. Doubt themselves. That's the way it was with people.

The last thing they would believe was that someone had sneaked in and only taken a little.

He'd come to realise over time that people fell into two categories. Those who blamed themselves for everything that went wrong, and those who blamed everyone else.

He suspected he knew what sort Sandra was. She was a blamer. He remembered her clearly enough.

His dad, though. He suspected he took the blame from his wife. Took it and took it.

So, Trevor would take the money and let Sandra blame his dad. There was no one else to take the blame.

After all, why would someone come into your house, your

home, only take a few notes, leave the TV, the priceless ornaments, the valuables left lying around? Why wouldn't they take it all?

He skimmed off forty pounds and slipped the notes deep into his front jeans pocket. He held the notes for a moment longer before taking another twenty and stuffing it into his pocket with the other notes. His dad owed him that much, if only for the fucking coffee.

Folding the remainder of the money, Trevor placed it back exactly how he found it in the little metal tin. The tin went back into the drawer, precisely where it had come from.

As he withdrew his hand, his gaze fell on what appeared to be a drawer liner. He edged his fingernail under one side and peeled the item out from underneath all the detritus. A bit like a magician who whips a tablecloth from under a whole table full of crockery to leave it immaculate in its wake.

He held the brochure in both hands, a small curl of recognition unfurled as he stared at it.

Like small, fast electric shocks, the memory returned full scale.

47

THIRTY YEARS EARLIER

Sandra's voice, high pitched, bordering on hysteria, raised as Trevor curled into a tight ball at the top of the stairs, his vision obscured, but the voices carried loud and clear.

'Trevor can't live with my parents. They live on a narrowboat, for God's sake. Have some common sense. He's a child who hasn't even been taught to swim. What on earth would they do with him? It's too small. There's barely enough space for the two of them and that scabby little dog of theirs. He can't live there.'

'But, Sandra, surely they can manage. Just for a while. Until we can make other arrangements.'

'What other arrangements, *Henry*? No, no, Henry, they will not have him. It's not fair even to ask them. They bought that narrowboat to retire on, not to take on a new family. One that's not even theirs.'

'Sandra...' Hurt laced his words.

'He's unruly, and I don't trust him. I do not trust him.'

His dad's voice dropped to a harsh whisper, so Trevor edged closer along the top step, straining to hear.

'Sandra, keep your voice down.'

She lowered her own voice, but it still caried weight. 'Henry, you must do something with him. He cannot go and live with my parents. What have they got to do with him? They're not even his grandparents. They're my parents, the grandparents of my *dead* baby.'

Her voice broke.

'Sandra. No, it's okay. It's okay. It's all right. Sandra.' His dad's voice thickened with emotion. 'He was my baby too.' The quiet rustle of clothing as Trevor imagined his dad taking that witch into his arms to comfort her as she got her own way once more with tears and blackmail.

'We'll think of something. I promise.'

Her voice stiffened and Trevor felt the almost physical pulling away. 'Well, he can't live on a narrowboat, for God's sake.'

'I know. I know. It was just a thought. I'm just trying to make things work. For all of us. It would have only been temporary.'

'You're not listening,' she snapped.

'Yes, yes, I am. I understand. I'm just trying to explain my thoughts.'

'Well, my thoughts are that no child belongs with a retired couple on a narrowboat for any length of time.'

Her voice smoothed, slid into a reasoning tone that made Trevor cringe. This was the tone that always won. The one his dad could never withstand.

'The space is way too small for a child. It's too restrictive. And his behaviour is just not good enough for my parents to look after him. He's disturbed. They're not young any more, Henry. They've done their bit. They don't expect to take on a child. Effectively a child who has nothing, nothing whatsoever to do with them. They've barely met him. Like me, they believe he murdered our baby. You want to palm him off onto them?'

The Stepson

'No, I won't be palming him off onto your parents. That's not what I said at all. It was merely a thought.'

'A thought of putting a child who can't swim on a boat. Well, that was no thought at all.'

In the long silence, Trevor waited, his breath held. She'd won again, but that could only mean one thing. They couldn't send him away. He was safe. He'd get to stay with his dad.

As he scooted backwards ready to go to bed, his dad's voice halted him again.

'I can't think of anything else I can do with him.'

'Well, let the social worker do what she suggested, then, Henry.'

'I can't let him go to another family to be fostered. He's my son.'

'He's not my son and he's not normal. You know that. He's evil.'

'Sandra, he's not evil. You...'

'We cannot go around this again. Henry, you do something. You do something, or I won't be responsible for my own actions. You've got to put it right.' Her voice gained confidence, control. 'The only way I can see is that you get the social worker to put him with a foster family. Just for a few weeks while we try and figure out something else. Respite. For all of us. We can do it, Henry. I need you to do it.' Her voice cajoled.

'All right, Sandra, you win. All right. I'll speak to social services tomorrow. First thing.'

48

FIVE DAYS EARLIER

Trevor weighed the small bundle of keys in his hand as he stared at the decrepit narrowboat, partially grounded on the bank, the tail end of it jutting out into the canal.

How could they have let it get to this state and not have it towed away by some canal authority? Were there canal authorities? Was there such a thing? He'd not got a clue. He'd never been on a narrowboat. Avoided canals, especially the lengths running under railway bridges.

The long-ago memory sent a shudder through him. All that humanity huddled together. Lost souls in a homeless world.

He leaned against a tree trunk, obscured by a thicket of bushes while he took his time studying it.

He'd found it more by luck than judgement. No longer in the mooring site listed on the brochure he'd photographed and slipped back into the drawer before he'd sneaked from the house the way he'd come in. He should have made note of the information when he first discovered the brochure in the drawer. Little did he know then that it would prove invaluable. After all, he'd been more focused on dealing with his dad.

He'd just needed to bide his time, make up his mind what further actions he wanted to take once his dad was dead and buried. Did he want to let sleeping dogs lie, or did he want to complete his revenge? Revenge on the woman who'd ruined his entire life. Revenge on the child who took his place.

He'd mulled it. Taken his time. Decided he didn't have it in him to let go. Not until the job was done.

Careful to check the old lady next door wasn't staring through the back window, he'd waited in the shadows. It was difficult to know with the sun lowering in the sky to reflect light off her dark windows, but he took the chance as he slipped over the fence at the rear of the property and slid quietly down the embankment to the main road to where he'd left his car. Technically, not his car. Toenail-picking Dave's brother's car who was currently doing time. For nicking cars. He'd let his older brother borrow it while he was inside. Dave didn't have a licence and was wetting himself at the thought of getting pulled over. Trevor had no such qualms.

He'd not expected to be setting off on a journey, but this was hardly an opportunity he was about to pass up.

Two hours was nothing in the scheme of things, when he'd spent years in prison. Besides. He needed to come this way anyhow. He'd soon be calling in on his Aunt Caroline on a regular basis. She was a soft touch. The guilt of his upbringing tethered her and made her an easy target for new clothes and a small bundle of money from time to time. After all, pot washing hardly paid enough to keep a grown man in comfort.

A comfort he'd half expected to find on the canal boat.

He was sorely disappointed.

He had time enough to check the wreck out from a distance, but the light was almost gone and the narrowboat looked like it belonged in a graveyard.

It wasn't possible someone still lived there. Not the way it listed to one side.

He grasped the weighty palm-sized torch in his hand that he'd brought from the car he'd left in a small car park in the woods.

Never without the tools of his trade somewhere close by. This was an efficient torch and a pretty handy weapon to boot.

The boat might look deserted, but who knew?

Trevor had slept in rougher places than this one as a teenager, just to keep well out of the way of predators.

With no one in sight, he made his way along the narrow towpath, keeping his torch switched off so that he remained invisible in the dark donkey jacket he'd managed to take from his dad's wardrobe on one of his foraging expeditions into his house. It might be early June, but the weather didn't seem to have warmed up this year. Or that could just be that he'd been living in stifling accommodation at Her Majesty's behest.

He paused beside the canal boat. *The Old Codgers.*

A reluctant smile curved his lips. How funny that Sandra's parents had a sense of humour. They were all right, from memory. But were they still around? Certainly not on this boat. Surely?

He tapped the base of his torch against the wooden slats of the narrowboat and held his breath, waiting for a reply. For movement.

Silence.

He knocked once more just to make sure. He didn't want to hit the wood too hard, or he'd probably knock a hole in it.

'Hello?'

No answer. Good. They'd been old when he was kid, they were surely dead by now. There's no way they could be living there. It didn't look habitable. Not for normal humans.

He waited another long moment, but there was nothing to indicate anyone lived there.

Until he stepped onboard, and the wooden slats creaked in

protest at his relatively light weight. The smell of fresh woodsmoke hit him as he levered open the unlocked door to the galley with the edge of the key.

Shock registered on the face of the old man as Trevor stepped inside. A moment of horror, until the face relaxed.

'Henry.' Warmth of recognition laced the old man's voice.

Trevor swallowed. Christ. This was Sandra's dad, his stepgrandad. A man he'd barely come into contact with. Possibly only seen four or five times on brief occasions where Trevor had been ignored while they came to coddle their one and only daughter.

The 'old codger' was still very much alive. Sallow skin stretched over knobbly cheekbones and dipped deep into the recesses of huge eyes with milky discs indicating cataracts. Which was probably why he couldn't get a good look at Trevor.

'It's been a long, long, time, boy. Come on in.' The old man's voice warbled as the thin, empty skin on his throat trembled. 'You're too late if you're after supper, I've already eaten.' He indicated the stack of dishes in the sink, grease floating on the top of the water as though it was stone cold.

Trevor grunted, pulled the door shut behind him, and stepped into the dim warmth of the cabin, taking care not to step too close to the one wall light that appeared to be working, its yellowed light casting heavy shadows across the small room.

The old man turned, a glass of golden liquid in his hand. 'Don't suppose you have time for a whisky?'

Trevor nodded, unsure whether the old man would realise it wasn't his son-in-law if he spoke. His sight might be shot and his hearing couldn't be good if he'd not heard Trevor knock.

The man's huge eyes blinked as he stared at Trevor. 'I can't remember the last time you came. You don't seem to have aged a jot.' He handed over the dirty-looking glass and turned to pour himself one, leaning heavily on one hip as he balanced himself against the sink. 'Yeah. Actually, I do remember.' He turned around and slipped into the booth, indicating for Trevor to take the bench opposite. 'Last time you came here was after the baby died.' He took a swig of his whisky and blew out a breath laden with it. Evidently not the first drink of the evening.

Heavy lids lowered over his eyes. 'Does that mean you've come to break more bad news?' His voice was scratchy with sadness. 'Is my daughter all right?'

Trevor nodded. 'She's fine.'

The old man lifted his head and stared off into the distance. Regret shimmering through the tears forming in his cloudy eyes. 'I haven't seen Sandra since my Doris and her fell out. Must be around twenty years ago now. If memory serves me right.' He leaned against the filthy back cushion on the bench. 'I've missed her so much.' He shook his head, tears trailing down his parched cheeks. 'Do you think Sandra's forgiven us yet?'

'Forgiven you?'

'For trying to help that boy when he wrote to us.'

Trevor sucked in his breath. He never knew his letters had even reached them. A desperate plea, a last-ditch attempt to reach his dad when nothing else seemed to have worked.

'They went at it hammer and tongs that day. Doris said Sandra wasn't welcome here ever again after she spoke to her like that.'

Sadness enveloped him like a heavy blanket. 'I never thought they would stick to it, but they did. My girl's never been back, even when Doris died. Unforgiving, the pair of them.'

He wallowed in his sadness, taking sips of his whisky. 'Three years gone since the old girl left me. Three years since I saw Sandra at her funeral. I never had a chance to even speak with her before she'd gone, like smoke on a breezy day.'

He squinted, a sad smile creasing his cheeks. 'I thought she'd change her mind and come visit me, but she's cut from the same cloth as her mother. Merciless. Single-minded, miserable old bitch.'

He spluttered out a laugh and then took another quick sip of his whisky. 'Course she was wrong. Silly old cow.' He pointed a grubby finger. 'She didn't know I sided with Sandra on that one. That boy of yours.'

He took a gulp of whisky and missed the narrowing of Trevor's eyes.

'A wrong 'un if ever I saw one.' He nodded at him as though taking him into his confidence. 'I know he was yours, but I knew the moment I met him he was trouble. Sandra knew it too, that's why the pair of them fell out. I kept quiet. Never had to say anything, but I would if I'd needed to. Henry, my boy, I said that lad of yours would come to no good, and I was right.'

Trevor's blood slowed as it chilled.

'Not only that, but he split a family. More than one. Little bastard. I bloody loved Doris and Sandra to bits. And now, look what I have.' He spread the fingers of one leathery hand. 'This. Doris's dream to retire on a narrowboat. Navigate all over the place.'

He rubbed his knuckles over his eyes, making the thinning skin around them stretch. 'I was never fussed. Loved our holidays on one and found myself easily swayed. Didn't really have an opinion at the time. She was so sold on the idea, I happily went along with it. But look.' He waved a hand around at the place. 'It's hardly bricks and mortar, is it?'

Regret shimmered in his almost opaque eyes. 'The old girl and I didn't think that one through when we sold our house to buy this. We couldn't afford a brand-new one. Couldn't afford to ditch it and buy another house, when the property market rocketed. So,' he grunted as he heaved himself back off the bench seat and reached for the bottle of whisky. Long, yellowing fingernails tapped at the glass as he picked the bottle up by the neck. 'When the rudder broke, and the bloody thing grounded itself, I had no option but just to sit in it and wait for my fate.' He sighed. 'At least Doris wasn't around to see what became of her beloved.' He barked out a strained laugh. 'I do mean *The Old Codgers*, not me.'

He poured himself two fingers' worth of whisky and slopped more into Trevor's almost full glass, pouring much more than he'd allowed himself.

'I'm just waiting for God now. You'd think at the age of ninety-one he'd want to come and collect me. Seems he's still got more in store for me, yet.'

He groaned as he leaned back and narrowed his eyes at Trevor. 'So, if it's not about my daughter, I have to ask, what is it you want? Because, for sure, neither of you are getting an inheritance. There's nothing left in the coffers, otherwise I'd go and buy myself a week in an hotel and hope I passed away before I was due to come back.'

Trevor picked up the glass he'd been cradling in his hands, hardly worried about the dirt on it. He'd had worse. Besides, 40 per cent alcohol was sure to sterilise it.

He took a swig. The warmth of the whisky circled his stomach, relaxing muscles he'd not realised had tensed.

The place might look a wreck from the outside, but inside it was snug and cosy, even if it did tilt to one side, the old boy had it nicely warmed through. Elderly folk often left heating off, but this man had the right idea.

Trevor circled his gaze around. Filthy dirty, but that didn't bother him much. It might suit him just fine. Somewhere to keep his head down.

He allowed himself a small smile. It wouldn't take much to rub a cloth over the surfaces, knock off some of the cobwebs in the corner the old boy obviously couldn't even see.

Trevor took another sip from the glass. Felt the burn. Smiled even wider. Yes, this might just suit him fine now he only needed to check in with Ken once a fortnight instead of weekly.

'I was passing. I thought I'd come and check up on you. But don't tell Sandra.' It wasn't exactly a lie. Although it barely skimmed the truth. He took a drink. No, it was a great big, whopping lie.

The old man surveyed him. 'Has she kicked you out?'

'No.' That wasn't possible. He'd not even seen her. Yet.

'No.' The old man grumbled, wriggling to get comfortable. 'Last time, it was her who walked out. Came here, didn't she? Always came back to her mum and dad. Up until that last time. She'd been here too long, you know. It was a good job you came and fetched her back when you did, otherwise her mum might have fallen out with her back then. As it was, I think that's what caused the rift. She was too long here, trying to change things for her mum and me, trying to dictate the way we lived. Back then, it wasn't even an option. We'd barely had the narrowboat for a few years.' His voice turned wistful. 'She was a real sweet boat, in her time.'

He stroked fingers disfigured from arthritis across the wooden panelling lining the inside of the boat, still glossy despite its age and lack of care.

Trevor could hardly agree with him, he'd never seen it before. Only on the sales brochure. Admittedly, she'd been in a great state of repair then, with shiny red and green paint on the outside he'd noted when he arrived. Paintwork that was now cracked and peeling.

Still, there might be hope for her yet. He wasn't averse to a bit of grafting. He'd had duties inside when he'd taken his turn to wash the pots, and peel potatoes. He'd been known to mop floors, too.

He wasn't so sure about his DIY talents, though. 'How bad is the rudder broken?' Would his knowledge tinkering on cars stretch far enough to do up a boat?

'Bad enough. She needs to go into dry dock to have it fixed. Not like you can just get under her and replace it. She'd have to be towed.'

'Otherwise, is she seaworthy?'

'Seaworthy,' he spluttered out, raising his hand to his forehead. 'It's only a bloody canal. If you mean watertight, then sadly the answer to that is also no. The steel has rusted. There must be a hole in the flat hull from when I grounded her. It's been a while, so I suspect it's deteriorating rapidly now.' He gave a vague wave in the direction behind him, the light showing up the dirt under his nails. 'I have a bilge pump going every morning for a couple of hours. Nothing major, but there's a little more water coming in each day.' He shrugged and slung the rest of the whisky back. 'Frankly, son, I don't have the wherewithal or energy to do it, but don't you go telling Sandra that. She'll be on the towpath giving instructions and I'm not like her mum. I'd end up caving and then she'd have me in a home soon as look at me.'

A little unsteady, he came to his feet. Swayed. He picked up his glass and placed it in the greasy water with the rest of the crockery.

Trevor's mouth curled with distaste. Gnarly old bastard. He was as bad as the rest of them. A coward who didn't dare to speak up against his over-powering wife.

Trevor suspected the old man had lost the thread of the conversation and forgotten that Trevor hadn't answered him as to why he was there.

'Well, Henry, my boy. It's past my bedtime, so I'll bid you farewell and let you out. Give my daughter my love, but don't mention the state this place is in. I know it.'

He sent Trevor a sad smile. 'Last thing I want, boy, is to finish my days in a home. I'd rather be dead.'

He turned his back and walked towards the door to let Trevor out.

Trevor came to his feet, glanced at the whisky bottle before he changed his mind and weighed the small torch in his hand. It would be such a waste of good whisky.

He followed the old boy to the door. 'In that case, let's see to it that you don't. I'm sure I can oblige.'

He brought the torch down on the old man's balding pate with a satisfying *crack*.

49

EIGHTY-SEVEN HOURS SINCE PHONE CALL

The resemblance was startling.

Lorraine's legs buckled under her, but she managed to right herself after a couple of staggering steps. She hitched Elijah up in her arms and hugged him tight to her chest.

'It's not Grandad, silly!' Sophia's giggling voice pierced through Lorraine's head.

It certainly wasn't.

Her dad was long dead. But this man held an uncanny resemblance to him. One whose genealogy couldn't be denied.

His face was narrower, leaner. But then, when her dad had been this man's age, perhaps his had looked the same.

What was more striking were the eyes. Not just the unusual colouring, and shape, but the intensity as they burned through her.

'Trevor?' She hadn't meant it as a question, but the name lilted upwards on her tongue regardless.

A spark of surprise lit those eyes.

'Yes. I've been waiting for ages.'

'I'm sorry? What do you mean?'

A slow smile of pleasure curved his lips.

'I've been waiting for you. I thought you were never going to pick up your daughter.'

50

THE DAY OF THE PHONE CALL

The curtains twitched and a slow smile spread across Trevor's face.

She knew he was there.

She had to know it was him. With the old car engine rattling away on her front drive.

He tapped his fingers on the steering wheel, deliberately not leaning forward to look up. She didn't need to see him.

He'd left hints. Tiny things no one else would notice. Moved an item here and there in her house so she thought she was going mad. Left the patio door open a crack while she was out shopping. Opened her bedroom window.

She had to know he'd come for her next. There was no way she'd believe Henry's death had been an accident. It had all been too coincidental. She'd found out. And now it was her turn.

She deserved it.

She deserved everything she had coming to her.

Maybe that's why she'd been pulling her curtains early before the evening light had faded. Maybe that's why she had more wine bottles piling up in her recycling than she'd had before. This was the kind of habit he took notice of when he staked out a place.

Trevor had been staking out his dad's on and off since the first time he met him after he'd been released from prison. Almost a year. He'd wanted to see. Wanted to know what a privileged lifestyle they'd lived without him.

Not so very privileged. It was an ordinary house. Nothing special. An ordinary three-bedroom house they'd brought one child up in. They'd hardly got rich off the death of his mum. Money that should have gone to him but seemed to have disappeared in a puff of vapour, without mention. He'd known nothing about it until he was in prison. Until it occurred to him there might be something. Funny what an education did for you.

He snapped on a pair of blue nitrile gloves, touched his finger to the interior light of the old car and switched it off so it didn't illuminate as he slipped out the door, barely letting it click behind him as he shut it.

She had to know he was coming for her. Would she hear his footsteps approaching up the drive? He hoped she did. Hoped she pissed herself at the mere thought of him being near.

He hesitated, then turned and tugged at the handle of the rear car door to leave it open a few inches.

There was no further movement from the window as he took a long moment to study it. She'd scarpered. Had she hidden? Run?

Next door was in complete blackness. At three o'clock in the morning, he hoped it would be. He'd waited out in the chill evening air, glad of the donkey jacket he considered an inheritance. It might be June, but the nights were still cold. A bit of an arctic blast from the jet stream.

He knew what Sandra would do, where she would go. Because she sure as hell wasn't going to come out the front door straight at him.

The woman was a coward. He realised that now. After all these years, he'd come to the conclusion that she'd been terrified of him as an eleven-year-old. So terrified, she'd never actually confronted him herself. Not from the moment she discovered his baby brother in his arms.

Now he was an adult, she had good reason to be even more petrified.

He'd taken the chance she wasn't going to phone the police. She didn't want them buzzing around, asking questions. Why would your stepson be stalking you? Aren't you the woman whose husband died last year? Nasty accident. Where were you at the time? Because he knew where she'd been. Knew what she'd done.

The clothes she'd dumped in her neighbour's bin were in the back of his car. He grinned as he remembered strategically placing the ruined slippers just under the bed, toes poking out. He would have loved to have been a fly on the wall when she'd found them yesterday.

Funny.

Who could she tell? No one. Because if she did, it would incriminate her. The police would know. Her precious daughter would know. That was the last thing Sandra would want.

He could almost guarantee she thought he was there to intimidate her, maybe blackmail her. But intimidation wasn't his gameplay this time. Blackmail, maybe. But he had a quicker, more efficient way of dealing with her. He wasn't a child any more, he knew what he was about. He wanted his share of what was left from his mum's house now his dad was dead. It didn't all belong to Sandra. It wasn't her right.

After all, his dad had taken all the money when Trevor's mum had died. It wasn't his. It should have been left to Trevor.

According to Aunt Caroline, it was supposed to be in a trust fund for him somewhere. She'd urged him to speak with his dad, but his dad hadn't mentioned it when he let him buy his own coffee, his own cake. He'd not mentioned it when he brushed him off and told him he could no longer see him.

Trevor ground his teeth as he waited and wondered. There'd been no evidence of any paperwork when he'd riffled through the drawers, the cupboards, even that little safe Sandra had at the back of the wardrobe, with nothing but their house deeds inside.

Had his dad spent all the money his mum had left to Trevor? On his precious family.

One child. A daughter.

What they wouldn't do for their one precious daughter.

How about they'd given it all to her so she could buy her own sweet little house that she had. Brand new it had been, too. Worth a fair amount. Nothing too lavish. Nice. Neat.

And she was on her own. No husband around.

Trevor had stalked her too.

After all, he wanted his money.

He'd stashed his own money, too. Before he'd been picked up by the police. Before he'd been sent to prison.

He'd not had the means nor the time to retrieve it yet. Too many check-ins with probation, although he'd been good enough to apply and have holiday approved.

He'd probably made a mistake asking to be housed in Shrewsbury, when it was The Wirral where he'd left his stash.

A mistake made in the naive hope that his dad would welcome him with open arms. Together with the distinct possibility that if he went for the money straight away, it would be a dead giveaway. He needed to plan properly. In a house-share, there was no way he'd risk bringing home that dosh. Not something an ex-con could open a new bank account for. He couldn't remember the exact amount. He'd had to act quickly. Twelve thousand pounds. Roughly. A lot of money ten years ago. Not so very much now.

That would have to wait.

Soon, though. All his plans were sliding nicely into place now. Everything coming together. A little more sorting out and he'd have it all.

Fate was dealing him a fair hand for once in his life.

He knocked on the front door.

Bang! Bang!

Two sharp raps. Short and threatening. Trevor smiled to himself as he surveyed the houses across the road. He could have let himself in, but he didn't know where she'd be.

All quiet in the street. Everyone safety tucked into their beds. A party down the other end had raved on, making the pavements throb with the sound of the bass beat. Thankfully, it had ended over an hour before. No chance of police being called out to that. It had been a risk he wasn't willing to take, which was why he'd left his move so late.

He'd made sure first as silence descended before he'd walked along the street and picked his car up from outside the party house, where it wouldn't have been noticed amongst all the other visiting cars. Then he'd driven it onto Sandra's driveway.

He didn't want to risk her screaming and waking the neighbourhood. Or even deciding it was worth her life to ring the police if she thought he was inside her house. Let her think he wanted her to come to the front door. And like a rat deserting a ship, he could guess the route she'd take.

Trevor paused before he entered the passageway that ran alongside the house, on the opposite side to the neighbour. He checked the curtains next door again. Not even a chink of light showed through.

Hopefully, the old bag would be fast asleep by now. More than likely. He'd watched as Sandra went in while the light faded and assumed she was putting the woman to bed for the night. Like she seemed to do every night. The quick routine. The hallway and landing lights went on, the living room lights off, followed by the bedroom and bathroom both illuminating. He'd watched as Sandra yanked what appeared to be heavy blackout curtains closed. Her body coming close to the window. Her face visible.

Fifteen minutes later, the lights would go out one by one as she retraced her steps through the house and then locked the door behind her, slipping the key in the pocket of her fleece jacket.

Each time she'd emerged, she'd looked like a rabbit in headlights, stepping over the small, dead hedgerow and dashing for her front door like there was something following her. Or someone watching. Then she'd perform a similar routine in her own house before all her lights went out.

She slept in the back bedroom. He knew that too. Had spent several hours looking over the hedge line of the back garden. Then down the slippery slope to the road.

She liked to peep out of the front bedroom curtains, though, before she went to bed. Like she was afraid of something.

Afraid of him.

With good reason.

If he'd just wanted to get his own back, be spiteful, he could have reported her to the authorities anonymously for what she did for the old girl next door. He might still, yet. Depending on how the whole scenario played out. After all, she wasn't a registered carer, but she spent a lot of time around there. Cleaning. He'd seen her hanging out clothes in the back garden. Heard the vacuum through the open back door. She brought the old girl groceries a couple of times a week. Took around what looked like meals.

He'd bet his sweet life she was taking a backhander from someone, even if it wasn't the old lady herself. Her bank statements had a regular payment in monthly. From the old girl. It was her name. Possibly one of her son's.

Probably some guilt-ridden member of the old girl's family who didn't want her living with them. They probably didn't want to stick her in a home either, so they lost all the money from the house they believed was their inheritance.

His lips gave a bitter twist as he waited one more minute.

Inheritance. Had his gone up in smoke? Or into the bricks and mortar of someone's house?

He'd soon find out.

Slick as a phantom, he slipped down the pitch-black passageway, his dark clothes and balaclava merging him into the darkness. He reached over the top of the gate, unbolted it knowing that she never bolted the bottom one. Was that because she had to lean down? She had a stiffness to her when she walked, a rigid gait as though she was in pain.

He hoped it was killing her.

He held his hand firm against the gate in case the light breeze caught it and banged it shut. He reached his gloved hands into his pocket and withdrew the small white cloth together with a bottle of clear fluid which he doused the cloth in.

She wasn't going to answer the front door, he'd bet his inheritance on it. But she might slip out of the back and over the low fence into the neighbour's garden to call for help.

If she didn't, he would have to go in after her. Drag her out from under her bed if need be. But he'd risk a moment, just to see.

He leaned against the back wall, his own body melting into the deep, dark shadows, obscured by the large household rubbish bin, placed as he'd expected. Exactly as it always was. Now he just had to wait.

Sandra whispered the patio doors open just enough for her to sidle out unobserved, or so she thought. The phone in her hand cast a bright pinprick of light to point her out to him.

Dressed in thick, fleecy pyjamas and sturdy grey moccasins she'd obviously had the foresight to slip on, then again, she was experienced in escaping in slippers. She raised her hand to her chest, looking one way and then the other.

He let her step past him before he slipped from the shadows, snaked his arm around her waist and yanked her body against his chest, pressing the cloth firmly over her nose and mouth.

Sandra's small body convulsed, those sturdy moccasins kicking him in the shins as he lifted her from the floor, surprised at how powerful she was.

Her scream vibrated against his palm until she drew in a desperate breath, her kicks getting weaker until her whole body went limp in his arms.

Breathless, he waited a long moment just to make sure. This wasn't his normal modus operandi. Kidnapping not one of his acquired skills. He made certain she was completely out before he swept her up, a lightweight, and threw her over his shoulder. He'd carried heavier than her in his time. Red had been a skinny thing, but he'd been a deadweight when Trevor had dragged him up the stairwell into their flat.

Keeping close to the wall, he hurried back along the passageway and hesitated at the entrance, scanning the street again before he made a dash towards his car. He pushed the cracked open back door wide with his knee and dumped her sagging body over his back seat. One hand flopped over and landed on the carpeted floor with a hard thud.

Closing the door as quietly as possible, he ran back through to the garden. His heart racing until he thought it might explode from his chest, he drew the small torch out of his pocket and scanned it across the ground, where he'd been sure he'd heard Sandra's phone clatter to the floor.

He picked it up and stepped inside the house. Lithe as a cat, he raced up the stairs on the tips of his training shoe toes so the woman next door never heard a sound.

He scanned the screen of Sandra's phone, irritated to see a crack from one corner diagonally across to the other side.

Had that been there before, or was it from when it had just hit the ground? It looked like a fresh break.

There was nothing he could do about it. He couldn't take it with him in case the daughter had one of those tracking devices on it. Sleek sophistication he was only just learning about. But he knew that. He'd watched plenty of TV inside and was aware of the ability of police to triangulate a phone too.

Not a risk he was willing to take if Sandra was reported missing.

If anyone bothered to report her missing. They might think she'd gone for a spa weekend. It seemed to be the craze with women these days.

He'd been away too long. Life had moved on like greased lightning while he'd been inside. He'd tried to keep up, but there was so much that was different.

Technology had come on leaps and bounds in the last ten years, but even before he served his time, there'd been some kind of tracking ability. Not as sophisticated as today, though.

Curious to know if she'd called the police, he touched the screen, irritated when the face recognition declined, and the keypad appeared requiring him to enter a code. He didn't have the code.

He flipped the cover over the screen and placed it next to her bedside table with a quick scan around the room. He checked that everything was perfect. As though she had just got up, walked out and forgotten to take her phone.

About to step out of the bedroom, he turned and made his way back to the bed. With one finger, he flipped the phone off the table and watched as it clattered between that and the bed to land with a dull thud on the carpet. He hitched the covers up and smoothed out the duvet as he imagined Sandra would, once she got out of bed in the morning. She was that kind of person. He remembered even when she'd just given birth, she used to do that. Anytime he'd prowled through recently, the place had always been immaculate.

He stepped back, a whisper of a smile on his lips. The phone couldn't be seen from where he stood. Anyone looking for it would have to get down on all fours and peer under the bed.

He made his way to the front bedroom, the one she'd spied out of, and gave it a cursory glance, before he tiptoed back down the stairs through the living room and paused.

He could afford a moment longer.

Curiosity got the better of him and he pulled open the kitchen drawer full of crap that he'd searched all those months ago. The only place in the house that wasn't tidy.

Surprised the little tin was still there, still stuffed with money. For some reason, he'd believed the money had been his dad's, but it appeared Sandra was the hoarder.

More than twice as thick as the last time he'd looked, the wad of money barely fitted in the small tin. Stupid woman.

Maybe she thought he hadn't touched it before. Maybe she didn't realise he knew about it. He knew everything. Almost.

As he withdrew it, it sprang open, unfolding in his hand. He didn't have time to count it, but he'd estimate in the region of five hundred quid this time. He pulled off a few notes. Contemplated them. Then he folded them, tucked them neatly back into the tin and placed it back in the drawer before stuffing the huge roll of notes into the deep front pocket of his jeans.

After all, who else would know how much she kept in there?

Her daughter? Maybe. Maybe not. If she even checked.

He pulled the patio doors closed behind him using the spare key he'd discovered under the birdbath near the back door the first time he'd entered their house. He'd used it numerous times. He thought she might have moved it after he'd placed her slippers under her bed, but maybe she never knew Henry hid it there.

This time, he replaced it where he'd found it and then disappeared along the passageway like a wraith.

He glanced up, caught the pale face of the woman next door up at her bedroom window, the curtains tight around her, watching as he reversed out of the drive.

Stupid old bag.

It wasn't a problem.

He wouldn't be returning.

51

EIGHTY-SEVEN HOURS SINCE PHONE CALL

Lorraine wasn't sure she could endure any more shocks. She swayed on her feet as the man took a step towards her, concern wreathing his face as it evidently occurred to him she was surprised to see him.

'Are you okay? I'm sorry. I've given you a fright.'

He reached out a hand and she stepped away. With a shake of her head, she found she was barely able to speak.

'You look like Grandad. Only not so wrinkly.' Sophia pranced towards him, and Lorraine hesitated, unable to decide whether to drag her daughter back, instinct telling her something wasn't right.

From the information she'd learned about him, she was torn.

He stepped forward. 'Hi, yes, I'm Trevor. Trevor Leivesley. I'm your half-brother.' His brow crinkled at her silence and an unsure smile curved his lips as he dipped his head. 'I assume you know about me, right? Dad must have told you.' His accent was not dissimilar to her dad's, only heavily laden with the Irish element of Scouse and more of a twang at the ends of his words, like bullet points.

Frozen to the spot, even her lips felt numb. What did she tell him? What could she say? Yes, she knew about him but literally only just. She was still in shock. 'Umm.'

Elijah became a lead weight in her weakened arms, and she moved towards the car, desperate to put him down. 'Excuse me. I need to...'

Trevor stepped to one side, and then reached out as she touched the key fob and unlocked the car. With unexpected politeness, he opened the rear door for her and stepped back to allow her plenty of room to move past and place Elijah in his seat.

Lorraine let out a sigh as she relieved herself of her son's weight. She strapped him in, handed him a bundle of teething rings and then backed out of the car.

'Why do you look like Grandad?' Sophia piped up again, having been ignored by both adults the first time. 'I thought he'd come down from heaven, but his skin was all smooth again.'

Trevor broke into a smile so familiar, Lorraine's muscles weakened. She dipped her head. 'Sophia, hop into the car, lovely.'

'But Mummy...'

'Sophia...' She kept her voice level. 'Hop in and show Elijah your books while I have a chat with this gentleman.'

Sophia scrambled onto her booster cushion on the back seat, her head twisted at such an angle to stare at the man through the opposite window so Lorraine thought if that was her, she'd have a crick in her neck.

Lorraine closed the door with a soft clunk and then turned and leaned against her car, folding her arms over her chest as Trevor walked around to the same side.

She resisted the urge to move back, fascinated by every angle of the man's face, the colour of his eyes.

He tucked his hands in the pockets of a donkey jacket so familiar, she bit her tongue to stop herself from mentioning it as he ducked to bring his face closer to hers. 'I'm really sorry, obviously I gave you a bit of a fright.'

She didn't move, didn't acknowledge, just gave a quiet hum of agreement in the back of her throat. A bit of a fright was an understatement. He'd scared the living crap out of her. She wasn't sure if she'd peed herself.

'I've been looking for your mum. I've been around a number of times to her house, but there's no one home.'

His shoulders moved in a self-conscious shrug, unfamiliar enough that it allowed her to move past his strong resemblance to her dad.

She almost replied *haven't we all*.

'Why?' she asked instead.

The sharp flinch was there and then gone before she could quite identify it, but it had been there.

Again, the shrug. 'Before my... before our dad died, I was in contact with him. We'd met up several times.'

Lorraine shook her head, her lips tightening in denial. 'That can't be true. He would have said. I would have known.'

His eyes bored into her. 'How much do you know about me?'

She chewed on her bottom lip as she studied him and then shook her head again. 'I had no idea you even existed until yesterday.'

This time the shock was tangible and genuine.

'What?' The single word croaked out of him, and she wondered if he felt as weak limbed as she did.

She pushed away from the car and came closer to him, trepidation evaporating. 'I only found out about you yesterday. I had no idea you existed up until then. I had no inkling that my dad had previously been married. Why would I? It was nothing to do with me.'

She found herself making excuses to this stranger for her

parents' lies. 'It was long before I was born. It shouldn't impact on me. Certainly not at the age of thirty.'

She placed her hand on her chest. 'I was this many years old when I found out I had a half-brother and I'm not sure how I feel about it.' Mostly because she had far more pressing things on her mind than a man she'd never met, nor really cared to.

Trevor wiped shaky fingers across his jawline in a mannerism similar to her dad's when he'd been asked by her mum to deal with teenage daughter problems years ago. Getting the job done, despite nerves jangling.

'Wow. That's incredible. Unbelievable.' A deep vertical crease appeared between his eyes. 'I'm sorry. It must have come as a real shock.'

'It did. It has.' She nodded. 'It is.'

Trevor wrapped his arms around himself, hunching his shoulders up as he glanced at the darkening sky full of bruised clouds from which a light drizzle had started to fall. Not exactly June weather.

'Look, our kid, you want to go and grab a coffee?'

Our kid. She wasn't his kid. Was that just a term people from Liverpool used? Too familiar for her liking. As though they had a bond. But they didn't.

Lorraine watched him, her eyes narrowed as she tried to decide whether or not she could trust him. Perhaps she should call the police and let them deal with him.

Call them about what, though? That he'd approached her in the street where he'd been waiting for her? That he'd been polite and asked her to talk about things over a cup of coffee? That like her, he wanted to know where her mum was?

'I'm so scared, but mostly for you and the children. Because once I'm gone, you'll be next.'

She sucked in her breath. It was ridiculous. He couldn't have done anything to her mum. After all, why would he be looking for her mum if he already knew what had happened to her?

He dropped his hands to his side. 'Look, there's a Starbucks along the street. How about there? Somewhere you'll feel secure, where there's lots of people and plenty of light. After all, you don't know me from Adam.'

'Or Tom, Dick or Trevor.'

But there was no mistaking whose son he was. He was definitely her dad's.

He gave a reluctant grin. 'You can follow me, or I can follow you, but let's get in out of this rain, looks like a bloody storm brewing. I'll buy you and the kids a coffee.'

Lorraine raised an eyebrow. Evidently the man wasn't accustomed to the ways of children.

Unsure why she even agreed, except he sounded reasonable, Lorraine found herself nodding.

'There's actually a small independent café, Just Joe's, further up from that. It may be easier.' She thought of the tight squeeze in the tiny Starbucks outlet. More of a grab and go place than sit and chat, unlike their bigger outlets. 'They do a small hot chocolate for children there. Sophia will love that. Elijah has a bottle, we can warm up his milk there.' She wasn't about to feed her baby herself in front of a complete stranger. Elijah was just crossing over to bottled milk in any case. She'd be returning to work in a couple of weeks' time. She couldn't afford to stay off any longer. It wasn't easy to survive on Maternity Allowance.

Lorraine waited for Trevor to walk away down the street before she opened her own car door.

She turned on the engine and waited while the demister did its job and the windscreen wipers swiped away the rain so she could watch him slide inside his own ancient-looking car.

'Mummy, who is that man?'

Lorraine met her daughter's eyes in the rear-view mirror as she tilted it down. 'He's related to us.'

'How?'

Lorraine paused. How the hell was she supposed to explain this? 'He's Grandad's son.'

It seemed to satisfy Sophia as Lorraine put the car in drive and pulled away from the kerb to follow Trevor.

'Mummy, how did he know where to find us?'

Lorraine met Sophia's inquisitive gaze once more and suppressed a shiver.

Sophia was right.

How had he known where to find them?

52

THREE DAYS EARLIER

He'd expected the old man to be dead by the time he got back to the narrowboat. The cosh with the torch to the back of his head was enough to have killed an elephant.

Trevor wasn't the type to beat the living crap out of a victim. He'd never had the stomach for it, but he had gladly left him there to slip away quietly. Best way for it. He didn't want blood spatter all over the walls for the police to find if they happened to come aboard.

The wooden decking groaned under the combined weight of Trevor and Sandra as he pushed through into the cockpit area. Despite being small and delicate, her deadweight in his arms made him puff out small bursts of breath after he'd carried her from his car, through the woods and along the towpath.

It wasn't like carrying a couple of carrier bags from the local supermarket. He'd had to put her down once. When he'd needed to again, he'd just leaned against the trunk of a tree for a couple of minutes. It was easier than hefting her back up again from the ground.

Sandra's dad lay stretched out along the length of the bunk seat, his bony limbs poking out of his clothes at odd angles.

Trevor would have thrown him overboard but for the chaos it would cause when the body was found further downstream. Then there'd be questions asked. The police would be all over the place like bees around pollen, and he'd be the focus of them, especially with his prison record.

Or he'd have to vacate quickly. He didn't want that. He needed time. Time to finish off everything he had planned.

The plan was still a bit sketchy, but he was getting there. One step at a time.

He'd played the good boy so far, turning up at every appointment with his probation officer, but there might come a time when he needed to sever all ties and find himself a new identity. Currently, there was no rush.

He was comfortable with that thought.

It had been so long since he'd been on the street, he no longer knew anyone in that trade. It's not like they kept in contact once one of them got caught. Not unless they served time in the same prison. He'd not known anyone. The guys he'd met while he was in were people he no longer wanted to be associated with. Even if they weren't allowed to under the probation regulations, he'd been happy to leave them behind.

Most of them weren't like him. *They* were downright evil.

He snorted. The irony of it. But he wasn't evil. It wasn't his fault, but circumstances.

He walked through the galley kitchen into the small box room and flopped Sandra's inert body onto the berth. He coughed as a grey cloud of dust engulfed her. 'Dirty old sod.' Her dad had evidently not washed the bedding in years. The dull brown of the material probably wasn't the pattern, but actual dirt.

He watched her for a long moment, the light throb of the pulse at the base of her throat indicating she was still alive. Just about.

He leaned in to listen for signs of breathing, then rested his hand on her heart.

Perhaps he'd given her too much. He'd completely doused the cloth and held it over her face for some time after she'd screamed before sticking her in the back of the car.

When he'd pulled over, oil light flashing to indicate the greedy guzzler of the car had drunk it all again, he'd drizzled more chloroform on a new cloth and left it over her mouth and nose the rest of the way in case she came awake while he was driving.

He wouldn't have put it past her to have attacked him.

Now he regretted it as he watched the shallow rise and fall of her chest slow.

He stepped back and rubbed chilled fingers over his forehead as he mulled over what to do next.

Bloody hell. What was he supposed to do? She was the only one who could possibly know what had happened to the money.

His money.

His inheritance.

He'd offed his dad too early. He should have made sure he knew all there was to know before he'd got rid of him. It wasn't his fault. He'd lost his mind, and his temper. It had flashed hot and he'd reacted without thinking the whole plan through.

He wandered through to the galley and stared down at the old boy. Still breathing.

How disappointing. Ironic. The one he wanted dead was still alive, and the one he wanted alive was almost dead.

Trevor leaned down, heaved the skeletal old man over his shoulder and kicked open the door to the box room again. There was no point having a body in each room. He needed to give the place a quick clean so at least he didn't catch anything.

'Say hello to your daddy, Stepmother, dear.'

They might as well be together for their last few breaths.

He dumped the bony frame on the bed and watched as another puff of dust filled the room.

He squinted at the two bodies, side by side.

As the dust cleared, so did his mind.

Of course. There was one other option.

He'd watched her at his dad's funeral from the back of a crowded crematorium. Seemed his dad had been a relatively popular man. Unless they were all his workmates, or car enthusiasts. It appeared to be predominantly men. Trevor had fitted in comfortably, slipping away before his aunt spotted him.

Lorraine had rocked one of those baby car seats. Her son must have only been a few days old. A son. His dad had said she was expecting a boy. Boys in their family were fated.

So, maybe there was someone else who knew. Someone who could track down the paperwork and lead him to the money that was his right.

His darling little sister.

Half-sister, to be precise.

53

EIGHTY-EIGHT AND A HALF HOURS SINCE PHONE CALL

Lorraine lowered her head into her hands, the dizziness of exhaustion taking hold.

She'd barely finished her decaffeinated flat white coffee before her eyelids started to droop.

Her emotions were being ripped apart by the man in front of her. The tragedy of his story, the life he told her he'd led. How had he managed to survive and still come through the other side undamaged?

Her aunt was right. It was all heart-breaking and her dad had been trying to help him settle into his new life, according to Trevor.

'Are you all right?'

She leaned back on the creaky chair, her hand on Elijah's changing bag, and glanced at her phone. They'd been there over an hour and half and the kids were getting fidgety. Sophia had started to run around, attracting slightly annoyed expressions from a table of four older women.

As though none of them had ever had children who charged around with laughter in their hearts. Perhaps they should have gone to McDonald's instead, but it was so much further away from home. A home she really needed to get back to.

'I'm so sorry. I'm completely exhausted. Quite honestly, I don't know what I'm doing with myself. I'm worried sick about my mum.'

'And you've been to the police?'

She nodded.

'Muuum.' Sophia charged towards her, a wild grin on her face. A child Lorraine recognised as overtired.

Lorraine came to her feet, scraping her chair back. 'I've got to go. Sorry.' She sent Trevor a weak smile. He'd been generous enough to buy the kids food, a little pot of chopped fruit for Elijah. She'd picked out the grapes and cut them in half and then taken a jar of baby food from her bag. Fruit based again, but it wouldn't do him any harm. He needed something and it would see him through until the morning. He'd eaten well at Aunt Caroline's.

Still ravenous, it appeared, he'd stuffed it down while Lorraine ate one-handedly the chicken Caesar salad she'd decided on. Perhaps healthier than she'd had in the previous couple of days.

The offer had been for coffee and cake, but he'd freely dipped his hand into his pocket bringing out a roll of notes and bought them a proper tea when she'd mentioned the time. At least she didn't have to cook when she got back home. Just a shortened bedtime routine and then she could sit with a glass of wine and empty her mind completely. For the sake of her own sanity. Maybe call the police officer to catch up. See if there was any progress.

Disappointment flickered through his eyes, but she needed to go. Sophia was about to go from frenzied to ballistic, and Lorraine owed this man nothing. Not her time, nor the kids' welfare.

'I need to get the kids to bed.'

'Oh. Okay. Sorry, Lorraine. I never gave it a thought. I'm used to adult company.'

She gathered up her belongings and took Elijah from the high

The Stepson

chair. 'Sophia, time to go.' Sophia charged from the end of the café and slithered onto her bottom to slide the last few paces to her mum's feet.

With a self-conscious glance at the other women, Lorraine hitched Elijah onto her hip and bent down to whisper at her daughter. 'Get up. You'll have your skirt filthy.' Not that it mattered. She'd be putting a load of washing in once the kids were in bed.

Sophia came to her feet and gave an over-exaggerated dust-off of her skirt and then sent the four women a bright smile and a happy wave as she skipped towards the door.

As she finished putting the children in the car, Lorraine backed out and tipped her head towards them. 'Sorry, if they get overtired, I'll be up all night trying to get them off to sleep.'

She made her way around to the driver's side and opened her door. 'It was…' What was it? Surreal? '…nice to meet you, but I have to go.'

'I feel like I've only been with you five minutes. The time's flown past.'

'It has,' she agreed.

'Look. What if I follow you home, and once the kids are off to bed, we can have a bit longer to chat?'

A nervous energy dashed over her. She didn't know this man. This stranger.

Her mum had been terrified.

Had she been more terrified, though, that once Lorraine met him, she would like him? Like her dad had?

From what Aunt Caroline had told her, her mum despised him.

But he was blood.

Not her mum's, but her dad's.

Aunt Caroline had trusted him.

Why would he be looking for her mum, if he already knew where she was?

Undecided, she stood, her muscles trembling with exhaustion.

At her hesitation, he shrugged. 'I feel like I was just getting to know you. Like, I could help you find your mum.'

She rubbed her brow. Her mind was a complete mess.

What he said wasn't unreasonable. At least she'd have someone to talk it through with. She could let the police know she'd found him. Or he'd found her.

Something Sophia mentioned earlier popped into her head. 'How did you know where Sophia went to school?'

Surprise lit his unusual eyes, but he barely hesitated. 'I've been a couple of times with our dad when he was picking her up from nursery.' He nodded towards the darkened car windows. 'When you were pregnant with Elijah. I guessed she'd carried on into the juniors at the same school. A lucky guess.'

He gave her a regretful smile. 'I never went in with him. Left him at the door. It didn't seem fair to meet her when I hadn't even met you. Bad manners.' He shrugged. 'Dad was going to arrange it. He was dead chuffed to have me back in his life, after all these years, but...' His mouth twisted. 'He was trying to persuade Sandra. Said she was coming around to the idea.'

Lorraine sighed. Really. If her mum had been coming around to the idea, when the hell had they planned to tell Lorraine?

Trevor bowed his head and rubbed the back of his neck. 'The day he died...' He raised his head and stared straight into her eyes. 'He was on his way to meet me. Your mum was supposed to be with him. I've no idea what happened, why she wasn't in the car with him. Lucky for her that apparently she wasn't.'

'Why haven't you contacted us? Since... you know, Dad's accident?'

He wiped a hand over a face strained with sorrow. 'I couldn't face her. Your mum. I knew she'd blame me again. Wrong place, wrong time. I've been having counselling to get through my own issues with him dying before I'd managed to resolve things. You can't imagine what it's like to find someone, only to lose them again.'

Lorraine choked back a sob.

What a mess. There was a slow burn of anger building. Not against Trevor, but the whole situation. Her mum. Her dad. For lying to her and leaving her exposed. Emotionally vulnerable. Why would her mum just take off like that? Disappear so she didn't have to face the situation. Just like she had all those years ago.

Her dad would never have brought Trevor to Sophia's school if he hadn't trusted him. Would never have exposed her daughter to his son unless he'd been sure. Comfortable. Ready to move on.

She needed to move on. Home. Now.

'Maybe tomorrow.'

This time it wasn't just his eyes, but his whole face fell. With barely a beat, he responded. 'Can't. I've gorra job in the city. I'll be leaving in the morning to move into my new flat so I can settle in before I start on Monday. I'm not going to be able to get back for weeks.' Regret shimmered in his eyes as he hunched his shoulders, his head giving a slow bob. 'I thought we'd have more time, but with you being late...'

Guilt nudged at her conscience. He wanted to talk about her dad. Their dad. He needed to know things about him. She'd had a lifetime with the man, but Trevor had nothing from the age of eleven and just when he'd had the chance of getting to know him, their dad had been killed.

Surely she owed him this much. A short amount of time and then she'd probably not see him again. Certainly not for a while.

There was nothing further she could do about her mum, just sit and wait for the police to contact her. Other than that, have a glass of wine and sit on her own while the kids were asleep upstairs. Worry.

'I need to get Sophia and Elijah to bed.' Her argument sounded weak to her own ears.

'I've gorra go and grab some stuff from Tesco. What if you give me your address and I'll nip around after. Is an hour enough to get them off?'

She hesitated, saw the concern.

He'd been meeting up with their dad. Making arrangements to meet her too. If Dad trusted him, surely she could. Couldn't she?

With a reluctant nod, Lorraine reeled off her address and watched Trevor tap it into his phone.

'Don't knock when you arrive. It'll wake the kids. I'll pop my car in the garage, if you want to park on the drive. There's never any street parking left at this time of the evening.' Mainly because most newbuilds only had one garage or a parking space, but most families had two or even three cars each. 'You don't want to get into a spat with one of my neighbours.'

'It wouldn't be an issue.' He grinned, the sorrow dropping from him as he tucked his phone into his jacket pocket and started towards his car at the other end of the car park. 'See you in an hour.'

54

NINETY-ONE HOURS SINCE PHONE CALL

By the time he arrived, Lorraine had already poured herself a drink, regretting the rash decision to let him call around. All she really wanted to do was go to bed. It might only be 7.30 p.m., but she was exhausted.

She took a sip and let him in the front door, her index finger up to her lips. 'Elijah is out like a light.' The warm bath she'd given them both had seen to that. Her guarantee to relax her little boy. 'Sophia is asleep, but if she hears you, she'll want to come down and investigate.'

'No worries.'

He stepped inside, shrugged out of his coat and hung it over the newel post at the bottom of the stairs as the warmth in the house probably hit him.

Chilled through when she arrived home, she'd stabbed the heating on for an hour so they were all warm for bath and bedtime in the hope it would make them sleepy. Regretting putting heating on at this time of the year, she'd felt the need to ward off the damp. The radiators still ticked as the heat dissipated from them. It had certainly had that effect on her. She'd have to open her bedroom window when she went to bed. A waste of heating she was kidding herself she could afford.

The lights in the living room gave off a warm glow and Lorraine made for the settee, curling up against the arm and hugging a cushion to her stomach. 'Sit down. Oh, I've not offered you a drink.' She indicated her wine. 'Can I get you one?'

He shook his head. 'I don't drink. Not these days.'

She nodded her understanding of why he might not drink, although in reality she had no idea. She knew relatively little about him. Only what her aunt had told her and what he had imparted in the last hour.

'What about tea, coffee?'

'I'm sloshing.' He grinned as he lowered himself to the other end of the settee instead of sitting on the single armchair. 'I've had enough coffee to last me a week.' He leaned back, by all accounts at home. More relaxed than she'd imagined. More relaxed than she was.

Lorraine picked up her wine glass, took a sip and said the first thing that came into her head to fill the silence. 'How come my dad never told me anything about you?'

Trevor spread his hands in a helpless shrug. 'You know most of what happened with us. I won't bad-mouth your mum, Lorraine. She's your mum. Honestly, you're nuttin' like her. You're just like our dad.'

She warmed at the flattery and cradled the glass between her hands. Truth be told, she looked very much like her mum, barely resembled her dad at all, but she suspected she had his more relaxed attitude. Under normal circumstances, she never became stressed or overwrought. But these were not normal circumstances.

'But when he started seeing you...'

'When I got out of prison?'

'Yes.'

She thought he'd be uncomfortable talking about being inside, but it didn't appear to concern him. Almost as though he was proud. It was his life, after all. He was quite open about it from what he'd told her in the café.

He leaned forward to bring himself closer to her. 'He didn't want to upset your mum.'

She understood that.

'She would have hit the roof if she'd known he was seeing me at first.'

'But why not tell me? I'm an adult. I could have taken it.'

A regretful smile tugged at his lips. 'I wanted you to know. Dad said your mum was coming around to the idea. That he thought it was cruel to deprive both of us of the knowledge we existed. That day he was going to bring her to meet me…'

A shudder ran through her, and Lorraine leaned forwards to rest her elbows on her knees and lowered her head. 'Oh, God. She said they'd had a fight. A huge argument. She blamed herself for his accident.'

'Ahh, no. Do you think they'd been fighting over me?'

She raised her head. She couldn't say. Her mum and dad rarely argued about anything. 'It would make sense.'

'I was so freakin' excited that day. I thought I was going to get to meet her. Then you. I couldn't believe it when I discovered I had a kid sister. One I'd known nuttin' about until I met with Dad.'

She goggled at him. 'What?'

'I only found out when I met him last year. He wouldn't come to prison to visit me, I understood that, but we met for the first time…' He paused, choked on his emotion. He wiped eyes filled with tears and looked away as though it was too much to meet her gaze.

'When we met for the first time, he told me I had a little sister.' He sniffed and looked at her from under his brows. 'I couldn't believe it. Knocked me on my arse.'

'How come Aunt Caroline never told you?'

'She said it wasn't her story to tell. That your mum and our dad's lives were private unless they wanted to let me know.' He lowered his head. Sadness weighed him down. 'It's been a bit shit if the truth be told. I lost both my mum and dad when I was eleven.'

His direct gaze hit her. 'Now, I've lost my dad again, just when I found him. I have nuttin'. Nuttin' but you and your kids.'

She tried not to show her discomfort, but suspected he saw her squirm. Honesty was probably best, even if she risked insulting him. She'd rather have it out there right at the beginning. 'I'm not sure I'm ready to take on a big brother, Trevor. I'm really sorry.'

She wondered how he would take rejection, but he simply nodded.

'It's okay. I know. I don't know how to be a big brother. I'll be out of your life tomorrow in any case, but I'd like to think we can keep in touch. Maybe keep in contact, so I know I have family out here.'

Relieved, she smiled. 'I'd like that.' She drained the rest of her glass and sat back, more relaxed from the wine than his company.

'It's a nice house you have here. Did your mum and dad help you start out?'

She cast him a quick glance, but his expression was guileless. A touch insulted, as she always was when people asked, she withheld the whole truth. 'No. I managed to buy it on one of those schemes.'

'What scheme?'

'Help to Buy. It's a government scheme, don't ask. Basically, there's a housing provider who part owns the house. In our case 20 per cent. Then me and Simon the skunk bought the provider out

The Stepson

and the mortgage is in both our names – presently. Until everything's finalised with the divorce. The house was in my name, though, when I met him. I put the full deposit down, out of my own savings.' That and the money her mum and dad had contributed, but she saw no reason to tell him that at this point. She felt the regret of it all grind at her. 'I should have kept it in my name, but you should be able to have faith in someone you love... or think you love.'

His lips twisted. 'I wouldn't know. I've always been let down by those I've loved.'

Horrified, Lorraine shuffled around and hugged the cushion closer, thinking that if he wasn't there, she might have had a second glass of wine. 'I'm so sorry.'

'Aww, Lorraine mate, I didn't mean to sound like a pity-party. Take no notice.'

She let out an embarrassed laugh, finding it funny that he called her mate. She might just get that glass of wine anyhow.

As she came to her feet, he got to his and rubbed his hands on his jeans in a self-conscious way that stirred that sense of pity in her again. 'I'd better get off and let you get to bed.'

'Oh. Yes.' She glanced at the time. He'd been there for almost two hours. 'Way past my bedtime. I want to call the police back first thing in the morning. Give them an update. Put things straight, if that's okay with you.' She repressed the yawn and let out a small laugh. 'Gosh, I'm sorry.'

'No worries.' He stepped towards the doorway. 'Any chance I can use your loo? I could do with a whizz before I set out. I might not make it home.'

She reeled a little at his openness and then pointed up the stairs. 'Sorry, my downstairs one isn't useable. I was halfway through decorating when my mum went missing. All the paint tins and ladders are in there. You'll have to use the bathroom upstairs.

Quiet as a mouse,' she prompted as though she was talking to Sophia.

He grinned as if he got the joke and took the stairs two at a time.

Silent as a mouse.

55

NINETY-THREE HOURS SINCE PHONE CALL

Trevor edged the door to the nursery open once he'd been to the bathroom and slipped inside.

Silent as a fucking mouse, he approached the cot and stared down at the baby boy. A soft smile curved his lips as he leaned over to get a closer look.

He trailed a gentle finger over the boy's downy cheek, allowing himself an even wider smile. 'Sleep tight, little one,' he whispered.

As he straightened, he glanced at the baby cam above the cot. Keeping his smile in place, he edged back out of the nursery and pulled the door closed behind him.

With his back to it, his eyes turned to flint and the smile dropped from his face.

It was different these days, since he'd come out of prison. Everywhere, there was a camera. Wherever you turned, someone was watching you.

Still, he could bide his time. After all, Lorraine, his half-sister, had fallen hook, line and sinker for his act. What a stupid, naive woman. Any respect he might have had skidded away. Not street savvy in any way. She'd fallen for every little lie he'd made up.

Even trusted him upstairs with her precious children. The baby.

That little monster demanded far too much attention from his mum. Attention Trevor craved.

Just like he'd craved attention from his dad all his life and never got it. First because his mum had demanded it, then his stepmum with that brat of a baby who never stopped crying from morning all the way through the night.

Trevor couldn't even recall his name. He was that insignificant.

Well, they were all gone now. Every one of them.

Except Lorraine and her kids.

His bloodline.

Trevor took four steps down the stairs before he glanced back at the door across the landing at his eye level. He gave a slow blink.

Sophia was safe. For now. Off at school most of the day, from what her mum said when she was making excuses for her brattish behaviour in the café, she was exhausted enough by the time she came home to just want food, bath and bed. No trouble at all.

Not much of a demand on Lorraine's time. Hopefully. For her sake.

But Elijah. He was too much like trouble. Like the baby before Lorraine.

Too time consuming.

It hadn't taken much to dispose of him, the baby before. Just a soft pillow to the face after he'd removed him from Sandra's bed when she'd fallen asleep after feeding him. Dad had already slipped off to work, popping his head around Trevor's door before he went to let him know Sandra was feeding the baby and to keep quiet.

'Take care of my two angels, won't you, son.'

His angels.

Fury boiled now even as it had then. But he was an adult. He had control over his temper these days.

He'd had no control then.

He'd never intended to murder him. That little baby. It was an accident.

All he wanted to do was hold him, which Sandra hadn't allowed. Hadn't let him touch his own little brother. He'd not even been allowed in his nursery.

He belonged to him, just as much as he did Sandra and his dad. He was his little half-brother. Trevor had a right to hold him.

At first the baby had been silent, a quiet snuffle, a gentle squeak as he removed him from where he slept beside Sandra and took him to the nursery.

But as Trevor stood for over an hour with the baby cradled in his arms, getting steadily heavier, he knew he had to put him down. He'd not wanted to take him back in case Sandra woke up. She'd have a hissy fit and tell his dad when he got home.

Instead, Trevor laid the baby in the cot.

As he took his arms away and the baby rolled, he let out a whimper, then a wail, so Trevor panicked.

He'd not even pressed down on the pillow, just placed it on the baby's face to stop the sounds, until his chest had stopped rising and falling.

Panic had ripped through him when he realised what he'd done. He'd swept the baby out of the cot and into his arms and was just about to run through to Sandra, regret in his heart, when she came through the door.

And she knew.

He knew, she knew.

His heart had tremored for days, and he'd slipped back into his catatonic state. Well, he'd chosen not to speak, but that's what they'd called it.

Of course, not much had been known about SIDS back then. So much more was known now. He'd studied it while he was in prison. Sudden Infant Death Syndrome. Hundreds of women had been blamed for the death of their babies, and then the tide had turned when experts had realised that placing a baby to sleep on its front put them at risk. Combined with the mother smoking, it could be a lethal combination.

He'd never get away with it these days. Not in the same way. Besides, Elijah was older. Much less likely to simply stop breathing for no reason at his age. He was strong and robust. It would be much harder to deal with.

He'd have to think it through carefully. After all, that's why he'd taken science while he was in prison and all those online courses that told you things.

Very handy.

'Trevor?'

He turned at the sound of Lorraine's soft voice.

'Coming. Couldn't resist checking on my nephew.'

The smile she gave him lit up the dark hallway as he took the stairs down to stand at her side.

He touched her arm as he reached the bottom step. A move designed to put her at ease. Nothing intimate, or overtly familiar. Simple. Friendly. Calculated.

'It feels like I've come home.'

She gave him a sad smile. 'How sad that you've never really had one.'

He shrugged his coat on and smiled back as she opened the door to let him out. With a wink, he stepped outside and turned to her. 'You never know what the future might bring.'

* * *

Lorraine wrapped her arms around herself as he backed his car out of the drive while she stood on the doorstep. The roaring sound of his cranky exhaust enough to draw complaints from neighbours as he drove off. Luckily it wasn't the middle of the night. Only 9.30.

The warm evocative smell that wafted from Trevor's coat as he'd hitched it on brought back memories of her dad and she held back a sob.

She stepped back inside, about to close the door when something caught her attention.

Light from the hall cast a long finger, splitting apart the darkness and illuminating something on the ground.

She stepped out onto the rain-wet drive in her carpet slippers and hunkered down in front of the black circle where Trevor had parked his car. She dipped her finger in it and sniffed.

Oil. Exactly the same as she'd discovered on her mum's drive the day she'd disappeared.

She turned her head in the direction of Trevor's departing taillights.

Her throat turned to dust.

56

ONE HUNDRED AND FIVE HOURS SINCE PHONE CALL

'Aunt Caroline?'

'Lorraine?'

'Yeah. Hi.' She spoke up as the phone connection between them crackled and fizzed.

'Hi.'

'Remember you said you'd happily babysit Elijah any time I needed it?'

An awkward silence was broken only by more soft crackle of static on the line.

'I think I said if you lived closer, then I could...'

'Yeah. That.'

Another beat of silence.

Lorraine scrunched her face up and held her breath as her fingers tightened on the steering wheel.

'But you don't live closer and it's a long way for me to drive.' Aunt Caroline's voice was slow and clear as though she was spelling it out.

Considering she was a virtual stranger, Lorraine appreciated that. This was different. This was urgent and Lorraine wasn't about to let go of it.

'I don't need you to come to me, you see, I have to come over there to check something out.'

'To do with your mum?'

'Yes.'

'She's still not turned up?'

'No.'

'You must be worried sick.'

'To put it mildly.'

'Which is why you want me to babysit Elijah?'

'Which is why I really need you to babysit Elijah and Sophia.'

'Oh.' The shock in the other woman's voice gave Lorraine pause. 'I know it's a big ask.'

'It's a very big ask. Sophia hasn't even met me.'

'I know, I know, but I've prepared her.'

'Prepared her?'

'Yes. I've told her you're my aunty and what a nice lady you are.'

'You have?'

'Yes. And about the dog. Ghost. I've told her about Ghost.' All of it was true. 'Sophia is very easy. Just give her a book and let her be with Ghost. Although the weather's lovely, today. It looks like it's made a turn for the better. Summer will soon be here.' She could hear the rambling in her own voice but struggled to stop. 'Perhaps she could play in your garden?'

'Err...' She sensed the woman wavering, looking for a way out. 'When are you coming over?'

'I'll be there in twenty minutes.'

The stunned silence this time hung heavy on the air. 'Today? You're coming now?'

'Yes. I'll see you shortly.'

This time, as the crackle burst in, she touched her finger to the screen on the car dashboard and pressed the call-end button before Caroline could conjure up an excuse why she couldn't help out.

If she really didn't want to, she'd call straight back, wouldn't she?

Guilt-riddled, Lorraine took a quick look at the kids in the back of the car. Did she trust this woman with them?

Well, who the hell else did she have to rely on?

She needed to get this done.

She'd meant to leave another message on Sergeant Willingham's phone this morning to let her know she was off to her aunt's just in case they tried to contact her, but it had gone to voicemail to say the sergeant wouldn't be back in until Sunday night.

That gave Lorraine time if she needed to check out her own theories.

After all, by all accounts her mum had done it before, why wouldn't she do it now? When she felt under threat from Trevor, why wouldn't she take off back to where she'd been before on more than one occasion to hide out? To avoid a man who she wanted nothing to do with.

Lorraine tapped her fingers on the steering wheel and then indicated to come off at the fast-approaching slip road.

If her mum wasn't at the narrowboat, then she could cross that off her list of suggestions for the police. After all, if her mum had sunk into some kind of depression, she didn't want the police turning up in force to drag her away. Her mum would never forgive her.

If her mum had nothing to fear from Trevor.

But she did.

'I'm so scared, but mostly for you and the children. Because once I'm gone, you'll be next.'

Why else had Trevor been at her mum's house the night she disappeared?

Why was the oil from his car on her mum's drive?

She shuddered.

When had Trevor started wearing her dad's coat?

57

ONE HUNDRED AND SIX HOURS SINCE PHONE CALL

'Excuse me?' Lorraine leaned down, hands on knees as she peered at the man flat on his back on the floor of his narrowboat, his head under what appeared to be some kind of steering mechanism that he was fixing.

He shot upright, smacking his head on an old piece of metal jutting out. 'Oh, shit.'

'Oh, sorry.'

He rubbed his head as he glared at her through half-closed eyes.

'I'm so sorry. I didn't realise you hadn't heard me approach.'

He reached and turned down the small portable radio he'd had next to his head, playing quietly. 'Don't worry, love. Happens all the time.'

He rolled to his feet and stretched as he stood tall. 'I could do with a break in any case.' His accent rolled pure Yorkshire. 'What can I do for you, lass?'

Hiding her disappointment that he wasn't a local, Lorraine gave him a smile, nonetheless. 'I don't suppose you know where *The Old*

Codgers is tied up?' She smoothed her hand along the route of the canal. 'I thought it was meant to be along here?'

'Moored,' he corrected.

'Moored.'

'*The Old...*?'

'*Codgers.*'

He scratched at his head where a small, red bump appeared to be forming and let out a quiet hiss. 'Les? Lesley?'

A small woman popped her head out of the cabin, like a jack-in-the-box. 'What?'

'Where's *The Old Codgers* moored? I've seen it recently. Can't think where.'

Lorraine plastered a smile on her face, resisting the temptation to look at her watch. She'd told Aunt Caroline she'd be no more than a couple of hours tops. It had taken her forty minutes to drive there and find the place where the narrowboat was supposed to be moored. Thirty years ago. It could be anywhere. She was running out of time and luck.

'That's old man Kijuk. You come to check on him, love?'

'Umm...'

'About time social services stepped in. I reckon he's in a right state. Needs some help, poor old bugger. Mind you, he might not be too pleased to see you, so don't be surprised if it's not a warm welcome. Last time we stopped for a chat, he told us to bugger off and he's known us for years. We come every year, this time. When it's nice and quiet.'

'Lesley,' the man barked out. 'Tell the poor woman where his boat is. She doesn't want to listen to you wizz-wazzing.'

Lesley slammed her hands on her hips and looked as though she was about to smack him on the other side of his head.

'I am in a bit of a hurry.' A bit was an understatement.

Lesley shot daggers at her husband and then pointed along the towpath. 'Beyond that bend, love. He grounded it ages ago, hasn't manage to get it afloat since. Too proud to ask for help, I think. We did try and offer...'

Lorraine had already straightened and was sidling away, wishing the woman would just tell her the instructions and stop the inane chatter. Her husband, evidently of the same opinion, sighed, so Lesley continued.

'Past the lock and then the canal widens and deepens. Mind your footing, it's a bit boggy. We've had a lot of rain in the last couple of days. We're due a lot more. Bloody June. It should have all dried up by now, and we should be in drought season.'

'Thank you,' Lorraine called over her shoulder as she started out at a trot.

'Mind your footing,' Lesley called after her and Lorraine raised a hand in acknowledgement.

Just as the woman had said, the canal widened out after the lock and a wash of mud slipped over the pathway, so boots made for shopping, not walking, slipped in the sludge, making her slow down.

Drizzle started just as the grounded narrowboat came into view and Lorraine squinted to get a better look. She'd told her aunt it was going to be a sunny day. Play out in the garden. How wrong could she have been? Not that she'd had any chance to look at weather forecasts in the last few days.

Paint that might once have been red and green was cracked and peeling so the boards showed naked underneath. There was no resemblance to the beauty on the brochure she'd brought with her. Other than the name emblazoned on the body of the boat in red, outlined with black to make it stand out against the green panel, which appeared to have resisted weathering, Lorraine would never have recognised it.

'Hello?'

From where she stood, it looked to her like a ghost ship. The windows so filthy, she didn't even want to try to peer inside.

Nor did she want to step onto it in case the floorboards gave way.

'Hello?' She raised her voice, hoping if anyone was inside they would hear her.

While she waited, she assessed the narrowboat. Tethered only with one rope, the other one looked as though it had frayed and broken. The boat listed away from her.

'Hello!' She yelled the word this time, aware that there was no one else around. The other boat she'd passed with Lesley on was a good ten-minute trot back the other way and they'd been moored up, so they wouldn't be coming in her direction any time soon.

Undecided, Lorraine stood there for another few minutes, her hair plastered to her head. She hadn't thought it through.

As usual, she'd seen to all the kids' needs, making sure she'd taken enough for them both to play with and eat when she dropped them off at a very surprised Aunt Caroline's. She'd not even stayed for a cup of tea, explaining that the little ones would be happier if she dumped them and ran rather than stayed for a while. They'd have expected to go with her.

Her rationalising didn't make her feel any less than a bad mother.

Lorraine pulled her phone from her pocket. Who could she call?

Normally it would be her mum. But that was out of the question. Her mum evidently wasn't here either.

Aunt Caroline?

Lorraine blew out a breath.

That was no good. Her aunt couldn't come. She'd got both the children and no car seats for them.

She pushed dripping hair from her eyes and looked at the screen now covered in raindrops.

Sergeant Willingham. She could call her.

No. Not yet. There was nothing to tell her. Except she'd found an empty abandoned narrowboat that quite possibly her mum had visited thirty years previously. And besides, it would only go to answerphone and she definitely didn't want to dial 999.

She pressed the button to highlight the number she'd been given the night before.

She hovered her finger over the dial key.

Trevor.

She could call Trevor.

58

ONE HUNDRED AND SIX HOURS AND TWENTY MINUTES SINCE PHONE CALL

A hard smack of tin on metal reverberated through the whole boat and Lorraine snatched at her phone as it slipped from her hands.

She caught it just below knee height and blew out a quick sigh of relief as another loud smash resounded.

She stared at the narrowboat, her chest tight enough to restrict her breathing.

There was someone on there. There had to be.

'Mum?' she called out.

She looked at the screen, and then flipped the case on her phone closed before she had a chance to dial. She slipped it safely into the deep pocket of her baby-blue puffa jacket, hardly suitable for the weather. Warm, but not waterproof.

With icy hands, she grasped a rail and lowered herself into the narrowboat, tottering a few steps towards the other side on the slippery, uneven surface.

'God, oh, God.'

The bang sounded again as she reached for the door and flung it open.

Heat rushed out from what looked like an old wood-burning

stove, stoked so high, the place could have been about to burst into flames.

Confusion hit her as an old man, doubled over almost in two, raised a ratchet above his head and slammed it down once more on what appeared to be a dented heavy-bottomed frying pan.

With a gasp, Lorraine rushed forward, her hand grabbing his frail arm to stop him doing it again.

'Grandad.'

Shock whitened his features as the old man stared at her with eyes gone opaque. 'Sandra?'

'No.' She shook her head, convinced she was as pale as him. It was him. It had to be him, but he was unrecognisable from vague memories of when she was a child.

A deep black and blue bruise seeped from the top of his knobbly, bald head, down his forehead, lightening in colour until it encircled both eyes in a sickly yellow.

'Grandad. It's Lorraine.'

'Lorraine?'

'Yes.' She waited for the recognition, but none was forthcoming. 'It's Lorraine, Grandad. Sandra's daughter.'

The old man peered at her through those dull, smoky eyes. 'Sandra? Sandra didn't have a daughter. She had a son. He died at birth.'

He dropped his hand to his side as if the ratchet had suddenly become too heavy for him to hold.

Sadness swept over her at his predicament. The poor delusional man. He didn't even remember his own granddaughter. Had no memory of her.

She could hardly blame him. She didn't even know the man herself. She'd not seen him since she'd been a girl and they'd moved from the area, never to return. Never to visit, it seemed. Her memories of him were vague snatches.

Weary, Lorraine looked around at the disgusting pit the poor old man appeared to live in. It wasn't fit for anyone. No human should live here. It was only fit for rats and mice. Lesley was right. He needed help and from the look of his head, he needed it urgently.

He'd kept himself warm and fed by the look of it, although not well, his stringy old body bent and twisted, and the fire looked perilously dangerous.

'Mr Kijuk?' She thought it might be less confusing if she dropped the 'Grandad' title for now.

'Yessss.'

'What have you done to your head?' She raised her voice.

He raised gnarled fingers and stroked them over the area, his eyes squinting. 'I must have fallen.'

Lorraine nodded.

'Why were you banging on the pan?'

'Help.' He nodded to the narrow window at head height and Lorraine realised that's where she'd been standing on the towpath. He must have seen her up there and decided to attract her attention.

'Why do you need help?' She wouldn't be surprised if he turned to her and said, 'Why would you bloody think? Look at the state of this place.' But he didn't.

He was silent for a long minute before he shook his head. 'I don't know. I can't remember.'

He touched his head again, fingers shaking harder this time.

'Is it because you fell?'

He nodded, but Lorraine felt his attention drift away.

She tried to pull him back. 'Has your daughter, Sandra, been to visit?'

His confusion appeared to multiply. 'Sandra? You're not...?'

'No. I'm not Sandra. I came when you banged for help.'

He wilted against the sink just as a dull thud came from behind closed doors, where Lorraine assumed the bedroom was.

'Mr Kijuk. Is anyone else at home?' Lesley had only mentioned an old man. Was Lorraine's grandma also still alive?

'On board?' he corrected.

'On board. Is there anyone else on board?'

At his blank look, she sidled past him, touching his arm reassuringly. 'Is it okay if I look in here?'

With a mute nod, he crumpled into the bench to stare into space, his hand resting on a duffle bag.

Torn between helping him or going to check on the bedroom, Lorraine hesitated. Her heart quailed at the hideous living accommodation the poor old man had consigned himself to.

She pulled her phone from her pocket ready to dial, she wasn't sure who, but she needed to get him help and urgently. It couldn't be Trevor. He'd take an hour and half to get there and she wasn't sure her grandad had that much time. He looked sallow and gaunt.

She bumped open the door with her hip and swallowed the gasp midway, her phone forgotten.

'Mum!'

59

Trevor had been surprised to find the old man pottering around the narrowboat when he'd arrived back earlier that morning. He'd considered smacking him over the head for a second time and having done with it.

He'd proved to be of use, though. While Trevor had been away, the old boy had been feeding his own daughter, confused into believing it was his wife. Possibly because of dementia, more likely from the whack on the head.

It seemed he was unable or unwilling to loosen the ties on her hands and feet, but he'd kept her alive while Trevor had been otherwise occupied.

Very handy.

If she'd managed to get loose, she'd have killed him. He could see it from the fire in her eyes.

But Trevor was back now. Properly.

He'd stay until he got the job done. Then he'd set the whole narrowboat on fire and send them both off on a Viking's funeral. It wouldn't matter if they knew who'd done it. Not really, although it was more likely they'd just think it was some dodderer who'd sent his boat up in flames by accident while his daughter was on board having had a nervous breakdown after her husband had died. They might even blame it on her.

If there was any clue that they were looking for him, though, he could be out of the country with a new name, a brand-new passport and the money he'd managed to retrieve. Something he'd never had before.

Like his driving licence. He'd never qualified to drive. But he'd learned before he was sent to prison.

He'd driven the car there first thing only to find the narrowboat freezing, the fire out and the stupid old man dithering around. No food in the cupboard, not a scrap in the fridge. Panic-stricken about not feeding his 'wife'.

Trevor wasn't sure, but he thought the old man had dressed ready to go out foraging for food. The little local supermarket was only a twenty-minute walk. Possibly longer for the scabby old boy with his pathetic shuffle and step.

Trevor couldn't risk that.

If someone had seen him in that state, they'd have called the emergency services. It was the last thing he needed. He didn't want to draw attention to what appeared to be an abandoned boat.

He'd carried the brown paper shopping bags from the small, empty car park through the woods, pausing for a moment at the edge to do a quick survey of the area. He'd not been for a couple of days before today as he'd had his weekly check-in with his probation officer, followed by the whole debacle with his dear half-sister. Hanging around hour after hour, waiting for the irresponsible cow to pick up her daughter.

He'd been going to drive up the night before, but she'd been keen to talk. To welcome him into her life. She'd been deprived of a brother, hadn't she?

Still, he felt satisfied that he'd cued the snooker table up nicely for his imminent return. A new job, back in the area. A great excuse to start reconnecting their family ties.

He'd see what he could get out of her before he disposed of her too. She didn't have anyone except Aunt Caroline and, by all accounts, she barely knew her.

He'd be her closest living relative if something happened to Lorraine and the kids.

He stepped onto the boat and froze as the small double doors opened and his half-sister stepped outside, horror filling her eyes as they met his.

'Trevor?'

60

Shock froze her to the spot as she stared at the man she'd least expected to see there.

'Trevor.'

Her mum bumped into her, barely able to stand on her own since Lorraine had untied her. Almost as confused as her own dad. Neither of them coherent.

All Lorraine wanted to do was get them off that narrowboat and keep them in sight as she called the police. If she left them on there, she was terrified the wood burner was about to blow, the heat from it pulsing throughout the cabin until sweat poured down her back while she cut the rope fastenings on her mum's wrists and ankles.

Had her grandad done this? Had the pair of them fought?

Her brain refused to compute as she stared up at her half-brother.

Lorraine opened her mouth as Trevor dropped three paper carrier bags on the deck, with a force that split them open, so the contents rolled out.

'What are you doing here?'

Pieces of the puzzle knit together, and her mouth dropped open.

The food on the floor, the carrier bags, the fire raging inside the burner. Her grandad's head. Her mum unable to speak as Lorraine untethered her wrists and ankles. Her skin almost as ashen as the old man's from lack of fluids.

The duffle bag on the seat that her grandad had swooped up, refusing to leave it behind as she'd almost dragged the two of them out.

The assumption that her grandad had tied her mum up when she'd come to visit because of his confusion, the sickness of dementia, melted away as she stared into the eyes of a monster and realised her deadly mistake.

'Trevor.'

Her mum whimpered from behind her, the only noise she'd made since Lorraine had discovered her. Lorraine half turned and wrapped a protective arm around her as her mind refused to believe the horror of the whole situation.

Trevor stepped forward, his hands curled into fists.

Lorraine held her breath. Her mum had been right all along.

'Now it's me. I'm so scared, but mostly for you and the children. Because once I'm gone, you'll be next.'

'Well, would you fucking believe it? Lorraine, I've really done everything I possibly can to protect you. You're my kid sister. I didn't want you to come to any harm.'

She saw the lie in his eyes. No longer able to hide his true feelings, evil permeated through.

What the hell had she done? How had he managed to fool her the night before? To soothe away the worries for her mum. Not that he'd managed that entirely, which was why she was there. But she'd been a fool, believing he'd not harmed her mum.

She squinted at him. 'It was you. All the time it was you.'

'Of course it was me. Silly cow.'

She gave her mum a squeeze as her frail body slumped against Lorraine. 'Mum was right all along. You did kill my dad.'

'Our dad. He didn't want anything more to do with me.' He spread his hands wide. An excuse, not an apology.

'That's not a reason to kill someone.'

His jaw tightened. 'He took my whole life away from me. I risked everything for him. Just for his love. A love that was never true. There was always someone else in the way of him being able to love me. Do you know what it took to remove those obstacles?'

Aghast, Lorraine squeezed herself against the doorframe and tried to push her mum behind her as Trevor stepped closer, his lips curled in a snarl.

'It wasn't easy to throw my mum down the stairs.'

The soft sob from behind her made Lorraine realise her mum was listening.

'And my brother?'

'That was easy. Regrettable. But easy. It was just a matter of keeping my mouth shut.'

'So, you did murder him.'

He never gave a direct answer, but his eyes took on regret Lorraine could only assume was for himself.

'And still my dad couldn't see fit to love me instead. Me.' He stabbed his chest with his forefinger. 'The child he already had.' He poked the same finger and pointed behind Lorraine, she assumed at her mum. 'She took it. All his love, she took. So, he had none left for anyone else. The greedy bitch.'

At her mum's whimper, Lorraine didn't deny it. She knew it was untrue. Her dad had lavished love on them all. Her mum, her, and Sophia. Had he been given the opportunity, he would have showered it on his grandson, Elijah, too, but Trevor had deprived them all of that.

Without warning, Trevor leaped forward and snatched at the neck of Lorraine's coat, hauling her towards him. 'So, now what am I supposed to do? It's your fault, if only you'd kept your long nose out of it.' He tapped the end of her nose as though she was a puppy being rebuked. She flinched as he spat out, 'Now, I'm going to have to deal with all of you.'

He gave her a shake and her mum rushed out into the open, Lorraine's grandfather close behind.

The narrowboat gave out a weary groan as though it had had enough of life, and listed to one side with the combined weight of all four of them.

Trevor staggered, but held on, his hands going around Lorraine's throat as he shook her, his fingers digging into her skin.

She choked out one word before he cut off her air supply. 'No!'

The raging sound of a bull elephant filled the air.

Her grandad raced from behind her at a staggering sideways gait, arm raised with the ratchet grasped firmly in his fist, the bag clutched to his chest as though he was protecting himself.

Trevor let out a snort of disbelief, cut short as he dropped his hands from Lorraine's neck to defend himself.

Her grandad brought the ratchet down and it crunched through Trevor's wrist bone.

Trevor howled, his uninjured hand automatically covering his damaged wrist.

Her grandad raised the weapon again. This time, Trevor side-stepped it easily, letting it clatter to the ground as his feet skidded across the slimy decking. The narrowboat gave a hard lilt and Trevor shot across the width of the boat and slammed up against the lower edge, which now dipped into the water.

Trevor's arms windmilled out of control.

Lorraine clasped her mum tight with one arm and snatched a rail with her other as her grandad straightened, slithered across the deck towards Trevor and, with a fast jerk, he ploughed his elbow into the back of the other man's ribs.

Head first, Trevor flipped over the edge of the narrowboat and into the deepest part of the canal.

Leaving her mum clinging to the rail, Lorraine scrabbled across the slippery boards and snatched at her grandad's arm, hauling him away from the edge as he was at threat of following Trevor over the side.

She dragged him to the centre and as their weight evened out, the keeling boat straightened, its rear end drifting outwards, tugged by the current.

Lorraine clambered to her knees and peered over the side, horror clutching at her sore throat.

Screams of terror burbled from Trevor's mouth as he reached out, stretching flapping arms towards the narrowboat. Towards them. In the hope they would save him.

Terror filled his face as his mouth opened and shut like a landed trout, desperately seeking oxygen.

'He can't swim. He never did like the water.' Her mum's voice squeezed out, rusty and dry, as they watched Trevor flounder.

Lorraine's gaze slid to where a lifebuoy butted up against the inside of the boat, its tether loose, so it flapped against the still rocking narrowboat.

She drew in a breath and turned away from the life saver, her attention back on her half-brother as his screams faded to desperate gulps. Taking in more water than air.

Trevor's arms slowed, became less frantic, as her dad's donkey jacket weighted him, dragging him down.

Lorraine turned her head to look the length of the canal both ways.

There was no help in sight.

No one to see him. No one to save him.

She stared, dispassionate as Trevor's white face disappeared beneath the surface of the murky canal water for the third time, those strange, familiar eyes wide. His mouth open in a silent scream.

The water stilled as his body melted away like a distant nightmare.

61

ONE YEAR LATER

Laughter filled the house as the children raced through, the eleven-week-old blue-coated German Shepherd puppy attached to Elijah's pull-up nappy by his teeth.

Lorraine scooped Ghost's nephew up and suffered the enthusiastic licking as the puppy discovered another face to clean.

'Time out, kids. Blue needs to sleep.'

They groaned good-naturedly as Lorraine took the puppy to the crate in the corner, more to give him protection from the children than the other way around.

As she straightened, she looked out of the window at the woman approaching the front door.

Lorraine switched on the telly to let the kids watch a cartoon while she answered the door. 'Sophia, let Elijah sit with you.' She smiled as her daughter huddled her little brother up beside her on the giant beanbag while he stuffed a thumb in his mouth, his attention already on the brightly coloured characters.

'Mrs Pengelly?'

A little tremor of trepidation filled her. There was always the risk something evil would raise its head again. She'd always be on her guard.

Following the traumatic events the previous year, she'd moved to The Wirral, leaving behind her ex, her job and her past to start anew, closer to her aunt, where she could ask her to babysit once in a while.

Her aunt had been horrified to discover her nephew had absconded with all her mum's money. Well, that's what they'd felt appropriate to tell her. There was no need to involve her in the trials they'd been through. There was no chance of her grandad mentioning anything. Not after the blow to his head. He seemed a little confused at the whole thing and quite happy to let it go.

Sergeant Willingham had questioned them briefly about her mum's sudden re-appearance and had found nothing out of the ordinary that Sandra had been with her own father on the narrowboat. According to statistics, 85 per cent of people turn up back home within a few days of going missing. It was nothing unusual.

Her mum had been desperately worried about Lorraine's grandad and taken off without thought when she'd received word he was living on a derelict narrowboat with failing health.

When it had set on fire, they'd both been dropped off by a friendly passing stranger at the nearest hospital A&E department. They'd received treatment and were discharged relatively quickly once they'd rehydrated. No lasting effects from their trauma.

Sadly, they'd been unable to obtain the stranger's details as she'd driven off. It wasn't important, but it would have been nice to have thanked her.

'Yes. I'm Mrs Pengelly.'

The woman produced a badge with her identity on. 'I'm Willa Marshall. I work for Lite Insurance Company. Do you mind if I come in?'

'I don't know. What's it all about?'

'It's a private matter, if you have a moment.'

Lorraine stepped back to let the woman inside and closed the door behind them to stand in the hall, reluctant to go through to the lounge.

'I believe you had a brother called Trevor Leivesley.'

Lorraine's throat tightened. 'A half-brother. Yes.' She shook her head, linking her fingers together and squeezing them tight. 'I don't know him, though, we've never had contact.' The lie slid from her tongue quite easily. 'He's from my dad's first marriage. Thirteen years older than me.' Aware she was at risk of rambling, she clamped her teeth shut.

The woman tilted her head to one side and gave a small smile. 'Well, in that case, this may actually come as a nice surprise.'

Lorraine raised her eyebrows.

'Sadly, the remains of your half-brother were recently discovered, washed up on a buoy along the Mersey estuary.'

Lorraine raised her hand to her chest and sucked in a breath. 'Oh, no. How awful.'

'Yes, well. You don't need to know the details and I don't know them. As I say, I'm from the insurance company. I'm surprised the police haven't already informed you.'

'I've just recently moved.'

'I managed to track you down. Through your aunt.'

Lorraine's forehead creased. 'I see.'

'Yes, I've just left her place. It appears she was unaware too of the demise of her nephew. She was very upset.'

'Mmm.'

'But my job is to inform you that Mr Henry Leivesley, your dad, had set up a trust fund for him with his late mother's will. He'd recently, well, in the last three years, made a change to that trust, that on the death of Mr Trevor Leivesley, the trust should pass to you.'

Weak-kneed, Lorraine slumped down onto the bottom step of the staircase. 'You're kidding.'

'No kidding, Mrs Pengelly. The trust was lodged with a local solicitor, but we're the insurance company. I just need proof of ID, passport, driving licence and something with this address, council tax, etc., and then I can process this.'

Lorraine heaved herself up, her limbs a lead weight.

She dashed a quick look at the children. A happy pair, it seemed, since they'd moved. Perhaps because their mum was happy. And they had a puppy.

Stunned, she turned to the insurance agent. 'How much...' Her voice faded. 'How much is it worth?'

'Well, that's the thing. Your half-brother never drew on it for some odd reason, so the interest has rolled up. Originally it was worth sixty-two thousand pounds from life assurances from his mum's death. Now, it's in the region of three hundred and eighty-three thousand pounds. Once you sign these papers and provide your ID, it'll take around ten to fourteen days to process.'

Still numb when she closed the door behind the woman, Lorraine picked up her phone and tapped the short dial.

'Hi, Grandad, is Mum there?'

His voice warbled as he called her mum.

This would make the world of difference to them. Her mum's house was sold subject to contract, and she'd already found a nice little bungalow with a granny – or in this case, grandad – annex attached just a mile along the road from Lorraine's new house.

Mrs Tindall would miss her, but she had a permanent carer now. A live-in. Registered, too. After all, her sons could afford someone. Her mum had cared for the old lady out of obligation and a long-standing relationship, never wanting to take Gareth's money. He'd been insistent, but all Sandra had wanted was to ensure Mrs Tindall was clean, safe and comfortable.

Lorraine glanced at her children as she waited for her mum to pick up. She left them, happy in front of the TV as she slipped into the kitchen to stare out of the window at her pretty back garden, the roses starting to bud.

There was no need for the children to hear what she had to say.

She wouldn't tell lies, but why drag out the skeleton in the closet in front of them when keeping silent was better?

She could keep a secret.

It seemed she wasn't so very different from her mum.

'Lorraine?' Her mum's voice was faint, filled with concern as she came to the phone. 'Is anything wrong?'

Lorraine let a long, slow smile spread over her face.

'Quite the opposite, Mum. You're never going to believe this...'

ACKNOWLEDGMENTS

For some peculiar reason, once the idea of *The Stepson* formed in my mind, it simply flowed. Never one to plot, I found the whole story already formed just waiting to be written. I hope you feel this in reading it. My wonderful editor, Caroline Ridding of Boldwood Books, certainly did and I want to thank her for the terrific support she has given me right from the outset.

As usual I have a list of people I'd like to thank. There are so many these days to whom I am so grateful, for their support in all manner of ways. If I've missed anyone, I apologise.

First, to those who let me borrow their names.

For some time now, I have gathered names of real people who attend my talks, and my book release parties, both on zoom and in person. I hold competitions for them and pick out a name or two on the understanding that the character I create can be anything from murderer to murdered, dog-walker to police officer.

I never realised how many people wanted their names to appear in a book. So much so that when two of my friends from college days came to the book release evening for *My Little Brother*, I was quite taken aback that they were so keen. In truth, Caroline was, but Lorraine had a certain reluctance. Evidently, she knows where my mind goes. So, to Caroline Hamps and Lorraine Pengelly, thank you for your names and for the immense support you've shown me. I hope you enjoy what I have done with your characters.

I had two Sandra's, both of whom I've managed to write into my manuscript. Sandra Leivesley who won one of my competitions and Sandra Kijuk who has been a great cheerleader for so long and reads everything I write, even the hard bits.

Occasionally, a reader will say 'I'd love to have my name in your book,' just at the right time. Lisa Willingham was one such reader, so thank you for coming along just when I needed you.

For the wonderful support of Andi Miller and her Facebook group, Books with Friends.

To the wonderful Lynne Belsham who knows all things roses and although I haven't used much of her knowledge, it was this that directed the season of the book.

Ross Greenwood, for his excellent critiquing.

To my amazing family, Andy, Laura and Meghan who when I say, don't bother me unless it's an absolute emergency, melt into the background and wait until I emerge from my writing cave, often somewhat dazed, and lavish me with love and encouragement.

To my sister Margaret, as always, for reading through my manuscripts and loving every story I write.

To the ever-precious Lola, Laura's beautiful black Labrador who came into our lives as we went into lockdown and kept everyone's spirits high. I do love to use our furkids names when I can.

Finally, as this is the last book in my current contract, I want to thank Boldwood Books from the bottom of my heart for having enough faith to contract me for another four, which is quite fortuitous as I'm already writing the next one.

What fun we're about to embark on together over the next couple of years.

MORE FROM DIANE SAXON

We hope you enjoyed reading *The Stepson*. If you did, please leave a review.

If you'd like to gift a copy, this book is also available as an ebook, hardback, large print, digital audio download and audiobook CD.

Sign up to Diane Saxon's mailing list for news, competitions and updates on future books.

http://bit.ly/DianeSaxonNewsletter

Discover more gripping thrillers from Diane Saxon.

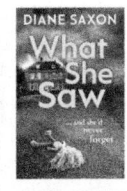

ABOUT THE AUTHOR

Diane Saxon previously wrote romantic fiction for the US market but has now turned to writing psychological crime. *Find Her Alive* was her first novel in this genre and introduced series character DS Jenna Morgan. Diane is married to a retired policeman and lives in Shropshire.

Visit Diane's website: http://dianesaxon.com/

Follow Diane on social media:

- facebook.com/dianesaxonauthor
- twitter.com/Diane_Saxon
- instagram.com/DianeSaxonAuthor
- bookbub.com/authors/diane-saxon

Boldwood

Boldwood Books is an award-winning fiction publishing company seeking out the best stories from around the world.

Find out more at www.boldwoodbooks.com

Join our reader community for brilliant books, competitions and offers!

Follow us

@BoldwoodBooks

@BookandTonic

Sign up to our weekly deals newsletter

https://bit.ly/BoldwoodBNewsletter

THE *Murder* LIST

THE MURDER LIST IS A NEWSLETTER DEDICATED TO SPINE-CHILLING FICTION AND GRIPPING PAGE-TURNERS!

SIGN UP TO MAKE SURE YOU'RE ON OUR HIT LIST FOR EXCLUSIVE DEALS, AUTHOR CONTENT, AND COMPETITIONS.

SIGN UP TO OUR NEWSLETTER

BIT.LY/THEMURDERLISTNEWS

Printed in Great Britain
by Amazon